To CALOY

Happy READING.

Jesse

Collections Of My Best And Most-Hated, "A Cup O' Kapeng Barako" Writings

Collections Of My Best And Most-Hated, "A Cup O' Kapeng Barako" Writings

Jesse Jose

ISBN:	Hardcover	978-1-4797-5172-3
	Softcover	978-1-4797-4399-5
	Ebook	978-1-4797-4400-8

This book was printed in the United States of America.

Rev. date: 03/20/2013

To order additional copies of this book, contact:
Xlibris Corporation
1-888-795-4274
www.Xlibris.com
Orders@Xlibris.com
107778

CONTENTS

ACKNOWLEDGEMENT

I wish to thank, first of all, **Bobby Reyes,** the publisher/editor of the online publication, www.mabuhayradio.com for publishing all my *Kapeng Barako* stories without fear, unfettered and un-censored. Other Fil-Am publishers have feared publishing many of my stories, for I tell it like it is. LOLO Bobby, as I call him, believes in FREE SPEECH and that every journalist must have the unfettered freedom to express his or her opinions, without fear . . . and censorship. Thus this book's subtitle is: "Collections of my Best and Most-Hated-Writings." Of course, there are some stories of mine here that are also pleasing and pleasant to read, but it's far and few in-between.

I also wish to convey my thanks to **Ray Burdeos**, an author of several books, for putting the idea in my head that I should also put together my own book, since I already have all the "tools," to write one, and for telling me that the words, "most-hated writings" within the title of this book, would surely attract the attention of readers.

My heartfelt thanks also to my dear friend and colleague, **Romy Marquez**, who is himself, a FEARLESS journalist, for all his positive comments on many stories I have written, no matter how "hateful" they were. Last, but not least, to **"Doc Lee" Lagda,** a prolific writer in his own right, for saying that my opinions on people, events and things much resemble some of his.

May I also mention **Annie**, a Film and Fine Arts international student from China, now attending Green River Community College of Auburn, Washington, for doing the sketch of the coffee cup that adorns the front cover of this book. Annie's Chinese name is **Jiajin Song**.

And, to **Mary Flores** of Xlibris for diligently downloading some of my stories from the mabuhayradio web site of LOLO Bobby. Without her help, this book would not have come to fruition.

—Jesse Jose

FOREWORDS

This book leaves out the likelihood that many readers of Jesse Jose also like the way he writes. "My Best and Most-Hated" are both extremes. Where "best" lies is where many of his admirers are; those who smile at every wry comment he makes whenever he finds reason to do so, which is hardly rare.

"Most-hated" would be a welcome avenue for those seeking to vent their dislike and contempt for this man who commands a big following in online media for all his irreverent commentaries. Bounding the "most hated" into a volume with the "best" provides a balance, an insight.

And it is in that balance where we see the man behind the bottomless cups of Kapeng Barako. The stuff he writes about are fairly everyday occurrence. It is in how he writes about them that generates the loudest whispers and the hateful screams. His commentaries aside, Mr. Kapeng Barako is a pleasant guy who is wedged between the best and the hated, easily likable.

The book should be a good way to while the time, specially when one can't make up who to like and who to hate; what to like and what to scorn. The book should provide the answer to that dilemma.

Romy Marquez,
Toronto, Canada-based journalist,
Poet and Author

This book is a collection of essays written by a salty submarine sailor author, Jesse Jose, from his column, ***A Cup O' Kapeng Barako*** that is published once a week.

I have to say that this book is worth reading not maybe because of its eye-catching cover, but rather the unique style of writing the author put into words that a reader is constantly mesmerized regardless of what subject is being told or critiqued. And it doesn't matter whether a reader may agree or disagree with the author's take on the subject or issue, because it is cleverly written that there is no room between words to be misunderstood or bored. In the end, a satisfied reader walks away with a smile.

—Ray Burdeos
Galveston, Texas

There is a glut of information in today's world, from the print media, broadcast journalism and in cyber space. I have neither the time nor the inclination to sort through the trite and unwanted pap. The advent of the computer era makes everybody think they can write and opine on everything. Many get the urge, very few are capable! Jesse Jose is capable and adroit in presenting his views on a wide range of topics. I enjoy the *Kapeng Barako* columns because they are meaningful, relevant and cogent. I like the passion and the fire in his columns and the way he tempers this heat with humor. Some of the columns bring me back to other places, happier times. The book should appeal to all Americans of Philippine descent and also to men and women who spent some time cruising the seven seas.

—"Doc" Licerio Lee Lagda
Cypress, California

INTRODUCTION

The time frame of these stories collected in this book, written in my column, *A Cup O' Kapeng Barako,* has a span of four years. The beginning chapters began in the year of 2012 when President Barack Obama was campaigning for his re-election, ending in the final chapters when Obama in year 2008 ran for the presidency of the United States.

But this book is not solely or merely about my opinions on politics. It's also about my take on current events, and my *Barako* thoughts on people and things that affected me personally. This book also contains conversations with people through emails, who came into my life during those four years. Some of those conversations were heated and hated, but some were also tender and kind.

But beneath them all, laughter abounds. For I write my column primarily for fun . . . meant only to be read by friends and comrades, and fellow Barakos. If at times I get corny, or my Pilipino English gets atrocious, they are puns intended, untended, and unintended, as in *"batu-batu sa langit, tamaan 'wag magagalit."* For my mainstream readers and friends, that means, "stones-stones thrown up in the air, don't get mad if they fall on your hair."

As y'all can see, I am a wanna-be humorist, *dyoking* a lot.

Some stories in this book also contains glimpses of my personal life, portions of which, are also hilariously funny, but tender and expressing love in places. *Okey ngarud,* happy reading, Dear Readers. **JJ**

An Economy Bumping Along the Bottom? It's the Economy, Stupid? The Economy Sucks? All Same-Same, right?

I agree.

"When half of the people get the idea that they do not have to work because the other half is going to take care of them and when the other half gets the idea that it does no good to work because somebody else is going to get what they work for, that my dear friend is about the end of any nation. You can NOT multiply wealth by dividing it. . . ."

A certain Dr. Adrian Rogers said that.

Who da heck this Dr. Rogers guy is, I dunno. I googled his name and from what I've read, he's some kind of a pastor, perhaps with a doctorate degree in religion, and that's probably why he's got a title of "Dr." before his name. Pastor or whatever, *doktor ng kabayo* or whatever, and of whatever church . . . I agree with that concept of his.

Because to me, it makes logical sense that you really can NOT multiply wealth by dividing it. Or, by redistributing it. You are a moron in my books if you don't agree with that. Of course, you don't have to agree with that. America is a free country, where you can be a moron, if you wish.

THE 47 PERCENT 'VICTIMS': Anyway . . . what I am saying is, those words of Doc Rogers, echo the words of Mitt Romney in a secretly-taped video from a small fundraiser for wealthy donors of Romney, where he blasted supporters of President Barack H. Obama as "dependent upon the government" *daw.*

So, I won't be accused by my critics and haters of my *Kapeng Barako* writings of taking something out of context, here's Romney's exact words:

"There are 47 percent of the people who will vote for the president no matter what," Romney said. "All right—there are 47 percent who are with him, who are dependent on government . . .

"Who believe that, that they are the victims . . .

"Who believe that government has the responsibility to care for them . . .

"Who believe that they are entitled to health care, to food, to housing."

Heck ya, Mitt, I agree.

It's exactly what I said in my previous two columns where I said that "half of the people in America do NOT pay taxes and these are the Welfare Queens and Kings, and the Disabled kuno, who knows how how to manipulate the system and suck America of monies and benefits."

These are the "47 percent," as Romney said. Who I called, the *palamunins* and parasites of America, the welfare queens and kings, and y'all know who I mean, right?

But being a gentleman, later in the day, in a press conference, Romney said that perhaps his comments about the 47 percent *palamunin* supporters of Obama, were not "elegantly stated."

Nonetheless, he insisted that "this is ultimately about the direction of the country." He asked: "Do you believe in a government-centered society that provides more and more benefits, or do you believe instead in a free-enterprise society where people are able to pursue their dreams?"

My take on that? Well, I am not an elegant man, so my words are certainly not elegant. I simply tell it like it is, and I am not taking back anything I've said.

TO BE A *PALAMUNIN* IS UN-AMERICAN: To depend on handouts from the government is un-American! To malinger of your INABILITY to work when you look so fit and strong, is un-American! To be a *PALAMUNIN* of this country is un-American. To work and to be productive and to take care of yourself and your family and to contribute to the greatness of this country IS the American way.

To say that there's no work to be had is a lot of bull!

There's always work to be had in this country, if you want work. When I retired from the Navy in 1981, there was a recession, too, in America at that time. It was a recession a lot more worse than in today's Obama recession. My pension from the Navy then wasn't enough to put sufficient food on the table for my growing family. So, I had to find work to supplement my meager pension.

I drove a taxi, I dug ditches with Mexican "day laborers," I worked as a night watchman.

AN INTERVIEW AT THE SAN DIEGO TRIBUNE: I was a Chief Journalist when I retired from the Navy. And I should have been able to find work as a journalist in the civilian world. I tried that. I was in San Diego, California then. So I applied for a job at the Tribune.

During my interview, I proudly presented my portfolio:Three Navy Chief of Information (CHINFO) awards for writing and a Thomas Jefferson award in photo-journalism from the Department of Defense. I showed clippings of my writings and published news photos I've taken.

Then they asked me if I have a degree in journalism. I said, "No, I don't. I didn't complete my studies. I joined the Navy, and they trained me as a journalist."

"We can't hire you then," they said. "We require a journalism degree for this position you're applying for."

"What about these awards and portfolio of my writings?" I asked. "They don't count?"

"Yes," they replied. "But we also require a bachelor's degree from you."

I was dumbfounded from the rejection of my writing skills that I've honed for many years while in the Navy. I wrote for Pacific Stars and Stripes, Navy Times, All Hands, Campus Magazine and other AP/UPI-oriented hometown newspapers. But all that didn't mean sh . . . t to them! I was furious.

Irate and desperate, I said, "I have an Honoris Causa in the Kama Sutra. I can show you all the positions. I am an expert. . . ."

They all walked away and loudly shut the door on me when I said that. While I was gathering my awards and writings together back into my briefcase, the door opened and one of the women—she had nice-looking legs and a full set of bosom—who interviewed me gave a note and said, "Here's my phone number, call me tonight."

I called her and that night I showed her the best positions from the Kama Sutra. Was I re-consider for the job after I've showed her the best and my most favorite positions from the Kama Sutra? Heck, no.

So, I went back to digging ditches with the Mexican laborers, driving taxis and doing night watchdog work.

I was never out of work.

I refused to belong in the "47 percent."

I didn't wanna be a *PALAMUNIN* of America.

AN ECONOMY BUMPING ALONG THE BOTTOM: I think I've gone off track again from what I was writing about. I was writing about those 47 percent supporters of President Obama, right? Let me get back on track.

So, this week in Florida, where he was campaigning to win the state's 29 electoral votes, President Obama—in response to Governor Romney's remarks about the "47 percent of Americans, who pay no income tax and believe they are victims and entitled to an array of federal benefits—blasted Romney as an "out of touch" presidential candidate.

"When you expressed an attitude that half the country considers itself victims, that somehow they want to be dependent on government, my thinking is maybe you haven't gotten around a lot," Obama said.

Romney, who was also in Florida, at that time, countered: "He's a very eloquent speaker, and so I am sure in the debate, as last time . . . he'll be very eloquent in describing his vision."

"But he can't win by his words," Romney continued. "Because his record speaks so loudly in our ears. What he has done in the last four years is establish an economy that's bumping along the bottom."

An economy bumping along the bottom? Hmmm. Though un-elegant, it's exactly what I said in my previous column: the economy sucks!!!

Sure, we all know that Mr. Romney has been dubbed "Mitt, the Twit" by the Brits, but . . . who was it who said that "it's the economy, stupid"? It was Bill Clinton, right? That was way back in 1992. When he won the presidency from the senior Bush, right?

So . . .

An economy bumping along the bottom?

It's the economy, stupid?

The economy sucks?

As Erap would say, same-same, right? Y'all get my drift? Hey, y'all don't get me wrong now. I like Barack. One of my cyberspace friends said, "Barack and *Barako* sound same-same." So how can I dislike someone who is a same-same *Barako,* like me?

PS: As to that MAD "elephant in the room," the MAD followers of Prophet MuhamMAD, rioting in the Middle East, killing Americans and burning US embassies and America's flags and MADLY screaming, "Death to America!" . . . hey, I MADLY say, too, nuke 'em!

Okey ngarud, Dear Readers and fellow *Barakos,* that's all. **JJ**

My Take on the Speeches of Michelle, Barack and Bill

I am writing this as the Democrats were having their national convention in Charlotte, N.C. Michelle Obama spoke Tuesday and Bill Clinton spoke Wednesday, and President Obama had his turn on Thursday. I only wanted to listen to these three speakers. The others are just BHO *bugaws,* I think.

What did Michelle Obama say, anyway? I wasn't really paying attention. I don't listen to lies and BS.

I think her well-known line among her speeches was when she said: "For the first time in my adult lifetime, I am really proud of my country. . . ." To translate those words in unique Filipino English: "Now that my husband, Barack Hussien Obama, has been nominated to run as president of the United States of America, I can now say that I can be proud of this country."

I'll always remember those lines of Mrs. Obama. The date was Feb. 18, 2008. And I'll always remember, too, my thoughts on her speech that day: "Say what? After what America had done for you and your husband? Send you both to expensive Ivy League schools, courtesy of American taxpayers. How ingrate can you get? You made Jane Fonda looked like a patriot, and Marie Antoinette as Mother Theresa."

MY COMING TO AMERICA: I said that, Dear Readers, because you see, I've been proud and have loved this country since Day One of my arrival here in America in 1960 as a U.S. Navy recruit bound for San Diego, California for my "boot camp" training.

Coming to America and pursuing the American Dream . . . had been my dream while growing up in the Philippines. And if in pursuing this dream I have to risk my life by joining the US military, I was willing to do it. The war in Vietnam then was escalating. But I was young, fearless and invincible. I wanted to experience battles in war. I wanted adventure. I wanted to see the world.

Several years later, when I became a U.S. citizen, and recited aloud my Pledge of Allegiance "to the flag of the United States of America and to the republic, for which it stands, one Nation, under God, indivisible, with liberty and justice for all," my pride and love for this country had grown ever more.

America took care of me through the years. It wasn't perfect. But I've traveled in several other countries and seen "things," and from what I've seen, I got to believe with all my heart, that America is the greatest country in this whole, wide world.

Back to Michelle O. I heard that she has expensive taste on clothes and she bought them like there's no tomorrow. She also gave lavish parties and went on lavish, expensive vacations with dozens of *alalays* and *tsimays . . . at kasama pa yung nanay niya*, paid for by you and me, the so-called middle class taxpayers.

And, as we all know, ONLY 50% of the people here in America pay taxes. The other 50% are the PALAMUNINS and the PARASITES and the WELFARE QUEENS and KINGS of America . . . and the "disabled" *kuno* who know how to manipulate and suck the system of welfare monies and benefits. Guess who pays for all that? Us, the middle class! But enough of that, because that only makes me mad and resentful.

I am not talking about America's disabled veterans. These veterans laid their lives on the line in defending the democratic ideals of this country. Some gave parts of their limbs and some gave it all. Whatever they are receiving now in benefits for their disabilities, they rightly deserve them.

ON PRESIDENT OBAMA: Y'all don't get me wrong. Just because I said these things about Michelle O, it doesn't mean that I also don't like President Obama. In my previous column, and I think it bears repeating, I said I like him. I said that he's done a lot of good things for America, despite all the bad press about him and the economy. He tried hard. I like his OBAMACARE. Affordable Health Care for all Americans is just and fair, and it's truly magnificent of Obama to offer that to all.

ON GAY MARRIAGE: I said I also like Mr. Obama's stand on SAME SEX MARRIAGE because it shows his depth of character. I am Catholic and I don't care what my fellow Catholics—the zealots, that is— say about same sex marriage.

These zealots said, "Marriage, according to the Bible, is only between a man and a woman." I say: Hogwash! The verses in the Bible shouldn't be read literally. Reading the Bible that way is the Fundamentalist way! The KKK's, with their Burning Crosses, read it that way.

Also, the Founding Fathers like President George Washington, said: "The United States of America should have a foundation free from the influence of clergy." Thomas Jefferson said: "Our civil rights have no dependence on our religious opinions."

And in the First Amendment to the U.S. Constitution, it says: "Congress shall make no law respecting an establishment of religion." It also implies clearly the separation of the church and state. To me, same sex marriage is EQUALITY for all! And, Lord Jesus loves us all . . . all the different people on this earth.

THE DREAM ACT: Another thing, when President Obama signed into law the Dream Act, I said, *"Okey ngarud,* my main man, you're a dawg." A dawg (dog) in street language is someone who's cool and an a-okay dude. Because signing that act into law is a show of compassion for young illegals and for our TNT's, giving them the opportunity to pursue the much-coveted American Dream.

BUT THE ECONOMY SUCKS: I also said, "But then the economy sucks. The unemployment rate has stood still at 8.3%. And the total national debt now stands at $15.9 trillion. President Obama has got a lot of explaining and convincing to do on this matter." Indeed, too many working Americans have been disillusioned by his promises and are angry at him. He failed them.

ON BILL CLINTON'S SPEECH: I like President Clinton. He's a brilliant man and one of the brilliant minds of the land. His wife, Hillary, is also one of the brilliant minds of the land. If only Hillary had won the Democratic nomination for president, she surely would have won the presidency over John McCain . . . and we would have had two brilliant minds of the land guiding America to more prosperity and greatness. But Obama won the nomination and eventually, the presidency.

Mr. Clinton's speech during the Democrats' convention was awesome, I think. He's a a gifted natural public speaker. He's a "folksy" speaker. Though he's delivering a speech to a multitude of listeners, he speaks like he's speaking personally ONLY to you. So you listen and pay attention.

He delivered a point-by-point rebuttal of the arguments made by president wannabe Mitt Romney and company during the GOP convention the previous week, warning America against the GOPs, declaring: "We can't let it happen."

Over and over, he endorsed the re-election of President Obama, saying there was no question that America now IS in a "better position than it was four years ago."

My reaction to that? Ain't no way, Bill. It depends "what is, is IS." The economy SUCKS now than four years ago. The economy was flourishing then during your time . . . and during the White House internship of, ahem, "Monica."

ON PRESIDENT OBAMA'S SPEECH: He's truly an orator. He's got magnificent charisma. He's a handsome black *mestizo.* Sharp dresser, too. He could be a model for GQ magazine. He's a magnetic speaker, and I thoroughly enjoyed watching him and listening to his oration of his party's oracles.

What's my take on his speech? Two words. As Erap would say: "same-same." Cut and paste. An exact copy of his nomination speech from four years ago. A couple of words were changed though. From "HOPE and CHANGE," it has become "FORWARD." But same-same. He's now forwarding the hope and change that he promised four years ago.

But in fairness to this very likeable man, this portion of his speech is the one I like very much:

"While I am proud of what we've achieved together, I'm far more mindful of my own failings. . . ." he said. Then added, "I have never been hopeful about America, not because I think I have all the answers, not because I'm naive about the magnitude of our challenges. I am hopeful because of you." Loud, long applause erupted from the multitude of listeners, when he said those words.

Then, with his voice breaking, he said, "if you share that faith with me, if you share that hope with me, I ask you tonight for your vote." My wife, who was sitting next to me on the family couch, said, "Not my vote, mister."

What about my vote? I dunno. I have a fickle mind, you see. My way of thinking on people and things is an evolving thing . . . *Okey ngarud,* Dear Readers, that's all. **JJ**

The Motherland's King of Comedy is Dead, But Pinoy Comedy Lives On

Dolphy is dead.

The King of Philippine comedy is no longer with us. He's been called home to the Lord. May he rest in peace. He was 84. Every Filipino all over the world knew of him. I knew of him when I was still a school kid at Rafael Palma Elementary in San Andres Bukid, Manila, way back in the 50's. I've seen him in many comedy shows with Panchito. I joined the US Navy in 1960, traveled the world, loved lots of women and fought in a war. Years later, when I retired from the Navy and came back "home" for a while, Dolphy was still on the scene making people laughed. Once again, I enjoyed watching him in that true-to-life, simple, comedy show, *"John en Marsha"* with Nida Blanca.

In terms of comedy, he was "it." He was an institution. He was a pillar. He was a natural. His talent in making Filipinos laughed was endearing and enduring, and his comedy endured through the years. Decades, in fact.

As Ms. Charo Santos, the president of TFC's (The Filipino Channel) ABS-CBN and host of of *"Maalala Mo Kaya,"* said: *"Nagbigay siya ng mga ngiti at halakhak sa gitna ng mga problema."* He gave us joy and laughter in times of trouble.

He was prolific, NOT only as a comedian, but also in "fathering" children. He fathered 19 children from several relationships. He said his children were his "pride and joy." He took good care of all of them.

He never married. His latest partner of 20 years was Zsa Zsa Padilla, a gorgeous award-winning actress and popular singer and recording artist.

Goodbye, Dolphy. Rest in peace. Thanks for the laughter. The Motherland sorely needed it through those years. . . .

In honor of this great comedian, what follows is dedicated to him. *Siempre,* it's something that we Pinoys can enjoy and laugh about. It was sent to me by a cyberspace friend, named "Doc" Lee Lagda. When Lee sent me this piece, he wrote:

This is great! To be a Pinoy is to be diverse and sometimes perverse but, most important of all, to be a Pinoy is to be funny! I think the Pinoy humor is what carries him through tough times. He knows how (ha ha ha) to laugh at himself. PS: Make sure it's PINOY, NOT Penoy.

Here it is, Dear Readers. Enjoy:

Are you a Pinoy? Enjoy, be Pinoy
Pinoy is what Filipinos call each other, a term of endearment. You're ***Pinoy*** from Pilipino just like you're *tisoy* from mestizo or *chinoy* from chino.

It's a nickname just as Minoy is from Maximo, Ninoy from Benigno, Tinay from Florentina and Kikay from Francisca. (But now they're Maxi and Ben and Tintin and Cheska.)

You've been called **indio**, **goo-goo**, **Negro**, **flip,** ***noypits***. Or **Filipino**, a biscuit that is brown outside and white inside, or a word stricken from the dictionary which means "domestic". **Ay,lintik!**

You're Juan de la Cruz or *Mang Pandoy*. You're *common tao*, *masa*, urban poor but also Cecile Licad and Don Jaime, **Jose Rizal** and Tony Meloto, Shawie and **Pacquiao** and Nick Joaquin—***galing-galing!***

Born June 12, 1896, the Republic of the RP is a **Gemini,** good at connecting, good at *loving-loving*, good at texting and interpersonal skills. **Filipinos like to *yakap, akbay, hawak, kalong, kalabit.*** We sleep side-by-side, *siping-siping,* we go out *kabit-kabit.*

There's lots of us to go around. Someone always to listen to a sob story, even in a jeepney, to share-a load or to share a TV.

A Pinoy family extends beyond nanay, tatay and anak. It includes lolo,lola, tito, tita, and so on. . . .

Who has a *hipag,* a *bayaw,* a *bilas,* a *balae,* a *kinakapatid*? Who has an *ate, dete, diche, kuya, diko?* The maids call her ***ate,*** the driver calls him ***kuya*** and everybody is *tito* or *tita.*

Who has a *Lola* Baby, a *Tito* Totoy, a *bosing* called Sir Peewee, his wife Ma'am Lovely and their kids Cla Cla and Cring Cring?

The ***Pinoy*** lives in a "condo", a mansion, an apartment, a *bahay na bato, ilalim ng tulay,* Luneta, Forbes Park,—and Paris, too!

He's a citizen of the world, he's in all the villages and capitals, colonizing the West, bringing his guitar and his *bagoong,* his *walis na tingting,* his *tabo,* his ***lolo*** and ***lola.***

Where there's a beat, there's a ***Pinoy.*** You'll find her singing in a nightclub in any Asian city, a musical in London, the Opera House in Sydney. Sure, they've got the infrastructure, the theaters and architecture. Who but ***Pinoys*** direct their plays, or trains their company managers, and imports our teachers, by the way?

Viagra to Victoria 's Secret:

Look at that baggage-all *pasalubong,* none for herself. From bedsheet to hair color, Toblerone to carpet, Viagra to paella pan, Victoria 's Secret to microwave.

Hey, Joe, don't envy me 'cause I'm brown, you'll get ultra violet from that sun and turn red not brown.

Just lucky, I guess. **GOD** put us all in the oven, but some were uncooked and some were burned, but me, I came out golden brown!

Hey, Kristoff! ***Hoy*** David and Ann!
Your ***Pinoy*** *yaya* makes your kids gentler, more obedient, she teaches them how to pray. Hey Big Brother! Hey Grandma Moses! Who but ***Pinoy*** nurses make your sick days easier all the way?

We made the **jeepney,** the ***karaoke***, the **fluorescent bulb**, the **moon buggy.** We invented People Power and *crispy pata*; popularized virgin coconut oil, **scaled the Everest** and made it with Cebu furniture abroad among the **best.** Ever trying for the Guinness World Record-with **the longest swim of a child**, the **longest kiss,** the **longest *longanisa.***

Linguist:

The ***Pinoy*** is a linguist.

"As in".

"As if".

"For a while".

"Open the light".

"Close the light".

"*Paki ganyan naman ang kuwan sa ano*?"

"Tuck in".

"Tuck out".

"Don't be high blood".

"If you're ready *na,* I'll pass for you".

Hayop; Hanep!

Bongga ka 'day, feel *na* feel *kita, kilig* to the bones *ako*. Don't make wala, don't make *tampo.*

Taralets na, *babes,* ***let's go,*** *nababato na ang syota mo.*

I'm inviting you to my party, please RSVP. *Oo* means 'yes' or 'maybe,' or 'yes if you insist,' or 'maybe if it doesn't rain.'

'Yes' is also a nice way of saying 'no.' Yes, *hindi kita sisiputin.* 'No,' ***eto na ako at ang barkada ko.*** Please don't ask a ***Pinoy*** a question like that!

Just flows and flows:

She's not so exact, not so **chop-chop**, she just flows and flows.

Filipino time? *Naku, huli din naman ang Kano!*

The ***Pinoy*** finds time to be **nice**, to be **kind**, to apologize, to be there when you're depressed, to help you with your *utang* and your wedding dress.

The Filipino is a giver, never mind what it does to his liver, never mind what it takes. **Hardships of the Third World don't dry up his blood, they just make him more compassionate, more feeling, of the other guy's lot.**

Note that the maid sends all her wages home to ailing daddy. She is the OCW whose labor of loneliness created the original **katas ng Saudi.**

'Bahala na':

The Filipino is fearless, *bahala na si Batman*, which actually means **Bathala na** or **'leave all to God.'** *Okay lang* if I die by *bitay, okay lang* if I live, *okay lang* if I survive by the skin of my teeth.

Saway ni Inay: Di ka naman Bill Gates, di ka naman French, mahirap nang magbuhat ng sarili mong bench. . . .

Be Pinoy. Enjoy! The Philippines' King of Comedy is dead, but Pinoy Comedy lives on. Okey ngarud, that's all. JJ

Title line: Pakyaw! Pakyaw! Laos na si Pakyaw!

Pakyaw lost!

I was reading the latest novel of John Grisham, *Calico Joe,* on the kitchen table when my son, Jonathan, announced quietly from the TV room: "Pakyaw lost." When my wife heard that, she said, "Pakyaw lost?" Then she repeated the announcement to me: "Hoy, Pakyaw lost!"

I looked up from Grisham's book, looked at her, smiled my crooked smile and made my own announcement: "Pakyaw lost, because he's LAOS." Then I went back to reading Calico Joe.

So . . . a *LUMPO* beat Pakyaw and took his title away. After all the media hype, that's all it took to take away the WBA welterweight crown and title from Pakyaw. Someone from the backwoods of California and unknown *pa* as a boxer. And to top that, while fighting Pakyaw, this underdog, named Tim Bradley got his left foot broken in the second round . . . then injured his right in the fifth. But he fought on.

I have the strong suspicion that Pakyaw did that. Anything goes in a fight. You've got to do what you got to do to win. Survival of the fittest, *ika nga* . . . and of the sneakiest. Surely Pakyaw is a smart guy, a fighter with lots of tricks at his disposal. And he has used them with a mighty fine finese.

After the fight, Bradley, as we've seen in news photos, was wheeled out on a wheelchair with grotesquely swollen feet. And said during a brief interview: "I heard my left foot snap in the second round, and then I injured my right in the fifth. . . ."

BRADLEY: I DIDN't FEEL PAKYAW'S POWER: He also said, "I thought I won the fight. I didn't think he was as good as everyone says he was. I didn't feel his power."

Pakyaw has no power? Pakyaw is a wimp? Hmmm.

What about the steroids? It didn't work for him this time? Hmmm. I heard that the fight did not start on time because Pakyaw had to watch first the NBA play-off game between Miami Heat and Boston Celtics. Perhaps in his excitement that the Miami Heat had won, he forgot to take the wonder drug, ha?

You see, Pakyaw roots for the Miami Heat, because the coach, Erik Spoelstra is a Filipino *daw.* And Pakyaw is a proud Filipino, who believes in TFC's (The Filipino Channel) mantra *na*: "Da best ang Pilipino saan man sa mundo." *Okey ngarud,* approve, *sige na, da bess na tayo.*

AN EMAIL FROM JGL: Anyway . . . when the blabbering of Pakyaw's loss began, Bobby Reyes, the publisher and editor of the online publication, www.mabuhayradio.com, wrote an email to all the DOMS and posted past controversial stories on the Internet that he wrote about Pakyaw, I wrote this response:

LOLO Bobby,

My next story will be titled: **"Laos na si Pakyaw!"** *When he was fighting pipitsugin Mexican boxers, it was written and opined by many Filipino journalists that they were "clean" fights, and that none were "fixed" and that the "mob" was not involved at all, and that Pakyaw was the "best boxer in the world."*

Now that Pakyaw lost this fight against an unknown boxer, these same Filipino journalists are now saying that the "mob was involved" and that the "judges were on the take and incompetent" and that it was "fixed." LOL. I'll have fun writing this story. Okey ngarud, take care.

Jesse.

It was JGL, who responded to my email. Out of the blue, after a year or so, my long lost friend and critic, and bantering buddy, and my favorite sparring partner in exchanging witty, hard-hitting punches, Joseph Lariosa's (JGL, for short) name flashed on my computer screen with this email:

JJ: Matagal nang laos si Manny Paquiao. Noon ko pa siya pina-reretire para ma-keep niya ang kanyang kinita at ma-enjoy niya. Pero, pag maglalaban si Manny at si Mayweather, kay Manny pa rin ako pupunta. My $500 bet with you at one-on-one odds stands. Take care. JGL

MY RESPONSE TO JGL:

Hello JGL . . . Long time, no hear. Thanks for your email. Sorry, I didn't get to reply to you right away. I've been getting lots of emails lately from my Kapeng Barako critics and fans and I've been writing back to them. So, how's everything with you, my friend? And how's everything in Chicago? How are the DOMS and the DAMS?

As to Pakyaw: It looks like a mere ***LUMPO*** kicked the shit out of him. *Eh papaano na lang kung si Marywweather ang makakalaban niya? Baka isang suntok lang, tulog na si Pakyaw.*

You're right about telling him to retire *na.* It's time for him to pursue his other dream: to be the president of the WaWa We Land. If Pee-Noy can do it, I am sure Pakyaw can do it, too. He's got a lot of Filipino fans, world-wide. He's a national hero in Pinas. Filipinos idolize him. They grovel at his feet and they hallelujah him. He's a Filipino god and Filipinos adore and worship him. To me, that's so *kadiri* to death.

You're one of them who treats this illiterate boksingero as a mighty god, aren't you?

But it's good to know that you've finally realized that Pakyaw now needs to retire. *Bago pa siya magulpi ni* Maryweather! And if I were you, my friend, I won't be betting and putting in jeopardy my hard-earned $500.

Because surely, Pakyaw will lose and you'll be a loser, too, of your $500. That's a large sum of money to bet on a sure loser, my friend.

No, I refuse to take that money away from you!

I am giving you this advise as a friend, JGL, my good friend. Keep the money. Wait and watch for the so called "fixed" rematch *na lang* between Bradley and Pakyaw. Pakyaw wil lose AGAIN, I am sure, but he'll make lots of money. Make sure to have lots of hankies with you to wipe your tears away, *dahil tapos na at laos na si Pakyaw.*

Next step *para sa kanya* is politics. He's now a Congressman of his province. He's got plans to run for Governor next. He'll easily win. Then president of Pinas, aka, the Land of Wawa We. Surely, he'll win that, too, ha?

Or, he can be the Army General of the Philippine Armed Forces. *Di ba Lieutenant. Colonel na siya ngayon?* Who knows he might be the next Lapu-Lapu in the fight against the Chinese "invaders" of the Scarborough Shoal? Then, he'll truly be a great national hero of the Motherland, perhaps. even greater than Jose Rizal, ha?

Okey ngarud, JGL, you take care know and send my regards to all the DOMS of Chicago. **JJ**

A Wedding Reception, a Birthday, a Gift and a Dyok on Obama Stamps

It was a blast.

In my previous column, "On Pakyaw, Miss Raj, Bristol . . . And On My Ripe Old Age," I mentioned that I recently celebrated my 70th birthday.

Indeed, it was a blast of a celebration, celebrated in conjunction with a second reception of my son Chris's marriage to Jaclyn Rostie. They got married in Boulder,Colorado. There was a grand reception there at the grand St. Juliene Hotel. But my wife and I held another reception a couple of weeks later here at the Emerald Downs of Auburn, Washington, for friends and relatives who were not able to make it to Colorado for the wedding.

I am not going to stop saying it. In fact, I want to scream it to the whole world. Chris and Jaclyn are both broadcast journalists. Chris now works for FOX News Denver, which is a big-time market in broadcast journalism, compared to those little TV stations in Cedar Rapids, Iowa, and Cheyenne, Wyoming, where he used to work right after graduating from the Edward R. Murrow College of Broadcast Journalism, at WSU in Pullman. Jaclyn graduated fromRegis University in Denver and now works for ABC News inColorado Springs.

So, in a way, it was three-event celebration.

It was a blast of a party. I drank several glasses of red wine. I can't remember how many. I think I got drunk a little. Well, I was celebrating. I was happy. Most of my friends were there. My wife's friends were there. My wife's relatives from Vancouver, Canada, were all there, en masse. And some of the people I go to church with in our church here in Auburn were there, too.

There was food galore and an "open bar." And there was a live band that played "disco" music, so I danced the "maski-paps" all night long . . . and celebrated to my heart's content. Heck, why not? It was my son, Chris's wedding reception. It was also a celebration and a toast to his success in his chosen, highly-competitive career. And it was my 70th birthday! Heck, yeah! I celebrated. Partied. And got drunk. Well, wouldn't you? And those people who were invited, but did not come, they all missed a good party.

GREETINGS FROM CYBERSPACE FRIENDS: To top all these, like icing on a cake, a couple of my cyberspace friends, **Romy Marquez of Toronto, Canada, and Ed Navarra, of Detroit, Michigan,** who are columnists themselves in their respective turfs, greeted me "Happy 70th birthday!" They also wished me more—many more—birthdays to come.

A greeting also came from **John "Bis" Bisbano of Port St.Lucie, Florida.** I used to work with Bis when we were sheriff deputies for the Martin County Sheriff's Office in Florida. I also a got a greeting from my friend and **next-door neighbor and walking partner, Jerry Lytle.** Jerry is a retired truck driver, who drove those 16-wheelers coast to coast in his heydays. When we take our walks, Jerry and I would talk and talk about politics and current events and about gossips in our neighborhood.

To me, it's a big deal when a friend has taken the time to greet and wish me a "Happy 70th Birthday." To me, these people are friends in the truest sense of the word. A 70th Birthday is a grand day in anybody's life. It means you have finally arrived at the crossroads of your life. The point where perhaps you can turn around and look back.

And remember.

And reminisce.

And savor the past.

And collect memories.

And perhaps, to collate all those memories into a book and experience them once again, if only in our imaginations, the exciting moments of one's youth and the many different indiscretions that comes with being young . . .

Ahh, those moments for me were aplenty, I tell ya.

FROM GERRY GARRISON: I also got this e-mail from Gerry, who I met in church and who became a close friend and a reader of my *Barako* column.

Jesse,

What a story! It is too bad the Filipinos keep voting these idiots in office. One good thing (?) that came out of the elections . . . litter is way down. This is due to new laws fining people anywhere from 50 pesos (for spitting) to 100 pesos (for littering). One has to wonder how long that will last.

Concerning Miss Bristol Palin . . . I say good for her. Idiots that call her names don't know her, or what she is all about. I give her many kudos for her bravery to even go on "Dancing With The Stars." How many of her so-called critics are willing to show up? Much less dance! I say put up or shut up.

As far as growing old: Age is a number, NOT a state of mind. You are only as old as you feel. From my perspective, you act and behave like a man half your age. With your peaceful neighborhood, along with your friends, I truly believe you have many more years to hang around.

Happy 70th Birthday!!!

Gerry

A GIFT FROM "LOLO": Now this one came from a very-special person. He's a prolific writer and a hard-hitting columnist from Los Angeles, California. He's also my publisher of my *Kapeng Barako* columns . . . and the nemesis of that infamous and corrupt Fil-Am organization, known, ahem, as "NaFFAA-A." LOLO Bobby is my idol. A long time ago, in my kanto boy days, it used to be Erap. Now, it's LOLO. He wrote, and to me, what he wrote here, is a gift:

Dear Ka Jesse,

I haven't greeted you yet, "Happy 70th Birthday," because I plan on publishing a tribute to you. Kaya lang baka sabihin ng mga readers ay parang "eulogy" na. LOL.

Of course, you know that I have given you the best birthday gift last year (on your 69th) and hopefully before your 71st BD, you will receive our Media Breakfast Club-Dean Reyes Award as "Columnist of the Years 2007-2010" sometime next year. Yes, for three years now, you have shown such a tremendous gift for irreverence but not irrelevance. And many readers, including me, like your style. Sometimes, you really piss off people but I am telling mutual friends (like our pals in Chicago) that you will mellow after you have reached 70. Hopefully, you will still be able to write classics like your Thanksgiving story, which we will put back on the Front Page this November. Yes, many Filipino-American publishers won't print sometimes your essays (controversial as they are) but for as long as we are operational, we will be honored and pleased to publish them. You are what a columnist should be and your fearless way of writing ought to be the model for Overseas-Filipino writers. Of course, our MabuhayRadio.com columnists are like you for they belong to a different breed of journalists, trained as they are.

Mabuhay ka, Jesse Jose, and may you live more-than a hundred years but your articles will be treasured forever, as long as there are men and women who care for literary relevance, if not absolute greatness.

Your fan,

Lolo Bobby M. Reyes

Someone who would write something like that about you is surely a gift, especially from someone like Bobby Reyes, the LOLO among LOLOS.

A STAMP MALFUNCTION, A DYOK: Dear Readers, before I go, let's *dyok muna*. Perhaps, some of you might might already have heard this, but we can still laugh at it, can't we? It's only a *dyok*, but I swear, it's true. My sister, Rosemary, who lives inNorth Carolina and works there as a mail carrier, told me it's true. I think postal workers though they go "postal" at times, don't tell no lie. Here's the *dyok*:

The Postal Services created a stamp with a picture of President Obama on it. But they noticed that the stamps were not sticking to envelopes. This enraged BHO, who demanded a full investigation.

After a month of testing and $1.73-million in congressional spending, a special Presidential Commission presented the following findings:

. ***The stamps were in perfect order.***

. ***There was nothing wrong with the glue.***

. ***People were spitting on the wrong side.***

And that's a blast of a *dyok*, I think.

PAHABOL: Oh, by the way, today, October 8, as I write this, marks the end of the 100-day honeymoon period for President Noynoy Aquino. As we all know, he has assumed the aka, "P-NOY." I suppose, just like the "BHO" aka of President Obama. From what I heard, the "P" in P-Noy stands for PE-Noy. Or PEE-Noy. Or PEK(2)-Noy. Hey, GMA was called with a "P" name, too, remember? What's good for the goose, should be good for the gander, *ika nga*. So, okey *ngarud*, let the P-Noy games begin *na*, ha? **JJ**

On Pakyaw, Miss Raj, Bristol . . . And On My Ripe Old Age

Acouple of days ago, I was quietly watching TFC's (ABS-CBN) news program, *"Bandila,"* when all of a sudden, Congressman Pakyaw, came on the screen swaggering as he entered the halls of Philippine Congress to attend one of its sessions, wearing a BRIGHT RED, body forming, long sleeve shirt with a bulaklakin tie . . .

First, I smiled, then I laughed, then I guffawed, then I felt sad for the Motherland.

Then, Miss Philippines, Venus Raj, the winner of the "Miss Little Perfect" title in the recent Miss Universe Pageant, came on next and announced that she would like to run, too, as a congresswoman of her province of Be Cool Land.

Talking about having a MAJOR, MAJOR heart attack, I thought I was going to have one from laughing so hard. And, do y'all know that that famous phrase uttered by Ms. Raj in the recent Miss Universe Pageant is now in vogue to say among the so called "in na in" crowd of the Philippines?

It's sad really. *Kaya kulelat palagi ang Pilipinas sa pag-unlad*because we have illiterate clowns getting elected as lawmakers of the land. Heck, even the country of Vietnam, totally destroyed by a war not too long ago, had surged ahead and surpassed the Philippines in progress . . .

Okay, enough of that.

ONBRISTOL PALIN: Have y'all seen the ABC show, "Dancing With The Stars" this Monday and Tuesday? I was curious on how Bristol Palin would fare? I like her, you see. So, I watched the show with interest. I always go for the underdog. Imagine competing against those movie celebrities, athletes and performers like Jennifer Grey, who danced with Patrick Swayze in the movie, "Dirty Dancing." Already, Ms. Grey is slated to win and that's not fair.

Also, before the show, people, bloggers, that is, were so mean toBristol.

They said that she's a "slut."

That she's a "hootchie."

That she's "hillbilly bitch."

That she's a "super tramp" and an "unwed teenage mother of a bastard, whose father is a punk . . ."

And that she's a "gold digger," like her mother, Sarah, the former governor of Alaska, and as we all know, the running mate of Senator John McCain in the last presidential election against BHO.

And that "she's no celebrity" and "what is she doing in a show called 'Dancing With The Stars'"?

On and on, those mean bloggers went. There were some kind words for her, but they were few and far in between those cruel and vicious words they said about her.

So I came on and joined the blogging, and said:

"I hope Bristol wins! She's THE show of this show. She'll dance all the way to the very last day of the show . . . and she'll win! Good luck, Bristol. Go knock 'em dead, especially those ugly, hate mongers who said those ugly things about you. I'll be cheering for you. Many will be cheering for you. So, go, Bristol, go!"

A couple of the bloggers commented on my comment and said they "agree" with me and that they are also "cheering" for Bristol. But one called me an "idiot." Can't win them all, I suppose.

Anyway, did you see that wiggle that Bristol did? Hmmmm.That was a winning wiggle, I think. A little more practice and little more weight off her, she'll dance all the way to the "finals" of the show, and hopefully she'll beat that old girl of "Dirty Dancing." Well, old man David Hasselhoff of the TV series, "Knight Rider" and "Baywatch" from a long time ago, has already been eliminated. So there.

ON OLD AGE: Talking about old age, I celebrated my 70th birthday this month. I don't feel old though. And I don't think old. But I am thinking of moving to North Dakota. According to Ms. Froma Harrop, a syndicated columnist of *The Providence Journal*, North Dakota—especially in a little town named Ashley—has one of the highest proportions of residents age 100 and older in America. Its older residents enjoy longer and healthier lives than in most parts of the country.

She said, this not a case of younger people having left the state. The proportion of people 65 and above is higher in Florida,Pennsylvania and West Virginia than in North Dakota, but they are more likely to die before 80.

And the SECRET she said of their longevity is that the people ofNorth Dakota enjoy the two things most associated with healthy aging: strong social ties and exercise. In Ashley, said Miss Harrop, if an older resident doesn't show up at a family restaurant where the old folks usually hang out, friends go look for that person.

The town's older population, she said, is weighted with retired wheat farmers and ranchers who've accumulated a lifetime of hard physical work. When they retire, they continue gardening.

IN THE NAVY: Well, I am fully retired now myself and I love gardening. When I was in the Navy, I worked my butt off, too, just like a wheat farmer. My first job in Uncle Sam's Navy was a "kargador," a job where I had to haul boxes of frozen meat weighing 50 pounds or more from a huge freeze box of the aircraft carrier I was on at that time, to the galleys (that's a kitchen) of the ship. And that freeze box was located seven ladders down (that's equivalent to seven stories of a building) in the bowels of the ship. And I had to make trips down there and up loaded with boxes of frozen meat on my back, like a mule, like 10 or 15 times a day. But I was young then and very strong. I could handle anything thrown at me and I could do anything . . . I did that kind of work for five years.

Then I was promoted to dishwasher, where I had to wash loads and loads of plates and heavy pots and pans in a steamy room. Then I became a cabin boy where I had to make hundreds of Navy officers's bunk beds. All these jobs were hard physical work.

Then I became a photo-journalist, where I had to jump from one ship to another, lugging my camera, and climbed steep ship ladders looking for stories . . . and then run to a typewriter to write those stories. That was very physical work, too.

Then I retired from the Navy. But I wasn't done yet in doing physical work. I became a cop in Florida, where I had to chase after "jits" and wrestle them down to the ground, handcuff them, pick them up bodily to haul their asses off to jail. And that was hard physical work, I tell ya!

Yes, I've had a lifetime of hard physical work in my heydays, just like those retired North Dakota wheat farmers that Ms. Harrop had written about in her recent column.

Miss Harrop also said that the rural Plains offer other advantages to a healthy old life: clean air and reduced stress; less traffic and less hurry. And that exercise and social networking are clearly the keys to quantity and quality of late life.

Well, I live in a place called Lakeland Hills, Auburn, Washington. And here in my neighborhood, it's very quiet and there's no traffic. And there's a Starbucks coffee shop a couple of miles from my house, where in between my gardening, I would usually walk, to and fro, to say hello to neighbors, old farts like me getting juice up on caffeine and flirting with all the young and pretty baristas that work there.

Heck, perhaps, I don't need to move to North Dakota after all. I've got a lot of friends here in Auburn. I am a member of our church's Knights of Columbus. I am a lector and I sing in a newly-formed all-Filipino choir, named after the one and only Filipino saint, San Lorenzo Ruiz.

Editor's Note: To read about Jesse Jose's latest avocation as a choir member, please click on this link, A Friend Named Gerry, a Church Choir, a Carrot, an Egg, and a Cup of Coffee

Yes, I am blessedly happy. And I thank the Lord that I've reached this ripe age happy and healthy . . . and horny, too, a few times a week. Well, thanks to Viagra I can get it up and keep it up. And I have this *Kapeng Barako* column, that acts as my bully pulpit and my soap box for laughter. And I have an indulgent, free-thinking editor/publisher to boot.

So what more can an old man like me ask from life? Well, perhaps, I'd like to live to over a hundred, just like those wheat farmers ofAshley, North Dakota. I've earned my keep, too, just like them. **JJ**

"Midget", "Whore" and "Chump" Labels for Pakyaw Are Not Racial Slurs to Us, Filipinos and Fil-Ams

Better late than never . . .

Nonetheless, I've got to have my say. My opinion on the matter, that is I've been wanting to say something about it for so long. But I've been so darn busy with other things in my life. That I just couldn't get around to sitting in front of my darn computer and writing about it.

Dear Readers, let me laugh first though: Ha! Ha! Ha!

Because I think it's really funny. No, better than that: it's hilarious! It's knee-slapping hilarious, I tell ya.

It's about those words that Boxer Floyd Mayweather said to describe our Pakyaw, the current national hero of the Philippinesand the number-one idol of many Filipinos.

A "midget."

A "whore."

And, a "little yellow chump."

Oh, my! I tell ya. That was so funny, I think. Hey, I've been called names, worst names, than that. And most of them were unprintable, too. I think there's nothing more hilarious than being called obscene, unprintable names. Because to me, the words merely reflect back on the name-caller's personality and mentality and the class of society that the name caller belongs to. You know, like the "patapon" class, y'all know what I mean? But let's move on to what I have to say.

From what I heard, the head honchos of NaFFAA had denounced Mayweather's comments as "racist" daw, and "a disgusting diatribe" against Pakyaw. And a "racial slur" and an "embarrassment to all Filipinos and Filipino Americans."

May I beg to differ?

Calling Pakyaw a "midget" is not a racial slur to Filipinos. Now if Mayweather had said that "Pakyaw, like most Filipinos, are midgets," then that would have been a racial slur to all Filipinos and Fil-Ams. Perhaps, to Mayweather, Pakyaw looks like a "midget." So, he called him a midget." And that to me is an opinion, but definitely NOT a racial slur.

Just like, for instance, calling a black man, a black man, would not be a racial slur, would it? For some, that would be a racial slur. I've been censored and "castrated," I mean, castigated for saying that. But then, how else would you describe a black man? There's no other way. Except, perhaps, with that "N" word. That's no longer allowed. If I use that word, I would not only be castigated, I would be, definitely, castrated. But back to the word, "midget."

The word, "midget," does not connote race. It connotes the size and looks of a person. Well, if Pakyaw looks like a midget to Mayweather . . . then a midget, he is, in Gayweather's, I mean, in Mayweather's mind. Y'all follow me, Dear Readers? If some of you find my logic faulty there, well, nobody is perfect. I am no midget though.

As to the word, "whore," from what I understand Pakyaw likes women and he's always surrounded by women swooning at him, and that he has "mistresses" galore, here and there and everywhere. It's an open secret, *sabi nga*. With all those millions of dollars that he has, heck, why not? He can buy women by the thousands. If you can "buy" elections in the

Philippines, you can easily buy women there for sex . . . or men, whatever is your preference. Or even with a child, for that matter. Believe me, I've seen it. Many foreign pedophiles come to the Philippines to buy child sex. The Almighty Dollar can buy anything in the Philippines, that's a fact, as we all know.

But back to the word, "whore." I think that's just a word of envy on the part of Maryweather, I mean, Mayweather, to describe Pakyaw. In the Philippines, anyway, the more women you have, the more macho you are. . . . In my younger days, I used to be a "whore," too. But I never made any buying though. I used my good looks to entice women. And the words then to describe men like me, were: "palikero o babaero."

Now, as to those words: "little yellow chump." In the dictionary, "chump" means "blockhead; a dolt." Once again, there's nothing racial about the word, "chump." It's merely a perception on the part of—Gayweather, I mean, Maryweather, sorry, I mean—Mayweather of Pakyaw. Y'all get my drift?

Colloquially, in American English . . . the word, "chump" could also mean, "monkey." But is Pakyaw a "little yellow 'monkey'"? Far from it, y'all know that. He is no chump nor chimp. He is the CHAMP! He's macho. He's an idol. He's "Pacman," the Filipino superman. He's a national hero . . . *at* congressman *pa ngayon, at artista, at bidang-bida.*

DISGUSTING AND AN EMBARRASSMENT: To me, what is disgusting and embarrassing to us, Filipinos and Fil-Ams are what the NEOs of NaFFAA have done: The thieveries and the fraud and the false and the convoluted financial statement meant to confuse . . . and their continuing refusal to come forward and come clean and acknowledge the theft.

And, their hypocrisies in presenting a goody-goody image, despite of it all!

From what I heard, the head "kurakuteros" and "kurakuteras" of NaFFAA (for the sake of uninitiated readers of my Barako column, NaFFAA means National Federation of Filipino-American Association, and from what I understand, there's now an added letter 'A' to the association's name and that added 'A' means "alcoholics").

Whether that's true or not, I dunno really. I've never met any of the NEOs of "NaFFAA-A." But I've heard and read a lot of things about them and what they have done—the shenanigans, the *nakawans*, the unaccounted money and all . . . and the sticky fingers of its leadership in the proverbial cookie jar.

And now, I am beginning to hear of its slow demise. *Dahil bankrupt na.*

I've also recently heard of new anomalies about monies that were collected for the Noy-Mar election campaign. Instead of the money going into the Noy-Mar campaign, *nawaldas na naman daw yung pera* on trips for "special" NaFFAA members who went home to thePhilippines. *Grabe. . . .*

And all these things that I've heard of NaFFAA or NaFFAA-A were written by three famed, award-winning Fil-Am investigative journalists and publishers: LOLO Bobby Reyes of Los Angeles, California; Joseph G. Lariosa of Chicago, Illinois; and my dear friend, Romeo Marquez, formerly of San Diego, California, but now of Toronto, Canada.

How can I NOT believe and echo what they have written? I am in awe of their fearlessness in exposing shenanigans within our Filipino community. Me? I am merely a irreverent joker, and a wannabe satirist, who likes to laugh at people and things, for he who laughs, the whole world laughs with him. Y'all can laugh at me, too, if you wish. And I'll laugh back at you. **JJ**

Battles Are Brewing, as My Coffee Brews . . .

Yes. Indeed, as my coffee brews, battles are also brewing, here and there, and everywhere.

But no, Dear Readers, I am not gonna be talking about my recent bruising battles with my siblings that I wrote about in my column last week. That's over and done with . . . I am moving on to bigger and better battles that give me neither grudge nor grief. I am a coward, you see.

So, I was at my favorite hang-out the other day, the Lakeland Hills Starbucks of our little town here in Auburn, Washington, drinking with gusto my "grande drip," mixed with a little Half and Half and two packets of Splenda, and leisurely reading my favorite newspaper, *The New York Times* . . . when I was jolted.

I mean, I was jolted by something that I was reading. I was reading the top news of the day, "Next Big Battle in Washington: Bush's Tax Cuts." No, that wasn't it that jolted me. What jolted me was what was written in the last sentence of the two lead paragraphs of this*New York Times* story.

To me, it was like, "what da heck are you talking about?" Let me quote these two lead paragraphs first:

"An epic fight is brewing over what Congress and President Obama should do about the expiring Bush tax cuts, with such substantial economic and political consequences that it could shape the fall elections and fiscal policy for years. . . ."

Okey *ngarud*, I'll buy that. Then the second lead paragraph read:

"Democratic leaders, including Mr. Obama, say they are intent on letting the tax cuts for the wealthy expire as scheduled at the end of this year. But they have pledged to continue the lower tax rates for individuals earning less than $200,000 and families earning less than $250,000 . . . (now, check this out): "what Democrats call the middle class."

Say what now? Those six words right there were the ones that jolted me. Not the words that Mr. Obama and company said that they "are intent on letting the tax cuts for the wealthy expire as scheduled at the end of this year." To me, that's the right thing to do. Spread the wealth, *di ba*? Screw the rich, stroke the poor.

But I think I got off track here. So let me get back on track: What JOLTED me were the words: ". . . what Democrats call the middle class." Y'all follow me? Or, are y'all confused? I am confused, too, Dear Readers.

Most people and majority of two-income families in America earn a lot less than that! In fact, most families probably earn ONLY a quarter of $250,000.

Like, for instance, in my household . . .

What I am trying to get at, is: If two-income families, earning $250,000 or perhaps a little less than that "is" the MIDDLE CLASS, where does that leave me and my two-income family? In the poverty level, correct?

I mean, my wife and I, with our incomes combined, don't even come close to that amount of $250,000. I mean . . . my wife has got a professional job that requires a master's degree and all that. And I have three retirement incomes that if added together could be the income of a degreed professional, too . . . YET we, as a family, hardly comes up to the income level that's considered middle class. Not even close!

What about the rest of the working people of America and those with college degrees, like teachers and lawyers and policemen and firefighters, and even journalists, print and broadcast . . . are they also WITHIN the poverty level?

I suppose so, ha?

Well, if that's the case, then we are also ENTITLED to the benefits that President Barack H. Obama has been SPREADING to the so-called "poor people" of America, the ones that I've dubbed the "PARASITES and *PALAMUNINS* of America."

Well, don't y'all think so?

THE IMMIGRATION BATLE IN ARIZONA: That new immigration law that was passed by the Arizona Legislature and signed into law by its governor, Gov, Jan Brewer, that majority of Arizonans and majority of Americans all over America approved of, was supposed to take effect Thursday, July 29, 2010.

But U.S. District Judge Susan Bolton blocked the state law and issued a temporary injunction against the core section of the law that called for Arizona law enforcement officers "to check a Mexican-looking person's immigration status while enforcing other laws and to require that person to prove that he or she is authorized to be in the country."

The law was designed to catch and deport illegal immigrants in a state that's considered the "principal gateway" for illegal border crossers from Mexico.

Judge Bolton issued the injunction in support to a legal challenge brought on by the Obama Administration. Eric Holder, Mr. Obama's Attorney General said the statute is "unconstitutional," since when it comes to setting the nation's immigration laws, "federal trump states."

Okay, that's fine. But the feds ain't doing their jobs!

Mr. Obama and his people are sitting on their butts on America's immigration problem. So Arizonans made their move to fix the problem for them within their state.

So, what's the problem there? This new Arizona immigration law ESSENTIALLY makes it a federal crime to be on American soil illegally, which is a state crime. So then, where's the conflict with federal law? In other words, it's a crime in the state of Arizona to be an illegal, which is also a federal crime all over America. If the feds ain't doing their jobs in Arizona, then the Arizonans will have to step in and do what the have to do for their state, right?

I really think that Arizona has taken the right steps in fixing this problem. In fact, seventeen states (and counting) have now made it known that they intend to follow Arizona's example. A couple of weeks ago, only FIVE STATES intend to follow Arizona's lead. Now, that has grown to SEVENTEEN STATES.

ILLEGALS COST AMERICA BILLIONS OF DOLLARS: This information was passed on to me by Jerry Lytle, a next-door neighbor and a friend and my walking partner around the hills of my Lakeland Hills neighborhood, and I wanna share it with y'all, Dear Readers. Please hang on to your seats while you read 'em:

. $11-billion to $22-billion is spent on welfare to illegal immigrants each year by state governments.

. $2.2-billion a year is spent on food assistance program, such as food stamps, WIC, and free school lunches for illegals.

. $2.5-billion a year is spent on Medicaid for them.

. $12-billion is spent on primary education and secondary school education for children here illegally and they cannot speak a word of English.

. $17-billion a year is spent for education for American-born children of illegal aliens, known as "anchor babies."

. $3-billion a day is spent to incarcerate illegal aliens.

. $90-billion a year is spent on illegals for welfare and social services by the American taxpayers.

. $200-billion a year in suppressed American wages are caused by illegal workers.

. The National Policy Institute estimated that the total cost of mass deportation would be between $206-billion and $230-billion or an average cost of between $41-billion and $46-billion over a five-year period.

The list of taxpayers' dollars spent on illegal immigrants goes on and on. The total cost is a whooping $338-billion a year. **More clearly, that's $338,300,000,000.00 which would be enough to STIMULATE the economy for the citizens of this country** . . . that, may I add, President H. Obama failed to do with those stimulus money that he gave to greedy Wall Street bankers and doled out to the PARASITES and *PALAMUNINS* of America.

The darkest side of illegal immigration are NOT only the millions of illegals that continually crossed America's Southern Border, but also the millions of pounds of illegal drugs, such as cocaine, meth, heroin, marijuana, that are continuously brought in to America. And the crimes generated from it all.

Need I say more? Ah, yes, one more. My coffee is now ready and freshly brewed. So talk to y'all later about my next "battle," as my next cup 'o coffee perks and brews. **JJ**

A Wedding and an Open Letter to my Siblings

My column this week is very personal. It's a letter to all my siblings in Florida and to a brother in the Philippines. And though it's personal, the human-interest aspect of this story is also universal. For I believe it can also happen to any family: the spats and the intrigues and all.

As y'all know, Dear Readers, the months of June, July, August and September are favorite months for couples in love to tie the knot. My son, Chris, my pride and my joy, and a broadcast journalist who's going to be news casting soon for FOX News Denver in Colorado is gonna tie that knot, too, with Jaclyn Rostie, who is also a broadcast journalist for ABC News in Coral Springs, Colorado.

They met four years ago in Cheyenne, Wyoming when they were both field reporters and anchors of the weekend newscast of KGWN, a CBS News affiliate. I suppose their proximity to each other and their common interests and team effort in bringing the news to their viewers . . . planted the seed for respect for each other that became love that sprouted.

When Chris moved up to a broadcasting job in Cedar Rapids in Iowa, Jaclyn followed. And again, I suppose, that love that sprouted, grew . . .

And grew . . .

And bloomed . . .

And ripened.

And that finally decided for Chris to buy a very-expensive diamond engagement ring and on his bended knees, offered the ring to Jaclyn and perhaps, with all the courage he could muster, finally uttered the words what every woman longs to hear from a longtime lover: "Will you marry me?"

So, the wedding date was set.

And it's going to be on August 8th of this year.

Detailed preparations got underway. The bride's maids and the best man and the grooms were painstakingly selected, as well as the venue of the wedding and the reception and the menu, the dresses for the entourage, the tux for the grooms, the theme color for the wedding . . .

And the guests, who are going to be invited to witness one of life's happiest occasions and to partake on the feast and to share in the joy of Chris and Jaclyn, were picked. It's a celebration! It's a celebration of love. It's a celebration of the joining of two loves.

It's also a celebration of the joining of two families: the Jose's and the Rostie's. So, invitations, carefully designed and lovingly worded, were sent out. Foremost of all, to the two families that will be joined together.

So, I made sure that each one of my seven siblings gets an invitation. Simply, but elegantly scripted, the invitation reads:

With joyful hearts we ask you
to be present at the ceremony
uniting

Jaclyn Eleonor Rostie
&
Christopher Navarro Jose

On Sunday, the Eight of August

Two Thousand Ten
at four o'clock in the afternoon
St. Julien Hotel
900 Walnut Street
Boulder, Colorado

Reception to follow

MY LETTER TO MY SIBLINGS: More-than two-hundred invitations were sent out. The deadline for receiving the RSVP's was on the 17th of this month. All responded, EXCEPT my brothers and sisters. I thought and thought about it. I asked myself several times, "why?" I asked my wife the same question. It was so embarrassing. My wife said, "I dunno, *pamilya mo yun mga yun . . .*" Since the only way I can express my emotional turmoil is to put pen on paper, I wrote this letter to them:

Hello Everybody,

I am going to let this forwarded e-mail by Jaclyn to Maribel speaks for itself. It's at the end of this letter to all of you.

Bakit naman LAHAT kayo hindi nag-RSVP doon sa wedding invitation ni **Chris at Jaclyn? Over two hundred invitations were sent out, but only the Jose clan did not respond.** ***Nakakahiya naman ang ginawa ninyo*****. The invitations were sent to Raquel to be given to all of you, except Soc's and Kirsten's which were directly sent to them by Jaclyn. Raquel said** ***na ibinigay ninya daw lahat sa inyo yung*** **invitation and you all got it.**

Maribel and I were all so embarrassed by everybody's non-response to Jaclyn. I really think that shows ***KABASTUSAN*****from all of you! And that made the JOSE CLAN look bad** ***at walang mga modo*****! All you had to do was check either yes or no and send back your response.** ***May selyo na nga at*****envelope enclosed in the invitation and all you had to do was to seal it and drop in a mailbox.** ***Mahirap bang gawin yun*****?**

I warned both Christopher and Jaclyn not to send the invitations out to you all of you there, *dahil alam kong hindi naman kayo pupunta.* But Jaclyn, who wanted to give to all of you her respect, insisted that the invitations be sent out, as you are all IMMEDIATE RELATIVES and it's the right thing to do. She was not asking for dole outs or money or anything like that. In fact, I even emphasized to Raquel *na ang "IMPORTANTE" diyan*, are your RSVP's.

But Jaclyn's attempt in reaching out to all of you was foiled. Y'all rejected her and ignored her invitation.

Hindi naman basta-basta itong Rostie family that Chris will be marrying into. In fact, the family is one of the pillars of the town of Brighton in Colorado. The family owns a professional plaza in town and real-estate properties. They have a private plane, a runway and a hangar in their backyard, and own the small-plane airport in town. In other words, the Rostie family is a wealthy family. A well-known and well-respected family in their town.

When Raquel told me that she had received all the invitations and said: "*O sige, magpapadala kami ng pera sa kanila,*" I almost laughed and wanted to tell her that that's not needed. But I didn't want to make *YABANG*, so I just said, "*Ang importatnte diyan, yung RSVP ninyo.*" I told her over and over, "RSVP, RSVP, RSVP." *Hindi PERA*!

This is really an EMBARRASSMENT for the Jose clan! We are going to be looked at as a socially-inept family. *Nakakahiya ang mga* "Jose." And it's a crying shame for Jaclyn that she's going to be a Jose, too.

Matuto naman sana kayong lahat ng konting urbanidad, mga kapatid ko. Learn how to open your hearts . . . and your mind. Learn how to respond and reach out to people who are trying to reach out to you.

At bawasan ang mga high-faluting na yabang, especially you, my dear Raquel! And I am going to say it again: *Kung meron masters si Jeje sa* nursing, she's an ARNP, who sees patients in an office and prescribes

medications to them. I use the VA hospital here in Seattle, so I know. ARNP's do not write out the nurses' working schedules. And there's no such thing as having a masters in "nursing technology." I am not knocking Jeje down. Please get me wrong. But I am not stupid either to believe that kind of *bola*. Let's stop all these high-faluting *yabang*. Because I am not impressed. *O naiinggit*. Please let's be truthful to each other. I am your brother, and whatever good things that come your way, I'll always be happy for you. I have no reason *na mainggit sa 'yo o sa mg anak mo*.

O sige na, pinatawad ko na rin kayong lahat dito sa kahihiyan na ibinigay ninyo sa amin*. But I had to say all these things that I've said. *Mabuti na yung tapatan, kaysa nagbobolahan. Tumatanda na tayong lahat. Tama na yun pa-impress-impress at mga high faluting ng mga bolahan.

God bless all of you and take care.

So what do y'all think, Dear Readers? Is this airing dirty laundry? My wife said it is. I don't think so. It's a Barako story. Blunt and honest and fearless and *orig . . . hindi Googled o kopya.*

My wife also said I am gonna get ostracized by my siblings for this. Ostracized for speaking the truth? Oh well, it won't be the first time and it won't the last time, for I don't have forked tongue . . . Dear Readers, thank you for reading my column this week. That's all. **JJ**

Is it Racial Profiling?
My Take on Arizona's New Immigration Law

Is it really racial profiling? No, it's not! I agree with it. It's the right thing to do. An illegal resident here in America is a criminal, a fugitive from the law. He or she must be apprehended and deported. No ifs or buts about it . . .

But before I go on, Dear Readers, let me tell y'all first this story. It's true. It happened.

When I moved to Florida in the early 1980's and was hired there as Martin County Deputy Sheriff, one of the first things I did was to open a bank account for the direct deposit of my paycheck. The name of the bank was the old Barnett Bank, the number-one bank then in Florida.

So I went to this bank and walked up to this young, pretty teller, and said: "I would like to open up a bank account."

She looked at me ("stared" would be the precise word) for several seconds, and then she said, "Can I see your drivers' license? And . . . your GREEN CARD."

I've never had that so-called "green card," so at first I honestly didn't know what she meant. Then it dawned on me that what she meant was that green card, the card that we, Filipinos, *na mga bagong salta sa Amerika,* eagerly long (even desperately, for some), to possess. It's the much-coveted pass to our journey in pursuing the American Dream.

But when this story happened, I was no longer a *bagong salta* or as my sons, Jon and Chris, would say, "fresh off the boat." I've already completed 20 years of active service in the U.S. Navy, seen most of America, from east to west, north to south, traveled the world many times over, and retired and transferred to the Fleet Reserve.

In other words, I've been around, done this and done that and, an American citizen *na*. In fact, "forced" to become one, so I could be granted a top-secret security clearance, as I was around top-secret military hardware and equipments aboard the nuclear submarine I was on. I suppose they just wanna make sure I wasn't a little Filipino spy for the Russians, America's number-one enemy at that time.

So, no, I've never had a green card. I became a citizen because I had to. But becoming one, I must confess, transformed me, slowly but surely, into a believer of this country and its ideals. I became, bit by bit, a loyal warrior of America, who was willing to fight and die for my adopted country.

Anyway . . . back to the bank: The only "green card" I had to show to that pretty, young teller was my Deputy Sheriff ID card and my shiny star-shaped badge next to it.

And, as I flashed them to her face, I said, with all the *Barako*coolness I can muster: "Will this be GREEN enough for you, Miss?"

She blushed red as a beet. Her pretty blue eyes opened wide. Her jaw dropped. And she stuttered, "Yes sir, I . . . I . . . think so." To put her at ease, I smiled at her. I felt so sorry for her. She was so pretty and so innocent . . . and so ignorant.

Then she asked, in a friendly, flirting tone, "When did you become aU.S. citizen, sir?

"Long before you were born, my dear girl." I replied with a DOM smile. She smiled back. She was so pretty.

Now, did this young lady commit racial profiling? Why did she ask for my "green card" when only a Florida driver's license was the only thing needed to open a bank account? Did that bank require green cards for people like me or for people who "looks" like me?

And, how did I feel when that teller asks for my "green card"? Well, honestly, I felt kind of slighted. But I saw the point why they "required" it, from someone like me. In Florida then and today, there are lots of Guatemalan agricultural workers and most of them are illegals. I suppose to this young, pretty honey, I might have been a Guatemalan illegal worker, so she asked for my "green card."

So, I showed her my "green card." Was it racial profiling? Of course, it was. Was it JUSTIFIED? Sure, it was. Because on matters like these, the chaff must be separated from the grain . . .

MAJORITY OF AMERICANS ARE IN FAVOR: Let's fast forward to 2010 and to Arizona's new immigration law. As I've said, I agree with it. It's the right thing to do.

In April, the Arizona legislature voted to "discourage and deter" illegal immigrants from staying in the state by authorizing law-enforcement officers to question Hispanic-looking individuals, WHEN caught breaking the law. Like for instance, for running a red light or for any kind of traffic infractions, or for whatever infractions committed.

When an officer has "reasonable suspicion" that a person is not a legal resident, he is to ask questions and can take into custody those who cannot show that they are legal residents. These illegal residents could then be convicted of a state crime and turned over to federal-immigration agents.

What the police CANNOT do is to arbitrarily stop a Hispanic-looking individual while walking down the street, grab him and ask him for his "papers." There must be a crime first or a violation committed BEFORE they can ask about his immigration status and proof of his legal residency.

I don't see anything wrong with that. There are sizable numbers of illegals in Arizona. There are also lots of legal and law-abiding residents. The chaff must be separated from the grain . . .

But President Barack Hussein Obama and his people in his White House said that they find the Arizona law "hateful," "pernicious" and "unjust." But 70% of Arizonans support the law. Majority of Americans all over America support the law, 69% to be exact. In fact, in five states—South Carolina, Pennsylvania, Minnesota,Rhode Island and Michigan—will soon follow this immigration policy that Arizona has spearheaded.

Within the same vein, if you're a Filipino in this country and a "TNT," which in our vernacular means, "tago ng tago," and in English means, "hiding and hiding" from the law, you're a fugitive from justice. And any person who helps hide a *TNT* "harbors" a fugitive . . . and that's a felony, too.

Arizona's immigration law does NOT symbolize cruelty.

It is NOT a form of racial profiling . . .
It is NOT unjust!
It is NOT pernicious!
It is NOT hateful!

It's a long-overdue reaction to the FAILURE of President Barack H. Obama's administration to preserve and protect the true meaning of citizenship, in America. That's all. **JJ**

A General Named McChrystal Versus the President Named BHO

Three words: He's got balls.

To me there are only three words fit to describe Gen. Stanley McChrystal, the head honcho in the battleground of America's war in Afghanistan—he's got balls.

No ifs or buts, but yes, indeed, he's got balls.

And I think the real reason he got "fired" from his job as the man in Afghanistan fighting the insurgents there and the Talibans, is that his balls are a lot bigger than President Obama's.

And Obama didn't like that.

Because, you see, on one side of this equation is the General, a proven brave warrior, a brilliant war general, a West Point graduate, a Marine and a Special Forces operations officer with all kinds of medals earned in fighting battles. He was the man in Iraq, as the LA Times puts it, "given the credit for undercutting the Sunni Arab and Shiite Muslim militias, and singled out for praise after the June 2006 operation that killed the leader of the militant group al-Qaida in Iraq, Abu Musab Zarqawi."

In other words, General McChrystal was the one who physically and completely broke the back of the insurgency there. He was the Man, the "Axman" of Gen. David Petraeus, who engineered the turnaround in the war in Iraq.

On the other side of the equation is President Obama, the so called commander-in-chief of the United States military, who has no military education or experience whatsoever, not even one course in high school of Jr. ROTC. The closest military experience he had ever had were saluting and shaking hands and paying lip service to battle-weary soldiers returning from their second, third or fourth tours fromAmerica's wars overseas.

I guess for Obama, vis-à-vis rendering military salutes toAmerica's returning warriors, is close enough to having a military experience.

POKING FUN AT OBAMA AND HIS AIDES: The reason daw the General was "fired" was because of disparaging personal comments that he and his aides made about Obama and his own civilian aides, who oversee *kuno* the war in Afghanistan from their air-conditioned offices in Washington, D.C.

These comments appeared in a Rolling Stone profile story, "The Runaway General," written by Michael Hastings, who reported that McChrystal is said to be "frustrated" with Obama and his top civilian leadership.

And that when McChrystal first met Obama, he was "disappointed" with the President's limited knowledge of the war and his complete "unpreparedness" for conducting a war against insurgents in Afghanistan. And during a meeting at the Pentagon with McChrystal and several other generals, Obama was clearly "uncomfortable and intimidated."

The General was also quoted saying that he found Obama "painful" when the president reprimanded him last fall for speaking openly about his desire for more U.S. troops inAfghanistan.

In this story, one of McChrystal's aides called White House National Security Adviser Jim Jones, who is a retired four-star general, a "clown," whose war strategy thinking is "stuck in 1985."

Hastings also wrote that McChrystal and his staff made fun of Joe Biden about "dismissing the vice president with a good one-liner."

And that McChrystal was quoted to have said: "Are you asking about Vice President Biden? Who's that?" Then an aide quipped, "Biden? Did you say, Bite me?"

The general was also portrayed as "exasperated" by e-mails that he had received from Richard Holbrooke, Obama's special envoy to Afghanistan and was quoted as saying: "I don't even want to open them."

Of Karl Eikenbery, the U.S. ambassador to Afghanistan, and McChrystal's harshest critic of his Afghan war strategy, the general said the ambassador's main preoccupation was merely to cover his butt: "The one who covers his flank for the history books."

THE "BETRAY US" GENERAL TO THE RESCUE: President Obama said General McChrystal's insubordinate conduct "undermines the civilian control of the military that is at the core of our democratic system."

YET, right after the firing of McChrystal, Obama RE-AFFIRMED his commitment to the same war strategy and policy that was drafted and proposed, and overseen on the scene by General McChrystal himself.

And then he ordered Gen. David Petraeus, the head honcho of Central Command—whom, if y'all remember, **Obama had called General "Betray Us" for proposing that surge inIraq**—to step down from his lofty position in Central Command and assume the position that McChrystal had vacated as battleground commander in Afghanistan.

Obama then called the appointment of Petraeus "a change in personnel but not in policy."

So, the REASON General McChrystal was sacked from his command was because President Obama didn't like the fact that he and his aides were mocked and made fun of by the general and his staff.

It's NOT for incompetence for handling the Afghan War, that's for sure. How petty *naman* the reason was. *Pikon pala etong si* Obama. *Pero, tinawag niya si* General Petraeus as General "Betray Us" during the troop surge in Iraq.

What's good for the goose should be good for the gander. But in this case, who's got the bigger balls, the goose, or the gander? And who's the goose and who's the gander? And, who's the better person here?

So, I've said all this. I am a retired U.S. Navy Chief Petty Officer. Is that being insubordinate, too? Speaking out my views? What's Obama gonna do? Force me also to retire? I am already retired. Take away my military pension? I am no FilVet who beg for "handouts" from the U.S. government for my wartime services. I am a U.S. military veteran. I've served this country for over 20 years, and in wartime, too. I earned my pension and disability benefits. Every bit of it.

But most importantly, I've also earned my right to speak out. And I think Gen. Stanley McChrystal was fired unjustly, and President Barack Hussein Obama's decision to sack him was a show of arrogance on his part.

It's true that one of the basic elements of the U.S. Constitution is civilian control over the military. But render to Caesar what belongs to Caesar. . . . And let the generals win their wars.

Let them speak out, too, fearlessly. That's all. **JJ**

Manny Pakyaw and Aling Dionisia Dyoks. An Old Farmer's Advice. And More.

Ahhh, finally it's summer.

And to me, a perfect summer day is when the sun is shining, the breeze is blowing, the birds are singing and . . . the lawn mower is broken, turning this day into a lazy day and the perfect time for***dyoks*** . . .

Wala na si Erap at si FPJ sa scene, kaya sina Pakyaw at si Aling Dionisia na daw ang uso ngayon that Filipinos love to make dyoks of. But some of the jokes are recycled ones from the glory days of Erap and pre-Erap politicians. Here are some of them. Enjoy:

Si Manny Pakyaw tumakbo sa pagka-Congressman sa Gen San . . .

Reporter: Manny, anong masasabi mo sa peace and order sa inyong lugar sa Gen San?

Pakyaw: Ah, yun ba? Uhmm . . . eh . . . ay . . .

Reporter: Ano?

Pakyaw: Ahh, kwan . . . maraming fish sa Gen San, pero wala masyadong umo-Order.

Reporter: Manny, ngayon nanalo ka ng "tongressman," anong ibibigay mong gift kay Jinkee?

Manny: Ibon syempre. Mahilig sya dun, eh.

Reporter: Ibon? Anong klaseng ibon?

Manny: Yung mga lipstek, pangmik up ba? Basta mga Ibon products. Yo know . . .

Pakyaw: Honey, buksan mo na yung sweets.

Jinky: Lambing mo talaga. Mwah!! Nasaan ang sweets, honey?

Pakyaw: Yung sweets ng ilaw. Di ako makakita. Ang dilim!!

Jinky: Manny, kung magkakaanak ulit tayo, ano ang magandang name?

Manny: Hmmm. Eh di combine na lang name natin . . . MANKY.

Aling Dionisia: Gusto ko naman pag nagka-anak uli kayo ni Jinky, di lang pangalan nyo pagsasamahin. Dapat kasali din pangalan ko.

Pakyaw: Oo naman, Nay, kasu midyu mahirap yun.

Aling Dionisia: Hindi ah, may naesip na nga ako, eh.

Pakyaw: Talaga, 'Nay? Anu?

Aling Dionisia: DIOMANJI (Dionisia-Manny-Jinky).

Aling Dionisia: Dok, gusto ko magpalagay ng breast.

Doctor: (Nagulat) Magpapasexsi ka na?

Aling Dionisia: Breast sa ngipen ba. Para umayos yun ngepen ko! Deba uso yon?

Pakyaw: Sabi ng titser ko, bakit daw an eggplant walang egg?

Aling Dionisia: Sabihon mo sa titser mo, na pag me egg yun, turta na, TURTA!

Aling Dionisia: Inday, akina yung seeds ko.

Inday: Bakit po, magtatanim po ba kayo?

Aling Dionisia: Anung magtatanim sinasabi mo? Nasisilaw ang mata ko kaya kailangan ko ng seeds.

Piolo and Manny were having a heart to heart talk.

Manny: Pare, ba't ba naman hanggang ngayon wala ka pang syota? Wala ka pa bang napupusuan?

Piolo: Meron . . . manhid ka lang!

Noodle!!! Noodle!! Noodle!

Pakyaw sa "Deal or No Deal."

Sa Las Vegas:

Waiter: May I take your order, Madam?

Aling Dionisia: Soup.

Waiter: Chicken, asparagus, noodle or soup of the day?

Aling Dionisia: Soup drenks.

"You is! You is! You is!," sigaw ni Aling Dionisia pagdating sa Amerika. "Andito na ako sa 'you is.'"

Sa isang birthday party.

Aling Dionisia: Blue! Blue de kick!

Sa Las Vegas, before the fight with El Kuto, as reported by CNN (Coconut News Ngayon).

Chavit: Manny, paki-acknowledge mo naman si First Gentleman, late dumating. Ayun kadadaan lang sa tabi ng ringside.

Manny: I would like to acknowledge the arrival of the late First Gentleman Arroyo who just PASSED AWAY!

And from the collection of Manny Pacquiao (MP) jokes from the humorists of the MabuhayRadio.com:

Foreign Reporter: "Do you have freedom of speech in Mindanao, Congressman Pacquiao?"
Manny: "Yes, we are free to spit here, there and enywhere."

Congressman Manny (as he addresses fellow freshman congressmen in a pre-session caucus): "My Dear Colleges . . ."

Another congressman (whispers to Manny): "Bai, hindi 'college' it's 'colleague' . . ."

Congressman Manny (correcting himself): "Colleague, singular, Colleges, plural."

Reporter: "What can you say about your primary job of filing bills in the House of Representatives?"

Congressman Manny: "Well, if there are bills, the Speaker should order that they be paid immediately."

Reporter: "I am referring to bills in the legislation process. What bills do you intend to file?"

Congressman Manny: "Oh, legislative bills? Well, I am filing immediately two bills: The first is to continue propagating the carabao for the farmers and, secondly, to propagate the Carabao English, so as to do away with 'Taglish' . . ."

Hahahahhahahaha! Want more of this? E-mail and ask my fellow **"DOM," Ed Navarra** of Michigan, who is now also a columnist with a newspaper published by Antonio Antonio, a former president of the National Press Club of the Philippines. Y'all know him, right? That's right, he's the Midwest Regional chair of NaFFAA. He sent me those dyoks, and I had a jolly good time reading them that I thought I'd share them with you, Dear Readers. I hope you had fun reading them, too. If you had read them somewhere before, well, reading them again—unless you're a scrooge—was really good for you. Because, you see, a laughter a day keeps the witches away. Laughter, I've found out, is also the best antidote for people who badmouth you. He, he, he.

Okey *ngarud*, enough of that. Stay with me. There's more, but this is serious now.

AN OLD FARMER'S ADVICE: I got this from a cyberspace friend, named Bryan, who is really a farmer, and the chaplain of the Martin County Sheriff's Office in Florida, where I used to work as a deputy. I think these are true gems of wisdom, worth your while reading and immersing yourselves in. I did, and my mind is still tingling from the wisdom of it all. If being a farmer gives you this kind of wisdom, I think I'd like to be a farmer, too, one day when I grow up. The ones IN ALL CAPS and in boldface, especially the last one, are favorites of mine that I intend to keep in my heart and mind. Here they are. Enjoy:

. Your fences need to be horse-high, pig-tight and bull-strong. Keep skunks and bankers at a distance.

. LIFE IS SIMPLER WHEN YOU PLOW AROUND THE STUMP.

A bumble bee is considerably faster than a John Deere tractor.

. WORDS THAT SOAK INTO YOUR EARS ARE WHISPERED . . . NOT YELLED.

. Meanness don't jes happen overnight.

. FORGIVE YOUR ENEMIES; IT MESSES UP THEIR HEADS.

. Do not corner something that you know is meaner than you.

. IT DON'T TAKE A VERY BIG PERSON TO CARRY A GRUDGE.

. You cannot unsay a cruel word.

. Every path has a few puddles.

. WHEN YOU WALLOW WITH PIGS, EXPECT TO GET DIRTY.

. The best sermons are lived, not preached.

. DON'T JUDGE FOLKS BY THEIR RELATIVES.

. Remember that silence is sometimes the best answer.

. LIVE A GOOD, HONORABLE LIFE . . . THEN WHEN YOU GET OLDER AND THINK BACK, YOU'LL ENJOY IT A SECOND TIME.

. Don't interfere with something that ain't bothering you none.

. If you find yourself in a hole, first thing to do is to stop digging.

. Always drink upstream from the herd.

. GOOD JUDGMENT COMES FROM EXPERIENCE, AND A LOTCOMES FROM BAD JUDGMENT.

. Lettin' the cat outta the bag is a whole lot easier than puttin' back in.

. If you get to thinkin' you're a person of some influence, try orderin' somebody else's dog.

. Live simply. Love generously. Care deeply. Speak kindly. Leave the rest to God.

. DON'T PICK A FIGHT WITH AN OLD MAN. IF HE IS TOO OLD TO FIGHT, HE'LL JUST KILL YA.

Okey *ngarud*, y'all have a great weekend. Oh, by the way, before I go, lemme say this, too: While President Barack H. Obama has the media on his side, he clearly does not have the will of the people—58% of Americans are dead set against his health care bill and 69% are for the Arizona immigration law that the Obama Administration calls "hateful."

And this: Al and Tipper Gore (y'all remember the lingering smooch in the 2004 presidential convention, right?). Well, they are now splitting, along with the BP oil that keeps on spilling. That's all. **JJ**

Magsaysay Redux: History Repeating Itself

As that worn-out cliché goes, history repeats itself.

But this story that was sent to me is far from being worn-out though. It's very true and it will be forever be true, that the automated, highly-spirited and highly-contested Philippine election of 2010 will be remembered in future Philippine History books, as fraudulent in many ways . . .

Mainly because the people's votes were counted by a Venezuelan-made Smartmatic machines that turned out to be *Palpakmatik* machines.

But most of all, it confirmed my suspicion that the election of Noynoy Aquino as President of my "belabed" Motherland, the Philippines, is CIA-orchestrated.

Just like the downfall of the late strongman, President Ferdinand Marcos.

Just like EDSA 1 . . .

Just like the "installation" of Tita Cory as President.

Now history is repeating itself, once more, as good old USA performs another "installation" of a Philippine President, this time around, of the "anointed son," Noynoy, dubbed by cynics (that includes yours truly), as the "second coming."

Uncle Sam has pulled a fast one, again, and Filipinos are cheering and worshipping this anointed son . . . courtesy of Uncle Sam. My Inang Bayan is truly a country of Wawa We!

This story recently appeared in the column, **"Strategic Perspective," of Rene B. Azurin** in the well-read Philippine publication, ***Business World.*** Enjoy. I am sure many will not agree with it, especially those true believers of the Noynoy phenomenon. Therefore, *ngarud*, may I suggest that you take your blood pressure pill first before reading it. Here's the story, en toto:

Magsaysay Redux?

The high-profile visit of American Ambassador Harry Thomas Jr. to Benigno Aquino, III's home to congratulate him on his election (before the official count had been completed) seemed to affirm the earlier contention of columnist Carmen Pedrosa (*Star*, March 20) that this election was characterized by "the intervention of a former colonial power." What it does, certainly, is recall the elections of 1953 when an Edward Lansdale-directed CIA operation got Ramon Magsaysay installed as President of this country.

As pointed out by (ex-CIA operative) Victor Marchetti and (ex-US State Department intelligence official) John Marks in their book, *The CIA and the Cult of Intelligence* (1974), that particular operation was "the prototype for CIA covert operations during the 1950's" and Lansdale became so well known that "he served as the model for characters in two best-selling novels" (*The Ugly American* and *The Quiet American*).

Multi-awarded journalist Stanley Karnow writes in his book, *In Our Image: America's Empire in the Philippines* (1989), that Lansdale "had in effect invented Magsaysay." In Karnow's telling, "Magsaysay listened reverently" while Lansdale would lecture him in a bedroom they shared after Lansdale and his bosses forced (with promises of aid) then President Quirino to appoint Magsaysay as Defense Secretary. The relationship of puppet master and puppet is reinforced by a story that (Karnow says) Lansdale would later tell

that he once "kayoed" Magsaysay when Magsaysay failed to deliver a speech Lansdale had written.

Among Lansdale's CIA associates (according to Karnow) were political operator Gabriel Kaplan, whose cover was head of what later became the Asia Foundation, and David Sternberg, whose cover was reporter for the *Christian Science Monitor*. Kaplan, interestingly, was the one who organized what became Namfrel (using Filipinos who were on the CIA's payroll) "to propel Magsaysay forward" and that group "enlisted civic leaders, teachers and students to act as poll watchers." The CIA effectively "underwrote" Magsaysay's presidential campaign against Quirino in 1953, channeling funds through JUSMAG and Kaplan's poll watchdog group.

Distinguished Filipino historians Renato and Letizia Constantino—in their book *The Philippines: The Continuing Past* (1978)—confirm the deferential attitude Magsaysay affected toward his American patrons—as well as toward his boss President Quirino—but paint a more nuanced portrait of him as a shrewd and calculating politician who was similarly manipulating his supposed "superiors" to achieve his own ambitious ends. One of the things he apparently learned from Lansdale's "psych-war" and "dirty tricks" operations was that, "with a cooperative press, it was easy to plant false information."

Part of Lansdale's buildup of Magsaysay involved organizing a well-publicized US visit, arranging meetings with American media, and getting him featured on the cover of *Time* magazine.

According to the Constantinos, "the choice of Magsaysay was part of a deliberate program supportive of Washington's designs in Asia. His rise, so much the product of a good press, was part of the tactics of the new Asian rearrangement that the United States was imposing." The highest priority was given at that time "to CIA efforts to elect Magsaysay President . . . (because) a new stage in American thrusts for world hegemony had started."

Once Magsaysay was elected, the CIA station in Manila "continued to assist Magsaysay with advice, drafted some of his speeches, and gave him all sorts of support with his various problems. One CIA-funded project coordinated press support for Magsaysay's internal programs and for his foreign policy in support of American objectives in Asia."

The CIA's manipulation of Philippine media was apparently so effective that it "was copied by CIA stations in Latin America." This manipulation continued well after the death of Magsaysay (in a plane crash) through the CIA's "press assets," meaning, "newspapermen in their employ or friendly to them whom they could use to plant news."

The point of this recollection of the Magsaysay story is that it sounds so eerily familiar more than half a century later. Of the building up then of Magsaysay, Karnow observed that, "In the Philippines at the time, to be called an 'Amboy'—'America's boy'—was a halo." Well, apparently, more-than half a century later, it still is. Is it possible that the recent elections made us all manipulated participants in a dusting off of the old Lansdale playbook, this time on behalf of Mr. Aquino? It would certainly explain the swagger and smugness of certain rabidly pro-Aquino journalists and spokesmen.

It would also explain the almost-ridiculous way the whole poll-automation exercise unfolded, beginning with the selection of an unknown and relatively inexperienced supplier (Smartmatic), through the suspicious one-after-the—other discarding of all of the system's supposed security features and the eve-of-the-election need to "reconfigure and replace" 76,000 memory cards unobserved by anyone, to the as-yet-unexplained use of the approximately P4-billion difference between the amount of the Smartmatic contract and the amount provided for the poll automation process.

If the US were involved, a conspiracy of this magnitude—requiring the sheep-like cooperation of all the Comelec commissioners and the quiet acquiescence of Mrs. Arroyo and her boys—would be plausible.

One might note that the world is in crisis and "American thrusts for world hegemony" is threatened today by the emergence of China as an economic power. Describing the Philippines after the installation in 1953 of Magsaysay, the Constantinos wrote, "United States control over the country was complete. The Americans not only had Magsaysay but also a panoply of personalities and organizations that attempted to remold thinking and implement projects favored by Washington because they jibed with the global designs of the United States."

Ambassador Thomas made a point of saying that he did not discuss the RP-US Visiting Forces Agreement with Mr. Aquino. Presumably, neither did he discuss the possibility of a permanent US base in Mindanao or oil concessions in the Sulu sea or the controversial Memorandum of Agreement with the secessionist MILF rebel group.

Were such discussions merely untimely? Or simply no longer necessary? Let's watch how events unfold.

So, what do y'all think, Dear Readers? *Si* Noynoy *ba, eh*, Amboy *din*? I thought it was Gibo who was the Amboy. And on his part, Gibo thought he was the "anointed one." But it turned out to be Noynoy. No wonder in his concession speech, Gibo said that the reason he lost, was because he was "betrayed." He didn't say who betrayed him though.

Now, we know, ha? History repeats itself, indeed. **JJ**

Congratulations to Noynoy, Et Al. Licking Wounds . . . and Women

The Filipino people had spoken.

So I, too, wish to congratulate Noynoy Aquino for winning the presidential election. I wish him well and our Inang Bayan.

I also wish to congratulate all the movie actors and actresses who, once again, were elected as senators, congressmen, governors, mayors, councilors, etceteras, etcetera. I wish all of them well and our Inang Bayan.

I also wish to congratulate Manny Pakyaw for becoming a "tongressman" of his hometown. He has come a long way. From panadero to boksingero to national hero and "symbol of the Filipino ethnic pride," and now one of the lawmakers of my native land. Yes, he has indeed come a long way. I wish him well and our Inang Bayan.

I also wish to congratulate all the dynasties of *kawatans* and all the old, useless *politicos* who got elected once again as leaders of my poor native land. Their political machineries are so finely-tuned that you cannot help but admire their tenacity and cleverness in "hanging on" to power. Yes, I wish them well, too . . . and our Inang Bayan.

And, to those die-hard *tutas* of Noynoy during this election, believe it or not, I also congratulate them and wish them well.

Pero sana naman, stop the gloating *na*. Move on *na*. Because the gloating is beginning to look ridiculous and *kadiri* to death *na*. Especially, The Filipino Channel (TFC) of ABS/CBN, which up to now still keeps flashing on the screen the million of votes that Noynoy has over the other candidates—like Erap, Villar, Gibo and the *kulelats*—rubbing it in and rubbing it in.

O, sige na ngarud, panalo na si 'Noy. . . .

LICKING WOUNDS: In a mass email to friends and ex-friends right after the elections, where I expressed my honest disgust on the results, a woman reader, perhaps one of my fans, said that it's time for me to accept the fact that my candidate of choice, Senator Manny Villar, had lost. After giving me a stern lecture on Noynoy's good qualities and what he would be able to do for our Inang Bayan, she said, "Lick your wounds now, Babe."

Now me, an all time smart-ass and a true DOM, gave her this quickie answer, "I'd rather lick your wound, Babe."

She responded, "I don't have any wounds. . . ." She also said that I can lick her next-door neighbor's dog, but she doesn't think her next door neighbor would allow that, as the dog is of a "high-class breed."

I laughed so hard when I read her response. Then I said, "I am an expert in finding women's wounds and I am sure I'll find your wound, no matter how well hidden."

She deleted my email. Well, cheers to the wound that never heals.

Y'all don't get me wrong now. I am not sexist. I love women, especially smart, intelligent and beautiful women, like my wife. I am for their equal rights and equal pay and all kinds of equality that they want to have. Yes, even in bed. And yes, they should be in combat, too, if they wish.

FIRST US NAVY WOMAN FIGHTER PILOT: I can't recall her name now, but when I was in the Navy as a chief combat photo-journalist, I interviewed and wrote a story about the first woman jet fighter pilot in the Navy. That story was published in several military and civilian publications. I followed her around for a couple of days during the interview. I watched her take off, do loops in the air and land and screeched her plane to a stop as if it was a toy, a million-dollar toy, it was. I was impressed. She was amazing that I took pictures of her. She looked gorgeous in her jet-fighter pilot uniform.

She looked like a true warrior. But she was all woman.

HORNY SAILORS: I just don't agree that women should be on Navy ships, teeming with horny, young sailors. I was in the Navy for 20 years. At sea for many months on end. Believe me I know how it is to be horny . . . and deprived. When you're deprived, you become depraved. Day in and day out, there's only one thing on your mind. At night you dream about it. You count the days and the hours, until that dream can be realized on "liberty." (Liberty is shore leave, for you guys who haven't sailed the seven seas, or any sea, for that matter).

Then this woman, a shipmate of yours, swishes and sways by you, enveloping you with that musky female scent that you dream about.

Now, can you imagine what that would do to a weak-willed and weak-minded man like me? As that daring first US Navy admiral during the Civil War, named David Glasgow Farragut, would say, or any daring, horny sailor, for that matter, would say: "Damn all torpedoes, full speed ahead!"

ELENA KAGAN: Seriously now . . . talking about "FIRST," as in first woman this and first woman that, President Obama's nomination of Elena Kagan, America's Solicitor General, to serve on the United States Supreme Court is, to me, a first-rate choice.

She was educated at Princeton, Oxford and Harvard. She has clerked on the U.S. Supreme Court of Appeals and the Supreme Court. She taught at the University of Chicago and Harvard law schools.

She's the first woman to be dean of Harvard Law School. The first woman to be Solicitor General. But the fourth woman on the U.S. Supreme Court, if she's confirmed by Congress.

It represents, as Justice Ruth Bader Ginsburg said on the day of her own nomination, "the end of the days when women, at least half the talent pool in our society, appear in high places as one-at-a-time performers."

As y'all know, for 12 long years, until Ginsburg joined the Supreme Court, Sandra day O'Connor was the only woman justice in the Supreme Court. Then for three years, after O'Connor's retirement and before Sonia Sotomayor's selection not too long ago, Ginsburg was the only woman justice in that Court.

The long era of "FIRST" among women has come to close. Not completely though. There are a few more ceilings yet to be cracked . . . like perhaps the presidency? I maybe a Republican in my political belief, but my personal choice is Ms. Hillary Clinton. No, not Sarah Palin. I think she's stupid. In an interview with Katie Couric, the primetime news anchor of CBS, during the presidential campaign, she was asked to name a national newspaper that she reads, she couldn't even name one. Dumb broad . . .

THE POLE DANCER: Another "first" among women is Rima Fakih (I wonder how her last name is pronounced), the newly-crowned winner of the Miss USA pageant contest. According to news reports, "It's historic" because she maybe the first Arab-American Muslim who had won this beauty contest. She's a Lebanese immigrant and a University of Michigan graduate and a wannabe lawyer.

But she's under fire now after "racy" photos of her *daw* had surfaced while competing in a pole dancing contest. I've seen that photo on the Internet, but I don't think it was "racy" at all. She was wearing gym shorts and a blouse up to her neck. She looked sexy in that photo, true, but it wasn't a racy photo. If you really want to see racy photos, get yourself a Penthouse magazine and see racy photos galore on its pages. . . .

CAMPBELL BROWN: One more woman I want to mention here, while I am at it: That's right, Talk Show Host Campbell Brown of CNN. We heard she's leaving CNN because of her show's low ratings. Good riddance. She acted like a schoolgirl during the election. Every time she spoke of Barack Obama, she drooled.

And talking about DROOLING, y'all know who that reminds me of. I've said it so many times. But as Bart T. of Chicago, a publisher of a Fil-Am publication, had said, "*tapos na ang boksing.*" The Filipino people had spoken. So, that's all. **JJ**

Obamacare Shows No Care for Military Vets and Retirees under Medicare

As I write this, Tuesday, March 23, 2010, President Barack Hussein Obama signs into law that "historic" *daw* **Health Care Reform bill that the House Democrats, led by Nancy Pelosi, had voted to pass over the weekend.**

The House voted for the measure 219-212, a mere seven-vote difference to get the bill passed. It was NOT voted on unanimously. Thirty-four Democrats joined Republicans in voting against the bill.

Nonetheless, in jubilance, Pelosi and company said, "It's history!"

Yeah, it's history alright! This history highlighted America's deep partisan and ideological divide! Yeah, it's history alright! Come November this year, in the midterm congressional elections, Pelosi and company are history! Come November 2012, Obama is history, too!

It would also be in history books the fact that VP Joe Biden added an unexpected touch to the signing of the health care bill, when he uttered the "F—bomb" after introducing President Obama at Tuesday's ceremony at the White House.

"This is a big (expletive) deal," Biden said to Obama privately, but his "effing" remark was captured on audio and video. Yeah, Joe Biden is history, too.

And the White House response to this "effing" by Mr. Biden? Nodding his assent, Robert Gibbs, the White House press secretary, said, "Yes, Mr. Vice President, you're right."

I tell ya . . . well, like any other rulers and kings, King Barack HUSSEIN Obama has got to have his court jesters, too.

THE BENEFICIARIES OF OBAMACARE: As we all know, the uninsured and the lowest-income families are clearly the beneficiaries of this legislation. It also meant to provide coverage to about 32-million people who have been pushed out because to insurers, they have been deemed as "too sick" or because they cannot afford the ever-rising premiums.

And that's a good thing. It's the American way to take care of those who are poor and needy.

But to MOST AMERICANS, working Americans, that is, the effect will not be as "significant." Like for instance, to my two sons, who in their daily grind work their butts off five days a week and sometimes more. And also, to my wife. They are not going to get anything out of this health care reform. (Me? I am retired. Twice retired, in fact. That's right, folks, I've put in my time in taking care of the poor and needy).

This Obamacare will be costly to consumers. Wealthy families will be required to pay additional taxes. And, whether they like it or not, most Americans will be required to have health insurance and face federal fines if they do not buy it.

In other words, this health care reform is being shoved down our throats!

It's the core of Mr. Obama's agenda for America: Spread the wealth! Give to the poor and lazy and to those on eternal welfare and screw the middle class and those who strive hard and work hard in order to get ahead.

To me, it looks like it punishes the achievers and rewards the losers . . . the *PALAMUNINS* and the PARASITES of America.

Now, check these facts out:

> **Millions of middle-income people will be pressured to buy commercial policies that cost up to 9.5 percent of income but cover an average of only 70 percent of medical expenses.**
>
> **Insurance firms will get at least $447-billion in taxpayer money in subsidies.**
>
> **People with employer-based coverage will be locked into their plan's limited network of providers.**
>
> **The bill will siphon off $40-billion from Medicare Payments to safety-net hospitals.**
>
> **Health care costs will continue to skyrocket, like they did in Massachusetts.**

And as the costs continue to skyrocket, who is going to be left holding the bag to pay up? The middle class! The working class who work their butts off to get ahead!

MILITARY RETIREES UNDER MEDICARE: Yours truly is a Legionnaire and I want to share with y'all this letter to the editor that was published in the "Legionnaire," an American Legion newspaper of the state of Washington, written by Charles W. Arnold, Lt. Col., US Air Force (Retired). The American Legion is a nation-wide organization consisting of military war veterans and retirees. I hope President Obama and Speaker Pelosi and those Democrat legislators pay attention to this. They better.

Dear Sir:

As you may already know, the Medical care retirees are receiving via Tricare and Medicare is under attack. With programmed reductions in the fees provided are paid, many doctors are now turning Tricare and Medicare patients away. One provider said they only took Tricare because they were Americans first. Unfortunately, not all doctors

think this way. My spouse was recently turned away from Inland Neurosurgery and Spine because they no longer accept Tricare, and are no longer taking new Medicare patients. This situation effectively limits the quality of the care a military retiree and his/her dependents can obtain.

President Obama's new health care bill only THREATENS TO MAKE THE SITUATION worse.

Retirees now have increasing co-pays for prescription drugs, and they cannot obtain brands name drugs because of the cost. While most generic drugs are OK, some are not, but it is virtually impossible to get Tricare to pay for a brand name prescription even when the prescribing doctor says the patient needs the brand name products. In addition, some of the generic drugs are either in part or in whole manufactured off shore, without good quality control to insure they are safe for the consumer. All of these problems are indicative of a health care system in crisis, and the LOSERS ARE THE MILITARY RETIREES who devoted their adult lives to their country and are now being disregarded.

Every veteran should be contacting their congressmen/women and senators and let them know the injustice that is being placed upon the military community. This is not just a retiree issue; it is an active duty and reserve issue, too. Everyone is being impacted, and the only way to fight back is to voice our dissent.

Now, this one came from Larry Nietmotka, also a military retiree and a Legionnaire from Vacaville, California:

Dear Sir,

Nancy Pelosi fails to address the fact that the proposed health-care bill will cut Medicare Part B. Cutting Part B will hurt military retirees under Tricare for life. I personally don't like anything about the health-care bill, but I find it most insulting when public servants assume military retirees can be fooled into believing Part B cuts won't affect our Tricare program.

Remember "stay for 20 and get free medical care"? Lie to me once, now lie to me twice? Sorry, but that dog don't hunt.

A DOGGIE DYOK FROM ED NAVARRA: Talking about "dawgs," this doggie *dyok* came from Ed Navarra of Michigan, the Midwest chairman of NaFFAA. Due to corruption and thievery among some of its national CEOs, this Fil-Am organization is now on the brink of getting debunked.

But that's another story. Let's go back to Ed's *dyok*. For propriety, I changed the name of one of the characters in the *dyok* and added a couple of choice Barako words (the ones in caps and in quotes). Here it is. Enjoy.

Joe Biden and Nancy Pelosi are on the same stage in Yankee Stadium in front of a huge crowd.

Mr. Biden leans towards Ms. Pelosi and said, "Do you know that with one little wave of my hand I can make every person in this crowd go wild with joy? This joy will not be a momentary display, but will go deep into their hearts and they'll forever speak of this day and rejoice!"

Speaker Pelosi replied, "I seriously doubt that. With little wave of your hand? Show me!"

So the "EFFING" Biden, with a little mighty wave of his hand, backhanded the "EFFING" bitch.

And what would be the morale of this *dyok*?

Yes indeed, forevermore the American people would speak of that day and rejoice . . . like the day the Democrats had rejoiced as one when President Obama signed into law the "EFFING" health-care bill, against the wishes of the majority of the American people. **JJ**

My Take on President Obama's State of the Union Address. And the Gays in the U.S. Military

So . . . did y'all watch President Obama's State of the Union Address last week? Well, I liked his tie. It's classy. Red with stripes of white, it's what you may call a power tie. Well, he's the man. He wields the scepter of power. He's Moses. He's the Messiah . . . and all that kind of crap.

And, he's truly one sharp dresser. In the old street language of my generation, a "dude," a "dog", a "hip," and a "homeboy made good."

And, he's an orator. An eloquent, brilliant speaker. As my wife said, "*mahusay magtalumpati.*"

But back to his tie: The color of red, in Chinese beliefs, connotes good luck. And white symbolizes death and mourning. Perhaps the statement Mr. Obama was making there was good luck to his agenda of "change" and death to the party of GOPs, the so called party of "NO." Y'all know what I mean?

What about his message to the American people? As Erap would say: "Same-same." Yep, same speech that we've all heard over and over during his presidential campaign. Same B.S. Same rhetoric. Same old promises . . . and to top it, he had the audacity to cunningly blame the failures of his promises to the past presidency of George W. Bush.

As y'all remember, he promised JOBS, JOBS, JOBS for America, but there were no jobs to be had. In fact, the unemployment rate, nationally, steadily rose to over 10 percent . . . and rising. That STIMULUS package had been a joke! Because as we all know, it was SPEND, SPEND, SPEND! The great bulk of the money went to bank bailouts and to the entitlements of America's PARASITES AND *PALAMUNINS*!

And the spending goes on. The federal government is now spending $2 for every dollar it takes in. America is on the fast lane of bankruptcy. The deficit now is in TRILLIONS! *Lubog na ang Amerika sa utang because of Mamang Obama . . .*

"I campaigned on the promise of change—'change we can believe in,' the slogan went," Obama said. "And right now, I know that there are many Americans who aren't sure if they still believe we can change—or at least that I can deliver. But remember this, I never suggested that change would be easy, or that I can do it alone."

Excuses, excuses . . . with all due respect, Mr. President, either you can do it or you can't. You have disappointed a lot of your supporters, who literally idolized and worshipped you when you came into the scene. They call you, "the Savior." You were so full of bravura. Now it seems that that bravura has become a bunch of brouhaha, so to speak, as in ha, ha, ha.

As my favorite newspaper, The *New York Times* sedately reported: "For a president who came into office with an expansive vision, the speech represented a dialing back. There was no sweeping new initiative or far reaching second year agenda. Instead, Obama vowed to continue pushing bills . . . that he tried to enact during his first year."

In other words, nada. Practice *lang*. Just empty promises, once again. A yawn. A snoozer of a speech.

Masarap lang siyang pakingan. And to look at. For Obama is a good looking man, really. FOR AN HOUR, I FORGOT HE WAS BLACK, he, he, he . . . hey, I didn't say that. Chris Matthews, that "Hardball" commentator on MSNBC said that. And really, I thought Motor-Mouth Matthews was an Obama lapdog.

GAYS AND LESBIANS IN THE MILITARY: I perked up though when Mr. Obama called for repeal of President Bill Clinton's 1993 "don't ask, don't tell" policy near the end of his speech.

"This year, I will work with Congress and our military to finally repeal the law that denies gay Americans the right to serve their country they love because of who they are," Obama said. "It's the right thing to do."

A few days later, America's top two Defense officials also called for an end to the decade and a half "don't ask, don't tell" law, ECHOING the call of Obama to allow gays and lesbians to openly serve in the military.

Navy Admiral Mike Mullen, the chairman of the Joint Chiefs of Staff and head honcho of all branches of the U.S. military, said: "No matter how I look at the issue, I cannot escape being troubled by the fact that we have in place a policy which forces young men and women to lie about who they are in order to defend their fellow citizens."

"It's my personal belief that allowing gays and lesbians to serve openly would be the right thing to do," the good admiral added.

Then, Defense Secretary Robert Gates said: "We have received our orders from the commander in chief, and we are moving out accordingly. . . ."

Then, in the background, Sen. Mark Udall, a Democrat from Colorado, dowapped, "You don't have to be straight to shoot straight." That's a good shot, Senator.

Sen. John McCain, that old maverick Republican from Arizona said, "Aint no way, Hosay. We ain't gonna do that." He also said that while the law was not perfect, REPEAL was too much to ask of a military stressed by two wars.

Now, me, a lowly retired U.S. Navy Chief Petty Officer, with 20 years of active service, may I have my say, too, about this matter? I agree with all those great intelligent leaders of our land. It's all true what they said and I agree with the profoundness of it all. But do they know the REALITY of it all?

Mr. Obama never had served in the military and he doesn't really know how it is in the military. Living conditions and living arrangements and all that. Same thing with Mr. Gates. Though he heads the military as the Defense Secretary, he's a civilian, and he's never been in the military. With Senator Udall, I don't know if he had seen military service.

As to Admiral Mullen, he's an officer, and I don't think he also knows how it is within the enlisted ranks. Officers usually get their own rooms and usually bunk in a room with another officer. Commanders and captains and above get their own private rooms. A top-ranking admiral, like Admiral Mullen, gets a suite, with Navy stewards, at his beck and call, waiting on him.

You see, in the military, among the enlisted ranks, you live in tight and confined quarters. You sleep next to each other and on top of each other. When you fart, those guys sleeping and living next to you, can hear and smell your fart. There's literally, no privacy. And guys run around naked all the time and nobody cares.

If there's a faggot (pardon my word, but that's how we called them when I was in the navy), looking and drooling at you, well, that would be kind of disturbing, wouldn't it? And it would kind of create a hostile, or maybe a violent reaction, from some of the guys, especially from the machos, like me.

If that had happened to me, you know, saw a faggot drooling at my nakedness and looking at me in THAT certain way, I would've kicked his butt and shoved his face in the commode. I mean, literally. And that's being kind. The other guys would've been more mean and brutal, and laughed about it, too.

That was the Navy I knew. It was like high school. A lot of bullies around. Woe to you, if you were effeminate.

GAYS ON MY SHIP: But doesn't mean that we didn't have any gays within our midst. On the last ship I was on, the aircraft carrier, USS Constellation, on our way home from a nine-month patrol, we held what we call the "Halfway Home" show. It was an all day circus-like talent show. There were boxing matches and martial-arts demonstrations, singing and dancing. And whatever talent you wanna put on the makeshift stage. The highlight of this show was the "Miss Constellation" beauty contest. Yes, you read it right: a beauty contest!

So, out came the gays on that warship. Several dozens of them. In their finest fineries, negligees and all. Shaved legs and shaved armpits and all. Red lipsticks and rogue and all. False breasts and silk stockings and all. And perfumed they were, too. They smelt of Jean Patou. They all looked mighty fine. I gawked. The whole crew gawked. They pranced on the stage. They showed their sexy-looking legs. They did the Can-Can dance. They flirted.

We hooted. We whistled. We applauded. It was a riot. Those gay shipmates of mine did it so OPENLY. There was no problem at all. We loved them.

Repeal? Repeal what? Hey, Mr, Obama, with all due respect, sir, may I say, please don't repeal what ain't broke. What you need to repeal are your broken promises *na lang*. **JJ**

The Words of a "Wingnut" Vs. the Words of the Lord

In the world of religious wingnuts, fundamentalism trumps compassion.

As scenes of the horrific destruction and gruesome death in Haiti from that monster earthquake a couple of weeks flashed on our TV screens and spilled into our living rooms, the Rev. Pat Robertson, the televangelist and founder of The 700 Club, came on his televised bully pulpit, and barked:

"Something happened a long time ago in Haiti, and people might not want to talk about it. They were under the heel of the French. And they got together and swore a pact to the Devil . . . They said, 'We will serve you if you get us free from the Prince.'

"And so the Devil said, 'Okay, it's a deal.'

"They kicked the French out, the Haitians revolted, and got themselves free. But ever since, they have been cursed by one thing after the other, desperately poor . . ."

Slave rebellions are the work of the Devil? Never heard that before. Reverend Robertson also said that the earthquake that devastated Haiti was **"a blessing in disguise"** because it will give that forsaken country the opportunity **"to rebuild its spiritual and physical structure."**

Oh, my Lord, I tell ya . . .

Instead of preaching to his one-million strong congregations, to open their hearts and their arms and their wallets, like the rest of mankind, this religious wingnut was spewing bile about a "pact that the Haitian people made with the Devil" and blaming that for the death and destruction that rained on those people.

Really, I think that's an ignorant statement that can be uttered only by an honest-to-goodness wingnut. In high-school science, we have learned that earthquakes are caused by the shifting of the Earth's tectonic plates, "not by vengeful deities," as Kathleen Parker of the *Washington Post* aptly said, "bearing malice toward any particular man, woman, or child."

After the 9/11 attack on America, Reverend Robertson also said that **"God had given us what we deserve.**"

And, as his Christian coalition colleague and fellow wingnut, the late Reverend Falwell, recited this litany, Robertson, at his side, nodded on vigorously his agreement: **"The pagans and the abortionists and the feminists and the gays and lesbians . . . the ACLU, the People of the American Way—all of them who have tried to secularize America—I point a finger in their faces and say, 'You helped this happen!'"**

When Hurricane Katrina devastated New Orleans, the Reverend Robertson, blamed that calamity on abortion. He said: **"We have killed over 40-million babies in America. We are unable somehow to defend ourselves against some of the attacks coming to us, either by terrorists or now by natural disaster . . . could they be connected in some way?"**

Yes, those are the words of a wingnut.

FROM THE BOOK OF GENESIS: I am not as you might say an overly religious man. I sin every day, even knowingly at times. I am weak. But I go to church regularly. I pray. I believe in God. I believe that the Christian faith, my Roman Catholic faith, at its heart, is about mercy and forgiveness . . . and redemption. And that God is full of kindness.

I am a lector at our Holy Family Church here in Auburn, Washington, and not too long ago, I proclaimed, with joy in my heart, to our congregation this reading from the Holy Bible:

A reading from the Book of Genesis . . . Then, the Lord said: "The outcry against Sodom and Gomorrah is so great and their sin so grave that I must go down and see whether or not their actions fully correspond to the cry against them that comes to me. I mean to find out."

Then Abraham drew nearer to Him and said: "Will you sweep away the innocent with the guilty? Suppose there were fifty innocent people in the city; would you wipe away the place, rather than spare it for the sake of the fifty innocent people within it? Far be it from you to do such a thing, to make the innocent die with the guilty, so that the innocent and the guilty would be treated alike! Should not the Judge of all the world act with justice?"

The Lord replied, "If I find fifty innocent people in the city of Sodom, I will spare the whole place for their sake."

Abraham spoke up again: "See how I am presuming to speak to my Lord, though I am but dust and ashes! What if there are five less than fifty innocent people? Will you destroy the whole city because of those five?"

"I will not destroy it," He answered, "if I find forty-five there."

But Abraham persisted, saying, "What if only forty are found there?"

He replied, "I will forbear doing it for the sake of the forty."

Then he said, "Let not my Lord grow impatient if I go on. What if only thirty are found there?"

He replied, "I will forbear doing it if I can find but thirty there."

Still he went on, "Since I have thus dared to speak to my Lord, what if there are no more than twenty?"

"I will not destroy it," He answered, "for the sake of the twenty."

But he still persisted, "Please, let not my Lord grow angry if I speak up this last time. What if there are at least ten there?"

For the sake of those ten," He replied, "I will not destroy it."

The Lord departed as soon as he had finished speaking with Abraham, and Abraham returned home.

The word of the Lord.

The Lord is kind, indeed, and patient. I believe in His words. He's full of compassion. His words trump the words of any wingnut in this world. **JJ**

A Win for Scott Brown as GOP Senator and a Kick in the Butt for President Obama

Then President George W. Bush said that to another Brown, FEMA Director Michael Brown, during the Katrina debacle in New Orleans, Louisiana a few years back. Y'all remember him, right? You know, that clownish guy who worried about what clothes he should wear and how he would look like on TV than doing something urgently for the victims of Hurricane Katrina . . . and then halfway on his way to the scene of the disaster, made a stop first in a fine restaurant to dine leisurely on lobster and steak.

This cretin dined while people died. He was a horse trainer before he became a FEMA director, a political appointee of Mr. Bush. Hah!

Now this Brown, Scott Phillip Brown, that is, Republican Scott Brown, a little-known state senator just a few weeks ago, Tuesday this week, beat in a big-time way Democrat Martha Coakley to win the Massachusetts U.S. Senate seat long held by Edward Kennedy.

This historic victory, the first time since 1972 that the GOP has won a Massachusetts Senate race, Brown will occupy the "Kennedy seat" that Edward held for 47 years before his death last year. This seat was once held by John F. Kennedy before he became President in 1961.

No doubt about it, this win by Scott Brown is a KICK IN THE BUTT for President Obama, who on Wednesday of this week marks the first anniversary of his inauguration. How fitting. How sweet for the party of GOPS (not GOOFS, mind you).

And the reason for this win, as Massachusetts election consultant, Dan Payne, ironically, a Democrat, said, "Scott Brown caught the wave . . ."

And what wave is that? Surely, NOT just a single wave, but several waves. And these waves, said Dan Payne, are:

. The people's worry about jobs.

. Their anger about Wall Street bonuses.

. Their upset about back-door deals that have been made for healthcare legislation, commonly known as, OBAMACARE.

. Their fear of nuts like the underwear bomber.

And if I may add, the huge DEFICIT, the overspending, the bailouts, the looming bankruptcy of America . . . and the recent appalling decision of Mr. Obama to try that fat-lipped Nigerian underwear terrorist as a "criminal" rather than an enemy combatant.

Rep. Steny Hoyer, the House Majority leader, rationalizes the failures of the Obama Administration. "We're all pretty unpopular," he said. "Why? Because people don't feel good. We're the leaders and we're in office and they expect us to do something about it."

Well, at least, the Democrats themselves are aware that they're messing up and in danger, politically. Hey, y'all can thank your leader, Mr. Obama, for that. He blew it. One year into his office, he blew it, he blew it all away, taxpayers' money, they were. Spread the wealth. Hah!

So . . . Scott Brown, who will be sworn in next month, will become the 41st Republican senator, just enough numbers to allow Republicans to derail the very unpopular OBAMACARE that divides this country . . . and to block any legislation in the Senate, if they stick together. The victory of Brown reduces the Democratic majority in the Senate to 59 votes, just short of the 60 needed to break GOP filibusters.

In other words, this win of Brown redrew the political landscape headed into the 2010 elections and a SWIFT KICK IN THE BUTT of Mr. Obama. Heck of a job, Brownie!

I like this Scotty Brownie. As my two sons, Jon and Chris, would say, "he's a cool dude." Cooler than Barack, that's for sure. He's the epitome of the regular guy. He drives a truck, just like me, and many other men, just like me. He was a soldier, a lieutenant colonel in the Massachusetts National Guard. He said he joined the National Guard when he was 20 to help pay for his law school at Boston College. Exactly the same reason for many young men and women of America in joining the military—to help pay for the rising cost of college tuition fees.

Rep. Steny Hoyer, the House Majority leader, rationalizes the failures of the Obama Administration. 'We're all pretty unpopular. Why? Because people don't feel good. We're the leaders and we're in office and they expect us to do something about it.'

Now, check this out: When Scott was 22, he posed as a centerfold model in the much-circulated magazine for women, "Cosmopolitan," the counterpart of the men's magazine, "Playboy." Cool. In this long ago issue of Cosmopolitan, Scott Brown was named, "America's Sexiest Man." And in the two-page centerfold photo, he's seen reclining on a blanket—naked and smiling, young muscles rippling—with merely a wrist acting as a covering, as written, "for his manly bits." Cool, indeed.

Right after the senator-elect's win was announced, he praised the Kennedys, and the first person he called was Victoria, Edward Kennedy's widow. That's magnanimity at its best. Surely, that's the coolest of all that is cool in this world.

According to news reports, when President Obama called to congratulate him, Brown challenged Obama to "a game of two-on-two hoops: he and Ayla (Brown's 21-year-old daughter, a senior forward on the Boston

College basketball team) against the president and a player of his choosing."

Indeed, this Brown has also got big cojones to challenge, "ALREADY," President Obama, a Black Man, to a game of hoops. Hoops, as we all know, is the game where black men naturally excel. The next challenge, perhaps, would be in 2012 for the seat that Obama sits on now. . . .

Let it be known, too, that Scott Brown at 50, is also an accomplished athlete who jumps into "frigid lakes at five in the morning for triathlon training" and a proud competitive athlete, who applied this competiveness in winning his senatorial race.

"I treated this campaign like a sprint triathlon," Mr. Brown said. You have to be good in everything, 18, 19 hours a day. We were just out there cranking."

Heck of a cranking job, Brownie!

It was a spectacular win. You're the man now. America has embraced you and year 2012 will soon be here. America is pondering now that it might be you who would be the right man to replace this man who promised "change" and "unity in America," promises that merely remained as promises, barren and unfulfilled. Beat him first in two-on-two basketball, then on 2012, beat him again in the presidential elections.

Yes, you can! You betcha, America will be cheering you on, just like it did in Massachusetts. **JJ**

"Game Change," a Book of Smut

Yes, it's grim. Chaos and destruction are everywhere. Dead bodies litter the streets. Survivors, if there are, and the dead, are still being dug from the rubbles . . .

But the Haiti tragedy is not my story this week. My story is about a book, a book of smut, that is, and what it contains.

Just before that monster earthquake struck Haiti, the buzz in every town and every TV and radio talk shows all over America was the book, "Game Change," written by two journalists, John Heilemann of *New York magazine* and Mark Halperin of *Time magazine.*

In it, they revealed that during the 2008 presidential campaign, Senate Majority Leader Harry Reid referred to President Obama, then a fellow senator, as someone who could win the White House because he was a "light-skinned" black man, "with no NEGRO dialect, unless he wanted to have one."

And that racial slur, of course, created an explosion of talks by TV and newspaper pundits all over America and by bloggers on the Internet. Mostly those pundits and bloggers were Black Americans . . . or are they now called, African Americans?

From what I understand, the Negro word, used to be uttered as, "Nigger." Then, it became "Colored." Then that word evolved into the words, "Black American." I believe that's no longer politically correct. It's now, "African American."

But why call America's Blacks, African Americans? They are not Africans? They didn't come from Africa? They were born here. They are Americans.

Really, what's wrong with the word, "Negro"? Or the word, "Filipino," for that matter? Or the word, "Hindu"? Or even the word, "Caucasian"? Or "Redneck"?

Editor's Note: It may be a happy coincidence that today, Bobby Reyes published also his latest article in this website's History Section: The Term "Caucasian" Is a Historical Aberration

The word "Negro," is still being used, like, for instance, "The United Negro College Fund." And the word, "Nigger," is still vogue among Black youths in calling each other by that name.

Let's call a spade a spade. I said this before and I'll say it again: If it quacks like a duck, walks like a duck, looks like a duck, well, to me (I don't know about you), it's a duck.

As to the words, "light-skinned," in describing the color of one's skin, what's also wrong with that? I am a "brown-skinned" Filipino. That's a fact. I am not offended by that. My good friend and neighbor and walking partner, Jerry Lytle, is a "white-skinned" dude. Sometimes, I would tell him, "Hey, good buddy, you better get some sun, you're beginning to look like a ghost. Your skin is too white." He's not offended by that.

When I used to live in Florida, I became good friends with a white dude there, named "Bis," whose neck would turn all red under the Florida sun, and I used to call him, "Red," for his red neck. I don't remember him getting offended by that, too.

True, America is moving further away from its racist past, but race and perceived racial slurs will always remain THE fault line of this country . . . like the color of one's skin, like the duck, that will always quack as a duck. And that's the reality of it.

THE SMUT ON SARAH PALIN: In this book, Sarah Palin was portrayed as an "ignoramus," who didn't know the difference between North Korea and South Korea and who believed *daw* that Saddam Hussein was behind the 9/11 attack. She was also depicted as "mentally unstable, with wild mood swings."

"One minute, Palin would be her perky self; the next she would fall into a strange blue funk," the authors wrote.

On the day of her disastrous interview with CBS' primetime news anchor, Katie Couric, they said that Palin's "eyes were glassy and dead" and that when make-up artists had prepped her up for the show, Palin said, "I hate this make up." She then "smeared the make up off her face, messed up her hair, and complained that she looked fat." Then, when she went on to give answers to Couric, she sounded "so incoherent" that the interview damaged her image.

The authors also said that when Palin's aides tried to quiz her preparedness in answering questions from the media, "she would routinely shut down—chin on her chest, arms folded, eyes cast to the floor, speechless and motionless, lost in what those around her described as a kind of CATATONIC stupor."

When Sarah Palin was asked in an interview with Bill O'Reilly on FOX news about this SMUT written about her, she slowly shook her head and sadly said, "How could they have known? They weren't there. . . ."

By the way, do y'all know that Ms. Palin is now a FOX News analyst/commentator . . . and check this out, second on the list as "the most admired women" in America. Topping the list is State Secretary Hillary Clinton. Last on the list is Michelle Obama, right after Erin Nordegren, the wife of Tiger Woods.

THE SMUT ON BILL CLINTON: The authors of "Game Change" also wrote in their book that during that presidential campaign, Bill Clinton, the "Big Dog," was rumored to be in his philandering self again. And that after some "discreet fact-finding by aides" concluded that "Bill was indeed having an affair, NOT a frivolous one-night stand, but a sustained romantic relationship."

Tee-hee, so what? He's THE big dick, I mean, the Big Dog. He can do that. I got no problem with that. Bill, to me, is the main man among little-minded men, if y'all get my drift.

Did you hear that a biography of Warren Beatty, also released this week with that smutty book, Game Change, claims the 72-year-old actor has slept with "12,7775 women, give or take, a figure that does not include daytime quickies, drive-bys, casual gropings, stolen kisses and so on"? The biographer, Peter Biskind says that Beatty was "insatiable" in his heydays as a Hollywood icon, having sex as many as seven times a day. . . ." Oh my! How many viagras did that take, I wonder.

Hey Tiger, you heard that? You only had nine mistresses, and you got into big time trouble that ruined your career and drove your greedy wife to claim most of your millions. Life ain't fair, that's for sure. Well, Tiger, you ain't Bill, the "Big Dog" nor Beatty, the "Hollywood FM," so there, suffer, dude.

For the record, Jesse Jose was the first Filipino-American columnist, if not the first Filipino writer in the entire world, to question on May 2, 2007, the character of then very-popular Democratic presidential aspirant, John Edwards . . .—MabuhayRadio.com editor

THE SMUT ON JOHN AND ELIZABETH EDWARDS: I think one of the smuttiest portions in the book, was when it was revealed that former Sen. John Edwards' affair with his videographer was an "open secret" among his aides.

Okay, perhaps, that's not too shocking. It happens all the time among famous men. The shocking revelation was when the authors described the cancer-stricken Elizabeth Edwards, a lawyer herself like her husband, as a "scornful woman," who treated her senator husband as "intellectually inferior" to her. The authors also said that Elizabeth Edwards was "an abusive, intrusive, paranoid, condescending, crazy woman."

And when her husband's affair was exposed, "she fought with him in public and tore open her blouse to reveal her lumpectomy." And then "wailed at her husband: 'Look at me!'" She then staggered and fell to the ground . . . like a scene taken out from a Filipino soapy opera.

I heard there are several more juicy bits of smuts revealed in this book. I tell ya, I must soon go to Barnes and Noble and buy this book, before it's all gone. America loves to read SMUT, especially smut on America's elite. **JJ**

Let's Speak the Truth on America's Enemies

Y'all can call me a "little brown American," but when it comes to my adopted country, the United States of America, I am prejudiced, I am biased, I am protective. Right or wrong, America is my country now.

I love America. It's a benevolent country and the most-generous country in this world. Whoever would hurt or attempt to hurt my country becomes my mortal enemy.

Editor's Notes: To read Jesse Jose's and this editor's writings on the "Brown Americans," please click on these links:

Is Jesse Jose "A Little Brown American?"

How Filipinos Came to Be Called as "Brown Americans"

I believe that if you live in this country and has become a citizen of this country, there's no other flag or other symbols that you should be pledging your allegiance to, or singing to . . . *o kailangan iwagwag* to show one's Filipino-ness, or whatever "ness" that is, that you want to show your loyalty to.

To me, there should only be ONE FLAG, ONE PLEDGE, ONE SYMBOL and a total and complete LOYALTY to this country of thee that takes very good care of us. To me, America is now our "*Bayang Magiliw.*"

I was a warrior of this country and had laid my life on the line, without question, for this country. Anytime it would call on me again to do so, I would heed that call, without hesitation.

And, anybody who would kill my fellow warriors and fellow Americans is also my mortal enemy. Hated to my very core.

On American soil, in June 2009, in Arkansas, Muslims killed a U.S. Army recruiter and wounded one. In November, also of last year, a Muslim, a major at that and a psychiatrist *kuno*, of the U.S. Army, killed 14 soldiers and wounded 31 in a "Jihad" in Fort Hood, Texas.

Then last December, on Christmas Day, a Nigerian Muslim boy with fat-looking lips, Farouk Abdulmutallab (pronounced Barok Ab-dool Full-of-Muta) almost blew up in mid-air an American plane, with 300 people on it, just over Detroit International Airport.

So when this little blurb was sent to me by Protacio, a good friend who resides in the Philippines, I believed what it contained . . . for it confirmed and strengthened what I believed of America's enemy. So here goes. Enjoy. I don't know who wrote it, but whoever wrote it is an American patriot. It's titled: "The Truth Is Out There!" (All rights reserved; all wrongs revenged).

CAN A MUSLIM BE A REAL AMERICAN? In light of the murders of soldiers at Ft. Hood by a Muslim officer (who had sworn to defend the people, our Constitution and the United Sates), this question becomes more timely and real than ever: ***Can a good Muslim be a good American?*** This is the result of that question to someone who worked in Saudi Arabia for 20 years. The following is his reply:

THEOLOGICALLY, NO. Because his allegiance is to Allah, the moon god of Arabia.

RELIGIOUSLY, NO. Because no other religion is accepted by his Allah except Islam.

SCRIPTURALLY, NO. Because his allegiance is to the five pillars of Islam and the Quran (Koran).

GEOGRAPHICALLY, NO. Because his allegiance is to Mecca, to which he turns in prayer five times a day.

SOCIALLY, NO. Because his allegiance to Islam forbids him to make friends with Christians and Jews.

POLITICALLY, NO. Because he must submit to the mullah (spiritual leaders), who teach the ANNIHILATION of Israel and DESTRUCTION of America, "the Great Satan."

DOMESTICALLY, NO. Because he is instructed to marry four women and beat and scourge his wife when she disobeys him.

INTELLECTUALLY, NO. Because he cannot accept the American Constitution since it is based on Biblical principles and he believes the Bible to be corrupt.

PHILOSOPHICALLY, NO. Because Islam, Muhammad, and the Quran do not allow freedom of religion and expression. Democracy and Islam cannot co-exist. Every Muslim government is either dictatorial or autocratic.

SPIRITUALLY, NO. Because when we declare "One Nation Under God," and the Christian God is loving and kind, Allah is NEVER referred to as "Heavenly Father," nor is he called in the The Quran's 99 excellent names.

Therefore, after much study and deliberations . . . perhaps, we should be suspicious of all Muslims in this country. They obviously cannot be both "good" Muslims and "good" Americans. Call it what you wish, it's still the TRUTH . . .

PRESIDENT OBAMA'S ORDERS: So, finally, after President Obama decided to come back to work from his vacation in Hawaii, he issued his orders to America's intelligence agencies, saying that they all have to respond aggressively to the "failures" that allowed a Nigerian boy to ignite an explosive components on a commercial jetliner on Christmas Day.

Mr. Obama also directed the Homeland Security to speed up the installation of a $1-billion worth of BODY SCANNERS at U.S. airports, and to work with international airports, worldwide, to see that they upgrade equipment to protect U.S.-bound passengers.

In my previous column last week, I said that these very expensive, high-tech body scanners, which I dubbed the "PEEPING MACHINE" will show your naked form in videos and will detect whatever foreign objects (components of explosives, etc.) that you're carrying next to your skin, underneath your underwear and such.

But check this out: If you're OBESE, those peeping machines would not be able to detect what's in the folds of your fat flesh. Nor can those machines detect objects or explosive components stowed in BODILY ORIFICES! And really, I don't have to spell out what those orifices are, in men and in women. As we all know, women have more of these orifices than men.

A SNIFFING dog would be able to detect what's inside those orifices . . . but would the women allow those dogs to sniff at them . . . at their orifices? LOL. Don't mean to laugh. Don't mean to be rude either, folks. Just asking a question. As President Obama said, "we are at war" and the enemy is the Muslim "extremists."

With all due respect, Mr. President: They're NOT extremists. They're terrorists. Let's call a spade, a spade, shall we? Those Muslim terrorists are out to destroy America and kill us. I don't believe in being politically correct with America's enemies.

Let's speak the TRUTH about them. . . . **JJ**

Air Security Is a 'Big Joke,' a Big Balloon Full of Hot Air

What a big joke! It's true. America's aviation security and its intelligence network, world-wide, is a big joke, like a big balloon, full of hot air. But let me tell this story first. It's true. It happened. I swear.

Not too long ago, I visited my mother, who lives in Florida. At the curbside of SeaTac Airport, my wife dropped me off. I gave her a kiss, and then went inside. With my boarding tickets in one hand and my small carry-on bag in the other, I followed a long line that leads to the airport's security.

I grabbed a gray plastic container, removed my cowboy boots, my belt with the big buckle, my blue blazer, my watch, my wallet, some loose change from my pockets . . . and placed them all in this container. Then I pushed this container on little metal wheels and watched it rolled away into a tunnel-like machine. Then I walked slowly through a narrow rectangular gate.

No problem. I got through without setting off any alarms.

Then a goofy-looking guy in a Transportation Security Administration (TSA) uniform on the other side of this little "tunnel" told me to step aside as I would be patted down and "wanded" and my bags searched further.

Now, me, always the wise ass in situations like this, asked this goofy-looking guy: "Why?"

"We saw a couple of things that we consider as dangerous weapons in your carry-on bag. Open your bag, so we can confiscate them," he ordered.

"If there's a weapon in my bag, it's not mine. . . ." I said. I was getting hot under my collar now . . . and SCARED that I am going to be mistakenly arrested as a terrorist and get thrown in jail with Muslim terrorists and Jihadists. With my fertile and cynical imagination working in overdrive, perhaps, I thought, even shipped to that CIA-run prison in Gitmo Bay, Cuba, and tortured! Water boarded and all, deprived of sleep with pit bulls and CIA interrogators growling at me, grilling me with Gestapo-like questions.

Cowed by that thought, I obediently unzipped my bag and removed my clothes and underwear that I would be wearing during my three-day stay in Florida with my mom. Finding not any so-called "weapons," I asked the goofy-looking guy, "So what weapons are you talking about here?

"Open you little black bag there and dump all its contents on the counter," he said.

"You mean my douche bag?" I said.

Despite of my fear of getting arrested, I was getting mad as hell, too, that I almost said to this goofy-looking guy, "What da f—k for?" But I shut my mouth and kept my cool, and dumped instead, angrily, the contents of my douche bag.

Then he picked out my little MUSTACHE SCISSORS and two little tubes of 'Just For Men' mustache coloring gel, and said, "I am confiscating these."

"Those are dangerous weapons! WHAT A BIG JOKE!" I exclaimed in total disbelief. "That pair of scissors is for trimming my mustache with and these two gels are for coloring."

"The scissors can be used to threaten passengers with physical harm, if you're a terrorist," the goofy-looking guy said. "And the gels could be mixed with some other chemicals to make an IED bomb to blow up the plane."

"I am no Muslim terrorist," I hissed at him in quiet anger.

"WHAT A BIG JOKE!!!" I screamed. Of course, I screamed those words after I've gathered my things, put on my boots, belt and blazer . . . and was madly running down the crowded aisle of the airport to the gate, where I would catch my cross-country flight. And I made it just before they shut the door of the plane on me. Huffing and puffing and sweating, I handed my boarding tickets to the ground stewardess, who sweetly said, "Have a good flight, sir."

I kid y'all NOT. That story is true.

THE 'UNDERWEAR' TERRORIST: I suppose you've all heard about this Nigerian boy, named "Barok" something, with a last name that sounds like "Abdul-Full-Of-Muta" (heck, I can't spell all them Muslim-sounding names), who as y'all know almost blew up a Northwest plane bound for Detroit, Michigan, on Christmas Day. This flight originated from Nigeria to Amsterdam to Detroit, with 300 passengers on it.

As security experts have said: "For all intents and purposes, Northwest Flight 253 exploded in midair . . ." That's true.

Okey *ngarud,* but how did Abdul-Full-Of-Muta get on board that plane when all kinds of red flags had already come up that this boy was a potential terrorist . . . targeted and spotted, and HIGHLY-SUSPECTED as one?

According to intelligence gathered days before Christmas from Yemen, a country where several Al-Qaida terrorists are based, their leaders there were talking about "a Nigerian" being prepared for a terrorist attack.

Barok Full-Of-Muta, the "Nigerian" came to the full attention of U.S. Intelligence officials when his father, a rich banker and a former member of the Nigerian government, went to the U.S. Embassy in Lagos last month to report that his son had expressed radical and dangerous views and had traveled to Yemen several times.

The Embassy then sent a cable to Washington and Barok's name was entered in a database where he was listed as a "person of interest," whose multiple-entry visa to America should be "revoked." If that was the case, why didn't the U.S. Embassy people in Lagos revoke his visa?

But THAT didn't happen, as we all know now. They were not able to connect the dots . . . the exact replica of NOT being able to, before the 9/11 catastrophic attack on America.

And simply that tells me that aviation security and the intelligence network, world-wide, and Homeland Security kuno here in America is a BIG JOKE, staffed by well-paid jesters and morons.

Janet Napolitano, America's Homeland Secretary, one of those "tax-evaders" appointed by BHO into his cabinet, said that "the system has worked really very, very smoothly over the course of the past several days." And Robert Gibbs, BHO's spokesman, used exactly the same words, saying that "in many, many ways, this system has worked."

Really? WHAT A BIG JOKE! What system is that? The "Bahala-Na-Kayo-Diyan" system? The reason Northwest Flight 253 did NOT explode in midair was because Barok Full-Of-Muta's intent was foiled and he was jumped on by passengers and crew members . . . and the fire that he started that burned portions of the walls of the plane was contained quickly by fire extinguishers on board.

How did he get the explosives on board? According to security experts, he hid the components of those explosives in his UNDERWEAR! That weren't detected by the X-ray machines, approved and installed by security experts kuno. WHAT A BIG JOKE!

A 'PEEPING' MACHINE: Now check this out: These same security know-it-all experts are proposing to install something better daw in detecting explosives hidden underneath clothings. The machines will show videos of your naked form and will detect whatever foreign objects you're carrying next to your skin. But if you're OBESE, the machines cannot detect what's behind the folds of your fat flesh.

Nor can the machines detect objects stowed in bodily orifices! Men have two of these orifices; women have three. WHAT A BIG JOKE! If that happens, the Al-Qaida will simply recruit more women airline bombers, because of that advantage . . . don't y'all think?

So, if that PEEPING MACHINE won't be passed by Congress and approved by President Obama because of PRIVACY CONCERNS, what are we going to do to improve aviation security?

My son, Jonathan said, we can all just remove and show our underwear to the TSA screeners, since that's where Barok Abdul Full-Of-Muta hid the explosives that almost blew up that plane.

Really, I thought that makes sense, because . . . remember Richard Reid? (No relations to Harry Reid, the Senate Majority Leader). Yeah, the shoe bomber from eight years ago, the one who hid his explosives in the sole of his shoes, and the reason why we now have to remove our shoes to be X-rayed? Remember him?

So, together with our shoes, belts, jackets, wallets and whatever we have in our pockets, let's also remove our UNDERWEARS and put 'em into that container. In that way, perhaps, we would be able "to defeat" (President Obama's words) America's enemies. Ha, ha, ha, ha!

Hah! I tell ya, air security is a BIG JOKE, indeed, like a big balloon, full of hot air. Happy New Year, folks! It's the Year of the Tiger. America: Let's roll . . . and roar with laughter at the BIG JOKE. **JJ**

JOY to the World!

Laugh, and the world laughs with you; weep, and you weep alone.—Ella Wheeler Wilcox (1883)

First this . . . and this is about Pakyaw. There was a blurb on him in this Sunday's (Dec. 20) issue of *Parade magazine*, **the supplemental insert that all newspapers here in America get to have. Did y'all see it? It was on page two, in the** *Personality Parade* **section. There was a mugshot of Pakyaw there, and below it are these words: "Pacquiao: Lord of the ring."**

Then this question that was asked by a New Yorker, named Rick Digno: "After winning his recent fight, Manny Pacquiao got his welterweight belt and another belt studded with diamonds. Why?"

***Parade*'s answer: "Pacquiao, who has won an unprecedented seven weight-class titles, fought Miguel Cotto at a catch weight—a boxing terminology for a subdivision within a weight class—of 145 pounds. The diamond belt was a special award for the catch-weight title. Some skeptics saw the bout as a way for the World Boxing Council, the promoters, and HBO to make extra money. We're thinking they might have a point."**

In other words, *PALABAS lang*! Like a FPJ movie production. It's all about money. Exactly like what California Fil-Am journalist Bobby Reyes had said numerous times in his writings. That I echoed in this *Barako* column quite a few times, too.

But this is now MOOT. *Tapos na ang boksing, ika nga.* I just want to bring out the fact that *Parade*, a well-read and credible, national magazine and an institution here in America, voiced out the same opinion on Pakyaw fights to that of LOLO Bobby Reyes' . . . and of yours truly.

LET'S LAUGH: *Pasko na.* Let's make merry. Yes, indeed, let's "*laugh, and the world laughs with you; weep, and you weep alone.*"

It's an old saying. Ella Wheeler Wilcox, who said it, was a genius, a thinker and a sage. She understood the world and what it needed. And what this world sorely needs, ever more so, is laughter. Especially laughing at yourself. And in my case, laughing at cretin-like comments hurled at me.

In writing my *Kapeng Barako* column and telling it like it is, I get cussed at and called all sorts of names and even threatened with physical harm. And . . . I get talked about daw. Dirty talk. Mean-spirited talk. Graphic talk. Talks that snowballed and turned me practically, comically, into a LEGEND. Maybe I am a sado-masochist. Maybe I am crazy. Or maybe, I am even a "sociopath," as one of my readers said of me recently.

Because, you see, I love to laugh at people who curse at me or who put the curse on me or wish my demise from this earth. My demise, your demise, or anybody else's demise is all within "God's own time." It's always been His call. NEVER from the whispered wishes of witches . . . nor from the call of cretins and clowns.

But, really, I think these people are a bunch of cowards because they all do their pernicious deeds from afar, through emails, and ANONYMOUSLY, at that. They won't reveal their true names and true selves. They would rather grovel in the shadows among their own kind.

And I can only pity and laugh at these people, like this one, who called himself, "Brian RoughSODy." I am sure it's a fictitious name. The word, "sod," I told him, means feces. Or . . . that good old American word that also begins with a letter "S," uttered with an exclamation point to express disgust.

Anyway, this is what RoughSOD sent to me that he BCC'd *daw* to his circle of 25 friends, quoted en toto and verbatim, misspelled words, incorrect punctuations, grammatical errors, warts and all. Get ready to laugh. Here goes:

To JesseJose,

Below WAS an actual email conversation between 2 guys ABOUT YOU. (About 25 people received the blind copy of this email)

1st Guy:
"This JJ's ego could have swallowed the asteroid that killed off the dinos. Besides being an egomaniac, he also sports paranoia, megalomania and a self-agrandizing monomania—needs his head and balls professional shrunk.

"I would have asked, "who is this guy anyway", but it's not worth it."

2nd Guy's reply:
"This guy is a vain retired US navy man, who forgot he's a Filipino and whose vile salty language belies his claim of having gone in several institutions of higher learning.

"You both know him through his Kapeng Barako writings which will hereafter be discontinued in the **FilamMegaScene** ***weekly paper in Chicago."***

Truthfully,
Brian RoughSODy

Ha, ha, ha, ha, ha! Yes, Dear Readers, I laughed, I howled, I guffawed when I read that. Surely, RoughSOD will need an army of professional "balls-shrinkers" to shrink my balls. Because I've got a huge set and it's made of steel. Ha, ha, ha, ha, ha!

When this sweet boy first e-mailed me, I thought his e-mail came from one of my fans, so I opened it. Curses and all sorts of dirty names littered his email. He called me a "SOCIOPATH" and other foul names that I can't remember now. Immediately, I placed his email address in my spam mail box, where it automatically deletes all his subsequent emails. I got this email from RoughSOD when Romy Marquez, a friend and a San Diego, CA., journalist, replied to one of his e-mails. Romy wrote:

Hi Brian,

If you have an issue with Jesse Jose, please discuss it with him. My perception of the man (as a true, fearless and topnotch journalist) will not change however uncouth your language is. Your sympathetic friends will not influence me either.

I do not wish to receive your e-mail exchanges simply because I don't know you and your friends. But if you let me know who you are and the circle you belong in, then I may consider reading your e-mail. Until that happens, please do not BCC me.

Can you also forward this e-mail to the 25 people you blind-copied? Thanks and best regards.

(Signed) Romy Marquez

I really don't think RoughSOD will blind-copy his 25 friends as Romy requested. He'll surely slink away now, blinded by Romy's brilliant words, his two minutes of fame gone forever, flushed down the commode. Ha, ha, ha, ha, ha, ha!

Ahhhh, yes, indeed, I am a wise ass. A sociopath? Good heavens, no! I am "smart and satirical," to borrow, momentarily, a phrase from another reader. This reader said her name is "Clarabelle." That's all the information she gave about herself. From the way she wrote her comments, big high-faluting words and all, she seemed to be a highly-educated woman.

I tell ya, my writings are read by people from all sectors of society. Her comment is a reaction from my column a couple of weeks, titled, "Noynoy looks like a retard." I'll just quote the important portions of Clarabelle's comment:

"Your writing is far from smart and satirical. It's mean-spirited, boorish and lacking any taste. Your use of the words "retard" and "moron" shows just how low your brow is, it's pretty much in the gutter, where it belongs. . . .

"However, you must be thanked for proving just how OBTUSE you are. We suggest you take a good dose of Exlax to rid yourself of the filth that fills you."

(Signed) Clarabelle

This Clarabelle, she's kind of classy, ain't she? She perches herself on a high pedestal. "Obtuse"? Oh, boy, I had to open the dictionary to know what that word means. And I had to study how it was used in her sentence, because the dictionary gave several contrasting definitions.

"Exlax" to rid myself of filth that fills me? Oh my, like as if Clarabelle has no filth in her that she also needs to void? Miss Clarabelle, may I suggest, PRUNE JUICE? It's not only more effective, but it's healthier. It's natural and it's full of good nutrients. It's what I use. Heat up the juice first before gulping a glassful. Stay close to a bathroom though, because in less than ten minutes, your own FILTH is gonna let go with merry, little fire-cracking sounds. . . . Ha, ha, ha, ha, ha! And Merry Christmas to you, Clarabelle! To you, too, RoughSOD.

And to all my friends, my ex-friends, my enemies, my critics and detractors, my fans, my admirers . . . and to all and to each of my dear readers: Merry, Merry Christmas! Ho, ho, ho! Yes, indeed, laugh and whole world will laugh with you! Ha, ha, ha, ha, ha, ha!

PS: There were many comments. I can't fit them all. But I'd like to mention **Mr. Jose de Jesus of New York, New York,** who said in his comment that I might be his "long-lost cousin, *kahit baligtad ang akin pangalan.*" But it does not matter, he said. "What matters is that my friends and I like your way of expressing your opinion with massive doses of humor and satire. Although you can use more politically-correct phrases from time to time. . . ." He concluded, "Let's drink more Kapeng

Barako, JJ. Let's have a toast of KB coffee to your continuing success as op-ed writer." (Signed) Ka Jose

Also, **Ed Navarra, the Midwest Chair of NaFFAA,** whose comment on my "Noynoy, the retard" story was simply this: "JJ, it's a super duper article. . . ."

Kind words always prevail at Christmas. Pareng Romy, Ka Jose and Ed, thank you for your precious gifts of kind words. Your kind words make me laugh with joy. Joy to the world! Laugh with joy, and the whole world will laugh with you. **JJ**

People Tell Us: "Your columnist Jesse Jose is crazy . . ."

This piece is a reprise. It's been published in several publications and I wanna dedicate it to all my fellow DOMs—a word I coined for this group—in Chicago, who, perhaps, because of my anti-Pakyaw stance and vulgarity have all stopped talking to me. They remind of my wife, who wouldn't talk to me for days when I've said something she didn't wanna hear. And THAT makes me laugh so hard. So here goes:

People tell me I am crazy.

I have a confession to make: I am crazy. I think I can see lots of heads nodding out there. Yeah, well, nobody is perfect. Each one of us has a flaw or two. I have many, and my biggest flaw is that . . . I am crazy.

Editor's Note: Please read a related article that explains also why the MabuhayRadio.com editors continue to publish proudly Jesse Jose's often classic commentaries even if some of our readers dub him "a crazy columnist . . .": Is it Better to Be Called "Crazy" than Be Dubbed "Stupid"?

Read on and I'll tell you why.

A couple of weeks ago, a dear reader from Kansas, Tom Martires, wrote: "I like the way you write and I like your sense of humor. You're funny . . . and very articulate. I like to write, too, but I am not as articulate as you. What school did you graduate from?"

Hmm, I thought . . . a fan.

So, I wrote back: "I attended the University of Santo Tomas and San Sebastian College in Manila, UConn and Connecticut College, the Syracuse University in New York, Palm Beach College in Florida and many others too numerous to list here, but I've always considered UST as my alma mater. I have a doctorate and an HONORIS CAUSA in the Kuma Sutra."

Nirvana, in layman's term, is the joy and the bliss of a heavenly, mutual climax. And Jesse Jose is a retired American Navy journalist of Filipino ancestry who practices the art of the Kuma Sutra, the Hindu philosophy. But then some of Jesse's detractors say that he is not a Hindu philosopher but a Filipino 'filosopo.' LOL.—Editor Lolo Bobby Reyes

Tom replied: "You're well-schooled. What is the Kuma Sutra? Also, may I ask, what's your hobby?"

"The Kuma Sutra is a form of a Hindu philosophy. It's a very physical philosophy actually," I answered. "But it's also spiritual, emotional and mental. You have to be totally focused when applying this philosophy in real life . . . because it takes the whole self to practice the techniques and its various sets of principles. You practice this philosophy only with someone you're physically and emotionally in tuned with. Your partner does not have to be knowledgeable with the techniques."

"The techniques can be easily taught," I said. "It's an exhausting philosophy to apply, but very satisfying and fulfilling. When you do it well, you and your partner can both attain Nirvana. Nirvana, in layman's term, is the joy and the bliss of a heavenly, mutual climax.

"The Kuma Sutra is also my hobby," I went on. "I used to be a macho dancer, but I've retired from that."

Tom replied: "You're crazy . . ." See, I told ya, I am crazy.

Now, this one came from a U.S. Border Guard, named Kura-Kura. My wife and I often go to Vancouver, Canada, to visit her relatives there and participate in orgies of eating, yaba-yaba talking and gossiping. It's only a three-hour drive from Seattle to Vancouver, and the ride is pretty and scenic all year round. So, on a whim, we often go. I always enjoy the ride and the orgies. It's crossing the border that sours the joyride and the orgies. The Border Guards ask too many questions.

Questions like: Where are you from? Where do you live? What's your citizenship? Why are you here? What's your occupation? What's the purpose of your visit? How long are you going to stay? Did you buy anything? What do you have in the trunk of your car? What are you bringing into the country? Etc, etc.

STUPID, irritating, Gestapo-like questions.

And I have to answer all their questions respectfully. Because those goofy-looking Border Guards on the American side work for a goof, named Michael Cherry Van Goof (sorry, I can't spell his last name). But y'all know who I am talking bout . . . you know, that Homeland Security honcho, who looks like a clone of CNN TV pundit, Larry King.

On the Canadian side of the border, the Guards there work for a cretin, I think. And whoever you work for is who you are . . . and vice versa.

The Border Guards, for some reason, always suspect me as a terrorist. It's probably because of my Erap-like mustache (Erap was my hero in my kanto boy days) and from the way I look at them as they grill me with their IDIOTIC questions: I always look at them . . . cross-eyed.

So, they always pick on me. A couple of weeks ago, on the way back to the American side of the border, I decided, for a change, to pick on one of them. As we approached the guard shack, I noticed that the Border Guard looked Japanese. So, I asked him: "Are you Japanese?"

"No," he curtly and officiously said, "American!"

In Pidgin English and pointing at myself, I said, "Me, too, American." Then I gave him the thumbs up sign and said, "Amerika-nese numbah one!"

He looked pissed. He barked an order, "Let me see your passport and open the trunk of your car." I showed him my U.S. passport and flicked the trunk of my car open. He closely scrutinized my passport, held it against the light and flipped through the stamped pages of my travels to various countries in Europe and Asia. Then, he went to inspect the trunk.

"There are dead body parts in there," I said.

"What!" he said, looking at me, his slant eyes widening in disbelief. I looked back at him, with my own semi-slant eyes . . . and I crossed 'em for effect.

That perturbed him even more.

For a second or two, he touched his automatic pistol in his holster, like he was gonna draw. For a second or two, I touched mine, too, a magnum .357, like Clint Eastwood's, which was stashed under my seat. And I thought that day was gonna be a Clint Eastwood "make my day, punk" kind of day for me.

For eternity-like seconds, my mind entered another time, the Japanese Occupation in the Philippines, and in my mind's eye, I saw a Jap in an Imperial Army uniform, whose face was my parents' oppressors and I blew him away with three wire cutters, his dead body parts plastering the walls of his sentry shack.

It was surreal . . .

Until that Jap, wearing a U.S. Border Guard uniform, spoke up again and said, "What did you say was in your trunk?"

"Dead body parts," I said. "They're in the big silver pot." I couldn't see what he was doing from where I was sitting, but he must have lifted the lid off the pot of our PABAON, because the garlicky smell wafted into the air.

"These are dead body parts?" he asked.

"Yes," I said. "Dead body parts of a pig, and the concoction is called, ADOBONG BABOY . . ."

"DOROBO?" he asked.

"No," I said, resorting, again, to Pidgin English. "You, Dorobo! That, adobo. Me, adobo eater, yummy, yummy, like sushi . . ."

At the mention of the word, sushi, Kura-Kura's slant eyes, slanted to slits. I stared back at him, crossed my eyeballs, uncrossed 'em and crossed 'em again. Then I wiggled my ears, one at a time.

Then I farted, LOUD. That did it. He said: "You're crazy . . ."

The crossing barrier to America flew up. I stepped on the gas and roared away, roaring with laughter. As I savored my mirth, Maribel said: "You're crazy . . ."

See, even my wife tells me I am crazy. Ha, ha, ha, ha, ha, hah! **JJ**

Pakyaw THE Symbol of our "Ethnic Pride"? Ain't no way, Hosay!!!

There is no such thing as objectivity . . . I actually think it is pernicious as a goal.—Molly Ivins, the late syndicated columnist, in her defense of being opinionated

I don't really know exactly what Ms. Ivins meant by that. Pernicious means deadly or lethal or destructive . . . something like that. As a columnist, yes, I am opinionated. But am I lethal? Am I deadly? Am I destructive? I don't think so.

Well, perhaps, I "stir up" emotions among the people within our placid Fil-Am community, and that fact perhaps bring out the worst in some, that they do things that are, well, "pernicious," perhaps?

I don't do things that are pernicious. And that's simply because, I am a coward, you see.

So . . . before some of you guys go pernicious on me and stomp on my column and apply feces on my photo again, let me wish y'all now a **Happy Thanksgiving.** (I kid you not, a couple of years ago, someone with a seething pernicious hate towards me cut the photo off my Kapeng Barako column, smeared feces on it and mailed it to me with cussing hateful words).

And guess what? That made me laugh so hard. And if that poor soul is still alive, I also wish him a wonderful Thanksgiving. But if he had kicked the bucket already, so to speak, may he rest in peace.

Okey ngarud, enough hating already . . .

Did y'all, by any chance, read the *MegaScene* "Flipside" column of my colleague and good friend, Nelia Bernabe, last week? Yes, of course, I was on cloud nine. She wrote about me and my opinionated thoughts. So I said to her:

Hello Nelia,

Read your story. Thank you so much for the "plug" of my infamous name and for my "much-hated" *Kapeng Barako* column.

It's an excellent piece. It's well-written . . . and truly one of your signature columns. I like your original version better though, where you said at the very end of your story, "Jesse, my friend, bring it!" That was a very powerful ending, I think.

I also think that I understand the reason why you decided to delete it. You don't want the "WOLVES" to be after you! But that's okay. It didn't take anything away from the overall excellence of your story. It's still a very powerful piece.

There's one thing I couldn't agree with you on though, no matter how much I tried. It's that portion where you said that Pakyaw is the "symbol of our ethnic pride."

May I beg to differ? To me, he's not!

Someone who is ILLITERATE and whose skill and aura are only in the world of boxing is not THE symbol of our so-called "ethnic pride." We can do better than that. I am sure there are many other Filipinos who are more WORTHY to be the symbol of our ethnic pride.

The fact that we are all groveling at Pakyaw's feet and doing all kinds of hallelujahs for him, point to the fact that we, as a people are SO LACKING and SO HARD-UP . . . and SO DESPERATE for a symbol.

To me, Pakyaw is merely a PUNY symbol of the Filipino people . . . NOT THE symbol at all as we claimed him to be. We are NOT a puny people! We are not that insignificant as a people "grabbing at straws" and fawning at a mere puny symbol, and an illiterate one at that!

True, he's a good *boksingero* and we thrill at his boxing feats. And we all rejoice when he knocks out his opponents.

But really, I think it's INFANTILE of us as a people to look up to him and grovel endlessly at his feet and put him on a pedestal as a "god" and install him as THE symbol of our ethnic pride just because of his boxing skill and feats.

As they say here in America: Ain't no way, Hosay!

Take care, my friend. Once again, thanks for the plug.

(Signed) Jesse

Yes, I am aware that many of my columns seem to consist of e-mails extracted from my e-mail box, but I think e-mails written spontaneously in reply are mini-essays written in splendid honesty.

So . . . here's Nelia's reply, en toto:

Jess, thank you so much! There's so many things that I would like to say but out of respect to you and those who think that Pacquiao is the symbol of our ethnic pride, I will keep those things to myself. But let me just say something briefly. It is really unfortunate that somebody who is "illiterate and whose skill and aura are only in the world of boxing . . ." has become that symbol. I agree with you that there are many out there who are deserving but right now, Pacquiao is "it." You are an exception Jess because most Filipinos in America won't think twice about throwing that phrase—ethnic pride—freely to describe how they feel towards Pacquiao. I think for these people and this is not an emboldened assumption on my part, they take Pacquiao's wins at their face value. No need for any

other explanation. It could even be as rudimentary as the fact that he is a Filipino. It does not matter that he is illiterate and he's rags to riches, he's a success story coming from a country that's been nursing a soiled image for decades and a country that badly needs to turn that soiled image around. You can call their hero-worshipping a DESPERATE AND HARD-UP FACT BUT IN THEIR MINDS, THEY'RE SIMPLY ELATED. It really does not take much to please or make a Filipino happy. Live and let live Jess. If that's what makes people happy, who are we to stop them?

Anyhoo . . . I like that ending a lot too but knowing you, I really didn't have to make it official. I know that the underlying allure to "bring it" exists regardless if I say it or not. The wolves don't bother me. I just rather not deal with them.

Again, thanks my friend! You make this world an exciting place that's for sure. Take care!!!

(Signed) Nelia
P.S. No rebuttal from me after this e-mail :O) . . . it's Friday and time to kick back plus my daughter from Los Angeles is flying in tomorrow with her dog. Life is short Jess. . . . Have a wonderful Thanksgiving everyone!!!

Nelia, my dear friend, you mollify me. Yes, let's all live and let live. And let's all have a blessed and a wonderful Thanksgiving with friends, families and loved ones. And let's all be thankful for all the blessings that this wonderful country had given us. **JJ**

The Sound and Fury of the Comments I Got after the Pakyaw/Kuto Fight

It is a tale . . . full of sound and fury, signifying nothing.—Shakespeare

And I believe what Shakespeare meant by that is that time spent on overheated rhetoric and debates don't mean nothing at all.

The other night I dreamt that a pack of wolves was circling me. Then just when the wolves were about to devour me, I woke up. Hmmmm, I mused. Why did I dream that? It's probably just a "tale" concocted in my subconscious mind while I slept, "signifying nothing."

But, let me tell y'all that the "sound and fury" of the comments that I received when Pakyaw won his fight against El Kuto did not "signify nothing."

It signifies SOMETHING. Many things. Even "ism" things, if y'all follow my drift.

Let me quote another well-known writer, a Filipino, this time: Conrado de Quiros, of the *Philippine Daily Inquirer*. Y'all know him, right? The most fearless, I think, and one of the most-prolific columnists that the Motherland has today. He wrote of the Pakyaw phenomenon in this way:

"There's always SOMETHING disquieting when a country (and the Filipino people in all parts of the globe, if I may add) pins its hopes, its future and its destiny on the outcome of a sports event . . .

"Having NOTHING to be proud of, having everything indeed to be ashamed of, we look up to Pacquiao as SOMETHING to prop us up, as a source of replenishment . . .

"He isn't just a hero (of the Filipino people), he's the savior . . ."

Can you imagine that? Pakyaw is the "SAVIOR" of the Filipino people. No wonder I dreamt of wolves devouring me because I chose to differ in my opinion about the ALMIGHTY Pakyaw and said blatantly in my previous column that "Hindi ako bilib kay Pakyaw."

And these "wolves" in my SURREAL dream, turned to be, in reality, my friends and colleagues that I usually have vigorous debates with. What follows are some of their e-mails. PLEASE don't get me wrong. Because, you see, I love them all to death! Along with these good people circling as wolves in my dream, are also the hate mongers, who wish my demise from this earth. I am not gonna include their hate e-mails because what they wrote me and the language that they used are unprintable.

The first e-mail came from Pareng Don Azarias:

"Per Yahoo Sports: Pacquiao's performance was so good that no one laughed when promoter Bob Arum said he believes Pacquiao is the best fighter he ever saw. And yes, Arum included Muhammad Ali, Sugar Ray Leonard and Marvelous Marin Hagler in that group . . ." Then Pareng Don quipped, "No doubt about it!"

Then, my Bestpren, Yoly T. and my Erapok, Bart T., followed, saying: "Long Live Pacquiao, the pride of the Filipinos!"

Then my good friend, Joseph Lariosa, came in and said: ***"I hope the cynics, the whiners, sour grapes and all anti-Pacquiao fans should now give Pacquiao the credit he truly deserves . . ."***

I love to argue with Joseph, so I wrote this: ***JGL, my friend . . . First, congratulations to your hero. I am happy for Pakyaw and for all Filipinos in the world, who hero-worship him. He should be installed*** *now as a national hero. The Philippines is so hard-up for a hero, and to me, that's a damn shame!*

I am neither a sour grape nor a whiner. It's you who's whining. Whinnying and gloating; drooling and groveling at the feet of Pakyaw. . . . Now that Pakyaw won the fight, and you can gloat about it, does that make you a better person? You ever heard of the word, "MAGNANIMITY"? I can only feel sorry for you, my friend, if you haven't.

Because I think, people who gloat in their little triumphs possess a glaring defect and a shallowness of character. (Signed) JJ

From THAT reply, Ting Joven, another friend that I love and respect, fired her own e-mail: ***Jesse, my friend . . . Just take a bow. PERIOD. No need for sarcasm. You had your time to gloat on your "heroes." It is our time to gloat. No need for personal attacks on anyone's character in this list serve because the current topic is all about Pacquiao's (and his supporters) HUGE victory—nothing else. And by the way, "little triumphs"??? C'mon, my friend, be a sport.***

Don't feel sorry for Joseph because he's gloating with us and the whole world! Tsk, tsk, tsk. How ironic, because after reading your posting, I actually felt sorry for you, my friend . . . BUT I AM STLL GLOATING!!!! LONG LIVE, PACQUIAO!!!! Take care now. God bless. (Signed) Ting

My reply to Ting:

Hello Ting, my friend, and all my other friends and all my foes, et al . . . I took a "bow." I said, "Congratulations to Pakyaw and to all the Filipinos in the world who hero-worship him." And I also said that I am "happy" for Pakyaw and for all his fans and admirers. What more do you want me to say? And what more do you want me to do? Do you also want me to grovel at Pakyaw's feet, just like what you are all doing?

No, thank you.

Also, I didn't start the sarcasm and the personal insults as you said . . . words, like, "whiners" and "sour grapes" and "shameless" and "anti-Filipino" and a "Filipino without an identity" and several other hurtful words. I am the one being deluged now with personal insults and all kinds of sarcasm. I merely tried to deflect all your collective blows and all your kicks to my gonads and countered to the best that I know how, you know, just like Pakyaw's celebrated "kumbinasyon". . . . (Signed) Jesse

Ben Giovanelli, who I thought I've lost as my only "paisano" in this world, because of my radical views that he considers as abomination, also chimed in: ***My friend . . . You seemed to be the center of controversy. You're like an investment company, with a slogan: WHEN JESSE SPEAKS, EVERYBODY LISTENS.***

It takes a real man to admit SOMETIMES to the main consensus that we disagree with . . . and lose! As a journalist, that is your role, so I can understand where you're coming from! Taking the so-called temperature of the "mainstream" is fun for you! I am sure, in most cases, you're laughing at all the attention that you stir up! Being we're both retired, what else is there to do? Have a good one, my friend. No harm meant. (Signed) Brother BG

"BG, I love you, too, my brother. Thank you so much for your gentle and kind, and wise comment . . ." There were several other comments, too, gentle and kind, and others that were "full of sound and fury." But I can't fit them all. So, that's all. **JJ**

Pakyaw! Pakyaw! Pakyaw!
Hindi Ako Bilib Kay Pakyaw!

If you are a Filipino and you dare say those words above, to another Filipino, you're liable to get "murdered" by that Filipino. Or, you can get ostracized and dubbed as an "unpatriotic" Filipino, who had turned his back on his "ethnic pride."

Or, you can get cursed severely . . .

My dear Erapok, Bart T., in a mass e-mail, verbalized it in pretty words that red-hot Filipino anger, in this way:

There's such a feeling we call "Ethnic Pride." We all have to respect that feeling. That's probably why the Irish people celebrate and flaunt their St. Patrick's Day in the USA, why Irish men still love to show their skirts on parades, why the Puerto Ricans or even the Mexicans trumpet their horns on US streets in exaltation of their independence back home.

If we cannot respect our own pride and heritage, we must not expect others to respect us. If we cannot even love the triumphs of your compatriots, do not expect others to recognize your own talents or just even listen to your message. (Signed) Bart

My reply to Bart:

Erapok et al,

I am a journalist/columnist, NOT a Filipino trumpeter. I write the way I see things, NOT the way others would like me to see things. If people don't want to "listen to my message or recognize my talents," as you put it, that's their prerogative . . . and their problem, not mine.

Just like it's also my prerogative *na ayaw ko kay Pakyaw at hindi ako bilib sa kanya.* I think his last two fights against De La Hoya and Hatton were "fixed" by the Vegas MOB. It's all about money. He's a good boxer, but not the greatest in the world, as his Filipino admires claimed him to be.

Let's don't get overly sensitive now and get personal about our comments to each other when discussing Pakyaw and his fight against "El Kuto" this Saturday. *Boksing lang 'to.* We are all just commenting and voicing out our opinions. You've got your own opinion and I've got mine. Many others, too, have their own thoughts about this matter, perhaps, similar to yours . . . or perhaps, different. Be cool, Erapok. (Signed) Jesse

Perry Diaz, a friend and a colleague and a fellow MegaScene columnist had also verbalized his thoughts, succinctly. Quoting an excerpt from his e-mail, he said:

Pareng Jesse,

. . . In my opinion, when you put down Paquiao, you're putting down yourself and all the Pinoys in the world. I wouldn't be surprised to hear a Redneck say, "Look at these people, one of them becomes the best pound-for-pound fighter and they pull him down!

Isn't that what we call "crab mentality"? (Signed) Perry

My reply:

Pareng Perry,

May I beg to differ with you? I don't agree with that opinion. That's putting all Pinoys in one "BOX," where everybody MUST think alike, talk alike . . . and even look alike. And that if you DARE think or say anything outside of that box, you're "putting yourself down and all the Pinoys in the world." And that if you don't align yourself with fellow Pinoys within that box, you're a "cock-eyed" Pinoy. That's limiting and confining yourself within that Pinoy box . . . don't you think?

We, Pinoys, or anybody else for that matter, should be free to think and talk and to voice our opinions freely on anything and on anybody, without fear, whether that person you wish to comment on is the ALMIGHTY Pakyaw . . .

That's the American way!

When George W. Bush was still the President, many Americans laughed at him and put him down. He was laughed at on comedy shows and he was fodder for late-TV comedians and pundits, print and broadcast. And he was the President of the most powerful country in the whole world.

Surely those fellow Americans who put him down did not feel that they were putting themselves down as Americans, do you? They were merely voicing out their opinions and acting like typical Americans.

Si Pakyaw, boksingero lang, pare. True, he's got a lot of fans and Filipino admirers and . . . he's one of our own. He's also a "public" person, and anybody who is a public persona, will always have plenty of detractors and critics.

If you remember, you yourself and several people on this list serve—*na mga* community leaders *pa kuno*—had also made fun of of Pakyaw's Visayan accent and singing "talent."

***Nasa* America *na tayo, pare.* We have chosen this country now as our country and our children's country. And it's a great, benevolent and generous country, may I add.**

We Pinoys should now think like Americans. NOT as Pinoys within that proverbial box, thinking alike and talking alike and perhaps, even wanting to look alike. Pare, it's time to leave that box and join Mainstream America . . .

As to that "crab mentality" of Pinoys, unfortunately, that's true. We also possess a "monkey mentality." You know, as in "monkey see, monkey do."

Not too long ago, Mariah Carey, that famous and very sexy American singer, attended a concert in her honor, where our Philippine singers from that popular TV musical show, ASAP, imitated her. I suppose they were able to ape her singing and stage antics so closely that she angrily called those Carey look-alike singers as a "bunch of monkeys."

She was right. Pinoys COPY and IMITATE everything and anything American. We are talented imitators. We are monkeys . . . Alimango na nga tayo, chongo pa. Que barbaridad! (Signed) Jesse

Romy Marquez of San Diego, Ca., another respected colleague and a prolific investigative journalist, chimed in, highlighting first what I said about "Pinoys within the proverbial box, thinking alike and talking alike . . ." Then he said this:

Pareng Jesse . . . That is so profound, so enriching . . . something that could only come from you, or somebody like you who possessed the knowledge, the understanding, the tolerance, the experience and the talent to articulate one's thoughts. Thank you so much. This one truly lives up to your reputation, fearless, barakong-barako! (Signed) Romy Marquez

Well, someone likes me. But back to Pakyaw, I dare say AGAIN, *hindi ako bilib sa kanya* and I think he's gonna lose this time! That's all. **JJ**

Okey Ngarud, Mag-dyok Muna Tayo

This *dyok* (joke) was sent to me by Bart T., a Chicago-based friend. It may be a *dyok*, but I think it's very true. "And God knows that . . ." I told Bart. I also told him that I enjoyed the *dyok* so much that I should share it with my Barako readers, especially those *macho-nurin types na mga DOMs.*

The title of this dyok is: "Two Types of Men." So here it is. Enjoy.

When everybody on earth was dead and waiting to enter Paradise, God appeared and said, "I want the men to make two lines: one line for the men who were true heads of their household, and the other line for the men who were dominated by their women. I want all the women to report to St. Peter."

Soon the women were gone, and there were two lines of men. The line of men who were dominated by their wives was 100 miles long, and in the line of men who truly were heads of their household, there was only one man.

God said, "You men should be ashamed of yourselves. I created y'all to be the head of your household. Y'all have been disobedient and have not fulfilled your purpose! Of all of you, only one obeyed. Learn from him."

God then turned to that ONE MAN and asked him: "How did you manage to be the only one in this line?"

The man replied, "My wife told me to stand here."

I really think I have something in common with this MAN. Because, just like him, I am an obedient husband. Honest . . . Okey *ngarud*, enough of that.

Editor's Notes: To read Jesse Jose's other classic "dyok" stories, please click on these links:

Okey Ngarud, mga Pare, Mag-dyok Muna Tayo . . .

Untitled pa . . . itong kuwentong kung ito

Mga Dyoks . . . Tungkol kay Barack HUSSEIN Obama

That "Funneeeee" Cartoon of the New Yorker Magazine

A Turkey Story for Thanksgiving Day

Hysterical hysterics of Desperate Housewives

So, you guys voted this past Tuesday? I did. And the guy I voted for mayor of our town, won. He's a GOP.

OBAMA GOT HIS BUTT KICKED: And we heard that the two GOPs, Chris Christie and Robert McDonnell, who ran as governors in New Jersey and Virginia respectively, both won, too. It was said by conservative pundits that Chris Christie's "gutsy" win in New Jersey puts his opponent, the "arrogant big spender Jon Corzine in his place."

And that obviously Christie's victory is a "body blow" to Mr. Obama.

And that Corzine's defeat sends a loud-and-clear message that America is "moving sharply against Obama."

And despite of the fact that Mr. Obama was in New Jersey so much that it almost looked like it was him who was running for governor instead of Corzine . . . "did no good." Loudly and clearly, President Obama's butt and his surrogate there in New "Joisey" got a beating big time. Ouch!

When a GOP candidate in Virginia wins by 20 points, it sends a message that Mr. Obama's mantra of "YES, HE CAN!" is beginning to sound like, "NO, HE CAN'T!"

But it's the win in Virginia, political analysts have said, that's considered as "the most important." For the "sudden switch" of loyalties in that state, which was a swing state that Mr. Obama carried in the last presidential election, "heralds tough political times ahead."

And that when a GOP in Virginia wins by 20 points, it sends a message that President Obama's mantra of "YES, HE CAN!" is beginning to sound like, "NO, HE CAN'T!"

And this, I believe, is THE change we can truly believe in!

As Dick Morris, a news commentator for *FOX News* commented: "The elections of 2009 . . . show the limits of Obama's appeal . . . a signal on how the public is reacting to his RADICAL agenda."

And, it's not only the GOPs that are incensed at President Obama's policies. A growing numbers of liberals—the pro-choice proponents, the gay activists, the immigration rights groups, the anti-war crusaders, the civil libertarians, etc.—are fed-up with him for betraying them on the liberal agenda that they elected him to enact.

So . . . so much ngarud for the AUDACITY OF HOPE of Barack H. Obama, ha? Okey *ngarud*, enough of that.

PAKYAW ON JIMMY KIMMEL SHOW, MY TAKE: Did y'all see Manny Pakyaw, live, this past Tuesday, on Jimmy Kimmel late-night TV show? I think that's awesome. He's now the most famous Filipino on Earth. *Nadaig pa niya si Willie, the "Wowowee."*

My fellow columnist, Joseph Lariosa of Chicago, a die-hard fan of Pakyaw, wrote an excellent story on Pakyaw's appearance on that show. His story has been published in several on-line and hard copy Fil-Am publications. Check it out. I wrote a comment on JGL's story (Pacquiao

Lives Up to His Name and Appears in Jimmy Kimmel Show), ribbing him in this way:

Hello JGL,

Good story and a good read. A multi-talented man like Pakyaw—boxer, singer, actor, pandesal baker . . . and writer kuno pa pala—should be, as Kimmel suggested, THE President of the Philippines. With Willie, the Wowowee as his VP, that Pilipino adage, "Ang Pilipino Angat Sa Mundo," will surely come true.

(Signed)JJ
PS: I bet you my piggy bank of pennies, he's gonna lose to "El Kuto." Because, you see, El Kuto is no Mehicano, he's a Negro. And Pakyaw can only beat up Mexican boxers, who have retired, and recycled to box Pakyaw for the money. Hah!

Gamely, JGL wrote a reply:

Hi, JJ:

Thanks for reading my story.

I also enjoyed reading your "Philippines: The Land of 'Wawa We'." I hope those foreigners you mentioned in your accounts who are taking over the businesses from Filipinos are paying their proper taxes para naman hindi "Wawa We" ang Pinas.

In the case of Pakyaw, itabi mo na lang ang iyong mga pennies para lumago pa. I hardly make any prediction because it is very hard to be accurate. But I think as a Puerto Rican who speaks the Latino language, Mr. Miguel Cotto is in line to be another "Mexecutioner" victim of Manny. Our Pakyaw may not only be able to "pa-pak" (I hope not bite the ear, like Mike Tyson did) Cotto, pero puede na rin tirisin na lang ni Manny si Cotto, na parang kuto. (Signed) JGL

There were several funny "Kuto" comments commenting on my "Kuto" retort. But, once again, I've ran out of space. Kaya, dear readers, use your imagination *na lang*, ha?

Okey *ngarud*, that's all. **JJ**

On a Letter, on Barack Obama, on Fox News and on Coffee

I don't have any idea at all.

For almost like half an hour now, I've been sitting here in front of my computer, looking at the blank screen, trying to think of the word that would untangle my jumbled-up ideas on what to write about, but that word wouldn't come . . .

I think writing those past four stories of what I've seen of the "Land of 'WaWa We'," kind of drained me out. I feel kind of empty right now.

Then while I was flipping through my beat-up notebook full of doodles and scratches of unreadable notes, I came across an email from a reader that I've printed and inserted between the pages . . . and quoting it here en toto, it reads:

Dear Sir,

I always enjoyed reading your column. I like it with a sense of humor. Looking forward this weekend again and I will read your column. Thank you!

Teresa Toledo

From the way it was written, I think a young girl wrote that letter. And yes, it was awkwardly written, but I think this young girl's missive is awesome and inspiring.

And, I am humbled.

For pro-bono columnists like me, whose labors, are labors of love, that's indeed, awesome and inspiring!

So, with gratitude in my heart, I wrote Teresa:

Hello Teresa,

Thank you so much for reading my column. It makes me so happy to know that you read my column and you like the humor that I inject now and then in my stories and that you've taken the time to write to tell me about it. For columnists and writers like me, feedbacks and comments from our readers are our rewards, and we welcome them.

Any time you wish to make a comment again on any of my stories, please feel free to do so.

Take care now, Teresa, and once again, thank you and God bless.

Jesse Jose

Moving on . . . Before I began to write this column, I had a phone conversation with my Bestpren. We talked about a lot of things. She asked me: "Ano ba ang topic ng column mo ngayon? WaWa We na naman ba?"

"No," I said, laughing. "Tapos na ako diyan. I am moving on to Barack naman."

ON BARACK OBAMA: So moving on . . . we heard that Barack Obama is failing. Failing big. And failing everywhere: Foreign policy, domestic initiatives, and most importantly, in forging connections with the American people. The incomparable Dorothy Rabinowitz in the *Wall Street Journal* put her finger on it: He is failing because he has no understanding of the American people, and may indeed loathe them. Fred Barnes of the *Weekly Standard* says he is failing because he has lost control of his message, and is overexposed. Clarice Feldman of *American Thinker* produced a dispositive commentary showing that Obama is failing because fundamentally he is neither smart nor articulate; his intellectual dishonesty is conspicuous by its audacity and lack of shame . . .

No, I didn't write that. It's an excerpt from an article titled, "Another Failed Presidency," written by Dr. Geoffrey P. Hunt, who is a social and cultural anthropologist and writer for *American Thinker.*

Do I believe that? No, I don't. I think it's hogwash. But those writers who were quoted in that excerpt are all within their rights to say their opinions.

I, too, have something to say to Mr. Obama: So, when, Mr. President? When will your deeds match your words? All those people who worked tirelessly to get you elected are getting tired of waiting . . .

You promised them jobs, but that didn't happen yet. You promised them health care for all, but that didn't happen yet.

You promised them that there won't be any more wars that America will be involved in, but as America prepare to draw down troops from that quagmire that was the war in Iraq, you have plans on committing more troops to another quagmire that is the war in Afghanistan.

Yes, Mr. President, you promised them a lot of things that are not happening! America's satisfaction with the way things are going has hit a six-month low, Sir! NOT only that. The federal deficit has also hit the $1.43-trillion mark! And that's more than the total national debt for the first 200 years in the history of this country. Hey, Mr. Obama, what's up?

ON *FOX NEWS*: Moving on . . . Do y'all know that the White House has declared war on *Fox News.*

White House communications director Anita Dunn said that *Fox* is "opinion journalism masquerading as news."

Senior Adviser David Axelrod declared that *Fox* is "not really a news station."

And, Chief of Staff Rahm Emmanuel warned the other networks not to be "led by and following *Fox.*

"Or else . . ."

Charles Krauthammer, a syndicated columnist, said that *Fox News* is a "singular minority in a sea of liberal media . . ."

In other words, in a sea of Obama lapdogs, like *ABC, NBC, CBS, PBS, CNN* and *MSNBC, Fox News* stands alone. The number-one lap dog among the news anchors of the liberal media is, I think, Brian Williams of *NBC,* followed by that motor mouth of a news commentator on *MSNBC,* named Keith Olbermann. His "Countdown" days are numbered.

ON COFFEE: Moving on . . . According to researchers at the Harvard School of Public Health, big-time coffee drinkers, those who downed more than six cups of coffee a day, have a 29 to 54% lower risk of developing type-2 diabetes. Sipping only one to three cups per day ain't gonna do it, they said. It must be at least six cups. And decaf coffee has no value.

The researchers said that coffee contains potassium, magnesium and anti-oxidants that help cells absorb sugar . . .

So, okey *ngarud,* talk to y'all later. I am gonna have my *Cup O' Kapeng Barako* now and watch *Fox News'* prime-time evening report. **JJ**

In the Land of "Wawa We," Who Is Gonna Win the 2010 Presidency?

Noynoy! Noynoy! Noynoy! The poor people of the Philippines, the masa, that is, scream their hearts out. Noynoy! Noynoy! Noynoy! They chant with reverence. How sad. . . .

Wherever he goes, the people reach out to him. Noynoy! Noynoy! Noynoy! How truly sad . . .

Y'all know whom I am talking about, right? That's right: that Noynoy, the only son and *panganay* of Ninoy and Cory Aquino among a brood of daughters.

It's said that he's going to be the next President of the "Land of 'WaWa We'." The people there said that he's their "salvation." And that he's going to bring the changes that are sorely needed to the Motherland. They said he's NOT corrupt and that he's going to wipe out the blatant corruption and poverty that pervades in the "Land of 'WaWA We'."

They said he's THE anointed one! They said he's got the genes of Ninoy, "the martyr" and Cory, "the saint." Yada, yada.

Recent polls and surveys revealed that Noynoy is leading the presidential field. You know what? I think the reason for his popularity is through name recall only. President Cory Aquino, his mother, the popular and much-revered "praying saint" of the Filipino people, recently died. And at the heels of her death was the commemoration of the anniversary of the assassination of his father, Senator Benigno "Ninoy" Aquino, the "martyr."

So, okay, he's the son of a "martyr" and a "saint."

But what are Noynoy's accomplishments? From what I've read about him in all his years as a Congressman, he was merely a BACKBENCHER, who didn't have a single bill attached to him!

Yeah, in other words, while in Congress, Noynoy didn't do anything . . .

But sat on his lazy butt!

Also, when there was this recent GREAT FLOOD all over Metro Manila and the outlying provinces that Typhoon ONDOY caused, where was Noynoy? *Hindi makita. Siguro, takot sa baha. Baka, hindi marunong lumangoy*. Or probably, he didn't want his pants to get wet and his shoes to be muddied. *Pero, kahit na, pakitang tao man lamang sana.* Just to show the people that he's with them, in sharing with their tragedies . . .

HACIENDA LUISITA: Hey, do y'all know that the Aquinos, from Noynoy's great grandfather, Jose Cojuangco, Sr., did not own the much-ballyhooed, Hacienda Luisita, and I am going to quote here the widely-read Philippine newspaper, the "*National Inquirer.*"

"The Aquinos were 'dummies' of the government. They were given $2.12-million from the Central Bank and P3.98-million from the GSIS to buy Hacienda Luisita, on the condition that the land would be distributed to the farmers in 10 years, or by 1968, at the latest . . ."

Forty-one years later, the *Inquirer* revealed that Noynoy cited "labor trouble and debts for the reason not to distribute the land by 1968" under the conditions for his great-grandfather's acquisition of Hacienda Luisita.

"It's a well-known historical fact," the Inquirer asserted. And it opined that Noynoy's morality campaign and his family's goody-goody image is merely a "BIG LIE . . ."

And the campaign's "BIGGEST SHAM."

When I visited the "WaWa We Land," a few weeks ago, I had an interesting tee-a-tee with the husband of one my wife's closest friend, Corazon, who is a school principal at a Christian school in Quezon City. Her husband, Froilan, is a lawyer and a former judge in one of the districts of Metro Manila. But because of "death threats" he had received, he resigned his position as a judge and now works as a Public Defender for Quezon City.

Over dinner at his home in Kamuning, Q.C., we talked about Philippine politics. I asked him who he thinks is going to be the next President of the Philippines.

Without hesitation, he said. "Teodoro."

And why is that?

"Because," Froilan said, "he's Uncle Sam's choice. *Kung sino ang susuportahan ng* America, *yun ang magiging presidente ng Pilipinas.*"

AMERICA IN THEIR HEARTS: Froilan ardently believes that it's NOT Noynoy that America supports, but Defense Secretary Gilbert "Gibo" Teodoro, Jr.

And why is that?

"Because Teodoro is a *TUTA* (lap dog) of America," Froilan said. "Just like Arroyo is a *tuta* of America. And Cory was a *tuta* of America. And Ramos was a *tuta* of America. So was Marcos was a *tuta* of America. Well, at first, Marcos was, but his head got too big and he stayed too long in power and his wife, Imelda, didn't know when to stop accumulating those shoes . . . that America finally got fed up and ran them both out of town."

"All these Philippine Presidents had America in their hearts . . . and had been brainwashed and mentored by America," Froilan said. "Ramos was a West Point graduate and a soldier of America. Arroyo studied in the United States and was an erstwhile classmate of Bill Clinton, at Yale, I believe. And Cory had lived in Boston, Massachusetts, for years. When she became the President, she had said several times that "Boston is my home and that's where I want to go and live when I retire . . ."

"And, Marcos was a FilVet during the Second World War, who fought for America," said Froilan. "He led a group of guerilla fighters . . . and as you know, he was the THIEF, who stole Yamashita's treasures."

Hmmmm.

"With Teodoro, do you know that he has a GREEN CARD?" Froilan said. "And that he has a Masters Degree in International Law at Harvard and has a license to practice law in New York . . ."

"And the reason," Froilan said, shifting his discourse, "Cory Aquino won so easily and handily the presidency was because at that point in time even if a monkey would run against Marcos, the monkey would win. And Cory naturally was better than Marcos or a monkey!"

So, dear readers, who do you think is gonna win the 2010 presidency in the "Land of 'WaWa We'"? Noynoy, Gibo, or a monkey? **JJ**

Final Chapter: "Philippines, my Philippines, the Land of 'WaWa We'"

It surprised the heck out of me.

Like that TV ad on a battery that keeps going and going and going, the comments and feedbacks on my "Philippines, my Philippines, '*WaWa We*'" story keep coming . . . and coming . . . and coming.

Not only from one group of people, but from different groups of people, from everywhere, from California to Florida, from Canada, from the Philippines and from the Middle East.

Majority of the comments were from Balikbayans, who have seen the Philippines up close . . . and their common comments were of the "EXTREME POVERTY" that they saw there. And that each time they would visit the Philippines, "the DETERIORATION there . . . *lalung lumalala*!"

"One after the other, the country has been ruled by useless and corrupt administrations," one fellow Balikbayan said. And another pointed out that "after President Ferdinand Marcos fell and got run out of the country, its slow demise and slide down the gutter, began."

"The Pearl of the Orient has become the armpit of Asia," another one added.

I think I hit a nerve of so many Fil-Ams with these stories, that if I am going to compile all the comments, it will take several pages of this publication to fit them all in. Heck, maybe, I'll compile some of them in my next column. I've never gotten so many comments for any of my stories I've written before.

Comments from Iowa

Even my son, Chris, a broadcast journalist and an Emmy-Award nominee of KGAN, an affiliate of CBS TV station, in Cedar Rapids, Iowa, who usually keeps mum on my Barako stories, commented: ***"Pops . . . I liked your story. I forwarded it to Jaclyn (Chris's fiancé and also a broadcast journalist) and her family, and they enjoyed it, too.***

"You simply reported the facts and truths about what you have observed there. That's what journalists do. You can't let your personal beliefs or biases skew the truth. It's like the slogan of Fox News: 'We report, You Decide.' I am looking forward to the next column."

Editor's Notes: To read the articles that the columnist has written about Chris, please click on the following hyperlinks:
More-than a Chip Off the Old Block
Jesse's Son Wins Wyoming Broadcasters' Awards

Comments from San Diego, CA

Another journalist, Romy P. Marquez of San Diego, California, the editor/publisher of *PhilVoice News*, said: ***"Pareng Jesse . . . Thanks for the heads-up.*** **Masaya at malungkot yung *story* mo.**

"As you said, so many things have changed, or have gone down the drain, among them the demise of Philippine Marines guarding Jose Rizal (his remains mainly buried underneath the monument; well, JR is now a security guard at Seafood City supermarket here) . . .

"One good thing though is your namesake **Kapeng Barako** ***which, happily, they still serve there. I would have done the same thing you did—gulp the brew cup after cup until the caffeine gives you a high. Well, mabuti hindi ka nalasing!***

"How could our people betray our very own* Kapeng Barako *for Starbucks? That would be a good story.

"I like the first part of your story as much as this second. Very informative, revealing and, as they say in journalism lingo, straight from the shoulder. Best regards."

So, now, where was I? Where did I stop in my last column? I think I was in Tagaytay, at the Taal Vista Lodge, looking at those beautiful God-made mountains and gulping cups of *Kapeng Barako.*

Yes, it was so beautiful up there, and so clean and the air so fresh and the quietness of the mountains so calming.

TAGATAY HIGHLANDS: While there, a tall, pleasant-looking young man approached us and offered us a free tour of Tagaytay Highlands, a new real-estate development of "condos" up there in the sky of Tagaytay. Curious to see what this young man has to sell, we went with him in a van.

Through winding narrow roads, we rode. Then, passed a gate guarded by armed guards, we followed more winding, narrow, manicured, rolling roads all the way to the inner sanctum of this development.

And I tell ya, what I saw took my breadth away. It was like a dream. It was like entering paradise. He showed us a model unit and I went straight to the patio and what I saw before me was "God's Little Acre." And if only I had then the million of pesos that was required to make a down payment on one of the condos there, I would have done it.

I wanted a piece of that acre and lived the rest of my life there. I think I am going to . . .

Leaving that place to go back to Manila was like waking up from a beautiful dream into a horrible real-life nightmare. On the way back to Manila, we passed through Imus and Bacoor . . . the pollution, the gutted roads, the holes in the roads, the chaos and the madness in those two towns, well, was like HELL! I looked around me. I did not see any trees or any plants growing. They all have perished from the pollution and from the thick layers of dust and from the stench of the trash and garbage that littered the road.

Grabe talaga . . .

Sen. Bong Revilla, a former action movie star, who championed in the halls of Philippine Congress the two PORNO women of the famed Kho-Halili/Kho-Maricas Reyes triple-x films . . . *hindi ba taga Cavite 'to?* Instead championing porno women and reviewing their performances on films, he should be championing for the infrastructure of Cavite and fixing those roads.

Editor's Notes: To read more of Jesse Jose's take on Senator Revilla and the Dr. Kho porno films, please click on this link, Why Do Filipinos Talk About the Kho-Halili Sex Video Instead of Foreign Pedophiles, the "Abortion Doctors" and the Arroyo Corruption Scandals?

KOREAN-OWNED PHILIPPINE BEACHES: With relatives tagging along, children and all, we went to Subic Bay, Zambales. Not bad. That former U.S. Naval Station that has become a Freeport Center seemed to be well-maintained, flourishing and thriving. Instead of people, we saw a lot of wild monkeys crossing the winding roads. That was interesting. There were trees and plants everywhere and very green.

A few miles from there, we went to a zoo as a treat for the children, and then we headed down to the beaches. Entry to the beaches has been walled in and has become private commercial properties owned mostly by Koreans . . . and so we had to pay to get in, to the beaches. When I was in the U.S. Navy, stationed at the naval base there, those beaches used to be free and opened to the public. Now, they are owned by frigging Koreans . . .

The Chinese own the mushrooming malls; the Japanese, the five-star hotels; the Americans, most of the resort areas . . . whereas the Filipinos in their own native land, own the small little stinking shacks that litter everywhere . . . that seems to be the picture I get there . . . So sad, indeed.

HAPPY MOMENTS WITH RELATIVES: Though it was sad for me to see the Motherland in such a sorry state, I had wonderful, happy moments seeing my brother, Soc, and his beautiful family. And I told him that. I also told him that I love him, "*kahit paminsan-minsan lang kitang nakikita.*" Together, we visited Itay's burial plot at the Holy Cross Cemetery in Novaliches. We uttered a prayer for Itay and told Itay that we were just dropping by. We left him a bouquet of flowers and two burning candles. I think Itay would have preferred a bottle of Ginebra.

I had fun talking with the nieces of my wife, the sisters, Khela and Joy. I had a wonderful time with Corey, who became our tour guide, and her son, Josan. And Corey's kasambahay, Aning, and Rio, the master cook of pinakbet. It was good to see Minda and her son, Ogie Boy, and his children, Patricia and Tim Boy. And Minda's 13-year-old adopted son, Gelo.

And . . . Protacio, my "partner in crime" here in Seattle, who went "home" there years ago and stayed. He looked mighty fine. Hiyang sa kanya ang Pilipinas.

It was also good to see Mycel, who is so grown-up now . . . and the old folks, Kuya Dads, Ate Meng, Ate Chit and Kuya Jun.

And, of course, Bianca, who was the reason for our trip to this **"Land of 'WaWa We', Philippines, my Philippines."** That's all. **JJ**

Philippines, my Philippines . . . the Land of "WaWa We" (Part II)

My column last week, the first part of this story, generated a lot of comments. Surprisingly, most were positive comments, agreeing with my observations and on what I wrote. The comments were from several Fil-Am community leaders, such as Ting Joven and Bart Tubalinal, Jr., of Chicago, Dr. Tom Bonson of Virginia, Perry Diaz of California, and several others.

They said they, too, have seen the extreme destitution there and the chaos and the filth . . . and smelled the stench, when they visited the Motherland a few years ago.

My Erapok, Bart T., asked about my son, Jonathan's reaction to his "exposure" to those "Philippine truths" that I wrote about. My son, who grew up here in America and visited the Philippines for the first time, said: "There's so much poverty there. And everything seems to be too small. And there are so many malls . . . malls after malls everywhere and they're always crowded."

A reader, named Sito Serate, said the Catholic Church is to be blamed partly for the poverty in the Philippines, a Catholic nation, for it preaches the sins of birth control and, therefore, condones the "population explosion" and that compounds the extreme poverty there.

There were "hate mails," too, of course, that I received, and a couple of the letters have even cursed me out with words that are unprintable here. Mac Flores, a reader from California, angrily said: "***No need to***

emphasize the dirt, noise, heat, unwelcome sights and other bad comments about RP. We knew it already. These bad images do not sell to the tourists. Every country in this world has its own unwelcome sights. Why comment about it, especially if it is your own country? Why not strain your eyes to the beautiful spots in the Philippines? Badmouthing about the country is not good."

I wrote him back:

"***Mr. Flores . . . Thank you so much for your feedback. But I don't work for the Philippine Tourism Industry. I am a reporter/columnist and I merely reported on what I've seen of the Motherland, while on a visit there. It wasn't my intention at all to 'badmouth' the country, but to write what I've seen and how it affected me personally.***

"***I agree with you that there are many 'beautiful spots' in the Philippines to see and get agog about. But unfortunately, they are only for tourists and*** **balikbayans** ***and for the moneyed people of the Philippines to go to and enjoy.***

"***What I wrote about were 'spots' where the multitudes, the majority, perhaps, of our*** **kababayans,** ***live. If that's 'badmouthing' a country, then so be it. As I said, I am a reporter and I merely wrote of what I've seen of the Motherland. If those truths have offended you, I am so sorry.***"

And so with that, let me continue on what I've seen of the "WaWa We" Land.

LUNETA, MAKATI AND TAGAYTAY: Luneta Park, which used to be one of the world's most beautiful parks and a tourists' attraction, is no longer that way.

In the 80's, when I was still courting my wife, we used to make *pasyal* there on some evenings and ride the Motor-Co, back and forth, along Roxas Boulevard, just to enjoy the sea breeze . . . and eat *balut*. It used to be a lively, enjoyable park, and a place for lovers, like me, to make *ligaw*.

It's poorly-maintained now, trashy and muddy and a melancholy place at night.

The monument of Jose Rizal, our national hero, which used to be guarded by smart-uniformed Philippine Marines, where at all times, two marines marched smartly back and forth and cut corners sharply around the perimeter of the monument . . . well, the marines are no longer there.

We strolled inside the historical Intramuros. That, I am happy to say, is well-preserved and well-maintained. There are flowers everywhere. The armed guards at the gate are garbed in Katipunan-like outfit. We took a lot of pictures there.

We also went to see Makati and walked around in that plaza-like square, where the two five-star hotels, InterCon and Shangri-La, face each other, and which I heard from the locals, are now the "watering holes of "foreigners and the moneyed class of the Philippines." My wife and I used to go disco dancing at "Where Else" of InterCon, so we went in there to check the place out. "Where Else" no longer exists. It was day time when we went there, so we went into the coffee shop.

For almost like half an hour, we waited for a waiter to approach our table. But nobody came. Then a foreigner, a white American dude, came in and sat a couple of tables away from us . . . and immediately, out of nowhere, a waiter materialized to wait on the white dude.

I went to the front desk of the hotel and demanded that someone wait on us, too. Soon, a pretty young woman, wearing a native costume and a wide, FAKE smile approached our table and apologized. She said the hotel didn't have enough wait staff to serve guests. Of course that was a lot of B.S., for I saw a couple of waiters standing idly at a corner but both of them disappeared when we came in . . . and magically popped out of nowhere, when that foreign dude walked in.

Wa Wa We!

We also went up to Tagaytay to look at the mountains there. We stopped at the famous Taal Vista Lodge. We went out at the hotel's back patio to look at the panoramic view of Taal volcano and the outlying mountains.

It was a sight to behold! It was breathtaking and I felt the presence of God, like when I saw the Grand Canyon. I uttered a prayer . . . and then, we did the usual *picturan.*

We went inside the dining area that overlooks the mountains for our merienda. I asked if they have brewed *Kapeng Barako*. Our waiter said it's the only kind of coffee that they serve there. I had two freshly-brewed cups one after the other. I gulped the brew thirstily. I tell ya, *Kapeng Barako* is coffee for the gods.

I asked our waiter why is it that this Batangas-grown coffee is served only in big, flashy, expensive hotels. Why won't they make it available to the common *tao*?

"*Kasi*, sir," our waiter said, "the people would rather drink Starbucks coffee."

Starbucks coffee shops have mushroomed all over Metro Manila, as well as Jollibee and MacDonald's . . . and Shoe Mart malls, where they sell, mostly foreign-made clothes and shoes. And the decorative posters on walls of those stores are of beautiful boys and girls of good, old USA.

Where are the Philippine-made products? *Bakit hindi tinatangkilik ng mga Pilipino 'to?*

Wawa We!

By the way, do you know how the words, "Wawa We" came about? It was derived from the word, "Wowowee." That's right, that very popular and IDIOTIC and *bakya* program, hosted by Willie Revillame, that is watched globally *daw* by Filipinos. When Willie said that he might run as VP for Manny Villar in the presidential election of 2010 . . . and boasted that if he does that, he'll surely win, Filipino political and opinion writers joked and scornfully laughed at Willie and coined the words . . .

Wawa We!

Hey, those writers can laugh as much as they want, but I bet ya, that if Governor Vilma Santos runs as a presidential candidate in 2010, with Willie, the Wowowee, as her VP, the people will vote for them and they will win . . .

Y'all remember FPJ, right? He won, didn't he? *Kaya nga lang, dinaya nila GMA, aka, Pandak at ni Garci si FPJ, 'di ba? Hello Garci . . .*

WaWa We!

I talk too much. I've run out of space, again. *Marami pa akong ikukwento tungkol sa Pinas. Kaya, may* sequel *pa 'to. Abangan po ninyo sa susunod na linggo.* **JJ**

Philippines, my Philippines, the Land of "Wawa We"

After twenty-five years, I paid a visit to the Motherland. And what I saw is an extremely poor . . . backward, third-world country.

My trek there, with my wife, Maribel and my son, Jonathan, began with a greeting of "welcome aboard" in heavy-accented English by a very pretty and petite and smart-looking Korean stewardess, in a brown form-fitting uniform, of Asiana Airlines.

Right on schedule, we were airborne

It was a long flight . . .

It took 11 hours to fly from Seattle, Washington to Inchon, Korea, where we had a lay-over and a change of plane. I had a book with me, a thriller, so I read that intermittently during the flight. But most of the time, I amused myself by watching the crew of petite flight stewardesses walked up and down the twin aisle of the plane. They walked like models on a ramp. They giggled and smiled as they served the food and drinks. We were fed three times during the flight and plied with drinks in between.

It was a very pleasant flight, I think.

The international airport at Inchon was sparkling clean and very modern and their staffs of workers were all very efficient. At one of the many fast-food restaurants in the airport, we had huge bowl of vegetable noodle soup . . . and it was super delicious.

After a two-hour lay-over, we were airborne again, on a smaller plane this time, but the service or the prettiness of the crew of stewardesses didn't lessen.

It was five-hour flight from Korea to the Philippines.

Then FINALLY, we landed at Ninoy Aquino International Airport . . .

The arrival area teemed with uniformed airport workers standing around, gawking at us stupidly. Nobody directed or guided us where to go for Customs and for Immigration and where to pick up our suitcases and luggage . . . unlike in Korea, where, as soon as we, the newly-arrived passengers entered the terminal, the airport staff shepherded us courteously to the "where-tos" of the airport.

One thing VERY surprising though at Ninoy airport: We cleared through Customs and Immigration with ease, without the usual *LAGAY* that this Philippine airport was so well-known for. We were outside of the airport in no time.

Then . . . the heat immediately assaulted me.

Then . . . the noise.

Then . . . the pollution.

The narrow two-lane street just outside the exit door was a picture of total chaos. Honking vehicles of all sorts and sizes and screaming people clogged the sidewalk and the street. I looked across the narrow two-lane street and saw hundreds of gawking faces, behind a steel fence, who were perhaps, relatives of those newly-arrived passengers, making *sundo*. Or maybe, they were just onlookers.

It was madness . . .

But it was the noise, the cacophony of noises, that overwhelmed and deafened me so. After about an hour, we saw our *sundo*, waving a huge placard with my wife's name written on it.

THE POVERTY AND THE FILTH: We were in the Philippines for two weeks. We stayed in a condo in Cainta, Rizal, that my wife "rented" through the Internet. It was called the Mayfield Park Residences. Though it was described in the Internet as a "condo," it was really like a tenement kind of housings. But it was quiet and clean within the property limits and there was a swimming pool that you can dip in if you want. There were two security gates to pass through, and the area is patrolled 24 hours by armed security guards.

From that place to Manila is only about 30 miles or so.

But to get to Manila takes about three to five hours!

Because you have to wade and crawl through the thick, crazy-like traffic, through the fumes and pollution, through all sorts of obstacles on the road, people walking and crossing the streets, cigarette vendors, chitcharon vendors, street urchins hawking sampaguitas, beggars, jeepneys and cars and tricycles and motorcycles and what have you, cutting you off or blocking your way.

There were no traffic rules. There were road lanes, but nobody paid attention to them. There were no stop signs or stop lights. There were traffic enforcers in every street intersection, but they just wave everybody through. And I don't know how they survive each day breathing in the poisonous black smoke belching from every vehicle on the road.

It was mad, mad, mad.

It was a good thing our hired driver was as deft and as crazy as those other crazy drivers on the road, so we managed each time to arrive safe and sound to wherever we were going.

Our driver was also street smart for he knew all the side streets and alleys and "short cuts," so to speak, of the streets of Manila. And this gave me the opportunity to see the Manila that the tourists and fellow *balik-bayans* don't really see . . . or will never see.

Poverty reigns supreme in the heart of Metro Manila!!!

And the filth is unbelievable!!!

I saw shacks after shacks, made of rusted *yero* as homes for many people.

I saw creeks and canals used as garbage dumps . . . and the stench was suffocating.

One time, while passing through an alley, I saw a kid defecate on the sidewalk, while his parents and elders squat nearby, gossiping . . .

And I saw a wake being held on the sidewalk and a feast, liquor and all, a couple of blocks away.

And while passing through a narrow street next to the Pasig River, not too far from the Post Office building in the heart of Manila, I saw a woman washing clothes, using the filthy, water of Pasig River as rinsing water for her *labada*.

And then not too far from there, I saw a young woman taking a bath from a faucet right on the sidewalk, where everybody can see her. She was fully clothed though, so that wasn't too bad . . .

I saw a lot of things, ugly and bad and not too bad. I saw beautiful things, too, of course. But this column is getting too long now. So, continued *na lang* next week. I have a lot more I wanna tell. *O, sige na muna, ngarud.* **JJ**

"Tita Cory," the Filipino People's "Uncanonized" Saint: A Dissenting Opinion

She (Tita Cory) retained a whiff of sanctity even as her government rotted . . .—Howard Chua-Eoan, TIME/CNN columnist

May she rest in peace.

Corazon Cojuangco Aquino, this political saint and former President of the Philippines, who the Filipino people fondly called, "Tita (Auntie) Cory," and who was accidentally catapulted to power after her husband, Ninoy Aquino, was assassinated . . . you are all familiar with her story, right?

It's been written and re-written that Tita Cory has now become like a legend and a myth . . . and a saint to most Filipinos. When she was still living, she was photographed many times on her knees, in prayerful repose. She was always praying. Perhaps, praying for her family, praying for Ninoy and praying for the Filipino people . . . or perhaps praying for her rebellious and promiscuous daughter and *bunso*, Kris. Tita Cory was a woman of prayers.

Yes, I, too, shed some tears when I watched her funeral services Tuesday on TFC (The Filipino Channel) of ABS-CBN. It was truly like a Filipino soap opera made for Filipino viewers.

And me being a Filipino at heart, I couldn't help myself shed those tears for Tita Cory. She was a good mom, a good housewife, a good person, a person of prayers and all that good stuff. But she was no leader!

As President, she was simply incompetent. Under her regime, *lalung naghirap ang Pilipinas* and if y'all remember, from BANGUS, GALUNGONG became the national fish and the staple *ulam* of many Filipinos.

And believe you me, I saw the worsening poverty in the Philippines when Tita Cory became the President. I was in the Philippines when all that happened. I've just retired from the U.S. Navy then and came home, and worked as editor of the Camp John Hay Newsletter in Baguio City.

TO HAWAII INSTEAD OF PAOAY: I also saw up close the first "people power" revolution in EDSA. We, at John Hay, were monitoring closely what was happening in Manila. And there was this colonel in the Philippine Army, who became a good friend and told me that "a THIRD PARTY had come in" between the Tita Cory/Juan Ponce Enrile/Fidel Ramos faction and the President Marcos/General Fabian Ver faction and that "all is lost" for Marcos and Ver. And, y'all now who the "third party" were, right?

A couple of days later, before the raging waves of mob at the Malacanang gates finally crashed in and looted the Palace, helicopters from this third party flew in and landed and whisked Marcos and Ver and their families and entourage away . . .

And brought in at Clark US Air Force Base, where they boarded transport cargo planes and told that they'll be flown to Paoay, Ilocos Norte, where the fierce and true Marcos loyalists were based. But, as y'all know, they landed instead in Honolulu, Hawaii.

Kasi, itong mga Kanuto, when they speak, they speak through their noses, and Marcos and company, probably misheard "Hawaii" for "Paoay." And that's how this part of Philippine History was made.

Let's go back to the funeral: Yes, *nakipaglibing din ako*. I silently paid my respects and uttered my prayers when Tita Cory was finally laid down to rest.

And I—just like the millions of Fil-Ams here in America, who watched and heard the whole episode on TFC—got carried away, too, with the emotions that Kris Aquino nakedly displayed, as she recited her eulogy for her Mom during that resplendent funeral services at the Manila Cathedral.

KRIS AQUINO'S EULOGY: It was a beautiful eulogy. She spoke about her feelings, openly, sobbing at times. She spoke about her relationship with her mom. She spoke about her late dad, the beloved Ninoy Aquino. She spoke of her parent's love for each other . . . and their love for the Filipino people. She spoke about the political legacy that her parents left to the country.

Though it was a eulogy, it was also, I think, a coming-of-age speech into the political arena. A hint, perhaps. A glimpse of a political ambition. It's in the genes after all. And, as Tita Cory said while she was still alive, her *bunso* is her "father's daughter" in many, many ways . . . Let's go back to the funeral.

POMP AND CIRCUMSTANCE FUNERAL: Yes, it was a resplendent funeral, with all the pomp and circumstance funeral fit for king or a queen . . . or for a praying "saint," like Tita Cory. Si Cory, from what I understand, was the first non-clergy *na ibinurol* sa Manila Cathedral. The church had only allowed clergies to be "viewed" there. But Tita Cory was special to the Filipino people. So the Catholic Church in the Philippines took an exception for her.

Watching the funeral rites that were held inside the cavernous, rich-looking church was like watching in panoramic detail the Philippines in a mammoth looking-glass bottle. Inside the air-conditioned church were the elite of the country—the old money, the landed gentry, the Cojuangcos, the Ayalas, the Aquinos, the Lopezes, the corrupt politicians, the movie actors and actresses—all in their finest threads and sparkling jewels . . . whereas outside of the fenced-in church, in the intermittent rain and steamy heat, there the UNWASHED stood and strained their necks and gawked.

It was the perfect portrait of the Philippines! The unwashed, always on the outside of the fence looking in, gawking and drooling at the displayed excesses of the rich and the privileged!

But back to Tita Cory. These are excerpts of her obituary as written by the *Associated Press*: "Mrs. Aquino left a mixed legacy as President . . . She proved an inept and indecisive leader in her country's high-pressure and political culture . . . She left agrarian reform to a newly-elected Congress dominated by rich landowners, and little changed hands in the feudalistic countryside . . .

"Her administration had VERY LITTLE success in alleviating the grinding poverty that affects more than half of the population or in stamping out the nation's endemic cronyism, graft and corruption . . ." that by the end of her term, "she had lost much of the global goodwill that accompanied her ascension to power."

But, of course, most Filipinos and Fil-Ams won't hear none of that. To them, Tita Cory was their SAVIOR and their SAINT. Well, to me . . . she was the "GALUNGONG" President.

But still, I say, may she rest in peace. She's laid to rest now. She's been blessed over and over. From what I heard, about TWO-HUNDRED Filipino priests, several bishops and the archbishop and a couple of cardinals blessed her. Can you imagine that? She's been made a saint.

But when will the Filipino people lay to rest and bury the remains of President Ferdinand Marcos? Tita Cory, the "uncanonized" saint of the Filipino people and the woman of prayer and healing and forgiveness . . . couldn't forgive to the very end. *JJ*

A "Stupid" Comment, a "Stupid" Cop . . . and a very "Stupid" Arrest

Y'all heard about it, right? About the arrest last week of Henry Louis Gates, Jr., Harvard's most-prominent professor and scholar of African-American studies, by a Cambridge, Massachusetts, white cop . . . and when President Barack Obama was asked to comment about it, said that that cop "ACTED STUPIDLY."

I agree. It was a stupid act! The cop who made the arrest was stupid! He's also a racist!

According to news reports, Prof. Gates, who has taught in Harvard for 20 years or so, arrived at his home from a trip in China to find his front door jammed. So, the professor asked his limo driver to help him force the door open.

Well, as the story goes, a neighbor who saw them thought they were breaking in to rob the place and called cops.

The professor was already inside his home for several minutes . . . when this cop, a sergeant, showed up at the front door. The professor told the police sergeant that he lived there . . . and he showed his Massachusetts driver's license and Harvard faculty ID card to prove it. Harvard University was just around the corner of the professor's house.

But the cop, Sgt. James Crowley, did not believe what the professor said that that was his home . . . and that according to the professor, the sergeant stepped passed him, and entered his house, "without his permission" and began looking around for evidence of forced entry and robbery.

Now, ain't that stupid? How could this cop NOT believe that? The professor's address is documented right there on the driver's license . . . and I don't think the professor would look like a criminal to anybody, especially to a cop like Sgt. Crowley, who has been a cop for 11 years. Unless, of course, Cambridge allows morons to become cops and stay as cops in their town that long.

So, the professor got mad at this cop and started yelling at him, demanding that the cop get out of his house. Perhaps the professor was so upset of the fact that the unwelcomed cop was inside his house, suspecting him of being a criminal, despite of the two IDs that he showed the cop, identifying him as a Harvard faculty member and the occupant of that house, which was owned by Harvard University.

So in frustration, the professor called Sgt. Crowley a "racist." And Crowley, the cop, didn't like one bit being yelled at and being called a "racist" that he radioed for a "back-up" to arrest the professor, describing the professor as "belligerent" and "uncooperative," then saying to the dispatcher "to keep the cars coming."

Professor Henry Louis Gates, Jr. is 5-foot-7. He weighs 150 pounds. He wears glasses. He's got a limp. He uses a cane. His mustache and goatee are graying. He's 58-years old. And, looks it.

And this police sergeant, who looks like he's in his physical prime, had to radio for a back-up in arresting the professor, and telling the police dispatcher "to keep the cars coming"?

To keep the cars coming? Now, that tells me that Sgt. Cowley is either a real stupid cop . . . or a coward. How many more back-ups did he need to arrest an undersized, diminutive, crippled man?

And why would he arrest someone who yelled at him in his own home and called him a racist? Sgt. Crowley is truly a stupid cop. That's not enough grounds for arrest. And that's the reason why the disorderly-conduct charges that was filed against the professor were dropped by prosecutors. They were just stupid charges concocted by a stupid cop.

You know, shortly after I've retired from the Navy, I became a cop in Florida. A deputy sheriff in Martin County. I have worked in the jail. And I have worked in the streets. Working in those two environments, you quickly learn who are "the scumbags" (a police lingo) and who are the law-abiding citizens.

Sad to say but true, but most of the calls that we had to respond to, involved mostly, black people. And the jails are usually populated by more blacks and Hispanics than whites. So, if you're not careful, you can easily get screwed-up in the mind and developed an assumption that criminal wrongdoings are mainly perpetuated by blacks and other minorities.

And believe me or not, I have seen a lot of "racists" among fellow cops that I've worked with. Whether they were racists or not, I am not really sure. They were buddies of mine and most of them are really good people. I've got their backs and they got my back. But I noticed that when dealing with blacks, these buddies of mine exude a different attitude.

They are more aggressive. They are rougher. They are more ready to pounce on them. And they were quicker to make their arrests. But when dealing with whites, these fellow cops showed more kindness and empathy.

Now . . . if you're going me to ask me what would I've done if I were the cop who answered that robbery in progress call to the house of the professor? Well, right off the bat, I'll know right away that the professor didn't belong to the "scumbag" class.

And the two IDs that the professor would have shown me would have been enough for me to quickly call dispatch to tell 'em that the call was a bum call and that there was no robbery at all and everything was 10-4 . . .

But Sgt. Crowley did not see that. He couldn't differentiate. He only saw a Black Man . . . and therefore a "scumbag" in his eyes.

Let me quote here excerpts from the column last week of one of my favorite columnists: Leonard Pitts, Jr. He's black man and a Pulitzer Prize winner columnist and I think he provided the best insight to this "incident."

He said: "It's important to see Gates—scholar, author, documentarian, Harvard University professor and African-American man—because that's what Sgt. James Crowley of Cambridge, Massachusetts Police DID NOT DO in the July 16 confrontation that has ignited debate about racial bias in the U.S. "justice" system."

In other words, that cop only saw his own perception of a black man and nothing else . . . He couldn't differentiate a "scumbag" from the law-abiding and educated citizen.

To Mr. Pitts, Sgt. Crowley is a racist. I agree. President Obama said, he "acted stupidly." I agree with that, too.

PS: When I wrote this story, the three: President Obama, Professor Gates and Police Sergeant Crowley were having a beer in the Rose Garden of the White House, talking "calmly" about what happened. News reporters were not allowed to get close and overhear their conversation. For the record, they reported though that the President sipped Bud Lights, the professor had Sam Adams Light, and the police sergeant gulped Blue Moon. Blue Moon is the favorite beer of Rednecks. Cheers . . . **JJ**

Cheating Hearts . . . and Sarah Palin, the Quitter?

I've got a question. What do the three Kennedy brothers, John, Robert and Edward, aside from their last names, have in common? And Rev. Jesse Jackson and John Edwards and (Los Angeles City Mayor) Antonio Villaraigosa and (former New York Governor) Eliot Spitzer and (former presidential candidate) Gary Hart and (Nevada Senator) John Ensign and (South Carolina Governor) Mark Sanders . . .

And, if y'all wanna go way back, Thomas Jefferson, Dwight Eisenhower, Martin Luther King, Bill Clinton . . . Y'all get my drift? The list goes on and on and on. This list of prominent American leaders, past and present, intelligent and powerful men, all of them . . . what do they have in common?

They all have cheated on their wives, right? They are all fools, right? They all have been caught with their pants down, right? And their peccadilloes exposed, right? Power must be an all-consuming, overwhelming aphrodisiac to risk so much . . .

* **Editor's Note**: Please read a related article, Ten Top Reasons Why Governor Sanford Went to Argentina

Many of these men were maligned and punished. But, as we all know, a handful got away, too. Because America wouldn't dare "catch" them . . . because it wasn't right at that time to catch them. Y'all know what I mean?

Like, for instance, America, at that time, wouldn't dare "catch" Thomas Jefferson—who was one of the Founding Fathers and who penned the U.S. Constitution—for his illicit liaisons with one of his black female slaves.

Nor . . . Dwight Eisenhower, when he was the War General in the European Theater and the man in charge in defeating the German Nazis in World War II, for his affair with that English female soldier who was assigned to chauffeur him around.

Nor . . . Martin Luther King, when he was the most prominent Black leader of the Civil Rights Movement of the 60's, for his harem of women.

Nor . . . John F. Kennedy, when he was the "King Arthur" of America's Camelot, for his strings of mistresses?

And many more. But oh, no! America wouldn't dare!

It's the same thing in the Philippines. Who would have dared say something against Manuel L. Quezon and Ferdinand Marcos and Elpidio Quirino and Fidel V. Ramos and Joseph "Erap' Estrada and so forth and so on, for their women, during their reign and height of power?

But, is the list of cheating hearts in high office, testosterone-exclusive? Or to put it simply, is cheating reserved only to men? Are women really the paragons of marital virtue?

According to Leonard Pitts Jr., a *Miami Herald* syndicated columnist and a Pulitzer Prize winner: "A 2008 study by the National Science Foundation found that 15 percent of women over 60 admit to having had an affair in their lifetimes."

"And that the rate of female infidelity," Pitts added, "is actually growing faster than that of males." Ha! Check that out!

ON SARAH PALIN: So, Governor Sarah Palin is going to give up her governorship 18 months before the end of her term. I don't care what you crazy Libs out there say about Ms. Palin. I like her. I don't care if y'all say that it was a wholly "selfish decision" on her part and a "puzzlement" and a "cop out" and all that. And, I don't care that you were all stunned and that her state of Alaska and the political world were all stunned by her announcement.

As we all know, her announcement left mounting questions about her future plans. Is she laying now the groundwork for a 2012 presidential bid? Hey, why not? (Nagkakalat na si Barack H. Obama. That's a fact. For one, his much-touted health care plan being drafted by congressional Democrats would INCREASE, rather REDUCE public spending, worsening the already-bleak budget deficit. That's kind of scary).

Will she find a high-profile position in the private sector, maybe on the speech circuit? Hey, why not? She's naturally eloquent. She doesn't use a teleprompter when she speaks.

Will she drop out of the limelight and focus on her five children? Hey, why not? She can do that, too, couldn't she? She's mom, a soccer mom, as we all know.

Sen. John McCain says, "Governor Palin will continue to play an important leadership role in the Republican Party and our nation."

As we all know, too, she gave many reasons for stepping down. She said she didn't want to be a "lame-duck" governor. She said she was tired of the "tasteless jokes" aimed at her and her five children, including her son, Trig, who has Down syndrome.

Sure, she stepped down, but she didn't "quit." She's no quitter. In fact, she stepped up! Sen. John McCain said, "She'll continue to play an important leadership role in the Republican Party and our nation."

"I am now looking ahead," said Ms. Palin, ". . . how we can advance this country together with our values of less government intervention, greater energy independence, stronger national security, and much-needed fiscal restraint."

Hey, if it's a bigger plan and a national agenda she planned to pursue . . . heck, why not? Whether you like it or not and you believe it or not, she's got a lot of admirers and supporters. Me, included. And millions more out there, that's for sure.

Ms. Palin has been a "victim" of repeated defamation. Palin haters have said in their blogs that the reason she quit was because she's under federal investigation for "embezzlement and other criminal wrongdoings," which are untrue.

She blasted the Obama lapdog media, calling their responses to her announcement as out of touch. "How sad that Washington and the media will never understand, it's about country," she said. "And though it was honorable for countless others to leave their positions for a higher calling and without finishing a term . . . for some reason a different standard applies for the decisions I make."

Lt. Gov. Sean Parnell, who would take Ms. Palin's position at the end of this month said he was "shocked" when he learned of the governor's decision.

"But then as she began to articulate her reasons, I began to understand better," Parnell said. "And nobody—unless they've been in her position and understood what she has gone through and dealt with and who she is as a person—really understands."

The question now is: Will Sarah Palin have a chance as a candidate for the presidency in 2012? An unnamed Republican strategist has this to say: "She has a base in the party that's motivated like no one else, and this decision (of quitting) won't bother them. I don't know if she'll run. I don't know if she could win. But I am sure she has a shot. . . ." Well, Ms. Palin has charisma and a personality that connects with people, and these are skills that are natural for her.

Hey, this woman who they called "Sarah Barracuda" when she was the star player of the girls' basketball team in her high school years, might have the last bite . . . I mean, the LAST LAUGH, yet. And when that time comes, I'll be laughing with her at y'all. So, go, Sarah, go! **JJ**

On Michael Jackson, the Man in the Mirror, My Take . . .

On Tuesday, this week, the world stood still to celebrate the life of Michael Jackson . . . and to bury him. A memorial that unfolded live on several TV channels, movie screens, computers and mobile phones, here in America and abroad.

***Nakalimutan ang guerra sa* Irag *at* Afghanistan. *Nakalimutan ang* Iran *at* North Korea. *Nakalimutan ang* deficit *at* health care *dito sa Amerika. At natabi sa isang tabi si* Barack H. Obama.** (People forgot the wars in Iraq and Afghanistan. They forgot Iran and North Korea. They forgot about the deficit and healthcare problems of America. And President Obama was on the sidelines.)

Yes, I, too, have a few words to say about Michael Jackson. But first, I'd like to say: May he now rest in peace. Or, shall I say, the media should now allow him to rest in peace. For two weeks, his unexpected death has been turned into a spectacle . . . like a Barnum and Bailey circus, with clowns and all.

Thank God, Tuesday this week, was the finale of that circus galore. On that Tuesday, it seems that the world stopped turning. All eyes were cast on the man who they called the "man in the mirror." Really, I don't even know why he was called the "man in the mirror." From what I understand, he had a CD/DVD and they dubbed that: "The man in the mirror."

Oh, yes, he was a dancer, all right. Like a *kiti-kiti*. And, oh, yes, he can moon-walked all right. But hey, I can do that, too. And I can also moon-talked. Just kidding, of course.

Seriously now, Michael Jackson was truly a brilliant performer. Way, way back when I was still in the Navy, I remember dancing the "sweet" with some cute Southern girls to some of Michael's Motown songs, like that sweet song, "I'll Be There" at the YMCA in Norfolk, Virginia.

And I remember so well that song, "We are the World," when it was sang by Bong-Bong Marcos and his sister, Imee, and their exclusive group of friends during one of Bong-Bong's birthday bash at the Malacanang Palace. It was televised and I saw it and I thought it was . . . well, a fitting and profound song for them at that time, because they were indeed "the world" at that time. For the Marcoses, though they ruled and "owned" the Philippines, were in another world of their own, at that time.

I also remember, "Billy Jean." Disco dancing was at the height of its popularity when that song became a top tune. And I used to dance to that music, too, at "Where Else," in Makati, my favorite hang-out during those days of wine and roses and real good disco dancing.

Yung mga taga "promdi" (from the province), I don't think they've heard of "Where Else." During those times, too, we didn't dance the cha-cha or the tango or the *kukuratsa*, or any kind of ballroom dancing for that matter. *Sa mga probinsiya lang isinasayaw ang mga indak na ganon.*

Now, where was I? I am supposed to be talking about Michael Jackson. As I said, he was brilliant . . . He composed his own songs. You have to be a poet at heart to be able to compose songs, I think. So, Michael, aside from being a complete entertainer, was also a prolific poet.

He was multi-talented. He sang and danced, like no other. And, as an entertainer, he broke the color barrier.

As the Rev. Al Sharpton said in a rousing sermon during Jackson's funeral, Michael Jackson had created a "comfort level" that opened the way for the achievement of others, including "a person of color to be president of the United States."

I agree. Although Michael's ever-lightening skin over the years had gotten much attention, his crossover appeal into the mainstream was hailed "as an achievement in civil rights." Yes, indeed.

But for many people, there were many Michaels. To many, he was also a pedophile. A child molester, as we all know. Was he, really?

He was accused twice and charged in the court of law for molesting children. In the first accusation, he settled out of court and paid mucho bucks—several millions, in fact—to the "victims" *daw*.

Years later, he was again accused of molestation, this time for molesting a 13-year-old boy, who was stricken with cancer, and who was staying at his Neverland ranch. The boy was staying at the Neverland on Michael's invitation. Y'all know the story right?

And, as y'all know, too, a Filipino couple—the man worked as a butler, and his wife, as a maid, in the Neverland—were the primary witnesses to this accusation. *Nakita daw nila. . . . Baka nakita, pera.* During the investigation, it was found out that these couple were both TNTs. *Kaya, mga* nadeport in the process. *Pero, mga nakakuha din ng konting pera* for their "paid" revelations of Michael's so-called depravation, perhaps paid for by Michael's envious, green-eyed enemies.

But the couple's statements were considered "incredulous," thus it was thrown out by the court overseeing the case . . . and Michael was acquitted.

Michael said that "true, he slept with children," but there's nothing "sexual" about it. He said, "it is sweet" to be sleeping with children. The problem, he said, were the people out there "who thinks that a bed is merely a place for sex."

I really dunno if Michael was a child molester or not. I know he was kind of weird. His clothes. His demeanor. His girlish voice. His increasingly whitening skin. His Pinocchio-like aura. His self-mutilation (facial-cosmetic surgeries) that transformed him from a handsome black man into an ugly "white" man. His whole self per se . . . was weird and out of this world. But all artists are weird and out of this world! Is there anyone out there who is not?

So on Tuesday . . . those who adored Michael Jackson, those who danced to his music and even those who thought he was a freak, came together to say good bye to the man who they called "the man in the mirror" . . . the man who mirrored their souls through his songs.

On that day . . . Maya Angelou, an American poet and writer, in a poem read by Hollywood Actress Queen Latifah, captured the day in this way: "*Today in Tokyo, beneath the Eiffel Tower, in Ghana's Black Star Square. In Johannesburg and Pittsburg, in Birmingham Alabama and Birmingham, England. We are missing Michael.*"

How true. So . . . goodbye, Michael. Thanks for all the wonderful memories. Most especially for "Billy Jean." For that was my favorite tune in dancing the "*maskipaps* with. . . . That's all. **JJ**

Okey Ngarud, mga Pare, Mag-dyok Muna Tayo . . .

Last week in my column, "The Yellows and the Greens . . ." I promised that I'll have a "funny" story, too, about Michelle Obama, for that "slutty flight attendant look" of Sarah Palin that David Letterman, the Cretin, cracked on his late-night show and that the Right had fun laughing about. I always try my very best to keep a promise. So, here it is. Enjoy:

A little girl wrote to Sarah Palin and asked, "How did the human race start?" Sarah Palin answered: "God made Adam and Eve. They had children. And so was all mankind made."

Two days later, the girl wrote to Michelle Obama and asked the same question. Michelle Obama answered: "Many years ago, there were monkeys from which the human race evolved."

The confused girl went to her father and said, "Dad, how is it possible that Sarah Palin told me that the 'human race was created by God,' and Michelle Obama said that 'they were evolved from the monkeys'."

Her father answered, "Well, honey, it is really very simple. Sarah Palin told you about her ancestors and Michelle Obama told you about hers . . ."

Ha, ha, ha, ha . . . I love it! You know what? If I had a little girl as precocious as this girl and she asked me that same question, I'd said the same EXACT thing, too. I kid you not.

Now . . . am I a racist for saying that? I believe in calling a spade a spade. If that's being a racist, so be it. I am a racist. I am no HYPOCRITE though. (That *dyok*, by the way, was sent to me by "tdb," a cyberspace friend from Richmond, Virginia).

Author's Note: The jokes, as edited and reproduced in this article, have been circulating on the Internet. The authors are unknown.

THE HARLEY—DAVIDSON FACTS: Here's another one from this friend of mine. This is a debate that Arthur Davidson, the inventor of the Harley-Davidson motorcycle, had with God, when he died and went to heaven.

At the gates, St. Peter told Arthur, "Since you've been such a good man and your motorcycles have changed the world, your reward is you can hang out with anyone you want in heaven."

Arthur thought about it for a minute and then said, "I want to hang out with God. So St. Peter took Arthur to the Throne Room and introduced him to God. God recognized Arthur at once and said, "Oh, so you were the one who invented the Harley-Davidson motorcycle?"

Arthur said, "Yeah, that's me . . ."

God commented, "Well, what's the big deal in inventing something that's pretty unstable, makes noise and pollution and can't run without a road?"

Arthur was a bit embarrassed, but finally spoke, "Excuse me, but aren't you the Inventor of woman?"

God said, "Ah, yes."

"Well," said Arthur, "Professional to professional, you have some major flaws in your invention. (Readers, since it's not possible for me to illustrate the flaws, please use na lang your imagination).

"One: there's too much inconsistency in the front-end suspension!
"Two: It chatters constantly at high speeds!
"Three: Most rear ends are too soft and wobble about too much!

"Four: The intake is placed way too closed to the exhaust!
"And five: The maintenance costs are outrageous!" "Hmmm, you may have some good points there," replied God. "Hold on . . ."

God went to his Celestial Supercomputer, typed in a few words and waited for the results. The computer printed out a slip of paper and God read it.

"Well, it may be true that MY INVENTION is flawed," God said to Arthur. "But according to these numbers, a lot more men are riding MY INVENTION than yours!"

Ha, ha, ha, ha, ha, ha, ha!!! God, He's so precious. He's got the greatest sense of humor of all.

SOME PINOY DYOKS: *Siempre, kung may dyoks ang mga Kano, may dyoks din ang mga Pinoy . . . at mas grabe pa sa sarap, lalung-lalu na kung Erap dyok.* Here's one, also told from heaven:

One day, Erap dreamt that he died and went to heaven. St. Peter gave him Ai-Ai delas Alas as partner, saying, "*Kung mabait ka sana, mas maganda ang partner mo.*"

Erap saw Chavit with Gretchebn Barretto and said, "*Bakit si Chavit, mas maraming kasalanan, si Gretchen ang partner?*"

"*Iho,*" St. Peter said. "*Parusa yan kay Gretchen. . . .*"

And here's another, *kausap naman ni Erap ay ang Cardinal ng simbahan*:

Erap to Cardinal: "*Hanggang ngayon galit pa ang simbahan sa akin.* This is unfair."

Cardinal: "Why did you say that?"

Erap: "*Meron Sabado de GLORIA, Sagrado de CORAZON, at Domingo de RAMOS. Bakit ako wala*??? Eh, I was also a president."

Cardinal (After a careful thought): "Okay, from now on, yours is ASS Wednesday!"

He, he, he. Y'all don't get me wrong now, I like Erap. He used to be my hero during my *kanto*-boy days in Kamias, Quezon City.

BABAE, SEXY, GUSTONG MAGDEMANDA: I always save the best for last. *Padala sa akin ni* Don Azarias 'to, a fellow DOM and a fellow *MegaScene* columnist from the windy and chilly city of Chicago. Don is a real cool guy, I think . . . *at macho-looking pa*, especially with those Elvis Presley dark glasses that he likes to wear. Here's the *dyok*:

ATTORNEY: "*Ano? Idedemanda mo ang boss mo ng sexual harrassment!!! Dahil lang sinabihan kang mabango ang buhok mo!!! Ano masama doon?*"

SEXY GIRL: "*Torni, UNANO ang boss ko . . . UNANO!!!*"

Ha, ha, ha, ha! O, *sige ngarud*, dear readers . . . till next week. Y'all have a safe and a Happy July Fourth. **JJ**

The Yellows and the Greens; the Slut and the Flower People

Let's talk about Iran. But first, tit for tat.

Do y'all know that Sen. John McCain was called a "yellow belly" by a newspaper editor (I am not gonna mention his name) because of the good senator's stand on Iran in which he said that President Barack Obama must be more forceful on speaking up on the unrest there?

I beg your pardon, but Senator McCain is no yellow belly. That's a misnomer. To me to call Senator McCain THAT is surely an ignorant remark. Mr. McCain is one of America's living heroes. He bravely fought for this country. He unconditionally loves this country. He came from a family of heroes, who fought bravely for this country. When he was shot down in Vietnam during the war over there and was captured and became a POW, he continued to perform bravely and admirably by defying the enemy and protecting his POW comrades from the beatings of their captors.

Let's give respect where respect is due. Sen. John McCain deserves America's respect. True Americans owe that to him.

I'll say again and again: Sen. John McCain is no yellow belly!

To this editor who called him that, please know your history. But then, of course, calling Senator McCain a yellow belly could also be an opinion of this editor. And no matter how ignorant the opinion is, he's entitled to that IGNORANT opinion of his.

Just like I am entitled to my own opinion to say it's BHO himself who is THE yellow-belly on the Iran issue. And timid and weak, and so early in his presidency has begun to show his true color beneath his dark skin . . . and that color is yellow!

Tit for tat . . . right, Mr. Editor?

GOVERNOR SARAH PALIN, "A SLUT'? Y'all heard about it, too, right? Aside from calling the Palin's family as a "clan of oversexed backwood hicks," David Letterman (you know, that cretin-looking, late-night TV jester) joked on his show that during the seventh inning of a New York Yankees game that Sarah Palin and her 14-year-old daughter Willow watched while visiting New York, Willow "got knocked up" by Alex Rodriguez, the womanizing Yankees third baseman . . .

And then this moron followed up his crass with a crack about Sarah Palin's "slutty flight attendant' look. Funny, huh? Imagine if some Right-leaning pundit made a similar remark about Michelle Obama, I am sure the outcry from the Left would be deafening. Hey, I have something funny, too, about Michelle O. in my column next week. Just wait and see . . .

PROTESTS IN IRAN: As we all know, the streets of Tehran, Iran have become the scene of upheaval and protest. Iranians alleging fraud in the presidential election between President Mahmoud Ahmadinijad (prounounced *Ah-mad-in-the-head*) and challenger Mir Hossein Mousavi (pronounced *Keh-mo-sah-bee*), have swarmed the streets of Tehran and clashed with police, defying warnings from Supreme Leader Ayatollah Ali Khamenei (pronounced *Ka-mo-nay*) that they were risking bloodshed.

But the protesters did not pay attention to the warnings. Urged on by the defeated challenger, they swarmed the streets like crazy and ran amok all over the place. So the police hosed them with water cannons and beat them with sticks to force them out of the streets.

It was said that Iran has not seen protests on such a massive scale since the Islamic Revolution three decades ago.

The unrest began immediately after Ah-mad-in-the-head claimed victory, that includes a landslide win even in the hometown of Keh-moh-sah-bee, the challenger. And this victory was endorsed by Ayatollah Ali Ka Monay.

Hey, this so-called election fraud reminds me of the Bush-Gore presidential contest when they counted the votes in Florida. Remember the hanging chads and the pregnant chads and the rigged voting machines and the rigged-election consulting firm of Howard Baker and Katherine Harris . . . and the endorsement of Mr. Bush by the U.S. Supreme Court as the winner, despite the blatant frauds and irregularities?

Y'all remember all that, right? Election frauds and cheating . . . that's everywhere. Yes, even here in America.

PEOPLE POWER: It's also been said that the unrests (revolution *daw*) in Tehran was exactly like the EDSA Revolution in Metro Manila in 1986. And that this "new brand of revolution" began there. Discovered *daw* and invented *daw* by Filipinos. Wrong!

The People Power Revolution was the brainchild of the HIPPIES (Flower People) of America of the 60's and 70's. It was during those years when this kind of revolution first begun. The Hippies, who were mostly young college students, were then protesting the military draft and the war in Vietnam.

They showed up in the streets and marched and demonstrated peacefully. The marches and the demonstrations happened on most major streets of America's cities. They sang and carried signs. Then the National Guards were called in to get them off the streets. The tanks came. The soldiers came with their rifles. The soldiers had live bullets in their guns and cannons in their tanks.

Some of the students were shot dead . . . just like what happened to that young Iranian woman, named, Yeda, who is now the face of the "Green Revolution" in Tehran. The color symbol of protests there is green, thus the name, the "Green Revolution." On EDSA, as we all know, the color of the revolution there is yellow, thus the name, the "Yellow Revolution."

Now many Third-World countries have aped and are aping this kind of People-Power Revolution. I only say this NOT to boast, mind you, but to set the record straight. I was one of the Hippies who "fought" in that revolution on the streets of America. And yes, we faced the tanks, the guns and the soldiers and fought them with flowers. As the soldiers came to us with their guns, the women among us would stick flowers in the barrels of the soldiers' rifles. That's how we earned the name, "Flower People."

The soldiers had their guns. We, the Hippies, our flowers.

The only difference of our revolution to the revolution of the copycats that followed after us, was the presence of the CIA. There were no CIA spooks in our midst. In EDSA, the CIA orchestrated the revolution there. Now, in Tehran, once again, the CIA guys are leaving their hand prints all over the place.

Once again, for the record: the People-Power Revolution was the invention of America's flower-carrying hippies of the 60's and 70's . . . NOT by the yellow-clothed Filipinos on EDSA in 1986, as claimed by many self-deluding kabayans. **JJ**

More than a Chip Off the Old Block

My wife, Maribel, said that "happy news must be shared." So, I am sharing this with y'all. But if you don't wanna partake in this happiness, which I am sure a handful out there won't, please flip this page and go away *na*.

Now . . . to my dear readers who are still with me, this little story began when I wrote my Bestpren, Yoly T. this letter last week:

Hello Bestpren,

Just want to let you know that Chris and his girlfriend, Jacklyn Rostie, who is also a broadcast journalist in Iowa, will be in Chicago this weekend, just "to check the place out," they said. They'll be staying at the Chicago South Loop Hotel and will be there from Saturday to Wednesday. I told him to give you a call and see you and Bart down there, perhaps . . . at magmano sa inyo. *Do you mind if I give him your cell phone number?*

When you see him, don't be surprised that he's no longer a boy. He's a man now and very self-assured and tall (6-foot-two). And his girlfriend is drop dead gorgeous . . . when on TV, that is. But in person, simple lang ang ayos. *Well, have fun with them. (Signed, Jesse)*

My Bestpren said that "if they have the time, they can give us a call. We have a full schedule Saturday and Sunday but we don't have any thing important going on on Monday and Tuesday. . . ."

The last time my Bestpren saw Chris was ages ago, when he was still in elementary school. In his high-school years and college freshman year,

Chris had a column in *Philippine Time* and *MegaScene*, called "Sports Talk." And this writing experience, plus Bart and Yoly's endorsement, had helped Chris get some scholarship money when he attended the Edgar Murrows School of Broadcast Journalism at Washington State U.

* ***Editor's Note***: To read an earlier story in this website about Chris Jose, please click on this link, Jesse's Son Wins Wyoming Broadcasters' Awards

So in a way Yoly and Bart were among Chris's many mentors, who had seen his growth from boy to man.

I am supposed to be telling y'all the good news, but you know, it never fails that when I begin to talk about this son of mine, I always get too chatty and diverted . . . and lost in thoughts. Though he's a "sutil," and my wife fondly calls him that, he's our pride and joy. I call him, "Bam" though, ever since I can remember, shortened from the name, "Bambino," that his Lola Menny (my wife's mom) gave him. His Lola said that he looked like Baby Jesus, the Bambino, when Chris was still a baby . . .

You see what I mean? I am lost, again, talking about this son of mine.

THE GOOD NEWS, THE GOOD NEWS: So the good news is . . . that while Chris and Jacklyn were in Chicago, Chris PROPOSED to Jacklyn, his girlfriend for almost like two years now.

Then he called his mom to tell her what he did. Then, of course, Maribel told me. When she blurted out, "I have good news from Sutil," I thought at first Chris won another broadcasting award or perhaps, took that job offer in California. But when my wife said, "Chris had proposed to Jacklyn," I had to sit down.

For all of a sudden, I felt old! Time had flown so swiftly by!

But Maribel was so happy. She was smiling from ear to ear, gushing with happiness. "*Magkaka-apo na rin ako*," she said. "If a girl, she'll be bright and beautiful, like Jacklyn. If a boy, intelligent and handsome, like Sutil."

Wishing to share her happiness and tell the whole world about it, my wife mass e-mailed "everybody." And that "everybody" are relatives from Canada to Florida to California to the Philippines. And dear friends, like Yoly and Bart, who would be happy, too, to hear our happy news. My wife wrote:

I would like to share the good news that Christopher has finally proposed to Jacklyn. I receive a phone call from Chris earlier today to share the good news. Chris shared that he proposed on his bended knees with the ring at hand on the shores of Lake Michigan in Chicago.

Time has really flown! We are so happy and excited for the two of them!

In droves, came the reply of "congratulations." My Bestpren and my Erapok were among the firsts to write back. They wrote:

Congratulations and Best Wishes to Chris and Jacklyn!

Finally the gorgeous couple will soon tie the knot! Let us know about the rest of the details as soon as they're available and we'll proudly make the announcement in our MegaScene! (Signed, Bart and Yoly)

Then Bart in an e-mail solely to me, said:

Erapok,

So now you will have your own manugang. Merkana pa!

Congrats! (Signed, BT)

As I said before, Bart and I call each other, Erapok. I replied:

Erapok,

At blonde na blonde pa. Tunay na blonde. Hindi bleached blonde. (Signed, Jesse)

After meeting Chris and Jacklyn, Bart wrote again:

Erapok,

We just came home from our meetings. The first one was with Chris and Jacklyn at the China Town. We had a late lunch.

Wow, the couple is gorgeous. Chris is impressive and someone who can mix well even with the older folks like us. One thing good about him is that you won't feel the generation gap. He is so conversant. Bagay na bagay sa kanyang piniling career. We talked about a lot of things. And certainly we enjoyed their presence. We told them to come again at anytime they feel like.

Chris agreed that his countenance is very much like his beautiful mom. That's what a lot of people say, according to him.

Regards. (Signed, BT)

I replied:

Hello Erapok and Bestpren,

Thank you very much for meeting Chris and Jacklyn. Chris said that he enjoyed your company and that both of you are a "good couple."

I am sure they would want to see Chicago again one of these days, especially the shores of Lake Michigan, where Chris proposed to Jacklyn. It's a happy and memorable place for them. And perhaps at that time we'll fly over there and see you guys, too.

Yoly wrote back:

That's a great plan and something to look forward to. We did enjoy their company as well. I think they really are very much in love with each other. We wish them the best. (Signed, Yoly and Bart)

Then . . . I wrote to my son:

Hello Bam,

Your mom told me the good news . . . the happy news. She was really gushing with happiness when she told me the good news. Congratulations to you and Jacklyn. I am happy, too, for both of you. Take care of yourself always and regards to Jacklyn. See you in August. . . . (Signed, Pops)

Chris's reply:

Thanks, Pops. It is an exciting time for both of us. See you in a few months. (Signed, Chris)

Yes, indeed, dear readers, happy news must be shared, and thank you for allowing me to share my happiness with y'all. **JJ**

Untitled pa . . . itong kuwentong kung ito

As I begin to write this story . . . I don't know what to write about yet. So, I titled this for now, "Untitled pa . . ."

What keeps turning over my mind is the Filipino dyok that follows. It's a classic now and rightly so. At first, it looks like a dyok, but if you're going to take a second look of it and analyze it a little, it's actually TRUE among many Filipino friendships. Here goes: short and sweet, but the message goes a long, long way, I think. Enjoy.

Dalawang mag-kumpare. Si Dong at si Bong. Parehong mayabang. Isang araw, nag-usap sila.

Dong: "Pare, ang galing ng aso kong si BHO. Araw-araw, tuwing umaga, pagka-magkakape na ako, dinadala sa akin yung diario ko."

Bong: "Alam ko . . ."

Dong: "Ha? Papano mo nalaman?"

Bong: "Sabi sa akin ng aso ko."

And that reminds me of a "DidoSphere" column, titled "Illegal Self Defense Techniques," written by Dido (last name unknown) that appeared last week in Chicago's Fil-AM MegaScene and on the Internet, and in a mass e-mail sent to the world of Yahoos and beyond.

No doubt about it, it was very well-written. Dido is a talented writer . . . or shall I say, a talented FANTASY writer. The BARAKO word for FANTASY WRITER, is . . . bullshitter!

Anyway . . . Dido said that he's trained in several kinds of martial arts: Muay Thai, Pentjak Silat. Arnis, Goju Ryu, Kempo, Tae Kwon Do, Gung Fu, Kick Boxing, Wrestling, Aikido and Brazilian Jujitsu.

He also said that he was an amateur boxer and a Division II wrestler in college and that he'd "beaten opponents with one hand." And that his best techniques are such exotic-sounding names like the "flying guillotine," the "kimura," the "rear naked choke," and many others too many to repeat and enumerate.

"Whether you're man or a woman, young or old, muscular or frail," Dido added, "I am confident that the self-defense techniques I will show you through these written instructions will enable you to walk away with your head up high and with confidence that you will be able to protect yourself in any physical confrontation."

Earn your Black Belt in five minutes through Dido's column, ha? I tell ya, I LAUGHED MY REAR END OFF WHEN I READ DIDO'S STORY! In fact, I swear, I almost choked from it. Dido reminds of Bong in that dyok above . . . that I couldn't help write this comment to him, CC the gang of DOMs:

Pareng Dido,

Wowowee! I am impressed. You're awesome. You're Bruce Lee-Jackie Chan-Chuck Norris-Pacman-Superman rolled into one. May I ask a question? Is your Manong Perry (Diaz) aware of your amazing feats?

Immediately, JGL came on line and said this:
You missed two others: David Carradine and Pat Morita."

Don Azarias came on next and said:
Pareng Jesse and Idol JGL,

You don't have to go very far. You both forgot our very own Bernard Belleza and Vic Vargas. And, of course, Idol JGL is a very humble man. But he holds a 6th degree in Karatan . . . ooops, I mean Karatehan.

Then Dido, sensing the brewing fun and laughter generated by his awesome fantasy story, jumped into the bandwagon and said:
Don't forget Tony Ferrer, Eddie Fernandez, Bernard Bonin and Roberto Gonzalez who just recently died . . .

Then I wrote Perry Diaz, aka, Scoop. Because of the way he would "outscoop" many of us, Fil-Ams ng mga journalists kuno, I nicknamed Perry, "Scoop." I also consider Perry a colleague, and a friend. I think journalists are good people. Most are highly intelligent, well informed and opinionated, and I like intelligent, well-informed and opinionated people. So there. Believe me, as enemies they're of the worst kind, but as friends, they're the BEST! So, I'd rather be friends with the lot of them. I am a coward, you see.

Anyway . . . Here's what I said to Perry:
Hey Scoop,

You copying all these traffic? Your silence is deafening. Say mo kay Dido, pare ko? Are you going to describe to us in detail, too, your secret weapons of destruction? You know, where in one swift, silent, quicker-than-the-eye move, you can send any of your foes—no matter how big and muscular they are—to their final resting place.

So, come out, Scoop and be heard by all, especially by Dido. Tell 'em about your one-hand "grab and crush" technique. And your "forefinger stab into the heart." Or that "middle finger up da nose" to rip up the face of your opponent. Go, Scoop . . .

Then, suddenly out of nowhere, my Erapok, Bart, aka, BTubalinalCPA or simply BT, came into the fray and said:
Erapok (we call each other by that name),

I really admire your style of EMBARRASSING people. Suaveng-suave. (Smiley, smiley, smiley) And you are good also sa pang-gagatong ng tao.

(Smiley, smiley, smiley) Talab na talab doon sa ginagatungan. I love the way you make them "pasok" sa mga pakulo mo! Lalo na si Lariosa. Ha, ha, ha! Continue sa iyong pang-aasar. You provide enjoyable comedies to everybody. Ha, ha, ha!

Okey ngarud . . . in whatever way I can contribute to da people, will do. But for now, folks, that's all. As to the title of this story . . . yeah, UNTITLED pa rin. **JJ**

Si Pakyaw, Namamakyaw, ng mga Laos na Boksingero

***Tapos na ang boksing.* There's nothing more to talk about. Manny Pacquiao (pronounced *Pak-Yaw*) won. True . . . the fight is all over.**

But surely, we can still talk about it. Hash it out a little, you know. And share with y'all my take on *Pakyaw*. You don't have to agree.

Yes, indeed, he won. He handily won and knocked out COLD, with a right cross, his latest boxing opponent, Ricky Hatton of England. *Talagang tulog. Sa second round pa lang, tulog na.* Right in the middle of the ring, Hatton was in dreamland, snoring away.

Filipinos all over the world were ecstatic and went wild with joy when they saw that.

***Pakyaw* is the world's greatest fighter, they screamed. He's the best. He's unbeatable. He's a hero. He's superman. A batman. A spiderman. A pacman . . .**

When he arrived home in the Philippines, President Gloria Macapagal Arroyo, AKA *Pandak*, declared the day a national holiday. For many days thereafter, Filipinos celebrated. They danced on the streets.

Sport writers wrote that Manny Pacquiao, AKA, Pacman, was like a fiesty "pit bull" in mauling Hatton. And Hatton was like a docile "mutt."

I saw the fight on Ru Tube. Some parts in the fight were shown in slow motion. Twice, I closely watched the whole thing.

Pakyaw was no pit bull. He was a runner. He was a clincher. A couple of times, he turned his back on Hatton and ran from Hatton's attacks.

And it looked like that THAT left cross that knocked Hatton out was delivered BLINDLY to the jaw of Hatton.

In other words, a lucky punch!

It was a mighty powerful punch, no doubt about that. *Napangiwi nga si* Hatton. And like a cut-down timber, Hatton fell heavily flat on his back, right there in the middle of the ring. I don't know how long exactly he was unconscious, but when he woke up, he looked UNSCATHED and UNHURT . . .

And RELIEVED that the fight was all over. *Kuwarta na kasi.* Like winning the lotto.

It was a FIXED fight. Like that fight with De La Hoya. *Palabas lang. Pera* . . . y'all know what I mean? *Para sa akin, si Pakyaw, namamakyaw lang ng mga laos na boksingero!*

Once again, Filipinos all over the world got fooled. And what's really bad about it, is that we blindly believe in something that only fools believe in. Filipinos are too naïve and too hard-up for a hero, that's why we easily believed in *Pakyaw*'s superman feats . . . and that's a damn shame!

As one mainstream American sports writer said of the Hatton/Pakyaw fight: "It's a CON JOB." It's the same thing with *Pakyaw*'s fight against De La Hoya. *Palabas lang,* a Manny Pakyaw Productions, just like the FPJ Productions, where the late Fernando Poe, Jr. was always the bida."

I say that because *Pakyaw* seems to fight boxers ONLY *na mga laos na. Mga* champion *nga. Pero mga dating* champion *na*. Has been. Sent to pasture. And retired.

Lured by lotsa money, they all came out to fight the Pacman. And all lost, of course. But, who's got the money? While the Pacman was acknowledging the Filipino worshippers lapping and groveling at his feet, the "losers" grabbed the money and ran.

Do y'all know that when *Pakyaw* fought De La Hoya, De La Hoya got paid handsomely? Much, much, more than *Pakyaw*. That's a fact. What does that tell you? I wonder if the same thing happened with Hatton.

Probably . . .

The Pacman should fight his "own size," fighters who are in their fighting prime and on top of their game, just like him.

True, he's a good fighter. Even a "great fighter." Sure, I'll concede to that. A great fighter, that is, among *pipitsugin* fighters. If he's one of the bests, he should be fighting the bests, NOT the *pipitsugins*. Why does he confine himself to fighting (to borrow my good friend, Joseph Lariosa's words) "the underachievers and the over-the-hills"? If he's really that good, he should expand his reach beyond his comfort zone into a fighting arena where the bests fight only the bests.

Kaso, champion *lang ng mga pipitsugin si Pacman, eh*. That's my take on *Pakyaw* as a boxer.

But readers, please don't get me wrong. I like *Pakyaw*. A couple of years ago, I wrote a story about him, praising him for his perseverance in reaching his goal, despite his humble beginnings as a *panadero* in his province.

"He's an inspiration to all young Filipino achievers, boxers and non-boxers alike," I wrote then.

His generosity to our poor *kababayans* in the Philippines is admirable. He shares with them his earnings and his wealth. He built a couple of schools in the province where he came from and a huge, well-equipped gym for aspiring world-class boxers to train in. He unselfishly and continuously donates to charities, and when he's home, he would sit in front of his mansion and hand out food and money to the poor and hungry.

That's awesome, I think. Sure, he might be the "*Pakyaw, na namamakyaw ng mga laos na boksingero*," but for his kindness and generosity, he can be dubbed, no doubt, the world's greatest champion. **JJ**

A Conversation with Nelia Bernabe, MegaScene's "Flipside" Columnist

Last week, Nelia Bernabe, a long-time friend and colleague, wrote an excellent and exciting story in her "Flipside" column titled, "Beware the Wrath of Old Men" that appeared in the Friday, May 1st issue of the *FilAm MegaScene* of Chicago.

It's about the squabbles and bickering of old men, acting like "old women" and so forth. It was good, it was funny and it was well-written. I thoroughly enjoyed it.

I have always enjoyed Nelia's writings. I like her style. She writes easily. Reading her writings always put a smile on my lips. She reminds me of my favorite columnist, Maureen Dowd, of *The New York Times.*

She bites. She scratches. She growls. She purrs. She's a lioness; she's a pussycat, rolled into one . . . or either one. She's a satirist. She's a storyteller. She's a journalist, a columnist and very opinionated. Columnists are like that. They opine . . .

Nelia seems to talk to her readers when she writes. And, she writes from the heart, I think. To me, that's the picture of an accomplished writer.

Most of the time, I'd read her column and just say, "hmmm" to myself or laugh aloud to myself. Other times, I'd shoot her a comment and simply say, "Hey, that was good. I enjoyed that."

Some of my comments are sometimes kind, but sometimes, they're not. Some are gentle, but some are blunt, coarse and rough. Her column last week compelled me to write this to her:

Hello Nelia,

Oh, come on, Nelia, my dear, don't be such a party pooper. Leave us, "old farts," alone. We're having fun, can't you see. Perhaps, it's disgusting fun to you. But to us, it's good old fun. The fun is called DOM's fun. It's a form of jiving. Like dyoking. You have to be a member of this exclusive club to understand our ways. You have to be an old fart, like us, to understand the ways of an old fart. Yes, indeed, my dear, you have to be an old fart to be able to appreciate and understand CORRECTLY the wisdom of old farts.

When you reach our age, you and your peers would be doing the same thing, too, I am sure . . . jiving and dyoking the way we do. I suggest that y'all should. Otherwise, you'll grow up to become bitter C's.

If I deserve a butt "spanking" for saying that, help yourself, my dear.

Nelia answered:

Not a party pooper at all, Jess, but if it was intended as a joke, I don't think anybody was laughing except you and me. Believe me, I laughed too but it got quite crass after a while. Not a question of me finding it disgusting either. I am a big girl, I can handle things way worse than the play of words. I wondered why you didn't jump in, but I figured you were in the sideline cheering and goading your ass off . . .

These guys gave me a topic to write about . . . But think about it—these pent-up emotions need to be channeled somewhere where we can reap some great benefits. A seminar would be good . . . now, don't pick a fight with me and start a volley of e-mails between us because I am a big fan of yours. Bitter C, ha! C'est la vie . . .

A few days passed by before I replied:

Hello Nelia,

I've been meaning to respond to your e-mail for the last five days now, but I keep getting distracted with flurries of e-mails from the "old farts." You know about the Hatton-Pacquiao fight . . . I told them it was just a con job and a "Manny Pakyaw Productions," just like the long-ago FPJ productions, where the late Fernando Poe, Jr. was always the bida. I also told them that Pacquiao likes to fight ONLY boxing champions who have retired and past their fighting primes. But because of the lure of big-time money, have come out of retirement to fight the so called Filipino "Pacman." Filipinos, all over the world, got fooled again by that fight.

After I've said that, I was immediately inundated with a tsunami of e-mails from the old farts and from a couple of die-hard fans of Pacquiao.

Your story last week seemed to have created a lot of buzz, too. Don Azarias, Romy Marquez, Joseph Lariosa, Bobby Reyes, Tom Bonzon and many others . . . including me, reacted to your story . . . as you said like a bunch of "old women." Ha!

You're a riot, I think. And you created one with your story.

Congratulations. I agree with your suggestion of a "seminar." It'd be fun to meet all the old farts in person, dyok and jive with them and join in the laughter of their DOM jokes. They're really a bunch of good people, I think. If you're game, let's do it. I wonder if the others, you know, the true, blue "bitter C's" would be game, too. What do you think?

Jesse

PS: I am a bigger fan of yours, by the way. And, for a long time now.

Nelia's response:

Hey Jess,

I really don't mean to create any buzz, that's the last thing I want but a buzz is good especially for a lightweight drinker like me . . . hahaha. I respect everyone especially the ones who were here way before me. People who are close to me (a handful) know that I do not call attention to myself just to do it. Believe me Jess, I have mellowed a lot. Gone are the days when I used to swear like a truck driver. Gone are the days when I would go toe to toe with a 6'2" American guy and verbally duke it out with him until he cried. No kidding but once in a while, the old me surfaces but I try to walk lightly now and I play 10,000 questions with myself first. If I feel that I have something to say and it's a perspective worth sharing, then I'll go ahead and do it. Otherwise, I am just here trying to quietly figure out how to make a difference in this crazy world.

The seminar is a great idea. Imagine having Joseph Lariosa and Perry Diaz in the same room. For as long as everything is professional and something good will come out of it, I say we should do it. Maybe FilAm MegaScene should sponsor it. In good jest and in the name of solidarity, a good ribbing will go a long way.

Thank you for believing in me—my writing, that is. It is encouraging to have you on my side. I still have a long way to go but I am slowly getting there.

All the best,

Nelia

My answer? It was short and sweet. "*Nelia, my dear," I told her, "as a person and a journalist, you've got a lot of class*." JJ

For President Obama's First 100 Days: A Grade of C+

My **wife was an English-Literature professor at the University of Santo Tomas (UST) when I first met her. It was in April 1981. I've just left the United States Navy after 20 years of service. Having nowhere to go, I went back "home" to the Philippines.**

While there, I goofed around a little and fooled around a lot, but pretty soon that got boring. Looking for something more interesting to do, I signed up for a summer course at UST, my alma mater when I joined the Navy in 1960.

I like literature courses, so I signed up for a course called, "Filipino Literature in English." And viola, it must have been fate. On the first day of class, the young teacher who walked in and stood before the class, and who the students call, "Miss Navarro," well, became "Mrs. Jose." It was love at first sight. I am a leg man, you see, and she had great-looking legs. After that first day, I was blindly in love that the rest of the summer became a blur . . .

Sorry to disappoint you, folks, but this is NOT a love story between my wife and myself. I just wanna tell you the final grade I've gotten from this Lit teacher of mine: C+. I asked her, "Why C+ only when I was the brightest student in that class?"

"*Ikaw na nga ang pinakamataas dyan, nagko-complain ka pa*?" she answered. "*At saka napasagot mo ako ng 'oo.' Ano pa ang gusto*?"

After classes, we reversed roles. I would become the teacher and she would become the student. Now, if you're going to ask me, what grade did I give her for the lessons I taught her after her Lit classes. Well, she was a very bright student and a fast learner, so I gave her A+++.

Talking about grades . . . for Mr. Obama's first 100 days in office Wednesday this week as President, what grade did I give him? Like that grade my wife gave me: C+.

And that's high considering that after campaigning as the agent of CHANGE . . . that campaign promise did not happen, as we all know. For what he delivered instead, were RECYCLED politics and same-same Beltway faces to head his cabinet. A couple of them were even known tax evaders.

For the last three months, spending was way up, with taxes soon to follow. To bail out failing financial institutions, $235-billion of taxpayers' money was spent by Mr. Obama. Plus $3.5-trillion in new spending; $1.3-trillion for defense and $13-billion for the wars in Iraq and Afghanistan, etcetera, etcetera . . .

That the deficit this year is projected to reach the $1.7-trillion mark.

I know I keep harping on these numbers. But we need to be aware of these numbers. We need to appreciate these numbers. We need to be scared of these numbers for our children's sake! We need to be on guard.

What about the numbers of jobs lost, nation-wide? Two-and-a-half-million and counting . . .

When Franklin D. Roosevelt was sworn in as President on March 4, 1933, America was a country "deeply troubled by a historic economic collapse." During his first 100 days, President Roosevelt accomplished legislative victories that helped set in motion the recovery from the Great Depression.

Not only legislations he got passed, Mr. Roosevelt changed the mood of the country. America felt more positive then. The Roosevelt accomplishments also set the tone for what would become "the first measuring mark" for Presidents.

Mr. Obama did okay. Like I said, a grade of C+.

According to Gallup polls, Mr. Obama's average approval rating puts him on par with other past Presidents from 1953 to the present, at 63%. Jimmy Carter was given a rating of 69%. Dwight Eisenhower had 74%. John F. Kennedy had the highest approval rating, at 79%.

I LIKE MR. OBAMA: Now, please don't get me wrong on what I say about Mr. Obama. As I said before, I don't dislike him. I like him in many ways. I like the way he wears his suit. He's a sharp dresser. I like the way he talks. He speaks eloquently. And I like the way he smiles. He has that toothy smile that disarms.

I also like his stance in giving more funding to stem-cell research.

And I liked it when he shook hands with Venezuelan President Hugo Chavez during his first Latin-American summit and offered to forge a new relationship with some of America's harshest critics and calling for an end to "old ideologies" that have dominated the debate in that hemisphere.

Mr. Obama also earned my respect when one on the things he did upon assuming the presidency was to shut down that horrible prison for Iraqi detainees at Gitmo Bay and those other CIA-run prisons, world-wide . . . that tortured detainees.

And, I like it a lot when he banned extreme techniques (torture, in layman's term) the Bush administration used to question terrorism suspects and his decision to declassify documents containing those torture tactics.

I only wish that he and his Attorney General, Eric Holder, would prosecute those people who carried out the torture program or the people who designed the program or the people who authorized the program or the people who said it was legal, even though they knew it wasn't legal.

Torture is illegal. And torturers should be punished, period. They broke the law and nobody should be above the law. If prosecuting them would appear like a form of witch-hunting, so be it. Let America hunt those horrible witches and burn them at the stakes!

A COWARDLY SHIP CAPTAIN: And . . . I liked it, too, when Mr. Obama gave the order to shoot those pirates who boarded to hijack the American cargo ship, the Maersk Alabama and kidnapped its captain. Those pirates are criminals and they should be treated as such.

Those pirates should not have been allowed to board that ship in the first place. The crew of 19 on that ship should have fought off those four teenage pirates and thrown them overboard. Richard Phillips, the captain of that ship is no hero. He's a COWARD!

What kind of a captain would allow his ship to be boarded by pirates without a fight and tell his crew to "hide and lock themselves in their cabins"? A coward, that's for sure. *O kaya, bakla* . . . **JJ**

Pathetic Jokes, Pathetic Jokes . . . and an "ID Ten T" Error

Let's not forget that at the same time they're looking for millions in savings, the President's budget calls for adding trillions to the debt—Senate Minority Leader Mitch McConnell, R-Ky.

Perhaps BHO was feeling kind of guilty with all that money—taxpayers' money, that is—that he's been throwing around.

As y'all know, in his first three months of office, Mr. Obama has seen his $787-billion economic plan enacted and the outlines of his $3.5-trillion budget passed. And all this money, albeit slowly but surely, is now being spent . . . and soon will be all spent.

So Monday this week, he gathered his Cabinet and told them to cut enough money from their budgets so as to set a new "tone" in Washington. But the amount the President set for the overall cuts, comes only to a small fraction: $100-million in trims. Y'all read it right, folks: $100-million!

That's from a budget expected to exceed $3.5-trillion! Y'all read that right, too: $3.5-trillion!

That's kind of lopsided, ain't it?

According to the *Los Angeles Times*, THAT merely would "cover 1/10,000th—or less than 53 minutes' worth—of the annual operating budgets for cabinet agencies, excluding the Iraq and Afghan wars and the stimulus bill . . ."

Mr. Obama conceded that "none of these things alone are going to make a difference."

But "cumulatively," he reasoned out, "That would make an extraordinary difference, because they start setting a tone."

"A cut of a $100-million there, a $100-million here," President Obama said, "Pretty soon, even in Washington, it adds up to real money."

What money? What kind of weed Barack O. been smoking these days? His math doesn't add up. As Mr. Bush used to say, it's "fuzzy math."

"To put those numbers in perspective," said Harvard University economist N. Greg Mankiw, "imagine that the head of a household with annual spending of $100,000 called everyone in the family together to deal with a $34,000 budget shortfall, how much would he or she announce that spending (be) cut? By $3 over the course of the year—approximately the cost on one latte at Starbucks. The other $33,997? We can put that on the family credit card and worry about it next year."

In other words, a penny wise, a dollar fool, this Mr. Obama.

Or as Senate Minority Leader Mitch McConnell, R-Ky, said: "Let's not forget that at the same time they're looking for millions in savings, the President's budget calls for adding trillions to the debt."

"That's a pathetic joke," said Grover Norquist, president of Americans for Tax Reforms.

It is, indeed, a pathetic joke.

"ISTS" ON FOX News: Sean Hannity is now my second favorite (my first favorite is Bill O'Reiley) news commentator. Sean said recently that "Obama is full of 'ISTS,' a Socialist, a Communist, a Fascist, a Typist, a Florist, a Manicurist . . . and a Bullshitist . . ."

By the way, do y'all know that FOX News is now the most-watched TV channel in America? And Bill O'Reilly has become the most-listened to as a news commentator? CNN and NBC and its sister channel, MSNBC, have dropped in ratings because of those disgusting Obama lap dogs that keep lapping Obama's butt.

GLIMMERS OF HOPE: More on Mr. Obama. He and his economic team, led by his Treasury Secretary Tim Geithner, AKA, "the tax evader," I mean, "the tax man," have said that the deep recession may have reached its bottom and that the economy is beginning to show "glimmers of hope."

Really? Or is that another pathetic joke?

Here in the State of Washington, where I am at, more than a third of a million are now unemployed and looking for work. Our state's unemployment rate has now reached the 9.2% mark. And a state forecast says the unemployment rate will continue to rise for the rest of the year . . .

Out of work Washingtonians have plenty of company in their misery. The national jobless rate is now 8.5 % and rising.

Here in Washington, construction had shed 5,100 jobs . . . and the shedding continues. Financial services are down at 1,800 jobs . . . and counting. Bars and restaurants cut 2,000 . . . and the cutting continues.

Health and social services were off 1,400 jobs. Aerospace, an industry centered on Boeing, lost 500 more jobs this month. And the software industry of Microsoft, plans to cut 2,000 to 3,000 jobs by the middle of 2010.

Glimmers of hope, indeed! What a pathetic joke!

"ID TEN T" ERROR: What follows is a little story, sent to me by "TDB," my cyberspace friend from Virginia. Here it is. Enjoy. If you've already heard it, well, read it again and laugh one more time. It's good to laugh.

I was having trouble with my computer. So I called Eric, the 11-year-old next door, whose bedroom looks like "Mission Control" and asked to come over.

Eric clicked a couple of buttons and solved the problem. As he was walking away, I called after him, "So, what was wrong?"

He replied, "It was an 'ID TEN T' *error."*

I didn't want to appear stupid, but nonetheless inquired, "An 'ID Ten T' *error? What's that? In case I need to fix it again."*

Eric grinned . . . "Haven't you heard of an 'ID Ten T' *error before?"*

"No," I replied.

"Write it down," he said, "and I think you'll figure it out."

So, I wrote it down: "I D 1 0 T".

I used to like Eric, the little bastard . . . JJ

At the GS-20 Summit Meeting, Michelle O. Takes Center Stage

President Barack Obama and wife, Michelle, are in London this week for the GS-20 summit meeting of world leaders. And though Mr. Obama is THE man on the world stage, it's First Lady Michelle who seems to be the center of attraction . . . the most-watched and the most-written about in tabloids and newspapers here in America and overseas.

They said she didn't curtsy to the Queen. They said she physically touched the Queen, that she hugged the Queen, which is a no-no from a "commoner." Unprecedented and all. Yakity-yak. . . .

I beg your pardon, lads, but Ms. Michelle is no commoner, she's the wife of the President of the most powerful nation on this earth.

The *Seattle Times* writes that while President Obama had an "eventful first day on the world stage, launching new arms-control talks and calming fears about the ailing U.S. economy, First Lady Michelle Obama, in contrast, attracted breathless attention with every stop, fashionable outfit and sip of tea."

The *Chicago Tribune* declares that Michelle Obama definitely is "one of the FAB FOUR in the political fashion world in the modern era—joining Jacqueline Kennedy, France's First Lady Carla Bruni-Sarkozy and Princess Diana . . ."

London's leading newspaper, the *Guardian*, opines that Michelle's choice of "ballerina-length black skirt with layers of net beneath and the pearls (around her neck) all play up to her youth . . . this rather results in her looking ever so slightly like she's dressed up to visit her grandparents . . ."

Another London paper, *The Daily Mirror*, a tabloid, published 14 photos of her and called her a "fashion belle." *THE BBC* surmised that the "Michelle Obama fever" had hit Britain.

My take on this? May I?

I think Michelle dresses like POKWANG, the Philippines' most prolific comedienne on *TFC's ABS/CBN* mindless comedy shows. Also, I think . . . magkamukha yung dalawa. No, I better take that back . . . *baka mainsulto lang si Pokwang*. Pokwang is a Lucy Liu look-alike. Whereas First Lady Michelle, is a Lucy look-alike . . .

CHINA, THE SLEEPING GIANT: It was also said that at this GS-20 summit, the Chinese, led by its President, Hu Jintao arrived at the meeting "riding a wave of nationalism and boasting an economy that, more than any other, is surfing the trough of a crippling recession."

According to *The New York Times*, three years ago, China did not have a single bank among the world's top 20. Today, the top three are Chinese owned. Three years ago, America had seven of the top 20 banks, including the top two. Today, America has three, and the biggest, Stanley Morgan, is rated 5th only. America owes China $1-trillion, and that is but half the foreign reserves generated by its huge trade surplus and investment inflows.

The rest of the world owes China money, too.

But even if China's economic clout is unquestioned and its cities are booming and its country's coast has become the world's factory, it remains a developing country. With a population of 1.3-billion, over 800-million of its people are FARMERS . . . and many, believe it or not, are still mired in poverty.

Also, China has no global military reach.

For now, yes, the giant's still half asleep. But surely, it won't be long now; the giant will be fully awake. Then, what will the world do, what will America do, and what will Obama do?

Me, I love *Pansit Luglug* and *Mami-Siopao*, and I know how to say Happy New Year in Chinese: *Kung Hei Fat Choy*. Also, my wife has Chinese blood in her. Her great grandfather was a full-blooded Chinese from mainland China. And my oldest son, Jonathan, is a Bruce Lee look-alike. On this, I kid you not . . .

ANOTHER OBAMA-CABINET PICK, ANOTHER TAX CHEAT: Y'all heard it, right? Unbelievable, I tell ya. Obama's cabinet teems with felons. This time, it's Kansas Governor Kathleen Sebelius, Obama's nominee to head the Health and Human Services Department. After she was caught, she RE-PAID the IRS over $8,000, including interest. Ms. Sebelius said it was "unintentional errors" and that it concerned charitable contributions, the sale of a home and business expenses.

Yeah, yeah, yeah . . . of course, it was UNINTENTIONAL errors. First, it was Treasury Secretary Tim Geithner. Then Senator Tom Daschle, who was Obama's first choice for HHS. Then that other guy . . . what's his face name now? Then this governor of Kansas. Whoo-hoo, who's next?

THE OBAMA BUDGET: The non-partisan Congressional Budget Office calculated that President Obama's $3.6-TRILLION budget would generate deficits of about $1-trillion a year for the next 10 years, for a total of, check this out: $9.3-trillion between now and 2019! More than $2.3-trillion that the Obama's White House had estimated.

So, what does that mean? An America that's BANKRUPT, that's for sure.

But Mr. Obama said THAT budget "I submitted to Congress will build our economic recovery on a stronger foundation . . . so that we don't face another crisis like this 10 or 20 years from now."

According to the *Washington Post*, "a massive deficit for the next year is inevitable, because it's essential to pump money into the economy during this recession. But the CBO forecasts "long-term debt that could trigger devastating inflation and American dollar devaluation."

So, how can America avoid deficits?

The *Chicago Tribune* opines that "to avoid massive deficits for the foreseeable future, we must INCREASE TAXES, CURB SPENDING, or both." But that ain't gonna happen under the Obama Administration.

So, what will happen? What would happen is "a ten-year deficit that's bigger than the combined economies of India, Russia, Brazil, Spain and Canada," said Kevin Hassett of the *National Review*.

Kind of scary, but no problemo, *ika nga. Nandiyan naman si Kabisi, na mauutangan ng Amerika*. So, don't worry, be happy. Buy stocks, said Mr. Obama. Go spend your stimulus money upon receiving it. Or better yet, buy a brand-new Jag, or a Hummer or perhaps, a Cadillac. From what I heard, if you can't make the monthly payments after three months, Mr. Obama will pay for it . . . that's right, just like those houses being foreclosed, y'all know what I mean?

Sarap naman, pabahay na nga, pakotse pa. Only in America. **JJ**

How Would You Know If You Are in a Filipino Party?

This is so hilarious, but true. It was sent to me by Ed Navarra, a fellow club member of an all-male, BARAKO-types only, known as "DOMs."

And because of this article's Filipino-ness, I wish to dedicate it to all my fellow DOMs, but most especially to Don Azarias, Chicago's most vocal Fil-Am community leader and the most prolific among the members of our most exclusive club.

It's clean reading . . . clean enough, I am sure, even for non-members of the DOMs Club. Here it is. Enjoy. It's titled: "How would you know if you're in a Filipino party?"

Editor's Note: The real author or authors of this humorous narrative are unknown.

When: You're an hour late and there is still nobody else there!

There's enough food to feed the Philippines.

You can't even get through the door because there's a pile of 50 pairs of shoes blocking the entrance.

You see a huge fork and spoon on the wall, a framed picture of the "The Last Supper," a huge Santo Nino, and a barrel man (or Buddha).

They start singing "Peelings" on karaoke . . . or you hear a male voice on the karaoke trying to emulate Frank Sinatra's "My Way." Or, they play "Achy-Breaky Heart" over and over again.

Or when everybody seems to have their own magic mike with "their" songs. . . .

The living room is tiled, not carpeted, because the furniture has been cleared out for karaoke and dancing. You're told only to walk on the plastic floor runners.

You're greeted by a *Tita Baby* and/or a *Tito Boy*.

The piano in the living room is just there for decoration and to display framed family pictures on. No one really plays the piano at the house, unless you count that one piano lesson the parents forced on one of the children to go to when that child was eight.

And when you enter, you "mano" half the old crowd and when you leave, you have to say goodbye to EVERYONE that's related to you as a sign of respect that you end up saying hello and goodbye for a total of 30-40 minutes.

Or when you hear an Uncle traumatize one of the female cousins by saying, "Oh, you're a big girl now!" instead of, "You're all grown up!"

And you have an Auntie that likes to grab your "thing" and calls it a "little birdie" or "*pitotoy*."

The older men are in the garage playing *posoy-dos*, the women are in the kitchen gossiping, the other people are in the entertainment room singing karaoke, and the kids are outside the streets running around unsupervised by any adults.

The drunken uncles in the backyard don't even bother going to the bathroom to take a piss . . . the rose bushes are designated to be the community urinals.

And when the old U.S. Navy retired Ilocano "Manongs" see old friends at the party, you hear: "UKI NAM! LONG TIME, NO SEE! SHEE . . . it!"

There's a goat-meat pulutan being cooked.

There's a crazy woman with a camera going around the house snapping away and yelling, "Uy peeeeek-chuuuur!"

Parents expect their children to be great friends with their friends' kids just because they (the parents) grew up as best friends back in the Philippines.

Parents also like to show off how talented their kids are by forcing them to sing or play an instrument in front of guests.

Someone tells you how much weight you've put on since they last saw you, and then hands you a plate and says, "go ETTTTT, go ETTTTT!"

Or someone, an Auntie or a Manang asks you, "Did you ETTTTT?" And you say, 'Yes, Auntie, I am full! And she says, "We hab kanin . . . you ETTTT!"

Or someone is encouraging you to eat the "chocolate meat" (*dinuguan*).

There's a token white guy there in the party that's responsible for bringing one of your aunts over from the Philippines by marrying her.

Chances are the hottest-looking chick there is only 14-years-old . . . and she ends up being one of your cousins.

The aunties like to show off their "designer" Louis Vuitton and Coach bags that they secretly bought at a swap meet in the Philippines.

They constantly ask you if you have a gf/bf, or if you're married yet . . . and when you say "No," they're like "Oh, why not?" and then they just so happen to know someone to hook you up with that's "perfect" for you . . .

You see banana ketchup.

* ***Editor's Note*:** Apparently this part of the narrative does not happen in Bicolano-American households. For to many Bicolnons, Tabasco is their equivalent of the ketchup. So, don't ask them what they use for Tabasco. To read more of the Bicolano traits, please click on this link, Top Twelve Reasons for Telling If a Filipino Is a Bicolano

The lumpia (spring roll) is gone in five minutes and they're frying up another batch.

Relatives will ask you where you work and if it's a retail job or if you workat an amusement park, they'll ask you if you can get them a discount.

Someone is always in the kitchen constantly cleaning up, and you're not sure if she's the maid or a relative, so you greet and kiss her or them on the cheek anyway, just in case . . .

After the party, you're helping out clean up and your auntie tells you, "Anak, put the kwan next to the ano."

The house is full of uncles and aunties that you aren't even blood related to.

When you say, "PSSSSSSSSSSTTT . . ." out loud, everyone turns to look because it's the universal way to get a Filipino's attention.

Last but not least: They have the Pacquiao fight on the illegal cable boxes on the 70' LCD in the movie room, the 10-year-old 50' CRT in the living room, the 15-year-old 30' tube in the breakfast nook, the 20-year-old 15' tube in the kitchen, the 30-year-old 13' tube in the garage and the little portable by the BBQ grill . . . because TVs are never retired in a Filipino household, they merely get demoted to whichever room doesn't have a TV yet . . . then it ends up in the balikbayan box to be sent to a relative back home. Only then it becomes the main TV at the house again . . .

Ang Pilipino, kakaiba at unique *talaga.* **JJ**

Hara-kiri for the AIG's Executives; Are the Obamas a Couple of Cheapos?

The problem with socialism is that you eventually run out of other people's money—Margaret Thatcher

The above quote is very true. The Obama administration, in form and substance, is a socialist administration. And the real bad thing about this is that the money Mr. Obama is now spending like crazy is money that America doesn't even have.

***Inuutang lang yan sa mga Intsik,* to be paid for by our children's grandchildren. And those "children" are the same children who voted for Mr. Obama, like my son, Chris. My son now said that voting for Obama was a mistake. He does not agree with Mr. Obama's Economic Stimulus Plan, especially the part about bailing out people, who can't afford their mortgages and that part about giving more and enabling America's perennial welfare people and such . . .**

I have no comment. It's a gloomy thought, I think. And I don't really wanna think of gloomy thoughts. It's better to think of funny thoughts and laugh.

Like this one: Y'all heard about President Obama's surprise phone call to President Gloria Arroyo early last Saturday morning, right? Reports say that Mr. Obama's daughters, Mahlia and Sasha, have yet to receive their new puppy from their poppa. And that MAYBE the reason why Mr. Obama called Mrs. Arroyo was that he was looking . . . for a "*tuta*" (lap dog).

HARA-KIRI FOR AIG EXECUTIVES: I agree what Iowa Senator Charles Grassley said about AIG executives taking the Japanese way of accepting shame and defeat by "killing themselves." Those remarks echoed what he has said in the past about other corporate CEOs, who have stolen people's money.

Senator Grassley said: "I suggest, you know, obviously, maybe they ought to be removed . . . but it would be better if they would follow the Japanese example and come before the American people and take the deep bow and say, 'I'm sorry,' and then either do one of two things: resign or go commit suicide."

As y'all know, the AIG received $170-billion in bail-out money from the government to remain afloat and "to avert a cascade of failures in the financial system." But instead of doing what they're supposed to do, it chose to pay their executives RETENTION bonuses. As reported, 11 of the AIG executives who received retention bonuses of $1 million or more—including one who received $4.6 million—were not even retained.

They're no longer working for AIG.

In all, 52 executives were paid bonuses and have left . . . and the funny thing is that these people who were given million-dollar bonuses were the same people who were responsible for the FAILURE of AIG.

As Maureen Dowd, my favorite columnist from *The New York Times*, said that Timothy Geithner, Mr. Obama's Treasury Secretary, a product of the cozy Wall Street club "believes it's best to stabilize the company and keep on board the same people who invented the risky financial tactics so they can unwind their own rotten spool." "Isn't that like giving bonuses to the arsonists who started the fire because they alone know what kind of accelerants they used to start it?" Miss Dowd asked.

Right on, Ms. Dowd.

"His (Obama's) lofty team of economic rivals is looking more like a team of small forwards and shooting guards,' Ms. Dowd added. "At the White

House on Monday, the President READ to reporters some tough talk from his teleprompter about the chuckleheads at AIG, accusing them of 'recklessness and greed.'"

Ms. Dowd suggested that what President Obama should have said to the bloodsucking bums at AIG, many of them foreigners, should have been this: "We stopped the checks. They're immoral. If you want American's hard-earned cash as a reward for burning up their jobs, homes and savings, sue me."

How about just a simple mass hara-kiri as Senator Grassley had suggested . . . that includes the AIG CEOs and executives and Mr. Obama's economic team, as well? The people are angry at AIG and at previous disclosures of large bonuses on Wall Street. The people are angry at auto executives who flew on corporate jets to Washington for Congressional bail out hearings. The people are angry at the rate President Obama spends taxpayers' money.

To appease the people's anger, the knighted nincompoops from Obama's round table must fall on their swords. It's the honorable thing to do. . . .

THE OBAMAS ARE CHEAPSKATES?: A couple of weeks, when British Prime Minister Gordon Brown and his wife, Sarah, came to America to pay their respects to President Obama and wife, Michelle, Sarah Brown gifted the Obama girls, with dresses and necklaces from the exclusive and trendy London store, "Top Shop," plus a basket of books penned by famous British authors.

In return, Michelle Obama, gave the Brown's boys, Fraser and John, models of the Marine One helicopter President Obama flies around in. Guess what? Those helo models sell for $15.00 on Amazon.com.

The British press can't seem to take a snub. Their journalists are hitting out. Thank goodness, they're just hurling words, NOT shoes—Jesse Jose

According to the London paper, *The Telegraph*, "while Sarah Brown had spent time choosing gifts for the Obama girls, Michelle had clearly sent an aide to the White House gift shop at the last moment."

As for the Prime Minister and the President, Mr. Brown presented Mr. Obama "a historically symbolic gift" of a pen holder carved from the timbers of the HMS Gannet, whose sister ship supplied the wood used to build the Oval Office desk. Mr. Brown also gave Mr. Obama a first edition of the biography of Winston Churchill, by Martin Gilbert.

In return, President Obama gave Prime Minister Brown a DVD collection of 25 movies that according to media gossips included the two American classics, "Deep Throat" and "Behind the Green Door."

According to another London paper, *The Observer*, "it is not so much the cheap prize tag that is wounding to British pride; it is the lack of thought."

Hey, mates, perhaps, the Obamas don't mean no offense. Perhaps, they're just simply a couple of cheapskates. Perhaps, they're waiting on their stimulus checks . . .

Or perhaps, Mr. Obama is no Anglophile. "How could he be?" asked Tony Parsons of *The Mirror*, another London-based paper. "As the son of a Black-African father, born in colonial Kenya, he carries the wounds and resentment of someone who has experienced British colonialism." I dunno about that . . .

The Brits can't seem to take a snub. Their journalists are hitting out. Thank goodness, they're just hurling words, NOT shoes.—**JJ**

On President Obama's Balat; an AOL Poll and a Marine

I am glad that I am free . . .

But I wish I was a dog,

And Obama was a tree

—A Filipino-American poet, who prefers to remain anonymous

In the Filipino culture, there's a belief that someone with a skin pigmentation known as the *balat*, brings bad luck. President Obama, I think, has a *balat*. Because today as I write this, on the 51st day of his presidency, his so-called Economic Stimulus Plan has gone catatonic.

And that's because so far:

* He has cost the American taxpayer about 100-billion dollars a day.

* Jobs continue to be lost. It's now in the area of four-million and counting.

* There's no transparency and bipartisanship in his administration that he promised will be achieved.

* It's business as usual in Washington. There's NO CHANGE at all.

* And . . . the stock market has lost 2000 points.

The Associated Press reports that the Obama Administration has "garnered the distinction no leader wants: the WORST ever stock-market performance for a new President."

"The Dow Jones industrial average has fallen 21 percent during Mr. Obama's first seven weeks in office," the AP writes. "Count back to Election Day and the results are even bleaker. That afternoon, the Dow Jones closed at 9, 625. Now it stands at 6, 547, a LOSS of 32 percent."

In other words, Wall Street has been disappointed by President Obama's $787-billion Economic-Stimulus Plan, as well as the ongoing financial bailouts for greedy bankers and their cousins in the AIG; the automakers and other troubled sectors of this free-falling economy.

And although the Obama Administration likes to say it "inherited" the recession and the trillion of dollars deficit from Mr. Bush and Company, the economic wreckage has worsened on Mr. Obama.

Kasi nga, as I said, *may balat . . .*

AOL POLL RESULTS: Now, check this out. What follows are the results of a poll conducted by AOL, also on the 50th day of Obama's presidency. About 800,000 people were asked at random.

Question #1: How do you rate Barack Obama's job performance so far?

POOR ------------------- 49 %
Excellent ----------------- 25 %
FAIR --------------------- 14%
GOOD ------------------ 12 %

Question #2: Will Obama be able to turn the economy around in the next four years?

PROBABLY NOT ----- 59 %
PROBABLY ------------ 31 %
NOT SURE ----------- 10%

FREE TATTOO REMOVAL: Got some tattoos y'all want removed? Hey, if y'all want your skin untainted again, Mr. Obama will do it for free. Y'all heard it right, folks. Free!!! As in free money.

Tattoo experts say that the average cost of tattoo removal is $50 per square inch per treatment. And it usually requires 12 or more treatments to completely remove them all.

And it's free, courtesy of Mr. Obama, to be paid for by you and me. Because, you see, the $410 billion spending bill Congress is sending to Obama includes $200,000 for people in California to get their unblemished skin back.

Hey, Mr. Obama, sir, if that's the case, how about some free botox treatment for vain old farts like me? And perhaps, a free ration of Viagra? How about a penis transplant, too, from a horse, if I could?

If that octuplet mom from California, named Nadya Suleman, can get a new four-bedroom, three-bath house, costing almost $600,000, because the house she has been living in is being foreclosed . . . plus FREE round-the-clock home care for her octuplets, I am sure me and my DOM friends, like Don Azarias and Jesse "Mr. Debonair" Farrales of Chicago, could also get our free rations of Viagra, our free botox treatment and our transplants . . .

THE FEW, THE PROUD, THE MARINES: I have a great respect for America's Marines. When I was still in the Navy, we used to call them, "Jarheads." In return, they would call us, "Swabbies." The Marines are a part of the Navy. And though they are of a different breed and wear a different uniform from us, I have a fondness for them.

Let me illustrate why:

Two radical Arab terrorist boarded a flight out of London. One took a window seat and the other sat next to him in the middle seat . . . Just before takeoff, a Marine sat down in the in the aisle seat. After takeoff, the Marine kicked his shoes off, wiggled his toes and was settling in when the Arab in the window seat said, "I need to get up and get a Coke."

"Don't get up," said the Marine, "I am in the aisle seat, I'll get it for you."

As soon as he left, one of the Arabs picked up the Marine's shoe and spat in it. When the Marine returned with the Coke, the other Arab said, "That looks good, I'd really like one, too."

Again, the Marine obligingly went to fetch another can of Coke. While he was gone, the other Arab picked up the Marine's other shoe and spat in it. When the marine returned, they all sat back and enjoyed the flight. As the plane was landing, the Marine slipped his feet into his shoes and knew immediately what had happened.

He leaned over and asked his Arab neighbors: "Why does it have to be this way? How long must this go on? This fighting between our nations, this hatred, this animosity, this SPITTING in shoes and PISSING in Cokes?

The Few, the Proud, the Marines . . . I have great respect for 'em. **JJ**

The Stimulus to Stimulate Welfare Money; Fil-Vets Beggars Cannot Be Choosy

The American public is NOT going to be waking up one morning four years from now and say: 'What a great economy! It all goes back to that vote that the Democrats passed on the stimulus bill.'"—Rep. Eric Cantor of Virginia, House Republican Whip

I totally agree with that quote above. Instead of JOBS, JOBS, JOBS, as he promised during his presidential campaign, President Obama's economic stimulus package ramps up: SPEND, SPEND, SPEND!

The bill includes BILLIONS in new money for food stamps, expanded child care and services for the homeless.

More money for welfare. More money for low-income and special-education students. New refundable tax credits for low-income workers. Expanded health-care coverage for the poor. And, an increase of $100 a month in unemployment insurance.

According to *The Washington Post* the package is a 'Trojan horse that will provide historic funding increases in a way that will prove to be politically difficult to stop once the nation emerges from its economic tailspin."

And that according to the think tank of the Heritage Foundation, this stimulus plan would be "creating new entitlements that are not likely to go away," and calling it the "undoing of welfare reform" that will eliminate "financial incentives for states to reduce welfare rolls."

In other words, the plan will encourage people to be lazy and to depend on government to give them alms, instead of encouraging people to get off their butts and work.

In Barako words, we are perpetuating the enabling of America's PALS (*palamunins*).

FEEDBACKS, FEEDBACKS: My story last week, "Finally, Alms Money for the FilVets," provoked several feedbacks from readers. Some blatantly cursed me; some cursed me under their breadths; some were unprintable.

But some were intelligent feedbacks, well-written and well-thought of. Here are two, en toto. This is the first one:

Jesse,

It must be lonely to be "a lone voice (crying out) in the wilderness. I applaud your courage to stick to your views on the FilVets Equity Bill. I am mindful that my taxes help pay for those benefits, and I am glad to know that they go to fellow Pinoys. They earned the benefits with their military service, and are, I believe, far more deserving than the unwed mom and her octuplets.

I ***share your deep reservation about distributing the wealth (taxes) through entitlement programs, such as welfare, food stamps, free or subsidized housings, tax credits, and the like. This mandated charity will, I believe, create a class of "mendicants" who will forever depend on the government for assistance.***

Meanwhile, like most taxpayers, I am struggling to make ends meet or maintain a comfortable lifestyle to which I am accustomed. After tightening my belt or making do with less, I am no better than my "brothers" whom I am supporting with my taxes.

Until such time that there are enough Americans outraged enough to flick the Socialists in Congress out of office, I guess we just have to learn to live with Obama's commandment, "Spread the wealth."

Take heart. You are not alone.

Connie Reyes,

A Concerned Filipino American

Here's the second one:

Dear Jesse,

I *don't have any problem with our FilVets getting something from the "generous" Uncle Sam. At least, as war veterans who fought alongside and died with American soldiers during World War I, World War II, the Korean War and the Vietnam Conflict, I do believe that they are entitled to some kind of compensation as originally promised by the U.S. government. If people from different countries, who had no previous allegiance to or alliance with the United States can come over and abuse the generosity of its welfare system, then why not those few remaining FilVets who had fought for this country in at least four wars. And you can even include the Spanish-American War.*

But I agree with you that the way in which the benefit was obtained had dishonored us, Filipinos. Why do we have to lower ourselves so much by begging the U.S. government for something that should have been given to our FilVets freely in the first place? Why do we have to go down on our knees for 60 years pleading for our FilVets if the U.S. government really feels that our FilVets truly deserved to be compensated? And now, after 60 years, it's either the U.S. government probably got tired of our constant nagging to finally capitulate or those Democrats decided that they can capitalize on this issue in terms of future political payback. Where is our national pride? Where is our amor propio?

The total amount of the FilVets' benefit is so miniscule compared to the billions of dollars in yearly outlays that the U.S. government provides Israel and Egypt and the billions more being sent in Iraq and Afghanistan. And let us not also forget the millions of dollars in debt that Jordan owed which the U.S. government forgave at the request of King Abdullah. And these countries did not even help the United States during those wars that I mentioned earlier. Yet it took the U.S. government six decades to finally provide our FilVets the alms that are nothing but nickels and dimes compared to the real money that they spend on other countries that had never helped them in the past, militarily or otherwise.

***One thing is perfectly clear:* "Tayong mga Pinoy ay niloloko ng mga Kano."**

Don Azarias,
Bartlett, Illinois

My reply to my friend, Don: "What really is very clear here is the adage that beggars cannot be choosy." **JJ**

Finally, Alms Money for the FilVets?

I think it's alms money. And all Filipinos should be ashamed of it. After six decades of begging to America for that money that the FilVets earned *daw* for fighting for their own country, it might be doled out finally.

In one big lump sum of—hold your breadth now: $15,000 for each recipient! I think that's a lot of money. *Parang tumama ng jackpot sa sweepstakes, o kaya, sa casino.*

It totals $198 million. It's money that many senators as well as print and TV pundits have railed against, including Sen. John McCain and Lou Dobbs of *CNN*... because that money will come out from that stimulus package, whose purpose is to stimulate the U.S. economy.

The payment is now in the "final version" of the bill, which President Obama hopes to sign Monday next week. This compensation was NOT in the House version of the stimulus bill. It was only INSERTED *daw* by Sen. Daniel Inouye of Hawaii when the bill reached the Senate.

At this point, *hindi pa rin sigurado*. Because the House will still have to agree to the final version. The House and the Senate will have to be in complete agreement of this bill.

President Obama, *kung ayaw niya*, can also veto it. *Kaya, tagilid pa. Pero*, there's a strong possibility *na lulusot na.*

Editor's Notes: Readers may want to visit again Jesse Jose's recent column entitled, The Dishonor of Having to Beg and Bobby Reyes' article, RP Must End Its Participation in the "Alms Race" (Part 6 of "Filipino Psyche" Series)

So, *kung lulusot na at sigurado na ang pera, mga tatang, balato naman.* Don't spend it all in one place. And don't forget to give *balato* also to those Fil-Am leaders who fought each other so hard in getting the recognition as to who should be the anointed one to lead the begging for this cause.

SIX DECADES OF BEGGING: This 60-year begging for this money stems from Pres. Franklin D. Roosevelt's decision in July 1941—when Second World War broke out and the Japanese invaded the Philippines—to integrate 140,000 Filipino soldiers into America's armed forces in the Philippines. The Philippines was then an American colony.

A year later, the U.S. Congress passed a law allowing those Filipino soldiers to become U.S. citizens, with full military benefits. But after the war in 1946, President Truman signed two bills RESCINDING the citizenship and full military benefits to those Filipino soldiers. Thus, the begging begun.

TWO VIEWS ON THE FILVETS EQUITY: This exchange of views began when an editorial, in a mass e-mail, extolling the generosity of America to the world, pop out on my screen a couple of weeks ago. The article contends that Americans are the most generous and possibly the least appreciated people on earth. Germany, Japan, and to a lesser extent, Britain and Italy were lifted out of the debris of war by the Americans who poured out in billions of dollars and forgave other billions in debts.

I responded:

"If America was so generous, how come it never gave those alms to the FilVets that our Fil-Am leaders have been begging for so long? *Hanggang ngayon namamalimos pa rin ba ang mga* Filipino? This FilVets Equity has only brought SHAME to all Filipinos. *Kailan matatapos ang kahihiyan na 'to?"*

Then, I hit "reply all." Lourdes Ceballos, a noted Fil-Am leader in Chicago, quickly fired back this answer:

Hi Jesse,

Interesting exchange of views on Uncle Sam's "generosity" or lack of it. As a U.S. veteran yourself (navy?), you might be able to explain for us laymen some gray areas. For instance, what about a comparison of the benefits other ordinary U.S. vets get compared to what the Filipinos' "Equity" demands as their "rights." You see, our kababayan vets are clamoring for "justice" as to recognition of their military service and the money equivalents entailed. As a writer, veteran and Filipino American, you would provide us with a unique opinion worthy of disseminating to our community.

Last Saturday evening, a friend's husband, a veteran of World War II, said how lucky our FilVets would be if they one day do get the Equity or similar privileges, compared to his kind, who just received $20 upon leaving the army!

Lourdes

For a week or so, I parked Lourdes' email. Then I drafted this answer:

Hello Lourdes,

First, I'd like to apologize for this late response to your email.

I think you know my stand on the FilVets Equity issue. I've said it many times to friends and foes alike. I've written about it many times in my column. I've sent letters about it many times to several U.S. congressmen. And many times, I've gotten hate mails and threats for it.

The FilVets don't deserve what they have been asking for. It has become a begging now actually, that it has shamed Filipinos and Fil-Ams alike. *Para sa akin nakakahiya ang ginagawa ng mga Fil-Am leaders natin,* who continue to perpetuate this shame.

These Fil-Am leaders who have been riding on this issue for so long should face the truth of the matter. The FilVets are NOT U.S. Vets. They don't deserve that so called "EQUITY." It's not the place of the U.S. government to give them compensation. And I don't think the U.S. government will ever give them the money. And rightly so. That money belongs to the wounded U.S. Vets coming home from the war in Iraq and Afghanistan. It belongs to their families. It belongs to those homeless U.S. vets . . .

Hindi nakakaawa ang mga FilVets natin* as we pictured them to be. They get all kinds of benefits: Social Security; Medicare/Medicaid; welfare money, food stamps; subsidized housings . . . da whole works, *ika nga.* They get much more than those homeless U.S. vets we see panhandling on city street corners. Perhaps, even much more than what you and I get as senior citizens of this country, who have honestly, labored all their lives pursuing the American Dream. *Sulit na at sobra pa ang naibigay na ni Uncle Sam sa mga FilVets natin.

I really think the FilVets Equity issue has brought DISHONOR to you and me and to all Filipinos and Fil-Ams alike . . . because it has turned us into hard-lined mendicants, the kind of mendicants who have learned how to manipulate the welfare system of this generous country.

Jesse

After drafting that letter, I hit "reply all." I didn't hear a word from anybody. Not even from Ms. Lourdes. I suppose my different opinion on this matter is like that so-called lone voice in the wilderness. **JJ**

President Barack H. Obama: "I screwed up . . ."

The other morning while I was at our neighborhood Starbucks lining up for my first shot of caffeine and to read my favorite newspaper, *The New York Times*, I overheard this from a man in front of me. He was talking to a woman who was in front of him. He said, "*Obama has no idea of what he's doing. He appoints people to office who do not pay their taxes, who are corrupt and who are felons . . .*"

The woman answered, "I *think he's a cutie and would look even better with a little more weight and a little more hair . . . I don't know what he saw in Michelle. He could have done so much better . . .*"

I nodded in silence.

For it's true: On Day 14 of Mr. Obama's tenure as President, his campaign mantra of "Hope" and "Change" and "Yes, we can!" has become: "*This was a mistake. I screwed up.*"

He can't afford to keep doing that so early in his presidency. He already had four screw-ups . . .

Ha!

* The first screw-up was his pick for Commerce Secretary: New Mexico Governor Bill Richardson, AKA, "the Backstabber," who is being investigated for corruption, just like that Blago dude of Chicago, AKA, "the Hair."

* Then his choice for Treasury Secretary, Timothy Geithner, who was found to have failed to pay his taxes from 2001 to 2004 and who had hired three undocumented immigrants as his domestic helpers and that over a decade had repeatedly failed to pay their Social Security and Medicare taxes. This man, by all counts, is a FELON. Yet, he was confirmed by the U.S. Senate.

*Then Tuesday this week former Sen. Tom Daschle, Obama's pick to be his Health and Human Services Secretary, withdrew his nomination, saying his failure to pay $146,000 in back taxes prevented him from serving "with the full faith of Congress and the American people."

In simple words, it means he got caught as a tax evader, too, like Geithner.

Another felon, roaming free . . .

* Hours earlier, Nancy Killefer, Mr. Obama's nominee for Deputy Director of the Office Management and Budget and Chief Performance Officer, also dropped out because of "unpaid taxes" and for failure to "pay unemployment compensation tax on household help."

Like that Geithner dude. Another felon, roaming free.

Ha!

Four screw-ups in two weeks? Hey, what's going on, O? In baseball, the batter is only allowed three strikes and he's out. In politics, I wonder how many screw-ups are you allowed to commit?

So, what's the next screw-up?

And when?

And who's next?

From what I heard, investigators are now eyeing Leon E. Panetta, Mr. Obama's nominee as Chief of the CIA. There are rumblings that are heard about, rumors that are thrown about . . . so to speak. A little odor of smoke *pa lang*. No fire has been detected yet. But if there's smoke, there's fire somewhere, right? Maybe, they'll contain it. I hope so. Because all these "honest mistakes" that we've heard one after the other are getting to be embarrassing for Mr. Obama. I am beginning to like him *pa naman*.

These mistakes, as *Washington Post* columnist David Broder said in his column this week "misjudged the political fall-out."

Especially, Daschle's withdrawal.

"Despite glaring contradictions," Broder said, "between Obama's proclaimed ethical standards and Daschle's lucrative expense-account life, Obama said he 'absolutely' stood by his choice. One day later, he accepted Daschle's resignation. That is a blow to Obama's credibility that will not be easily forgotten.

"It leaves Obama and his administration with egg on their faces," said Broder.

Well, an egg ain't too brutal compared to those pair of Muslim shoes that were thrown at Mr. Bush during his last press conference in Baghdad . . . *na may kasama pang mura na*, "You dog!

OBAMA'S STIMULUS PLAN FOR DUMMIES: To better understand Mr. Obama's Economic Stimulus Plan, it has been formatted into Q and A as follows:

Q: What is the Economic Stimulus Plan?
A: It is money that the federal government will send to taxpayers, and to non-taxpayers, too.

Q: Where will the government get the money?
A: From the taxpayers.

Q: So the government is giving me back my own money?

A: No, they are borrowing it from China. Your children are expected to pay the Chinese.

Q: What is the purpose of this payment?
A: The plan is that so you will use the money to purchase high-definition, digital TV set, thus stimulating the economy.

If y'all think that's dumb, I agree. That's why it's called "Economic Stimulus Plan for Dummies," y'all follow?

Below are some helpful hints on how to best help the U.S. economy by spending your stimulus check wisely:

If you spend that money at Wal-Mart, all the money will go to China. If you spend it on gasoline, it will go to Hugo Chavez, the Arabs and Al-Qaeda. If you purchase a computer, it will go to Taiwan. If you purchase a car, it will go to Japan and Korea. If you purchase fruits and vegetables, it will go to Mexico, Guatemala and Honduras. If you purchase heroin, it will go to the Taliban in Afghanistan. If you give it to charitable cause, it will go to Nigeria and Kenya.

We need to keep that money here in America. How? Beats me. All the consumer products here in America are now imported from somewhere, except home-grown pot that Michael Phelps, the winner of eight gold Olympic medals in swimming, was snorting—as caught on the camera. Ha! **JJ**

I, Barack HUSSEIN Obama Do Solemnly Swear . . .

Starting today, we must pick ourselves up, dust ourselves off, and begin again the work of remaking America—President Barack Obama

So ***O*** **(Oh) is in and** ***W*** **(Dubya) is out. I wish both men well. Dubya as he's led to pasture and** ***Oh*** **to carry on and clean up the mess that** ***W*** **had left behind. Whatever . . . my respect and best wishes to President Obama. I mean that. Honest, I do.**

It's true I've said a lot of negative things about Mr. Obama before, but that's politics. The shifting of loyalties is always constant. As Winston Churchill once said, "***In politics, there are no permanent friends, only temporary allies.***"

To those who will yell at me and accuse me of having no core because of my change of loyalty, I am sorry, but I will give our new President, my new President, Barack HUSSEIN Obama, the benefit of the doubt and wait to see how he will govern.

A GREAT DAY FOR AMERICA: This past Tuesday was indeed a great day for America. As tears streamed down faces of old and young alike, here and around the globe, the son of a white American woman and of a Black-African immigrant, ascended to his place of history as the first Black American to have become the 44th President of the United States.

As written and recorded by multitudes of journalists: "***Taking the oath on the steps of a capitol built by slaves, Obama became the first African American to reach the pinnacle of American political life, fulfilling the promise of a nation born with the pledge that all men are created equal . . .***"

That's awesome. I think. Only in America. I am moved. It's a great day for America.

I am proud of my adopted country. I am proud of President Obama for breaking the barrier for all people of color . . . for breaking down racism and the insane hatred and intense dislike of people who are "different from White America."

I am not saying racism will cease in America from here on, but it's the beginning. A promise . . .

So this man who was called a Messiah, a rock star, a wannabe Abe Lincoln, an FDR, a JFK, and a Moses who parted the Red Sea, told America and the world: "***Today I say to you that the challenges we face are real. They are serious, and they are many . . . they will NOT be met easily or in a short span of time. But know this America***:

"***They will be met***!

"***On this day, we gather because we have chosen hope over fear, unity of purpose over conflict and discord. On this day, we come to proclaim an end to the petty grievances and false promises, the recriminations and worn-out dogmas, that for far too long have strangled our politics.***"

Right on.

He urged Americans to step up into a "***new era of RESPONSIBILITY.***"

He said: "***Our challenges may be new. The instruments with which we meet them may be new. But those values upon which our success depends—hard work and honesty, courage and fair play, tolerance***

and curiosity, loyalty and patriotism—these things are old. These things are true.

"***What is required of us now is a new era of responsibility—a recognition, on the part of every American, that we have duties to ourselves, our nation, and the world, duties that we do not grudgingly accept but rather seize gladly . . . This is the price and the promise of citizenship.***"

These words echoed President John F. Kennedy's words, when he said during his own inauguration in 1961: "***Ask not what your country can do for you. Ask what you can do for your country.***"

President Obama also told Americans:

"***This is the source of our confidence, the knowledge that God calls on us to shape an uncertain destiny," he said. "This is . . . why men and women and children of every race and every faith can join in celebration across this magnificent mall, and why a man whose father less than 60 years ago might not have been served at a local restaurant can now stand before you to take a most sacred oath.***"

Those words gave me goose bumps.

He promised policies to create jobs, and to his detractors who question his expensive plans to stimulate the economy, he said:

"***Their memories are short . . . they have forgotten what this country has already done, what free men and women can achieve when imagination is joined to common purpose, and necessity to courage . . .***"

And to the Muslim World, he said:

"***We seek a new way forward, based on mutual interest and mutual respect. To those leaders around the globe who seek to sow conflict, or blame society's ills on the West—know that your people will judge you what you can build, NOT what you destroy.***"

"***To those who cling to power through corruption and deceit and the SILENCING OF DISSENT, know that you are on the wrong side of history; but that we will extend a hand if you are willing to UNCLENCH your fist.***"

And to those who wish to destroy America, he warned, "***You cannot outlast us, and we will defeat you.***"

It was an awesome speech, a promising speech, a somber speech, and these lines will forever be etched in my memory:

"***Let it be said by our children's children that when we were tested . . . we did not turn back nor did we falter; and with eyes fixed on the horizon and God's grace upon us, we carried forth that great gift of freedom and delivered safely to future generations . . .***"

It was like a Lincoln in tone.

To me, it was like a prayer. **JJ**

Folks, y'all Have a Great Life this New Year!

Whenever you find yourself

on the side of the majority,

it's time to pause and reflect.

—Mark Twain

And so, I reflect:

Another year will soon be gone by . . .

And so swiftly at that . . .

Whether I should be glad or sad . . .

I don't know that . . .

As y'all can see I am also a poet. *Dyok lang*, of course. But as I write this, I am sad. For once again, Israeli warplanes are on the attack, dropping bombs on the Palestinian people of Gaza City, hitting a mosque, a university and a television station, killing three hundred Palestinians so far. And Israeli soldiers and tanks have massed along the border getting ready to move inland for "ground operations."

In war, ground operations could mean indiscriminate killings and a slaughter of non-combatants. But Hamas officials said, no matter what the consequences were, they would fight back and call for more suicide operations to counter the Israeli strikes.

The air strikes, Israel said, were in retaliation for the "sustained rocket fire" that came from Gaza into its territory. They said the Hamas were to blame. They claimed the Hamas fired first. But why did the Hamas fire those rockets into Israeli territories? News reports didn't say.

Maybe those Hamas were just cruising for a bruising. Just like the Hezbollah of Lebanon. Remember that war a couple of years ago? The Hezbollah fired those rockets first into Israel. I suppose they were also cruising for a bruising then. Israel retaliated and annihilated the country of Lebanon with U.S. made bombs. . . .

Ms. Condoleezza Rice, Mr. Bush's Secretary of State went over there to stop the bombings and the killings and the insanity and idiocy of that war, but to no avail. As the firebombs seared Lebanon and the Lebanese people, she shrilled uselessly. While her boss, Mr. Bush, twiddled his thumbs.

I don't really wanna talk about the bombings and the killings of people and the insanity and idiocy of war . . . or the uselessness of shrills. It's depressing. I am so glad that this administration is on its way out.

BARACK H. OBAMA IS MOST ADMIRED: So I heard BHO won another election. This man is awesome: According to *USA Today/Gallup* polls, he dethroned Mr. Bush as the nation's most admired man this year. I don't think we all need national polls to know that. Just like we all don't need polls to tell us that Mr. Bush is America's worst president since Richard Nixon.

But in 2001, right after the 9/11 terrorists attacks on America, Mr. Bush was THE most-admired man. What goes up, must come down. It's the law of nature. Mr. Obama will come down, too, one day from his media-made perch.

But right now, that's unthinkable yet. Because right now, the man can walk on water.

Despite dirty Chicago politics where he sprung from, he's unassailable, he's flawless, and he's said to be gifted.

And though NOT God, he's nevertheless the Messiah in many people's minds. Or, THE Moses and the "mostest" of all.

As described by *The New York Times* Columnist Nicholas Kristoff: "*American voters have just picked a president who is an out-of-the-closet, practicing intellectual . . . an Ivy League-educated law professor with a fertile mind . . . who is actually interested in ideas and comfortable with complexity . . . who speaks in paragraphs rather than sound bites . . . and who seems to understand that the world abounds with uncertainties and contradictions . . .*"

Yeah, yeah, okay, okay, he's THE MAN *na.*

On women, the one who was voted the most-admired, according to national polls, was: Hillary Rodham Clinton! And guess who took second place? I kid you not: Governor Sarah Palin!!! So, you miserable Palin Bashers, eat your hearts out. True, her selection as John McCain's running mate appalled many, but it also energized a lot of people. Me, included.

EXCERPTS OF A PHONE CONVERSATION BETWEEN BLAGO & RAHM: Y'all know who these two are, right? Blago is Governor Rod Blagojevich of Illinois. Rahm is Rep. Rahm Emanuel of Chicago and President-elect Obama's choice as Chief of Staff of the White House he'll soon occupy. And, y'all know what's going on, right? The guv wants to sell to the highest bidder the seat that Mr. Obama has now vacated. From what we heard, Rep. Jesse Jackson, Jr. of Chicago . . . that's right, the son of Reverend Jesse Jackson, wants the seat and was found to have offered $1-million for it. But, of course, Jackson Junior has denied that.

Chicago politics is out of this world, I tell ya. Corruption and the profanities of its leaders are profound. Positions in government, elected and appointed, are sold and bought and bartered . . . like street drugs.

What follows is an excerpt of a phone conversation between Blago and Rahm that was wiretapped by the FBI on Nov. 10, 2008. The phone that was tapped was Governor Blagojevich's home phone. Their conversation was about to end here. The bleep-bleep words were the "F" words and the "A" and the "S" words that these twerps used to talk to each other.

BLAGO: ***Oh, now you're bleeping Godfather. Bleep-bleep!***

Emanuel: ***No, bleep-bleep, bleep-bleep, bleep-bleep!***

Blago: ***Bleep-bleep!***

Emanuel: ***Listen up, bleep. The bleep's gonna hit the fan, maybe tomorrow, maybe next month, and when Fitz brings down the hammer, it's gonna be my name that's going through your head. You won't know the hows and the bleeping whys, but it's gonna have my bleeping fingerprints all over it. Have a great life, FATSO!*** **(Click)**

My dear readers, y'all have a great life, too, this coming New Year! Cheers. *JJ*

I Am Dreaming of a White Christmas

I'm dreaming of a White Christmas . . . te-dum, te-dum. But this "White Christmas" is no longer a dream. All over this great land, except swampy Florida and the "negger" land of California, this white powdery dream has turned into a nightmare.

Here in God's Little Acre, known as SEATTLE, that dream had disrupted almost every aspect of life throughout our region: travelers have gotten stranded in our airports and bus stations, Christmas shopping have practically come into a standstill to the consternation of retailers, schools have closed down to the delight of children . . . and going to work said my wife is like trudging and climbing up the Alps.

Me? As y'all know I am retired, twice retired, in fact, so I am home, with my steaming cup of *KAPENG BARAKO* in my hand, humming along with Bing Crosby as he sings his song. Of course, there are other Christmas songs that I like to hum, too, as I watch the snow flakes fall from my window like the songs, "Let it snow, Let it snow" and "Winter Wonderland."

But like all things in life all this snow will come to pass and melt, and life will be normal again . . . and the trees will be green again here in Washington.

ON PASTOR RICK WARREN: So . . . Rick Warren, the famed author of the best-selling book, "The Purpose Driven Life" and the anti-gay, anti-abortion and the famed homo hater pastor of a church in California, has been chosen by President-elect Barack H. Obama to deliver the invocation at his January 20th inauguration.

Well, thank goodness, it wasn't THAT Chicago pastor, named Jeremiah Wright.

SENATOR CAROLINE KENNEDY?: Heck, why not? But the real question is, as asked by *Washington Post* syndicated columnist Ellen Goodman and many others like her: Would Caroline Kennedy be considered for the seat being vacated by Ms. Hillary, a senator who was pilloried herself in 2000 for being NOTHING but a FIRST LADY, if Caroline's last name were, say, Schlossberg?

As one pol barked, she has "name recognition, but so does J-Lo. Is this all about entitlement?" Hey, who da heck is J-Lo? Is she more famous than M.O., the wife of B.H.O.?

"As a lawyer, writer, fundraiser and mother of three who worked for many causes," says Ms. Goodman, "she was always dutiful and gracious about her role as a Kennedy . . . She was famously private, an oxymoron without irony. She can walk down the street without a hat and sunglasses. She enjoys that. . . ."

Like a princess would.

Goodman adds: "She described her reasons for supporting Obama, saying, 'My reasons are patriotic, political and personal and the three are intertwined.' So are the reasons for seeing her as a Senator Caroline Kennedy."

I agree. She would be the perfect choice to take Ms. Hillary's seat. I hope that Governor Patterson of the state of New York, the totally blind governor, who ascended from his position as vice governor to governor when the elected governor of New York, Gov. Eliot Spitzer resigned when he was found out to have had a tryst with a prostitute . . . would be able to see Ms. Caroline as she is: "the emblem of a generation—and maybe a country—coming back to life."

Yes, indeed, she is.

FACTS ABOUT CHRISTMAS: What am I doing talking about politics, when it's Christmas. Let's talk about Christmas, shall we?

Do y'all know that the Puritans so mistrusted Christmas that its celebration was outlawed in the 17th century? And that around the same time, the German theologian Paul Ernst Jablonski asserted that Christmas amounted to a PAGANIZATION of the authentic faith because the date, December 25, had been appropriated from the festival for a Roman solar god?

And, that many Christmas icons, like the decorated Christmas Tree, the Mistle Toe and the Yule Log originated from the Celtic pagans?

And, do y'all know, too, that from 1558 until 1829, Roman Catholics in England were not permitted to practice their faith openly? So someone from that era wrote this Christmas Carol as a catechism for young Catholics. It has two levels of meanings: the surface meaning and the hidden meaning known only to church members.

The Partridge in a Pear Tree **was Jesus Christ**.
The Two Turtle Doves **were the Old and the New Testaments**.
The Three French Hens **stood for Faith, Hope and Love**.
The Four Calling Birds **were the Four Gospels of Matthew, Mark, Luke and John**.
The Five Golden Rings **recalled the Torah or Law, the First Five Books of the Old Testament**.
The Six Geese a-laying **stood for the Six days of Creation**.
The Seven Swans a-swimming **represented the sevenfold gifts of the Holy Spirit: Prophecy, Serving, Teaching, Exhortation, Contributing, Leadership and Mercy**.
The Eight Maids a-milking **were the Eight Beatitudes**.
The Nine Ladies **were the nine fruits of the Holy Spirit: Love, Joy, Peace, Patience, Kindness, Goodness, Faithfulness, Gentleness and Self-Control**.
The Ten Lords a-leaping **were the Ten Commandments**.
The Eleven Pipers piping **stood for the eleven faithful disciples of Jesus**.

> The Twelve Drummers drumming **symbolized the Twelve Points of Belief in the Apostles' Creed**.

That's what the song says . . . and I believe in songs. Because songs are written from the heart.

Call me naïve, but my belief of Christmas is simple. **To me, Christmas is about Christ.** It's about His birth. It's about His coming to bring PEACE on Earth and GOOD WILL TO ALL MEN. I cannot think of a better way to apportion that peace than for us to quit fighting so much . . . or arguing so much about STUPID things like the election of BHO as president. Let's move on. Let's stop gloating. Let's stop sulking. Our lives ain't gonna CHANGE because of Obama. We'll still have the same bills to pay, the same amount of paycheck, the same car, the same house. Nothing ain't gonna CHANGE. Everything will be SAME-SAME. Like Christmas.

So, dear readers, Merry, Merry Christmas *po sa inyong lahat!* And peace to y'all. **JJ**

"F" words, "N" Words, "C" Words; Bush Dodges Shoes Hurled at Him

I think it's funny. There seems to be a lot of cursing and cussing going on. From Chicago to Manila to New York to Baghdad, the "F" words and the "C "words and the "N" words and even our own "PT" words are being heard and uttered by political leaders and celebrities and journalists alike.

I am sure y'all heard about the expletive and the bleep-bleep words of Governor Rod Blagojevich of Illinois that was caught on tape, right?

How about Philippine Senator Mar Roxas' outburst of his "PT" words, the most-often heard curse words of Filipinos world-wide? That was so eloquently said, wasn't it? And this guy is supposed to be of presidential timber . . . and could be the next President of the Philippines. And who was he cursing? From what I heard he cursed on camera, while delivering a speech, at the current President of the Philippines, Gloria Macapagal Arroyo, AKA, "*Pandak*," in English, "the Dwarf."

So, in retaliation, a congressman-son of President Pandak and her obese husband, First Gentleman Mike Arroyo, AKA, "Baboy," in English, "the Pig," called up Roxas and cursed at him too: "*P . . . T . . . Ina mo rin*!"

I think that was hilarious. These people are the elite and the highly-educated in the Motherland. But . . . hey, I'd do the same thing, too, if you curse at my wife. Not only that. I'll also kick your gonads and give you a "Filipino Haircut." What is the Filipino Haircut? It's a process somewhat like the "Mafia Necktie." No need to explain that kind of haircut and that kind of tie. They're deadlier than curses, trust me on that.

And, did you hear about the C-word and the vagina-like monologues that Actress Jane Fonda, AKA, "Hanoi Jane" uttered this week on NBC's "Today" talk show? That was so funny, too.

And, of course, we will never forget the "F" words that VP Dick Cheney screamed at Senator Patrick Leahy in the sacred halls of the U.S. Congress. That's right, those "F" words boomed, loud and clear, within those walls that they echoed and reverberated nation-wide . . . and world-wide.

And, did y'all hear that Rep. Rahm Emanuel, President-elect Obama's choice to be his White House chief of staff, is also very fond of using the "F" words?

MR. BUSH, THE SHOE DODGER: I know I shouldn't be laughing at the President of the United States of America. But I laughed and laughed and laughed so hard, when I saw on TV, on CNN, where they showed the film, over and over, in fast reverse and fast forward, how Mr. Bush dodged these shoes thrown at him.

Mr. Bush is surely an expert dodger. He's got a reflex like that of a cat.

According to news reports, the drama unfolded Sunday during Mr. Bush's farewell press conference, inside the Green Zone in Baghdad with Prime Minister Nouri Kamal al-Maliki to highlight the newly-adopted security agreement between the United States and Iraq that includes a commitment to withdraw all American soldiers by the end of 2011.

Then, all of a sudden, one of the journalists named Muntader al-Zaidi, from the Iraqi TV station Al Baghdadi, stood up about 12 feet from Bush and shouted in Arabic: "This is a gift from all Iraqis; this is a farewell kiss to you, dog!"

Then, he threw a shoe at Bush. Like a cat, Mr. Bush ducked.

Then, while Mr. Bush's Secret Service Agents and Mr. al-Maliki's Security Agents stood frozen, with their mouths wide open, al-Zaidi threw his other shoe, once again shouting in Arabic: "This is from the widows, the orphans and those who were killed in Iraq!"

Cat-like, Mr. Bush, once again, ducked and (the second shoe) **narrowly missed Mr. Bush as Mr. al-Maliki stuck a hand in front of Mr. Bush's face.**

Then, chaos reigned, as everybody jumped on the poor Iraqi journalist, dragged him into another room to beat him up. Mr. Bush called the whole incident "a sign of democracy" in Iraq. "That's what people do in a free society," said Mr. Bush.

Oh, pleeeeeez *naman*, Mr. Bush, shut up *na*.

In the Muslim world, throwing shoes at someone is considered THE supreme and absolute insult. Because it means that the target is even lower than dirty shoes. As y'all remember, crowds of Iraqis threw their shoes at the mammoth statue of Saddam that once stood in the center of Baghdad when U.S. Marines pulled it down during the early part of the Iraqi invasion in 2003. But that was another time when Americans were not considered yet as occupiers.

To many people in the Arab world, al-Zaidi, the shoe-thrower, is a hero for hurling his shoes at Mr. Bush.

To show their solidarity and support for the shoe-thrower, people in many towns and cities in Iraq, removed their shoes and sandals and placed them in long poles, waving them high up in the air, calling for the immediate withdrawal of U.S. troops from their land.

In Saudi Arabia, a sheik offered $10 million to buy one of the shoes that were thrown at Bush.

In Libya, one of the daughters of Libyan President Moammar Gadhafi awarded al-Zaidi, the shoe-thrower, the prestigious Medal of Courage.

In Syria, the shoe-thrower's picture was shown all day long on state-run televisions, with Syrians calling in to share their admiration for his heroism and bravery. In the streets of Damascus, huge banners hung, hailing al-Zaidi, the shoe thrower: "Oh, heroic journalist, thank you so much for what you've done!"

In Mosul, an old Sunni teacher there said, "I swear by God that all Iraqis with their different nationalities are glad about this act."

I understand the hate and anger of Iraqis toward Mr. Bush: The U.S.-led invasion has left tens of thousands of Iraqis dead and millions of people without homes . . . and their country and its infrastructure, destroyed.

"F" words, "N" words, "C" words, which as I said are merely funny, or those filthy shoes that were hurled at Mr. Bush, ain't nothing compared to what happened in Iraq. To me, what happened there IS what obscenity is all about. Not the "F" words, not the "N" words, not the "C" words, and certainly not the "PT" words of Filipinos, world-wide. **JJ**

A Satire but a True Tale of American History

One of my favorite novelists, Khaled Hosseini, who wrote the powerful and lyrical and hauntingly beautiful books, "The Kite Runner" and "A Thousand Splendid Suns," once said: "Describe things as better than they are and you'll be called a ROMANTIC; describe them as worse than they are and they'll call you a REALIST; describe them as exactly as they are and you'll be thought of as a SATIRIST."

I believe Novelists Amy Tan and John Steinbeck both said that, too. So did Novelist Quentin Crisp.

So, Dear Readers, with that in mind, what follows is then a satire. Because the words that were quoted are EXACTLY as they were uttered. But so as not to offend the effeminate sensibilities of some of my non-*Barako* readers, I used ellipsis on some of the words that were used in this tale.

And believe or not, this is a true tale. It's American history as recorded by historians and investigative journalists. Here it is. Happy reading.

It was the first day of school in USA and a new student from India named Chandrasekhar Subramarian entered the fourth grade class of Miss Sandra Jones.

Miss Jones said, "All right class, let's begin by reviewing American History. Who said, 'Give me liberty or give me death?'"

She saw a sea of blank faces, except Chandrasekhar, who had his hand up. "Patrick Henry," he said.

"Very good," said Miss Jones. "Who said, 'Government of the people, by the people, for the people shall not perish from this earth?'"

Again, no response from the class, except from Chandrasekhar, who said, "Abraham Lincoln, 1863."

Miss Jones snapped at her class, "You should be ashamed. Chandrasekhar, who is new to our country, knows more about its history than you all do."

She heard a loud whisper, "F . . . the Indians."

"Who said that?" she demanded.

Chandrasekhar put up his hand and said, "General Custer, 1862."

At that point, a student in the back row, said, "I am gonna puke."

The teacher glared at the class, looked around and asked, "All right, who said that?"

Again, Chandrasekhar said, "George W. Bush to the Japanese Prime Minister, 1991."

Now furious, another student yells, "Oh yeah, suck this!"

Chandrasekhar jumps out of his chair, waving his hand and shouting to the teacher the answer, "Bill Clinton to Monica Lewinski, 1997!"

Now with mob hysteria, someone said to Chandrasekhar, "You little sh . . . , if you say anything else, I'll kill ya!"

Chandrasekhar frantically yells at the top of his voice, "Michael Jackson, to the child witnesses testifying against him, 2004!!!"

Miss Jones fainted.

"Oh, sh . . . ! We're screwed!" the class said in chorus.

Chandraheksar said quietly, "THE AMERICAN PEOPLE, November 4, 2008 . . ."

PS: By the way, this was sent to me by "TDB," a cyberspace friend from Virginia and a SATIRIST, like me, but in many ways, more prolific than me. **JJ**

Change . . . Is It Change We Can Truly Believe In?

*It is impossible to defeat an ignorant man in argument . . ." **Jerry Lytle**, a neighbor and my walking partner*

Change. Change we can truly believe in. Change, change, change. So, this is what change looks like: Joe Biden. Rahm Emanuel. Tom Daschle. Bill Richardson, the Backstabber. Eric Holder. Robert Gates. Hillary Rodham Clinton.

The list goes on. **Remnants. Retreads.** Hey, hey, the gang's all here. Hey, where are John Kerry and Dennis Kucinich and Al Gore and Jimmy Carter and the Kennedys . . . and what's his face's name? And Ms. Brazille? And John Edwards, or is he gone for good? And that millionaire Mormon, Romney? And also that Baptist Minister from Arkansas, Huckabee? How come they're not in the team?

And where's Chuck Norris, Governor Huckabee's sidekick and action star of B-rated movies and the All-American Karate champion and master? And Reverend Jesse Jackson? And Reverend Al Sharpton? And Reverend who-you-ma-call, whose name I'd rather not mention before I am accused again of being a racist. How about Bill A.? And Joe, the Plumber, who I heard is now Joe, the Painter?

But seriously now . . . by re-creating Abe Lincoln's "team of rivals" and staffing his cabinet with America's best brains, President-elect Barack H. Obama may be already fulfilling his vision of a "unified" United States of America.

And really and truthfully, as a Democrat and an unabashed Clintonite, I am happy to see Mr. Obama staffed his cabinet with . . . well, Clintonites.

Mr. Obama's transition from Messiah to Moses to JFK and now to Lincoln, has really been dazzling. Try to imagine that, really. I dunno about y'all, dear readers, but I am THRILLED that Mr. Obama could also be another FDR. Why? The NEW DEAL, remember? That was FDR's mantra. Just like Obama's mantra of CHANGE.

Mr. Obama's unprecedented political personality had been aptly put this way by Rich Lowry, a columnist for the New York Post: "We still don't know who Obama is—he's been a SHAPE-SHIFTER throughout his career. But he's showing a ruthless pragmatism as he morphs into an establishment Democrat."

Hey, whatever it takes. Ruthlessness or whatever. Unprecedented or whatever. One thing for sure though: Mr. Obama displays an unprecedented air of command for a president-elect in defining his agenda for January 20 and beyond. We don't know him now, but we shall soon know who he is.

What we know of him presently is that he has sent a message that he doesn't really have enemies. He has FORMER enemies, and he has the smarts to turn his former political enemies into . . . subordinates. That's a dazzling move, I think. Definitely, Mr. Barack H. Obama is a brilliant man, with an enormous quantity of finesse and cool, and I wish him well in January and beyond. . . .

GOV. SARAH PALIN IS WANTED: T here are three political personalities that intrigue me—Mr. Obama, Ms. Hillary and Ms. Palin. Do y'all know that in addition to more than a dozen offers to write a book, Alaska Governor Sarah Palin has 800 requests for interviews and appearances, and she's considering them all? And the list includes invitations to make appearances in 20 foreign countries, all expenses paid for, PLUS a new set of wardrobe in each of her appearances. I kid you not. That was reported by the *Associated Press.*

So . . . you Palin bashers out there, who demonized this sexy and gorgeous and enigmatic woman and called her a "dingbat" and "stupid," eat your hearts out! And just like what I have wished for Mr. Obama and for Ms. Hillary, you betcha, I also wish Ms. Palin well. And more so, because she's swell and she swells in the right places.

ON PACMAN VS. DE LA HOYA: T here's a lot of buzz going in the Fil-Am community all over America about the Pacquiao/De La Hoya fight tonight in Las Vegas. Some say that Pacquiao will win the fight. Others say that Pacquiao will lose. Here's my take on it:

De La Hoya will make HOYA out of Pacquiao, that's for sure. Ain't no way a little man, like "Pacman," as he's called by fans in the Philippines and by Filipinos world-wide, can defeat a much bigger man, like Hoya. All the odds are against the Pacman: weight, height, experience and class.

I think this is merely an EGO and MINDLESS thing for Pacquiao to be fighting this fight. His many easy wins in the past against *pipitsugin* fighters have gone into his head, and he begun to believe he's now the INVINCIBLE Filipino version of Superman. As we all know, the American version of Superman, Christopher Reeves, fell off his horse while riding and became a paraplegic and was confined to a wheelchair for the rest of his life until he died a couple of years ago.

I really hope that Pacman would still be awake after the first round to realize his mistake. And, I pray that they won't cart him away on a stretcher after a few rounds with La Hoya. Please don't get me wrong, because I really wish Pacman well.

And to all my critics, who wish me NOT well for my political and non-political views, let me quote my good friend and my neighbor and my walking partner, Jerry Lytle, who said: ***"It's impossible to defeat an ignorant man in argument, Jesse."***

If that's true, then my critics win in all respects. And ignorant or not, I wish them all well, too. **JJ**

Politics, Like Dust, Never Settles . . .

"I'll get right back at ya! I'm still adorable, America—Gov. Sarah Palin

"Politics, like dust, never settles." Now, where did I hear that from? Can't seem to remember. A lot of things I cannot seem to remember anymore.

What about this? Who said it? "In politics there are no permanent friends, only temporary allies." If my memory still serves me right, I believe it was Marcos . . . yeah, that's right, former Philippine Dictator-President Ferdinand E. Marcos. It was he, who also said: "I'll die a thousand death for my country." Or did he merely dip his hands a thousand times in the cookie jar?

> ***Editor's Note:*** It was not Ferdinand Marcos but Winston Churchill who said what Mr. Jose quoted. Here are the links: There are no permanent friends and no permanent enemies. . . . Churchill once said that countries did not have permanent friends and permanent enemies. . . . just permanent objectives! How true!
>
> http://www.arguewitheveryone.com/u-s-foreign-policy-issues/33546-there-no-permanent-friends-no-permanent-enemies.html

Long dead, but his body not YET buried six feet under the ground; Mr. Marcos is still being blamed for the ills that presently beset our motherland.

Why not blame Gloria Macapagal Arroyo, aka, *Pandak*, and her obese, *baboy*-like husband, Mike Arroyo, aka, First *Kawatan*? They have dipped their fingers in the cookie jar NOT only a thousand times, but a million times, a trillion times. They are the KLEPTO couple now who is looting the cookie jar. It used to be the McCoy/Imelda partnership. Now, it's the *Pandak/Baboy* partnership. Philippines, my Philippines, *kawawa ka naman*. As Erap used to say: "Same-Same."

Good old Erap. *Pogi at macho pa rin hanggang ngayon*. It's the magical wonder of Botox and Viagra. I like Erap. He used to be my hero when I was still a Kamias *kanto* boy in Quezon City. Erap's fall from grace came about when he became the President of the Philippines. As an actor, he was superb. As mayor of San Juan, he was prolific. As VP to Ramos, he was fine. When he became the President, he got drunk with power and fell flat on his face . . .

But really, I don't wanna talk about Erap or Pandak, or McCoy and Baboy. I wanna talk about President-elect Barack H. Obama. Yeah, let's talk about him. He's the hottest news item right now. Kung baga sa ice cream, he's the flavor of the year, and for many years to come. Everybody now wants to take a lick of him and taste him. The whole world, in fact, wants to do that.

OBAMA'S CABINET: A couple of days, while I was flipping and browsing through our local Sunday paper here in Seattle, I came across a political cartoon about Obama that was so hilarious, I think . . . but so true. And I don't think the cartoon was meant to mock Mr. Obama. It was to present the current news in a light-hearted way and I don't think you Obambis out there can dispute the cartoon as phooey.

The whole idea of the cartoon was captured in two frames. In the first frame, we see Mr. Obama, standing in front of his president-elect podium with the logo, "CHANGE," written on it and two American flags framing him, saying this:

"As I prepare to take on the responsibilities of president, I recognize that the American people said they did NOT want a third Bush term. . . ."

Then on the second frame, he said this: "So you're getting a third Clinton term instead . . ."

Well, it's true, isn't it? Would I tell y'all a lie?

As y'all know, there's Ms. Hillary, whose appointment as Secretary of State for Obama's administration is now in the bag.

And, Eric Holder as Attorney General. Mr. Holder was a senior official in the Justice Department in the Clinton administration.

And, in introducing his economic team this week, Obama said he had chosen Timothy Geithner as his Treasury Secretary, and Lawrence Summers as his Director of the National Economic Council. Both served in the Clinton Treasury Department—Mr. Summers as secretary and deputy secretary and Mr. Geithner as a top aide. The leading candidate for another top post in the NEC is Jacob Lew, who was Clinton's budget director.

And, there's Richard Danzig, the former Navy Secretary under Clinton, who Mr. Obama has chosen to hold a senior position among Obama's National Security Advisors.

And, Grey Craig, a former lawyer for Clinton, as Obama's White House Counsel. And John Podesta, who was a Clinton loyalist and top aide, as co-chair of Obama's transition team. And Gov. "Backstabber" Richardson, who will become Obama's Commerce Secretary.

And, former Senate Majority Leader Tom Daschle, a Clinton buddy and top lobbyist, to serve as secretary of the Dept. of Health and Human Services. And, I suppose many others, too, who at this time we don't know yet.

IS MS. HILLARY THE RIGHT CHOICE?: In selecting Ms. Hillary as America's top diplomat, Mr. Obama stunned many people who were riveted by the epic primary battle between these two strong personalities.

Among the concerns that were raised were: Why did Obama choose someone he frequently criticized for voting for the U.S. invasion of Iraq to be the face of his administration's foreign policy? And, why would Ms. Hillary subordinate her strong personality and views to be the global face of Mr. Obama?

As y'all know, throughout the campaign, Ms. Hillary had repeatedly said that Mr. Obama didn't have the experience to be president and she mocked his willingness to meet with rogue leaders, like Hugo Chavez of Argentina and Ah-Mad-in-the-Head of Iran, as "irresponsible and frankly naïve."

According to news reports, Mr. Obama's advisers have said that the strengths Ms. Hillary would bring to the job outweigh the drawbacks.

"Hillary Clinton is a demonstrably able, tough, brilliant person who can help . . . advance the interests of this administration and this country," said Obama strategist David Axelrod.

I agree with that. Ms. Hillary, I think, has the chutzpah for the job. She has the stature. She has the respect and the admiration of the world. She's tough. I really think, she can be relied upon to take on America's adversaries with aplomb and flair, with no problem at all. That was a wise choice for President-elect Barack H. Obama.

"I've been spending a lot of time reading Lincoln,' said Obama in a recent interview on "60 Minutes," adding that President Abraham Lincoln's strategy of appointing political rivals to serve in his administration was "very wise."

Yeah, that was very wise, indeed. Yeah, politics, like dust, never settles, indeed. Yeah, just like car treads, when recycled, become retreads . . . yes, indeed. **JJ**

On Dogs, "Dawgs," Mutts and Bulldogs, Shepherds and Yorkies

The world has gone doggone ape over President-elect Barack H. Obama. Nobody can say bad things about him anymore, especially about the color of his skin because that can be misconstrued as a racist, bigoted, politically-incorrect remark. That's kind of scary to me. Shoot me, but don't muzzle me, please.

In Italy and in many parts of Europe and here in America, people reacted with shock and outrage after Prime Minister Silvio Berlusconi of Italy called the first African-American president-elect in U.S. history as "young, handsome . . . and sun-tanned."

The word, "sun-tanned" didn't go too well to a lot of people that many Italian newspapers gave the comment front-page attention to condemn the prime minister. They said that Mr. Berlusconi is an "imbecile" and "infantile" and a "psychological case" and one who "never fails to live up to our worst expectations."

Mr. Berlusconi, who is a multi-billionaire and one of the richest men in Europe, said that his remark about Mr. Obama was a "compliment" and that his critics "lack irony," telling them that "if you all want to get a degree in IDIOCY, I won't stop any of you. I say whatever I think."

"The Italian left is wrong about everything," Prime Minister Berlusconi added, "including their lack of sense of humor. Too bad for them . . . God save us from imbeciles."

Hmmm. I like this guy. He is a real Italian stallion. A fellow BARAKO. Big balls and all. He speaks his mind. A true "DAWG."

Just in case y'all don't know what a dawg is, in the 'hood lingo, a dawg is an all right guy, a cool guy, a fair guy, a good looking guy . . . yeah, he can be suntanned and all, too, like Barack O., y'all know what I am saying?

ON MUTTS AND SUCH: In his first news conference since winning the presidency, Mr. Obama said his top concern is passage of a multibillion-dollar stimulus package to create jobs, and to lend a helping hand to America's teetering auto-making industry. He also said he would tackle the nation's financial crisis "head-on."

Well and good then.

During this conference, Mr. Obama also talked about picking the First Dog for the First Daughters of the First Family. He promised his daughters, Malia, 10 and Sasha, 7, a puppy after the election, and "finding one has become a major issue," said Obama. Malia has allergies, so the Obamas are looking for a low-allergy dog that can also be a "rescue dog." Malia reportedly wants a "golden-doodle' dog.

Mr. Obama said that his family would prefer to adopt a puppy from the dog pound. And in an apparent self-deprecating humor that referred to his mixed-race heritage said that "hopefully we'd pick out a MUTT, just like me."

So, THE MAN describes himself as a "mutt."

So . . . if Ms. Hillary is the "bitch" and Bill Clinton is the "Big Dog" and Gov. Sarah Palin is the "pit-bull with lipstick on" and VP Dick Cheney is "Bush's attack dog" and all those lefty TV pundits of CNN, NBC, MSNBC, ABC and CBS are the "Obama lap dogs," I wonder what kind of a dawg is Michelle O? Does it begin with a letter "D," perhaps, as in Doberman?

Or, would that be unthinkable for many? And, racist. And, inappropriate. And, bigoted. And, politically incorrect. And, etcetera, etcetera . . .

I like dogs. They're amazing creatures, I think. Many dog years ago, before I became a deputy sheriff and worked in security as a canine handler, my employers gave me a German Shepherd as a working partner. His name was "Bandit." Once a week for many, many weeks, I trained with Bandit. Though this dog was supposed to be a work dog and an attack dog, he was very gentle and very affectionate and he liked children. Bandit, at my command then, could instantly turn into a killer and rip anybody's throat apart. He could also sniff drugs, and chase and take down, with any problem at all, a fleeing felon. Bandit not only became a working partner, but also a friend. I had to give him up when I joined the Martin County Sheriff's Office as a deputy. I remember that day when Bandit and I separated as a very lonesome day for me.

Editor's Notes: Readers may like to read articles in this website that are about dogs and "dogmestic (sic) violence." These are the links to the said articles:

China Continues "Dogmestic Violence"

Michael Vick Can Never Be Guilty of "Dogmestic Violence" in the Philippines (As Updated)

MAXIE AND CHLOE: My wife's niece, Cherry Ann, who lives in Vancouver, Canada, owns a bulldog. It's the ugliest bulldog I've ever seen. And the cuddliest, with a patience for humans, like the patience of Job. My wife would use this dog as her footstool whenever we would visit Cherry Ann. When I first met this dog, I scratched her behind her ears and rubbed her belly. Then she sniffed at me. I guess she liked the way I smell, because from that day on, whenever we were in Cherry Ann's house visiting, that dog would follow me around, smitten like a puppy

Cherry Ann named this bulldog, Bertucci, you know, like the name of that world-famous Italian soccer player, Bertucci . . . "Too-zie," for short. But this dog was so ugly and cuddly, that the Too-zie didn't really suit her. So, I renamed her, "Maxie," in honor of Max Alvarado, that famed-and-ugly favorite *kontrabida* (villain) of Philippine movies in the 1960s. So, Too-zie is now Maxie.

Then, there's "Chloe," a pure-bred Yorkie, owned by my son, Chris, who is now a reporter for CBS/KGAN in Cedar Rapids, Iowa, and his girlfriend, Jaclyn Rostie, who is also a broadcast journalist for NBC in Davenport, Iowa.

Talking about cuddly dogs, Chloe was made to be cuddled and petted and played with. Her favorite game is the tug of war, with her biting the other end of a tightly-rolled cloth and the other player, a human preferably, pulling the other end of the cloth.

She's a real doll, long-haired, does not shed, sweet smelling . . . a doll, indeed, just like her mistress, and handsome, just like her master.

What's amazing about Chloe is her little tinker bell and time-out chair. When she needs to go outside to pee or whatever, she rings a bell that's installed by the door. When the door is opened for her, out she goes, then returns, wipe her paws and comes in. And when she "misbehaves," and is told to go sit on her time-out chair, she obeys quickly, then she looks at you with those doll-like eyes, as if to say: "Hey, is it time yet? Can I get off now from this stupid chair?"

Maxie and Chloe, they're real dawgs, I tell ya. They both kill me. You may ask: what about THAT ONE who proclaimed himself as a MUTT? He, too, is a dawg, I think, "sun-tanned" and handsome and all . . . and though I don't go doggone ape over him, nonetheless, I really wish him doggone well. In fact, to honor him as the President-elect, I've adopted a mutt from the dog pound and named this mutt, "BHO." **JJ**

America Has Spoken: Hail Barack!

America has spoken. All over the land, there were shouting and screaming, celebrating and partying, crying and weeping with joy and happiness. People said: "It's a dream fulfilled. It's the dawning of a new era. America has spoken."

Okey ngarud, I am with that.

Here in Seattle, an African-American lady said, "Obama is Moses to us. We have been waiting 200 years for this."

Another said, "It's an Earth-shaking moment for me. As a black person, we vote for everybody else but we get the short end of the stick. We've cried the same cries. We have the same heartbeat . . ."

The *Washington Post* says that the 2008 election is the result of a "coincidental marriage of a powerful personality and a terrible political and economic environment . . . and to deny that would be to deny reality."

And another said, "This will go a long way toward healing the open wound that is racism in America. This was Dr. King's dream—to have someone in the black community to represent us, and bring the races together."

Okey ngarud, I am with that, too.

In a phone call, minutes after polls closed in the west of the United States, Sen. John McCain congratulated President-elect Barack Obama, then delivered his gracious concession, saying to his

supporters, "We have had and argued our differences, and he had prevailed . . ."

Yes, sir, Senator, I hear you. You've fought a good fight, and I honor you for that. You'll always have my respect and my admiration. In my heart, you've won this fight. As we, warriors of America, have said over and over: "It's not how you lost the fight, but how you fought the fight." And you fought honorably and valiantly, sir.

President Bush, speaking at the White House, said, "Many of our citizens never thought they would live to see this day. This moment is especially uplifting for generations of Americans who witnessed the struggle for civil rights with their own eyes—and four decades later see a dream fulfilled."

Okey ngarud, Mr. Bush, we hear you, too.

I do like Mr. Bush. I think he's a good person. HE TRIED SO HARD. . . . And it's sad to say that this election was in many ways a referendum on him, who polls show is the most unpopular President since 1930, because of his handling of the economy, Hurricane Katrina and the war in Iraq and Afghanistan. The McCain-Palin rout, according to *The Washington Post*, is the result of a "coincidental marriage of a powerful personality and a terrible political and economic environment . . . and to deny that would be to deny reality."

"Senator McCain fought a good fight, and I honor him for that. He will always have my respect and admiration. In my heart, Mr. McCain won this fight. As we, warriors of America, have said over and over: 'It's not how you lost the fight, but how you fought the fight.' And you, Mr. McCain, fought honorably and valiantly."—Jesse Jose

THE WORLD IN AWE: And there's no denying that this powerful personality, Barack Obama, this juggernaut, this Moses, this Caesar, if I may say so, is being hailed, not only in America, but also all over the world for wresting the bull by the horns, so to speak. And may I also say that it was a mighty way to wrest that bull by the horn. It left the world breathless and in awe.

From the cafes of Rome, to the streets of Kenya to the town in Japan, named Obama, people chanted, "Obama! Obama! Obama!" The world seems to view Mr. Obama's election victory as a "transformative event that could repair the battered reputation of America, lift the aspirations of minorities everywhere and renew the chances for diplomacy rather than war."

In Japan, they said, "Americans overcame the racial divide and elected Obama because they wanted the real thing: a candidate who spoke from the bottom of his heart. I think this means the United States can go back to being admired as the country of dreams."

In Bangkok, a man said. "What an inspiration! He's the first truly global U.S. president the world has ever had."

In France, a woman there said, "This is the fall of the Berlin Wall ten times over. Today, we all want to be American so we can take a bite of this dream unfolding before our eyes."

So all over this great land and all over this great wide world, people are celebrating, hailing the new Caesar. Here in my own little corner of world, among my fellow DOMs and cyberspace friends, emotions were also high. We wept . . . not because of victory, but perhaps because we saw an era slid by before our myopic, bespectacled eyes. Hear us also, please. . . .

From Don Azarias: "I have to admit that I shed a few tears as the impact of Barack Obama's victory begins to sink in. It's not because I dislike Obama. He seems to be a likeable guy. But it's because I like John McCain better.

"How could you not like a war hero whose love and loyalty to his country had remained undiminished even when he was a POW in North Vietnam and had every reason to be bitter during the time of his captivity where he was tortured and placed in solitary confinement?

"My heart bleeds for John McCain. It will continue to bleed for a long, long time. At his age, he lost his last chance to prove his ultimate love for his country by serving as president of the United States of America."

From Ed Navarra: "My phone has been ringing off the hook since the media declared Obama as President-elect. They (the callers) have been analyzing, commenting, and then crying on why this happened. Don, dugo ang niluluha ko dito. I am sure God has his intentions why this all came about. Let the passions die now. Meantime, no matter how difficult, we must go on with our lives. This will all come to pass, like kidney stones. LOL."

From Jesse Farrales: "My dear friend, Don, you said it perfectly well. I sympathize with you. We have the same mind set on this political issue. But at this point, let us pray that our new president will be serious in his promise to initiate the real CHANGE that will benefit the entire nation and not just selected sectors. Let us just embrace the positive outlook for our nation and for everyone. Take care, my friend."

From me, JJ: "Pareng Don, I feel your pain. But like my Bestpren, Yoly T. said, 'America has spoken.' The MAJORITY, the fifty-two percent of America, that is. The forty-eight per cent of America has spoken, too, but with a different lingo and voted for John McCain. Like you and me and those millions of others who sang a different tune, we bleed, yes, we bleed. . . .

"For now, let's lick our wounds and stem the bleeding . . . and join up with the victors. We are all Americans, them, the victors and us, the vanquished. The day will also come when "them" will become the vanquished and "us," the victors.

"As Ed said, 'Let the passions die now.' You know, like when you just made love to a beautiful woman, you lay back down to rest to catch your breadth and to savor the afterglow of that FIERCE and INTENSE and FORCEFUL and LUSTY bout of love. Pretend it was that kind of love, Pareng Don, and you won't bleed no more."

From Martin Celemin: "Hi Jesse. You aroused me by your advice to Don—"fierce, intense, forceful and lusty"! If Don follows that, he would forget the election all together. I'm sure he must have smiled and you brighten his forlorn condition and bleed no more."

Yes, indeed, America has spoken. Hail, Barack! **JJ**

TWO MEN: John McCain, the Phoenix; Obama, the Barnyard Mama

Y'all know the story of the phoenix, right? The phoenix was a legendary bird that was burned to death and became a pile of ashes. But this bird had magical powers and out of the ashes, resurrected itself to become its magnificent self . . . again. This magical bird reminds me of Sen. John McCain.

I am not saying now that Senator McCain has got magical powers. Maybe he does. I dunno. But he seems to have the knack to keep on resurrecting himself.

As y'all know he was a Navy jet fighter pilot during the Vietnam War, flying off from flight decks of aircraft carriers, day or night, to bomb military targets in North Vietnam. One day while on a mission, he was shot down by enemy surface-to-air missiles and was presumed KIA (killed in action).

But, like a phoenix, he survived. He crash-landed his plane and suffered a concussion, a broken arm and a broken leg. From a small lake where his plane crashed, he was fished out by enemy soldiers, beaten and hog-tied and became a POW in that infamous North Vietnamese prison, called by its inmates, "Hanoi Hilton." It was a POW camp reserved for captured flyers.

When McCain's captors found out that he was a son of a Navy Admiral, they offered to release him. But John McCain defiantly told his captors: "Release those others first who were here before me."

His captors hated him for that defiance. Repeatedly, they savagely beat him . . . and tortured him. They broke his body. But like a phoenix, John McCain survived the torture. Five years later, when the war ended, he was released, broken in body, but not in spirit. Yeah, just like a phoenix.

After retiring from the Navy, he ran under the Republican banner as senator of his home state of Arizona, and won. In Congress, he had a fondness for "reaching across the aisle." He developed a reputation as a "MAVERICK" among his fellow Republicans. He butted heads against the Bush/Cheney/Rove team. He clashed against his peers. He fought for what he believed was right for this country that he unquestioningly loves . . .

The silence of the Silent Majority of this country has a sound. And you'll hear its roar come November Four. Its roar is: COUNTRY FIRST!!! And out of that, John McCain, the phoenix, will emerge from the ashes of media biases to victory.

Fast forward to this presidential race. During the primaries, John McCain, the phoenix, was also given up for "dead" and buried, under the proverbial totem pole. As y'all know, on top of the pile, were Huckabee, the Baptist preacher and Romney, the Mormon, and Rudy Giuliani, the former rough-and-tumble mayor of a rough-and-tumble city, known as New York City, "the city that never sleeps."

But, like a phoenix, and yes, indeed, you've guessed it; John McCain crawled out from under the pile to become the candidate to battle the so-called "Anointed One," the "Messiah," the "Rock Star," B. HUSSEIN Obama. The battle now rages. Four more days, this epic battle will be all over.

And once again, John McCain, a true American hero, and MY HERO, has been written off by the Obama lapdog media as "dead." The polls said so, they said. In the 1980 presidential race, when Ronald Reagan fought against Jimmy Carter, the polls also said so, that Reagan "trailed" Carter in double digits . . . but the polls were proved wrong. Reagan came back from behind to win the White House.

The same thing happened in 2000 between Bush and Gore. Bush, according to national polls had 48%, while Gore had 43%. Gore came back to win a 0.5 percentage points, but lost the Electoral College. Polls are ALWAYS wrong, and whoever would believe polls as gospel truths are total morons.

The silence of the Silent Majority of this country has a sound. And you'll hear its roar come November Four. Its roar is: COUNTRY FIRST!!! And out of that, John McCain, the phoenix, will come riding in from the ashes of media biases, smiling from ear to ear, flanked by two gorgeous-looking women. On his left would be the quiet and gentle, Mrs. Cindy McCain, and on his right, his VP, the Alaskan warrior princess and corruption slayer, Ms. Sarah Palin.

THE BHO DOCTRINE IN THE BARNYARD: What follows was sent to me a cyberspace friend. He told me that my "admirers" might enjoy reading it. It's food for thoughts, I think. It's easy reading. Enjoy:

There was a little red hen who scratched about the barnyard until she uncovered quite a few grains of wheat. She called out all of her neighbors together and said, 'If we plant this wheat, we shall have bread to eat. Who will help me plant it?'

'Not I,' said the cow.

'Not I,' said the duck.

'Not I,' said the pig.

'Not I,' said the goose.

'Then I'll do it myself,' said the little red hen, and so she did. The wheat grew very tall and ripened into golden grain. 'Who will help me reap my wheat,' asked the little red hen.

'Not I,' said the duck.

'Out of my classification,' said the pig.

'I'd lose my seniority,' said the cow.

'I'd lose my unemployment compensation,' said the goose.

'Then I'll do it myself,' said the little red hen, and so she did. At last it came time to bake the bread. 'Who will help me bake the bread?' asked the little red hen.

'That would be overtime for me,' said the cow.

'I'd lose my welfare benefits,' said the duck.

'I'm a dropout and never learned how,' said the pig.

'If I'm to be the only helper, that's discrimination,' said the goose.

'Then I'll do it myself,' said the little red hen. She baked five loaves and held them up for all her neighbors to see. They wanted some and, in fact, demanded a share. But the little red hen said, 'No, I shall eat all five loaves.'

'Excess profits!' cried the cow. (Nancy Pelosi)

'Capitalist leech!' screamed the duck. (Barbara Boxer)

'I demand equal rights!' yelled the goose. (Jesse Jackson)

The pig just grunted in disdain. (Ted Kennedy)

And they all painted 'UNFAIR' picket signs and marched around the little red hen, shouting obscenities. Then the farmer (B. HUSSEIN Obama) came. He said to the little red hen, 'YOU MUST NOT BE GREEDY!'

'But I earned the bread,' said the little red hen.

'Exactly,' said Obama, the farmer. 'That is what makes our free-enterprise system so wonderful. Anyone in the barnyard can

earn as much as he wants. But under our modern government regulations, the productive workers must divide the fruits of their labors with those who are LAZY and idle.'

They all live happily ever after from that OBAMA DOCTRINE. But the neighbors of the little red hen in the barnyard became quite disappointed in her. She never again baked bread because she joined the 'PARTY' and got her bread free. And all the Democrats smiled. 'FAIRNESS' had been established. Individual initiative had died, but nobody noticed. Perhaps no one cared . . . so long as there was 'FREE BREAD' that the 'RICH' were paying for. **JJ**

If What Is, IS . . . Then Mr. Obama's Associations Are Who He Is, Isn't It?

So many questions, yet not one answered truthfully. First, there was this awful, demented man, Rev. Jeremiah Wright, damming and cursing America, spewing saliva and hate, who said: ***"No! No! No! Not God Bless America! God Damn America!"***

And as y'all know, this crazy man was B. HUSSEIN Obama's pastor for twenty some years, who married him and Michelle and then baptized their two daughters when they were born. Mr. Obama even named this man his "uncle" and his "mentor" and his "inspiration" in his two memoirs that he wrote.

But did we ever get a truthful answer from BHO why Reverend Wright stayed his pastor and mentor for twenty years?

Then Tony Rezko, Chicago's slum lord and convicted felon, who donated mucho bucks to Mr. Obama's political campaigns as state senator, U.S. senator and then as presidential candidate . . . and who helped Mr. Obama buy that million-dollar house that he now lives in. Yeah, I remember those words that Mr. Obama used to explain away why he accepted Mr. Rezko's help in acquiring his mansion. He said, "It was a BONE-HEADED decision that I made." Oh really? How many more bone-headed decisions will Mr. Obama make? Kind of scary to think if he becomes President of the most-powerful country in the whole world.

Then came Bill Ayers, the "unrepentant terrorist," who blew up military installations, including the Pentagon, and other landmarks of America. He has shown no remorse for his crimes and said, his "only regret" is that "he didn't do enough." Can you imagine that? And as y'all know, Mr. Obama's political career was launched from Ayers' living room.

Mr. Obama said he "knew Mr. Ayers only" when he was just eight years old. Was Mr. Obama only eight years when he launched his political career? ***Si Obama naman talaga, nangbobola pa! But the sad part here, is that: Kahit na bola, naniniwala ang maraming iba. Katangahan na lang yan, di ba? And, what does that tell you about Obama's supporters? Susmaryusep! I don't wanna say nothing na, baka may sumabunot na sa akin. Ngayon pa lang bugbug sarado na ako ng maraming mura. Nag-uunahan pa sa mga email nila.*** My email box is always full of hate mails, I tell ya. For self-defense, I just hit the DELETE button. Delete, delete, delete.

Now, where was I? Yeah, that's right, we were talking about Mr. Obama's associations with execrable characters.

"Associations are important," said Charles Krauthammer, a *Washington Post* syndicated columnist and Fox News TV political analyst. "They provide a significant insight into character. They are particularly relevant in relation to a potential President as new, unknown, opaque and self-contained as (Mr.) Obama. With the economy overshadowing everything, it may be too late politically to be raising this issue. But that does not make it, as conventional wisdom holds, in any way ILLIGITIMATE."

I agree. Nobody could have said that any better. And, why are these associations important?

"First, his cynicism and ruthlessness," said Mr. Krauthammer. "He found these men useful, and use them he did. Would you attend a church whose pastor was spreading racial animosity from the pulpit? Would you even shake hands, let alone serve on two boards, with an unrepentant terrorist?"

"Most Americans would not, on the grounds of sheer INDECENCY," Mr. Krauthammer said. "Yet (Senator) Obama did, if not out of conviction, then out of expediency . . . He played the games with everyone without qualms and with obvious success."
Washington Post's Charles Krauthammer said: "(Senator) Obama is a man of first-class intellect and first-class temperament. But his character remains highly suspect. There is a difference between temperament and character. Equanimity is a virtue. Tolerance of the obscene is not."
He played dirty politics. Mr. Obama is not the first politician to rise through a "corrupt political machine in Chicago," said Mr. Krauthammer. "But he is one of the rare few to then have the AUDACITY to present himself as a transcendent healer, hovering above and bringing redemption to the old politics."

The second reason why associations are important, Mr. Krauthammer continued, "even more disturbing than the cynicism, is the window these associations give on Mr. Obama's core beliefs." Granted, as Mr. Obama had claimed that he doesn't share Reverend Wright's hateful views on race nor Mr. Ayer's views about the evilness of America, "but Obama clearly did not consider these views beyond the pale. For many years he swam easily and without protest in that PETID POND . . ."

Mr. Krauthammer is truly a powerful, beautiful writer. Fierce, like that warrior/reformer princess from Alaska, Ms. Sarah Palin. And poetic, like that prince among fighters of the 60's, Muhammed Ali, who "floats like a butterfly and stings like a bee."

Here's how Charles Krauthammer ended his article: "(Senator) Obama is a man of first-class intellect and first-class temperament. But his character remains highly suspect. There is a difference between temperament and character. Equanimity is a virtue. Tolerance of the obscene is not."

Would you want that kind of a man to become the President of this great country? Indeed, I say, no way, Hosay.

O BAMA, THE SOCIALIST: Last week another scary word came about and got tagged on the front of Obama's tailored suit: SOCIALIST.

This was triggered by Mr. Obama's comments to a guy in Toledo, Ohio named "Joe, the Plumber." Y'all heard about Joe, right?

Joe told Mr. Obama that he hoped someday to buy a plumbing business, so he asked: "Your new tax plan is going to tax me more, isn't it?"

"It's not that I want to punish your success," Mr. Obama answered. "I just want to make sure that everybody who is behind you, that they've got a chance for success, too. My attitude is that if the economy's good for folks from the bottom up, it's gonna be good for everybody . . . I think when you spread the wealth around, it's good for everybody."

To mainstream America, spreading the wealth around is socialism, plain and simple. It's un-American. It's an idea far from the extreme left of America.

"Obama wants to talk about giving pieces of the pie to everyone," remarked an Ohio woman who witnessed the conversation between Joe, the Plumber and Obama, the Socialist. "But he never wants to talk about growing the pie. I don't want to share my pie. If I earn it, I want to keep as much as I can."

And so do I. So many questions have been posed at B. HUSSEIN Obama, yet not one has been answered truthfully. **JJ**

John McCain Dropkicks B. HUSSEIN Obama in Final Round of Presidential Debates

"***Senator Obama wants to spread the wealth around . . .***"
Sen. John McCain

First, please allow me to say this: Several of my readers, friends and foes alike, have accused me of being a BIGOT. They said that the reason that I "hate" B. Hussein Obama is because he's BLACK. Or "colored" or something like that.

Wrong.

First of all, I don't hate Mr. Obama. I am colored, too, just like him. *Pinoy na Pinoy*, in fact. The reason for me in not wanting B. HUSSEIN Obama to become the President of America is NOT because he's Black. Honest. Or, because he's a closeted Muslim, you know, as in closeted gay.

Okay, don't get me wrong now. I don't have any problems with closeted gays, or cross-dressers, or whatever. Hey, to me, whatever turns you on, it's fine by me (that is, as long as you're not hurting or scaring the kids or bothering anybody, or you're not my next door neighbor, de-valuing the prices of homes in my neighborhood), live and let live.

But really . . . I am coming away now from the reason why I don't want Mr. Obama to become the next President of America. Let me get back on track. The reason for me, dear readers, is because he's a LIAR, like George W. Bush! And liars cannot be trusted at all.

Since the beginning of his presidential campaign, he has LIED and changed his positions on issues several times, depending where the winds of public opinions shifted.

I don't like Barack HUSSEIN Obama, is not because he's BLACK, or because his middle name is HUSSEIN, or because his last name, OBAMA, sounds like, well, like OSAMA, America's public enemy number one, but because he's a LIAR!

He sways. He grooves. He dances. He's so smooth, a real dude, sleek and slick, even slicker than the Big Dog, Slick Willy himself. Y'all know who I am talking about, right? Again, please don't get me wrong. I like Bill Clinton. And I like his wife, Ms. Hillary, too. I like both of them VERY much. They have done a lot of good things for this country. But what has B. HUSSEIN Obama done for this country? Pray tell me.

VOTING FOR THE PARTY IS BLIND LOYALTY: I also like, believe or not, Sen. Joe Biden, Mr. Obama's running mate. And of course, Sen. John McCain and his VP, Gov. Sarah Palin. All three—Senator McCain, Senator Biden and Governor Palin—are my kind of Americans. God-fearing and patriotic Americans to the core. They have sons, who are now fighting in Iraq. Yeah, that's right, I am not a Democrat nor a Republican. I am not even an Independent or Green. I am a registered Democrat, but that doesn't mean I vote strictly Democrat. I vote for the person, the candidate himself or herself, NEVER for the party. Voting for the party is blind loyalty. . . .

And as I said, the reason I don't like Mr. Barack HUSSEIN Obama, is not because he's BLACK, or because his middle name is HUSSEIN, or because his last name, OBAMA, sounds like, well, like OSAMA, America's public enemy number one, but because he's a LIAR!

So early in his political career, he epitomizes the typical politician, who promises expensive goodies to voters to win their votes. Like: Education for all! Health care for all! Lower taxes for all! All the freebies and the goodies for all, except the rich. In other words, spread the wealth. Ala Robin Hood: rob the rich and give it to the poor. That's not my concept of America.

In America, you work your butt off. You take care of your family with your hard-earned money. You save part of your hard-earned money for the future of your children and for your retirement. In other words, you pursue the American Dream by working hard. To me, that's America.

But if you're lazy and you'd rather get handouts from the government . . . and develop this sense of entitlement because you're a minority in this country, then shame on you. And shame on any political candidate, too, who would perpetuate and ENABLE those kinds of people in eternal handouts and ENTITLEMENTS. I suppose that's also America. But I don't belong to that kind of America. I don't want to belong there.

And that's one of the reasons, my friends, why I am NOT voting for B. HUSSEIN Obama. He wants to enable lazy people and parasites in America. How would he do that? Through taxes. By raising our taxes. By squeezing us, the middle class, with taxes. He said he's going to cut taxes for the middle class. I say he's a damn LIAR!!!

As Gov. Sarah Palin said in a GOP rally in Richmond, Virginia: "America, doggone it, unfortunately we're deep in debt, and Barack Obama would put us even in deeper debt. We've got to reverse this. America, we cannot afford another big spender in the White House."

Mr. Obama epitomizes typical politicians, who promise expensive goodies to voters to win their votes. Like: Education for all! Health care for all! Lower taxes for all! All the freebies and the goodies for all, except the rich. In other words, spread the wealth. Ala Robin Hood: rob the rich and give it to the poor. That's not my concept of America.

MCCAIN'S DROP KICKS OBAMA: In my younger days in the 60's, I deeply immersed myself in the art of Tae Kwon Do, as taught by the father of American Tae Kwon Do, Mr. Jhoon Rhee. Tae Kwon Do at that time was not taught to children and teenagers, but only to responsible adults who were of "good moral character" because the techniques that were learned then could be used as deadly weapons. The two most lethal techniques that I liked the best and spent most time on in honing to perfection were the side kick and the drop kick. The side kick was easy to learn. It was the drop kick that was the most difficult to learn because it involved a lot of agility, balance and strength . . . and perfect timing to turn it into an effective weapon. But perfecting it was all worthwhile.

Just like what the name of the technique implies, you drop on the floor and on your side as your opponent delivers a kick at you . . . and then you kick up with a side kick to your opponent's most vulnerable body area, which is the groin area. And, that's it. The deed is done. Hasta la vista, baby!

In the final debate between Sen. McCain and Sen. Obama, there were two successive side kicks that McCain delivered to Obama. The first was when McCain, who was fed up with accusations by Obama as a mirage daw of Mr. Bush, leaped at him and said: "I am not President Bush. If you wanted to run against President Bush, you should have run four years ago."

The second side kick came at Obama in this way: "I have disagreed with leaders of my own party," McCain said, then adding his support to curb global warming, the way the Iraq War was being waged and an HMO patients' bill of rights.

Then . . . the DROP kick came swiftly and deadly when McCain said: "Yes, real quick now. Mr. Ayers. I don't care about an old washed-up terrorist. But as Senator Clinton said in her debates with you, we need to know the full extent of that relationship. . . . We need to know the full extent of Mr. Obama's relationship with ACORN, who is now on the verge of maybe perpetrating one of the greatest frauds in voter history in this country, maybe destroying the fabric of democracy."

Yeah, that was a picture of the perfect DROP KICK to BHO's gonads, which left him stuttering. As Ah-nold, the Terminator would say: "*Hasta la vista, baby!*" In Japanese, Sayonara *ngarud.* **JJ**

Sarah Palin Shines in VP Debate; Master Shames Grasshopper in Rematch

She's goofy. She's 'stoopid.' She's an airhead. She's incompetent. She's despicable. She speaks in incomplete sentences. She speaks without syntax. She's a liar. She can't spell. She has an old-fashioned hairstyle. She catapulted into the national scene with a Bible in one hand and an assault weapon in the other. She's dubbed the Failin' Palin. The list goes on and on . . . and on. The smears thrown at Gov. Sarah Palin never stop.

Governor Palin was mocked in America's most-watched comedy show, "Saturday Night Live," and by David Lettermen in his own late show. She was attacked from all sides by TV talk heads and print pundits.

She was even alluded to as a "pig with lipstick" by the Democratic presidential candidate himself, B. HUSSEIN Obama.

She was PILLORIED. Her family was pilloried. Her pregnant daughter was pilloried. Her youngest son, with Down Syndrome, was pilloried. Her husband, too, was pilloried as a "drunk" for getting a DUI ticket years and years ago. I don't know if the Palins own a family pet dog, but I bet ya, if they do, Obama's media lapdogs would have pilloried the family dog, too.

For Palin bashers, critics and detractors (*nag-kukumpulan sa dami*, like crabs and cockroaches in a bucket), they expected to see a Sarah Palin meltdown on the national stage in her first-and-last vice-presidential debate last week.

But, they were VERY disappointed! And so wrong.

Sarah Palin was strong. Articulate. Folksy. Warm. Assertive. Poised. She wore a bright smile throughout the exchange and carried herself with confidence. And, she was gorgeous in that black dress and stiletto heels.

She battled Senator Biden on a lot of issues—the economy, taxes, Iraq, Afghanistan, gay marriage, global warming, foreign relations, etc.—and she more than held her own.

On Iraq, she said to Senator Biden, facing and looking at him: "Your plan is a white flag of surrender in Iraq and that is not what our troops need to hear today, that's for sure." Absolutely! I am with that. No retreat. No surrender.

On taxes, she said: "Barack had 94 opportunities to side on the people's side and reduce taxes and 94 times he voted to increase taxes." Right on, and if I may add, on other issues, BHO merely voted "present."

On gay marriage, she said, addressing both the moderator and Senator Biden, she said: "Your question to him was whether he supported gay marriage and my answer is the same as his and it is that I do not . . ." Yes, me, too, I do not, but in civil unions, I do.

And I liked it so much, for she was so appealing, when she invoked her small-town roots, her status as a "Washington outsider" and her connections as a hockey and soccer mom.

Watching the debate from my living room, I stood up and clapped, when she said: "If you want Washington changed, send two MAVERICKS to clean things up . . . I think we need a little bit of reality from Wasilla Main Street there, brought to Washington, D.C."

When Senator Biden sought to link Senator McCain to Mr. Bush, I hooted with delight when Governor Palin said: "For a ticket that wants to talk about change and looking into the future, there's just too much finger-pointing backwards to ever make us believe that that's where you're going."

"Positive change is coming though," she added, "Reform of government is coming. We'll learn from the past mistakes in this administration and other administrations. . . ."

Yes! Yes, I think, Sarah Palin was smashing during this debate. And she smashed her detractors. It was her show. She was wonderful. She's READY to be VP.

True, she struggled with questions in televised interviews by the hostile media, but she has learned fast. And she will learn fast as time goes on. She will be a quick understudy of a President John McCain, I am sure. During the debate, she asked: "How long have I been at this? Like five weeks?"

Five weeks! Five contentious weeks! She has learned a lot. More likely now, after November 4, four more years in the McCain/Palin administration. Within those four years, she will definitely learn more. To Palin bashers, eat your hearts out!

THE MASTER AND THE GRASSHOPPER: Okay *ngarud*, let's talk now about the second debate between Senator McCain and BHO this week. It's more of the same, I think. Once again, Senator McCain clearly clobbered Mr. Obama.

If there is one thing that is very clear to me in watching debates between Senators McCain and Obama is that there's a reason Mr. Obama is called a "Junior Senator from Illinois." He's a junior in attitude and experience; vision and knowledge.

Mr. Obama compared to Senator McCain, is a *pipitsugin*. An empty suit *lang, ika nga*. In Kung Fu lore, Senator McCain is the MASTER, and Mr. Obama is GRASSHOPPER, the eager-beaver pupil. And once again, the master shamed the grasshopper for his brashness and clumsiness. He suggested that Mr. Obama simply would not be able to find his way through the maze and chaos of this world. Like a little boy,

Senator Obama hasn't seen nothing yet. Nor done nothing yet. While the MASTER knows. Been there. Done that. Ten times over. He knows the way through the maze and chaos of this world.

Mr. Obama talked about health care for everyone and government-paid college education and cutting taxes for the middle class. On and on, he promised all kinds of goodies for America. And it all sounded great. But who's going to pay for all that? The Chinese? America will be sunk!

The best part of the debate, I think, was when Senator McCain said this to picture Mr. Obama as a reckless spender, like the Bush/Cheney team: "By the way, my friends, I know you grow a little weary of this back and forth. There was an energy bill on the floor of the Senate loaded down with goodies, billions for the oil companies . . ."

"And it was sponsored by Bush and Cheney," Senator McCain continued. "You know who voted for it—you might never know?" Then pointing toward Senator Obama, Mr. McCain said, "THAT ONE!" Then he asked, "You know who voted against it? ME."

Yes, indeed, the ME, the MASTER, he knows. And he shows 'THAT ONE,' the GRASSHOPPER, the pupil, the way. **JJ**

The Dishonor of Having to Beg

What follows came from the September 26th issue of "This Week" magazine in its "Best Columns: International" section and I just want to share it with y'all. This condensed version, almost like to the letter, echoes my thoughts on the matter and mirrors several of my published writings, e-mails (to friends who became enemies and non-friends who became allies) and letters that I have sent to many members of U.S. Congress.

It was written by Jose Montelibano of the *Philippine Daily Inquirer.* Enjoy.

QUOTE: *Filipinos have lost their pride, said Jose Montelibano. We have been reduced to begging Washington to give compensation to our World War II veterans. These men fought alongside Americans "with the liberation forces of Douglas MacArthur" to drive the Japanese out of the Philippines. Yet "America did not consider the sacrifice and courage of Filipino war veterans of equal value to those of their own."*

Six decades after the war, Filipino-Americans have finally succeeded in getting a bill before the U.S. Congress that would authorize payment to surviving Filipino veterans.

The bill should be dropped!

Such payment would be HUMILIATING, since it would be offered only grudgingly, after a huge lobbying effort, and far too late. If Filipinos have any pride, they would donate to a veterans' fund themselves. Just $100 from every Filipino American, plus a smaller sum from everyone in the

Philippines, would ensure a comfortable retirement for WWII veterans. "Perhaps, instead, of BEGGING in the U.S. Congress, we can simply go into self-reflection, chew on our propensity to live in SHAME, and decide whether we wish to go on like this or seek the courage to be honorable . . ." **UNQUOTE.**

As reported by my colleague, Romy Marquez, this "claim against the U.S. government" will now be in the form of "lump sum payment" of $15,000 for those FilVets who are now U.S. citizens and $9,000 for non-citizens. Eighteen thousand of these FilVets are still alive.

This money will come from the coffers slated for the equipment of U.S. soldiers now fighting in Iraq and Afghanistan and for the care of wounded soldiers coming home from those two war fronts, and for their families. The American people should NOT allow this to happen, because it's NOT right at all. America should take care of its soldiers and veterans first before those FilVets. And, for heaven's sake, we FilAms, must stop the begging now, please. **JJ**

Sarah "Barracuda" Palin, America's Next VP, Rocks

"She's exactly who I need. She's exactly who this country needs to help me fight the same old Washington politics—Sen. John McCain

She rocks. She's a WOW! Simply and truly, a wow. Sarah Palin's speech Wednesday night was a wow.

She who rocks the cradle, rocks the world. It's true, the hockey mom of five, rocks. Wednesday night, she rocked, rolled and rattled the Obama bin Biden team off their grandiose perch. I bet ya, BHO's supporters are now shaking in their boots and shooting their mouths off to degrade and demean and belittle Sarah Palin's speech.

And that's because it made all those PLAGIARIZED speeches of Obama bin Biden sound PUNY and insignificant. As one fellow Seattleite said of Ms. Palin's speech: "Excellent! It is a case of little America calling the bluff of superficial BIG America."

Portions of her speech still ring in my ears, especially this eloquently-said quip on BHO: "This is a man who has authored two memoirs but not a single major law or reform, not even in the state Senate. This is a man who can give an entire speech about the wars America is fighting, and never the word "victory" except when he's talking about his own campaign. . . ."

Yes indeed!!!

To all those HOSTILE reporters of CNN, MSNBC, NBC, like Campbell Brown, Brian Williams and Keith Olbermann, who bad-mouthed her and her family, she said, coolly and with utmost subtlety: "Here's a little news flash for all those reporters and commentators. I am not going to Washington to seek their good opinion. I am going to Washington to serve the people of this country."

Yes indeed!!!

It's an absolute home run. A star is born. And she's a woman. She's one heck of a woman. And I adore her. And I believe million of others have fallen for her, too. Even surpassing the 18-million voters, who still cling tenaciously to Ms. Hillary's skirts. But mind you, she has only but praises and agreement for Ms. Hillary Clinton. She said, "It turns out the women of America aren't finished yet, and we can shatter that glass ceiling once and for all."

WHY JOE POTTER AND JESSE JOSE ARE VOTING FOR JOHN MCCAIN:

For this week, this columnist is giving way to a guest writer. The following piece has circulated among online circles in Illinois. It is now also being forwarded and re-forwarded in this country, from sea to shining sea.

Here is my guest columnist, Joe Porter. Unlike Mr. Porter, who is an independent voter, this columnist and his wife are both Democrats. Mr. Porter gives most of the reasons in his essay why we are all voting for John McCain.

QUOTE.

My name is Joe Porter. I live in Champaign, Illinois. I'm 46-years old, a born-again Christian, a husband, a father, a small-business owner, a veteran, and a homeowner. I don't consider myself to be either conservative or liberal, and I vote for the person, not Republican or Democrat. I don't believe there are "two Americas"—but that every person in this country can be whomever and whatever they want to be if they'll just work to get there. And nowhere else on earth can they find such opportunities. I believe our government should help those who are legitimately downtrodden, and should always put the interests of America first.

The purpose of this message is that I'm concerned about the future of this great nation. I'm worried that the silent majority of honest, hard-working, tax-paying people in this country have been passive for too long. Most folks I know choose not to involve themselves in politics. They go about their daily lives, paying their bills, raising their kids, and doing what they can to maintain the good life. They vote and consider doing so to be a sacred trust. They shake their heads at the political pundits and so-called "news", thinking that what they hear is always spun by whoever is reporting it. They can't understand how elected officials can regularly violate the public trust with pork-barrel spending. They don't want government handouts. They want the government to protect them, not raise their taxes for more government programs.

We are in the unique position in this country of electing our leaders. It's a privilege to do so. I've never found a candidate in any election with whom I agreed on everything. I'll wager that most of us don't even agree with our families or spouses 100% of the time. So when I step into that voting booth, I always try to look at the big picture and cast my vote for the man or woman who is best qualified for the job. I've hired a lot of people in my lifetime, and essentially that's what an election is—a hiring process. Who has the credentials? Whom do I want working for me? Whom can I trust to do the job, right?

I'm concerned that a growing number of voters in this country simply don't get it. They are caught up in a fervor they can't explain, and are calling it "change".

"Change what?" I ask.

"Well, we're going to change America," they say.

"In what way?" I query.

"We want someone new and fresh in the White House," they exclaim.

"So, someone who's not a politician?" I press.

"Uh, well, no, we just want a lot of stuff changed, so we're voting for Obama," they state.

So the current system, the system of freedom and democracy that has enabled a man to grow up in this great country, get a fine education, raise incredible amounts of money and dominate the news and win his party's nomination for the White House—that system's all wrong?

No, no, that part of the system's okay—we just need a lot of changes.

And so it goes. "Change we can believe in." Quite frankly, I don't believe that vague proclamations of change hold any promise for me. In recent months, I've been asking virtually everyone I encounter how they're voting. I live in Illinois, so most folks tell me they're voting for Barack Obama. But no one can really tell me why—only that he's going to change a lot of stuff. Change, change, change. I have yet to find one single person who can tell me distinctly and convincingly why this man is qualified to be President and Commander-in-Chief of the most-powerful nation on earth other than the fact that he claims he's going to implement a lot of changes.

We've all seen the emails about Obama's genealogy, his upbringing, his Muslim background, and his church affiliations. Let's ignore this for a moment. Put it all aside. Then ask yourself, what qualifies this man to be my President? That he's a brilliant orator and talks about change?

CHANGE WHAT?

Friends, I'll be forthright with you—I believe the American voters who are supporting Barack Obama don't have a clue what they're doing, as evidenced by the fact that not one of them—NOT ONE of them I've spoken to can spell out his qualifications. Not even the most-liberal media can explain why he should be elected.

Political experience? Negligible.

Foreign relations? Non-existent.

Achievements? Name one.

Someone who wants to unite the country? If you haven't read his wife's thesis from Princeton, look it up on the web. This is who's lining up to be our next First Lady? The only thing I can glean from Obama's constant harping about change is that we're in for a lot of new taxes.

For me, the choice is clear. I've looked carefully at the two leading applicants for the job, and I've made my choice.

Here's a question—where were you five-and-a-half years ago? Around Christmas, 2002. You've had five or six birthdays in that time. My son has grown from a sixth-grade child to a high-school graduate. Five-and-a-half years are a good chunk of time. About 2,000 days. 2,000 nights of sleep. 6, 000 meals, give or take.

John McCain spent that amount of time, from 1967 to 1973, in a North Vietnamese prisoner-of-war camp. When offered early release, he refused it. He considered this offer to be a public-relations stunt by his captors, and insisted that those held longer than he should be released first. Did you get that part? He was offered his freedom, and he turned it down. A regimen of beatings and torture began.

Do you possess such strength of character? Locked in a filthy cell in a foreign country, would you turn down your own freedom in favor of your fellow man? I submit that's a quality of character that is rarely found, and for me, this singular act defines John McCain.

Unlike several presidential candidates in recent years whose military service is questionable or non-existent, you will not find anyone to denigrate the integrity and the moral courage of this man. A graduate of Annapolis, during his naval service he own son is now serving in the Marine Corps in Iraq. Barack Obama is fond of saying "We honor John McCain's service . . . BUT . . .", which to me is condescending and offensive—because what I hear is, "Let's forget this man's sacrifice for his country and his proven leadership abilities, and talk some more about change."

I don't agree with John McCain on everything—but I am utterly convinced that he is qualified to be our next President, and I trust him to do what's right. I know in my heart that he has the best interests of our country in mind. He doesn't simply want to be President and he wants to lead America, and there's a huge difference.

Factually, there is simply no comparison between the two candidates. A man of questionable background and motives who prattles on about change can't hold a candle to a man who has devoted his life in public service to this nation, retiring from the Navy in 1981 and elected to the Senate in 1982.

Perhaps Obama's supporters are taking a stance between old and new. Maybe they don't care about McCain's service or his strength of character, or his unblemished qualifications to be President. Maybe "likeability" is a higher priority for them than "trust." Being a prisoner of war is not what qualifies John McCain to be President of the United States of America—but his demonstrated leadership certainly DOES.

Dear friends, it is time for us to stand. It is time for thinking Americans to say, "Enough." It is time for people of all parties to stop following the party line. It is time for anyone who wants to keep America first, who wants the right man leading their nation, to start a dialogue with all their friends and neighbors and ask who they're voting for, and why.

There's a lot of evil in this world. That should be readily apparent to all of us by now. And when faced with that evil as we are now, I want a man who knows the cost of war on his troops and on his citizens. I want a man who puts my family's interests before any foreign country.

I want a President who's qualified to lead.

I want my country back, and I'm voting for John McCain.

PS: At this point, I want to add that I don't want a First Lady that has to be shown how to really love America. I want a First Lady who thinks more about people beyond herself and takes on tasks like Cindy McCain does. Have you read about her trip to Rwanda and Zaire? Look it up. She thinks far beyond herself and "her" people. She would be a very important asset to the presidential office also. **JJ**

B. Hussein Obama, the Wannabe Messiah

Question: What do Britney Spears, Paris Hilton . . . and B. HUSSEIN Obama (BHO) have in common? Answer: All three are celebrities and a fascination to the lapping media. All three are examples of famous people who are famous for being famous but with no real accomplishments.

So . . . if BHO is merely a celebrity within the class of Paris and Britney, should the presidency of the United States of America and the leadership of the free world be handed to him on the basis of his star power?

I have another question: What do Charlton Heston as Moses and BHO as a world celebrity have in common? Answer: As y'all know, the biblical Moses parted the seas for his people, so they can go home to their Promised Land. Of course, we have not seen BHO part the seas yet, but he's talking like HE CAN, so we, the lowly and the wretched throngs, can also be delivered to our own Promised Land.

He said HE CAN stop the WAR and that in a jiffy, HE CAN bring the troops home. He said HE CAN talk to all the leaders of the enemies of America and pacify them with his charm. He said HE CAN unify the red states and the blue states of America into one red, white and blue color of the flag of the United States of America.

He said HE CAN balance the budget and make the budget deficit disappear. He said HE CAN give universal health care to all Americans, without raising our taxes. He said a lot of things that he said HE CAN. He even said HE CAN stop global warming. Can you imagine that?

He also said that HE CAN solve America's energy crisis and the rising gas prices. He said that the "offshore drilling" for oil that Sen. John McCain endorses is merely a "gimmick" and that the real solution to the rising gas prices is the "tire gauge." Yeah, that's what he said. By keeping our car tires inflated, we all CAN keep gas prices down low.

Hey, y'all remember that day during one of Mr. Bush's 2004 campaign speeches, when he asked America: "Got wood?" Now it's BHO's turn to ask America: "Got tire gauge?" I am telling ya, these two are SAME-SAME.

The difference between them is that Mr. Bush claimed he can talk to God and God talks to him and it was God who told him to invade Iraq. With BHO, he thinks he's the Messiah. Or Moses. Because he said HE CAN . . . do it all and deliver us to our own Promised Land.

Don't mean to sound like a heretic, but I have one more question: What do BHO and Jesus Christ have in common? Answer: Well, they don't really have anything in common. As we all know, Christ is the Messiah. BHO merely thinks he is.

BHO, CNN'S ANOINTED ONE: When BHO came into America's consciousness, people asked: "Who is he?" Before he became known nationally as a presidential candidate, he was locally known in Chicago as a state senator of Illinois who had a penchant for voting "present" during legislative sessions. He was also known at that time as having a close association with Tony Rezko, that felon and notorious slumlord of the city of Chicago. It was also during this time when he sat week after week in the pews of that "Southside" Chicago church to listen to Rev. Jeremiah Wright rant and curse "White America."

Now, thanks to the pawing left print media and mostly Black news analyst kuno of CNN and the left-leaning biased talk heads of NBC and MSNBC, like Brian Williams, David Gergen, Andrea Mitchell, Chris Matthews and Keith Olberman, BHO metamorphosed into a national figure, who can walk the walk and talk the talk of the Messiah. They anointed him as the ONE. And he began to believe that he's the one. Now people asked: "Who does he thinks he is?

PRIDE AND PREJUDICE, THE BOOK: My favorite columnist, Maureen Dowd of the *New York Times* has the perfect answer to that question. She said in her column last week: "The odd thing is that Obama bears a distinct resemblance to the most cherished hero in chick-lit history. The senator is a modern incarnation of the clever, haughty, reserved and fastidious Mr. Darcy.

"Like the leading man of Jane Austen and Bridget Jones, OBAMA CAN, as Austen wrote, draw 'the attention of the room by his fine, tall person, handsome features, noble mien. He was looked at with great admiration for about half the evening, till his manners gave a disgust which turned the tide of his popularity; for he was discovered to be proud, to be above his company, and above being pleased.'"

Yes, indeed, ABOVE . . . everyone else. Prayed to, pawed at, like a god. Like a wannabe Messiah.

A SPEECH IN MISSOURI: Not too long ago, Obama was in Missouri to deliver a speech. Speaking evenly, with a touch of humor, to a nearly all-white audience, he told them: "What they're going to try is to make you scared of me. You know, he's not patriotic enough. He's got a funny name. You know, he doesn't look like those presidents on those dollar bills, you know. He's risky.'"

As Ronald Reagan used to say: "there you go again." With all due respect, Senator BHO, sir, but it's true, that's how many people perceive you. You might think that you're the one, but you ain't. Also, why do you have to keep on insinuating your race? People can see that you're BLACK. Well, I suppose you're not completely black, but only half and half. But why do you keep on introducing the race factor and playing the race card into your campaign? Then you turn around and accuse Senator John McCain of playing the race card. It's you who's very adept in playing the race card . . . Sir BHO.

A DIALOGUE WITH A READER: A reader from Virginia asked me: "You had wanted Hillary to be the Democratic nominee and have been lambasting—nay, ridiculing—Obama since he became the obvious presumptive nominee. Now would BHO be palatable to you if he chose Hillary as his VP?"

I answered: "Even if Hillary will run as BHO's VP, I still will not vote for him. I don't trust this man. I think he's liar, like Mr. Bush. BHO have said repeatedly that voting for Sen. John McCain for president would be a vote for a Bush's third term. That's not true at all. It's the other way 'round. A vote for BHO is a vote for a Bush's third term. And that's because, they're alike. Both, as I said, are big time liars. And both have a Messiah complex. That's dangerous. Anyway, I don't think Obama will pick Hillary as his VP. I heard Oprah is his choice.

"Seriously, I think the surest way McCain can win this election is if Hillary becomes his VP. The Democrat Party then will get split in the middle, with the other half voting surely for the McCain/Hillary ticket. Ms. Hillary has 18-million voters under her belt that she can deliver to McCain. My wife and I are both registered Democrats, but we made up our minds to vote Republican this year. We don't want a president who has a Messiah complex . . ." **JJ**

Arroyo Dispensation's Legacy: "Pagpag" (AKA "Kanin Baboy") Meals for Poor Filipinos

The YouTube video called, "Pagpag" is the latest indictment against the presidency of Gloria Macapagal Arroyo. It is actually a documentary film by "*Sine Totoo*," or "Cine Reality." Jacel Arqueros wrote and produced it, as based on the research of Nick Samson.

The video is really disgusting! Thanks to President Arroyo and her clique, the Philippines is no longer known as the "Pearl of the Orient" but the "ARMPIT of Asia." The medical/sanitation people in Arroyo's government have claimed that they didn't know that this exists? Because of hunger, poor Filipinos have been reduced to eating "kanin baboy." Pagpag is only a pretty term for "kanin baboy," which is the colloquial term for left-over food that is fed to hogs.

This film must be shown to the whole world. People, especially Overseas Filipinos, must know how bad the situation in the Philippines is. Clearly, there's a hunger crisis that's going on there now.

Here are the other comments about the Pagpag video posted in a e-forum that I participate in:

From Jess Farrales of Chicago, Illinois:
"Pagpag is now getting popular as a good source of business and food on the table for the common people in the Philippines.

"I agree with you, Jesse Jose, dahil kay President Arroyo's corrupt governance . . . our people are going to the dogs . . . whether you call it Pagpag is a source of business/income . . . it is still the 'kanin baboy' business that we know of during our time in the Philippines."

From the screen name, Ccayamanda:
"First time I heard of 'pagpag' and it is very upsetting to see our people in the lower-economic level reduced to this level of urban existence. It may get worse because of our unabated population growth (90 million and counting with a growth rate of 1.8%!). Our government should have initiated a 'zero population growth' program yesterday!"

From Don Azarias, also of Chicago:
"I still haven't looked at it because I don't have the guts to handle what's in there based on the comments that I've read. My heart bleeds for our kababayans who are eating 'kanin baboy' while we, fortunate ones, have everything we can ask for in this land of plenty. Our less-fortunate brothers and sisters back home have to do what they are doing in order to survive. Never before had this happened to our people; not during the Spanish regime; not during the American and Japanese occupation and not during the administration of all our previous Presidents but only during the administration of the most-corrupt President in the history of our country, the shameless midget, Gloria Macapagal-Arroyo and, of course, her cohorts and all her partners-in-crime. Hell is even too good of a place for her to go. She is devoid of a soul and conscience.

"We should do something about this. You newspapermen should spearhead the move in bringing this to the world's attention or, at least, to the attention of the incompetent United Nations Organization. What do you think? Do we do something about it or do we look the other way?

"Jesus Christ once said: 'Whatsoever you do to the least of my brother you do unto me.' Isn't that enough to inspire us?"

From TDB of Virginia:
"It was very painful to watch. I couldn't bear to finish it.

"Years ago, three of my kids and I climbed the infamous Smokey Mountain on North Bay Blvd. in Metro Manila. We were accompanied by a couple of Christian missionaries. I wanted my children to see first hand how our poor people try to survive as scavengers as truck after truck of Manila garbage were dumped on that mountain of garbage. They thought it was unbelievably pitiful. When we got back to USA, they had a better perspective of life . . ."

From Manny Belbis, also of Chicago:
"This is terrible. Can't believe this will happen to our country of origin. How in hell the Philippines can produce smart people, if they eat 'kanin baboy.'? Our dogs here in America eat better than our poor kababayans there."

My answers to the comments above:

Seeing that "pagpag" film brought a lot of emotions out of me. It made me mad, it made me sad, it made me cry and many other kinds of disturbing emotions in between. How the Arroyo gov't can allow this to happen is beyond belief. This is worst than violation of human rights. It's a form of degradation of our people to sub humans.

We, Fil-Ams and our Fil-Am associations, must do something about this. Instead of stepping on each other's toes, demanding from the US gov't the UNDESERVED pensions that the FilVets have been asking for, we should all join forces, redirect our focus and condemn this disgusting phenomenon. **JJ**

That "Funneeeee" Cartoon of the New Yorker Magazine

You're allowed to laugh at Obama, you know—Jon Stewart, comedian and host of 'The Daily Show'

Yes, indeed, it was funny. It was so deliciously funneeeeee. Y'all know what I am talking about, right? Honestly, I thought that what the Rev. Jesse Jackson said was funny. You know, what he said about cutting B. Hussein Obama's (BHO) "nuts out" for talking down to Black Americans and telling them how to behave.

It happened in Chicago about a week ago, when Reverend Jackson was speaking to Dr. Reed Tuckson, a healthcare official, when a microphone picked up THE REVEREND saying in part: "See, Barack been talkin' down to black people on this faith-based situation. I want to cut his nuts out. He's talking down to black people. . . ." Yeah, man, I thought that was funny.

But that cartoon on the front page of the *New Yorker* magazine this week was a lot funnier. It portrays BHO and his wife, Michelle, standing in the Oval Office after winning the presidential election. BHO wears his tribal Muslim attire: turban, white robe, sandals and all. Michelle, in fatigue pants and combat boots, sports a combed-out Afro, wears a semi-automatic rifle on her back and gives BHO a "terrorist fist-jab" beneath a painting of Osama Bin Laden that hangs above a fireplace. And in the fireplace, the American flag burns.

As my cuz, Manuel, would say about outrageous dyoks: "*Pare ko* . . . Funneeee!" Yes, indeed, it was very, very, funneeee.

But, of course, the Obama camp went ballistics over it. BHO's spokesman, Bill Burton, said: "The *New Yorker* may think, as one of their staff explained to us, that their cover is a satirical lampoon of the caricature Senator Obama's right-wing critics have tried to create. But most readers will see it as TASTELESS and OFFENSIVE."

Nah, I don't think so. In fact, many readers have found the cartoon very funneeeee. That's what cartoons are for. To make people laugh. It was a brilliant lampoon, a bull's eye, in your face cartoon of BHO and Michelle.

All the stupid Hillary cartoons were okay then for the Obambis, but picking on their golden child is NOT okay now . . . come on, y'all, let's not be hypocrites! It was a work of art.

Ms. Elaine Miller, a retired professor who gives talks on political cartoons, said that "once you launch a work of art it belongs to the reader. The artist's intent is very interesting, but the reader owns the interpretation."

And the interpretation of the majority of people of that cartoon of BHO as a Muslim and of his wife, Michelle, as the picture-perfect image of a terrorist of the 70's was . . . right on. The effect was simply funneeee! Many people loved it.

As we all know, a cartoon reflects and exaggerates reality, like one of those funny mirrors that you see in fairs. Sure, what you see is NOT really the image of you . . . but it's you. In other words, yes, it's true that the New Yorker cartoon exaggerates, BUT that's what a lot of Americans believe about BHO and Michelle . . . y'all get my drift?

Asked about his decision to run the cartoon on the front cover of the *New Yorker*, its editor-in-chief, David Remnick, said:

"Obviously I wouldn't have run a cover just to get attention—I ran the cover because I thought it had something to say. What I think it does is hold up a mirror to the prejudice and dark imagining about Barack Obama's—both Obamas'—past and their politics. I can't speak for anyone else's interpretations. All I can say is that it combines a number of images that have been propagated, not by everyone on the right but by some, about Obama's supposed 'lack of patriotism' or he "being soft on terrorism or the idiotic notion that somehow Michelle Obama is the second coming of the Weathermen or the most violent Black Panthers. That somehow all this is going to come to the Oval Office.

"The idea that we would publish a cover saying these things LITERALLY, I think, is just not in the vocabulary of what we do and who we are. We've run many satirical political covers. Ask the Bush administration how many."

In other words, anybody is fair game. The *New Yorker* front cover cartoon this week merely reflects what many Americans think of the Obamas . . . and if that offends you, well, T.S.!

DO RETIREES HAVE MORE FUN?: Talking about jokes, what follows was sent to me by "tdb," a fellow retiree and a cyberspace friend from Richmond, Virginia.

"Working people frequently ask retired people what we do to make our days interesting. Well, for example, the other day I went downtown to go to the News Stand for the Wall Street Journal so I could track my investments. I was only in there for five minutes. When I came out, there was a cop writing out a parking ticket.

"I said to him, 'Come on, man, don't you have anything better to do than write a retired person a ticket? Why aren't you chasing crooks or child molesters . . . that's out of your league obviously!!!'

"He ignored me and continued and continued writing the ticket. I called him a 'Nazi.' He glared at me and wrote another ticket for having worn tires. So I called him 'Barney Fife.'

"He finished the second ticket and put it on the windshield with the first. Then he wrote a third ticket. This went on for about 20 minutes.

The more I abused him, the more tickets he wrote. Personally I didn't care . . .

"I came down on the bus. The car that he was putting the tickets on had a bumper sticker that said: OBAMA in '08." I try to have a little fun each day now that I am retired. It's important to my health!"

Funneeee! Right, cuz? **JJ**

On Watermelons . . . and B. Hussein Obama (BHO)

First thing first. Before we talk about BHO, let's talk about watermelons. That's right, folks, y'all read it right: WATERMELONS! And to those people, who idolize BHO, please don't go ballistic on me now and smear feces on my column.

I am not calling BHO . . . I repeat, I am NOT calling B. Hussein Obama a watermelon! I know that the word watermelon is a SLUR, if used to call or describe or to connote to a black person. Why? From what I've learned from ignorant Rednecks I used to know and worked with, it's because blacks have a fondness for watermelons, thus they're called, "watermelons." One is the other, they said. How silly. I have a lot of fondness for watermelons, too. But nobody had called me "watermelon."

They have called me "pineapple" though.

In the old days when I was still in the Navy, Filipinos then were called, "pineapples." There were a great number of Filipinos in Hawaii who were pineapple pickers. They also picked fruits in California and in many states in the South. So at that time, whenever ignorant Americans see a Filipino, they see a fruit or a pineapple picker.

Or simply, a "pineapple."

But let's go back to watermelons. Paul Newman, you know, that handsome and great Hollywood actor of the 70's and 80's, who starred with Robert Redford in that classical cowboy movie, "Butch Cassidy and the Sundance Kid," has also a great fondness for watermelons, and he's not black.

Years ago, he was quoted in a People magazine story to have said, "One of my many joys in life is submerging my face in a watermelon and lapping and drinking the fruit's juice that way. There's nothing like it. It's heavenly . . . and EROTIC."

I tried it and it's true, guys. It was, indeed, heavenly . . . and EROTIC.

VIAGRA-LIKE EFFECTS: According to Associated Press reports, a group of scientists in Texas said that "watermelons contain an ingredient called CITRULLINE that can trigger production of a compound that helps relax the blood vessels, similar to what happens when a man takes Viagra."

"Found in the flesh and rind of watermelons," they said, "citrulline reacts with the body's enzymes when consumed in large quantities and is changed into ARGININE, an amino acid that benefit acid the heart and the circulatory and immune systems."

"The arginine boosts nitric acid, which relaxes blood vessels, the same basic effect that Viagra has, to treat erectile dysfunction and maybe even prevent it," the scientists touted. "Watermelon may not be as organ-specific as Viagra, but it's a great way to relax blood vessels without any drug side effects."

Well, in that case, instead of planting veggies and flowers and fruit trees in my backyard this summer, I am just gonna be planting watermelons, so come harvest time I can drown myself in bliss as I submerge my face in a ripen fruit to drink and lap up the juices, the way Paul Newman used to do. And, pop the magic dragon, no more erectile dysfunction for me, forever and ever.

BHO, THE CANDIDATE OF CHANGE: Okey *ngarud*, let's talk about Obama now, the candidate of change. FIRST, THE PIN. Yeah, that miniature lapel pin of the flag of the United States of America.

During the primaries, while seducing the hard core Democrats that delivered him the caucuses and the nomination, BHO not only "disdained the pin, he disparaged it," said *Washington Post*'s columnist Charles Krauthammer. "Now that he's running in a general election against John McCain, and in dire need of a gun-and-God-clinging working class votes he could not win against Hillary Clinton, THE PIN IS BACK."

SECOND, THE CAMPAIGN FINANCE REFORM: Both before and during his candidacy, BHO virtually made himself a walking symbol for campaign finance reform. He touted it on TV, in speeches and in interviews. Then, as y'all know, as the cash began flowing in from the Internet, and he raked in nearly $290 million, an amount that tripled the $85 million in public funds that he would have been restricted, and to which John McCain has pledged himself . . . BHO announced that he's backing out of that promise and commitment. He'll be the first presidential candidate since the time of the Watergate scandal to reject campaign finance reforms.

THIRD, THE ILLEGAL WIRETAPPING: Last year, BHO won praises and accolades from his supporters when he opposed legal immunity for telecommunications companies that participated in Mr. Bush's warrantless wiretapping program. So strongly were his feelings (we thought, but he fooled us) that he promised to FILIBUSTER the bill if it contained the immunity clause. That promise now ain't no more. He now supports legislation that includes immunity for the telecoms. In other words, just like Mr. Bush, he'll now allow spying on you and me, looking into our emails and listening in to our phone conversations.

FOURTH, THE BAN ON HANDGUNS: Last week when the U.S. Supreme Court declared as UNCONSTITUTIONAL the ban of handguns in Washington D.C., BHO said that he agreed with the decision. Last November, he explicitly told the *Chicago Tribune* in an interview that that Supreme Court gun ban is CONSTITUTIONAL.

FIFTH, IRAQ: This is the biggie. BHO had said and continues to insist that he wants a phased withdrawal from the war—two divisions a month—until all the soldiers are home in 16 months. But now, check this out. In advance of his upcoming visit there, he tells us: "I am going to do a thorough assessment when I'm there. When I go to Iraq and

I have a chance to talk to some of the commanders on the ground, I'm sure I'll have more information and will continue TO REFINE my policies."

Refine my foot! Most likely, he'll continue to refine his lies. This is the BHO who dumped his pastor of two decades, then his church, after saying he could "no more abandoned his pastor than abandoned his own grandmother . . ."

BHO, the candidate of CHANGE. So what's the next change for this candidate of change? What's the next flip-flop? What's the next lie? What's the next dance? The cowboy cha-cha-cha, perhaps, like Bush's? Or the hip-hop moves, like Karl Rove's?

Mag-watermelon muna kaya tayo, ha? **JJ**

Lighting a Candle in the Dark for OFWs

This story came about when a lady named, Dr. Carmelita C. Ballesteros, a teaching fellow at Nanyang Technological University in Singapore sent a mass email and I was one of the recipients. She's a colleague in another publication that also publishes my column. And this is what she wrote . . .

Dear Family and Friends,

A group of Overseas Filipino Workers (OFWs) to which I belong has just launched a blog site. Please help spread the word among your family and friends who might be interested in OFW matters. The URL is http://barangay-ofw.blogspot.com. I hope you'll soon visit and leave a comment.

Many blessings.

Signed (Carmel)

I got curious, so visited the site, then I emailed her:

Hello Carmel,

I visited the site and read all your posts. Got a couple of questions: What happened at Ninoy Aquino International Airport (NAIA) when you left for Singapore that day? What did they do to you? And what did those people say to "DEMEAN" you and other OFWs who were leaving for overseas? Why did those airport officials harass you? Why would they do that?

Take care,
Signed (Jesse)

If readers of Jesse Jose and the MabuhayRadio.com want to help, too, in lighting the candle for OFWs, please log on at: http://barangay-ofw.blogspot.com . . . post your comments and be heard around the Internet world.

Camel answered:

Dear Jesse,

Thanks very much for visiting Barangay OFW. I wanted to forward to you my original email to former Chief Justice (CJ) Artemio V. Panganiban on June 6, 2008, but I must have deleted it.

Anyway, I've attached four columns by the CJ. They answer your questions and explain the beginnings of Barangay OFW.

The Immigration and POEA personnel detailed at the NAIA seem to have a THRIVING INDUSTRY at harassing and/or coercing OFWs.

My brother was going to Oman last February 21st as a tourist and had a return ticket. Our sister whose family is in Oman has sponsored his visit.

But the immigration people refused to let him through. Forewarned about my experience, he called my son for help. A lawyer-cousin of my daughter-in-law works at the Bureau of Immigration. He called one of the CROCS (buwayas) at NAIA and told them, "Ibalato ninyo sa akin iyang tong iyan. Pinsan ko iyan."

My brother who had left the queue was sought out from the crowd and was escorted through the gates. It was 30 minutes before his flight.

What's the thriving industry? From what I hear and read in emails, the Immigration/POEA personnel at the airport ask for a boarding

fee of Philippine pesos 10,000 Philippine pesos or 200 U.S. dollars. OFWs going to places like Nigeria where there's a Philippine travel ban are milking cows.

The catch is they tell you to rebook your flight, but it means losing your job. So you pay up. So if I had been prepared for the scenario, I would have offered to pay or called for a VIP to help me.

Being treated as if I were dirt was unspeakable to me then. I really felt as if I were a bug. (From hindsight, it was nothing compared to what others have endured.) I did call on Someone. I composed myself in a corner and prayed. Then I fell in line again toward a counter staffed by a kind-looking elderly man. With no questions asked, he stamped my passport and boarding pass, "Departed."

When was the last time you went home to the Philippines? It's a BATTLEFIELD. And yet it's home.

Let's keep the faith,
Signed (Carmel)

I answered:

Hello Carmel,

I read those four columns of the CJ. Really, what's new? Got another question: Now that the CJ had pointed out and exposed the anomalies at the Immigration/POEA at NAIA through his columns and President Arroyo and the Secretary of Labor were already made aware of those problems, do those problems still exist? If they do, then nothing has changed. It's still a country as corrupt as ever.

When I joined the U.S. Navy in 1960 and left the Philippines, big time corruption already flourished! When I came back for a visit 20 years later, it was still corrupt! Ten years later when I went back for another visit, it was still corrupt! It's now 2008, it's still corrupt! Only much worst from what I hear and read.

Everybody in the government are THIEVES, from the Arroyos to the small time politicians. Poverty and hunger pervade all over the land. I can only weep, Carmel, for our Motherland and for all those Filipinos who are still back there, yearning to leave the Motherland behind so as to seek better lives for their families and themselves. It's so sad.

Take care,
Signed (Jesse)

Carmel answered:

Dear Jesse,

Maraming salamat. You've invested time and heart in reading the files I attached. I understand how you feel about corruption and Filipinos dreaming of leaving the Philippines for a better place.

I'd like to ask you for an immense favor. Won't you please write about our Barangay OFW, our grassroots movement? I've attached a column of mine which shows why I feel committed to "Reforming the Present, Creating the Future." I can never move a huge boulder with my frail hands. Neither can you. But we can use a lever. If we do, we can move the boulder of corruption and hopelessness. Won't you help us light a candle in the dark?

Most sincerely,
Signed (Carmel)

I hope that in quoting verbatim my email exchanges with Carmel, I have somehow contributed in "lighting that candle in the dark." If readers of this column want to help, too, in lighting the candle for OFWs, please log on at: http://barangay-ofw.blogspot.com . . . post your comment and be heard. **JJ**

Mga Dyoks . . . Tungkol kay Barack HUSSEIN Obama

M*ga katoto, mag-dyok muna tayo*. When Joseph "Erap" Estrada became the President of the Philippines, all sorts of hilarious *dyoks* proliferated, and we all had a frolicking good time hearing about them and telling them to families and friends. He was laughable.

When George "Dubya" W. Bush became America's President, all sorts of *dyoks* proliferated, too, and we also had a jolly good time. Not so much now . . . because he's on his way out and has become irrelevant. Like Erap, Dubya was also laughable.

Mr. Obama is not yet THE President of Amerika (dream *pa lang*), but all sorts of *dyoks* about him had already proliferated and almost everybody is already having a grand good time. Bit by bit, as we begin to know him, his gaffs and flip-flops and his little white lies, he, too, has become laughable.

Here's one, titled "Snow White & the Seven Dwarfs."
"SENATOR OBAMA AND THE SEVEN DWARFS" JOKE: The seven dwarfs always left to go to work in the mine early each morning. As always, Snow White stayed home doing her domestic chores. As lunchtime approached, she would prepare their lunch and carry it to the mine.

One day as she arrived at the mine with the lunch, she saw that there has been a terrible cave-in. Tearfully, and fearing the worst, Snow White began calling out, hoping against hope that the dwarfs had somehow survived.

"Hello! Hello!" she shouted. "Can anyone hear me? Hello!" For a long while, there was no answer. Losing hope, Snow White again shouted, "Hello! Is anyone down there?"

Just as she was about to give up all hope, she heard a faint voice from deep within the mine singing: "Vote for Obama! Vote for Obama!" Snow White fell to her knees, crossed herself and prayed, "Oh, thank you, God! At least DOPEY is still alive."

Ha, ha, ha.

Here's another one, titled "Post Turtle."
THE "POST TURTLE" JOKE: While suturing a cut on the hand of a 75-year-old Texas rancher, whose hand was caught in a gate while working cattle, the doctor struck up a conversation with the old man.

Eventually the topic got around to Obama and his bid to be our President. The old rancher said, "Well, you know, Obama is a POST TURTLE." Not being familiar with the term, the doctor asked him, "What is a post turtle?"

The old rancher said, "When you're driving down a country road and you come across a fence post, with a turtle balanced on top, that's a post turtle."

The old rancher saw a puzzled look on the doctor's face, so he continued to explain. "You know, he didn't get up there by himself, he doesn't belong up there, he doesn't know what to do while he's up there . . . and you just wonder what kind of a dumb idiot put him up there."

Ha, ha, ha.

Editor's Notes: This online publication has also the following articles about Mr. Obama in its "Humor and Satire" Section:
Even if Ms. Clinton or Mr. McCain Wins the Election, Mr. Obama Can Still Be President
Top Ten Reasons Why Senator Obama Is a Foreign-Relations Expert

By the way, those *dyoks* were sent to me by Tom Bonzon, a fellow happy-go-lucky retiree and gardener, who lives in Virginia. He tells me he's also a fisherman, and I am sure at this time of the year, the fish there now are hungrily biting.

"DOG KNOWS BEST" JOKE: You know, I always save the best for last. The next one was sent to me by my tokayo, Jesse Farrales of Chicago, who is a fellow DOM and famously known in Chicagoland as the "Debonair." This one is titled, "Dogs Know Best." It's kind of a serious dyok, because it's true. I am not lying either, I swear. Here it is. Enjoy:

Have you ever heard that a dog "knows" when an earthquake is about to hit? Have you ever heard that a dog can "sense" when a tornado is stirring up, even 20 miles away?

Do you remember hearing that, before the December tsunami struck Southeast Asia, dogs started running frantically away from the seashore at breakneck speed? Do you know that dogs can detect cancer and other serious illnesses and danger of fire?

Somehow they always know when they can "go for a ride" before you even ask them. And, how do dogs get home from hundred of miles away? It's because dogs have keen insights into the "truth of the matter." They can sense a potentially terrible disaster well in advance.

Simply said, a dog knows when something isn't right. When a pending doom is upon us, they'll always try to warn us. . . . (There's picture right after this, and the picture is of a male dog with one leg lifted, peeing at a red, white and blue lawn poster that reads: OBAMA '08. With a bold caption underneath the photo that says, "Good dog!")

Ha, ha, ha. I wish I had the picture of the dog peeing at the Obama poster. That would've been funnier.

I READ THIS IN A BLOG AND I AGREE: "Obama will lose in November, and when he loses, Obama's people will say it's because this country is racist, when, in fact, Obama will lose because he's the weaker candidate. Obama is not qualified to become President. He has no grasp on the harsh realities of the world. He's ignorant on economics and foreign policy. He's arrogant and he feels as though he's somehow entitled to be elected to a job he's not qualified for. He had no business seeking the office in the first place with the thin resume he brings with him. He's also a FAR LEFT LEANING LIBERAL and his views do not reflect the thinking of the majority of Americans . . ."

True, very true, indeed, I could not have said that better. But dyoks are a lot clearer and lot more fun in delivering the message. *Kaya, mga katoto*, keep those Obama dyoks coming, let's get down and let's have some fun. Okey *ngarud*, talk to y'all later. **JJ**

Dis and Dat: On Russert, Hillary and Michelle O

First this: Last Wednesday, Tim Russert of NBC and MSNBC was laid to rest. May he rest in peace. And I am sorry that I've called him a "Mongoloid-looking moron, with a fat face" in my column.

But, you see, I didn't like the way he disrespected Senator Hillary Clinton when he had her as a guest on his "Meet the Press" talk show. He tried to make Ms. Hillary look bad. He was so unkind to her. It was so obvious that he favored Senator Obama's candidacy. I have a lot of respect for Ms. Hillary and I earnestly supported her candidacy. So when I saw this kind of treatment that Mr. Russert gave Ms. Hillary, I got so angry that when I wrote my column that week, I called him a "Mongoloid-looking moron, with a fat face" to spite him.

Yet, I felt bad when I heard of his sudden passing away last week. For indeed, he was a "giant" of a man and will be terribly missed by many of his fans, who watched his talk show on Sunday mornings, or the re-runs, late Sunday evenings.

Tim Russert was NOT a journalist! He was a pundit, a talk head, and very opinionated at that, like those two other MSNBC talk heads, Chris Matthews and that bespectacled guy with a German Jewish name . . . Olberman.

I usually watched the late evening re-runs of his show. You see, even though, I didn't like him, I still admired him. I admired his candor and bluntness and direct no-frills questionings . . . and the way he would give that quizzical STARE at the person he was interrogating. He was a lawyer, so he interrogated like a lawyer.

He was brutal, ruthless and merciless.

"He was really the best political journalist in America, not just the best television journalist in America," said Al Hunt, the Washington executive of Bloomberg News and former Washington bureau chief of the Wall Street Journal.

May I beg to differ? The best television journalist in America, I think, was the late Peter Jennings of ABC. And the best political journalist, whether print or broadcast, is Maureen Dowd, of the *New York Times*. Tim Russert was NOT a journalist! He was a pundit, a talk head, and very opinionated at that, like those two other MSNBC talk heads, Chris Matthews and that bespectacled guy with a German Jewish name . . . Olberman, I think is the way his name is spelled. These two are really obnoxious! Ya man, even more obnoxious than me. And much more obnoxious and opinionated than Mr. Tim Russert. Again, may this giant of a man in TV punditry rest in peace. And may I also say "thank you" for the many maddening, but stimulating late Sunday nights that I've spent watching his talk shows.

MS. HILLARY IS A WITCH? As y'll know, a lot of people have called Ms. Hillary a witch. Could that be true? I mean, a real witch, a witchy witch, who casts spells and magic on people and things. You know, there's a belief that if you've hurt or offended a witch, you'll have to pay for it. Now, I am only speculating. Don't take my word that Ms. Hillary is a witch.

But check this out:

. Iowa, the state that made Hillary "cry," so to speak. This state that voted overwhelmingly for Senator Barack HUSSEIN Obama, is now under water. Rising floodwaters inundated its cities and towns, creating widespread destruction. Last week, Iowa's nine rivers were above historic flood levels.

. Senator Ted Kennedy, who endorsed Mr. Obama at the most crucial time for Ms. Hillary . . . was found to have malignant brain cancer, a few weeks after that endorsement.

. Tim Russert, who made Ms. Hillary looked bad on his show, suddenly died of a heart attack.

As I said, these are just speculations. You witch hunters, don't y'all grab Ms. Hillary now and burn her on the stakes.

MICHELLE OBAMA IS FAIR GAME? Mrs. Obama said that America had gotten "downright mean." Now, facing a barrage of attacks, her husband's campaign is coming to grips with her new status as a target for attacks. "Leave my wife alone!" Mr. Obama angrily said.

Really, I don't think critics should leave her alone and treat her with kid's gloves. She's fair game. Picking on potential first ladies is nothing new.

In the early months of this presidential campaign, Judith Giuliani, the third wife of Rudy Giuliani, was the subject of merciless write-ups and profiles that depicted her as a "husband-stealing social climber."

In 1992, when Bill Clinton made his run for his second term presidency, Ms. Hillary was mocked, ridiculed and belittled when she said: "I suppose I could have stayed home and baked cookies and had teas, but what I decided to do was to fulfill my profession, which I entered before my husband was in public office." Conservative critics called her a "bitch" for that remark.

The conservative hate-mongers loved to hate Hillary Rodham Clinton. They loved to hate Teresa Heinz Kerry. Will they also love to hate Michelle Obama? They do already. For saying: "For the first time in my adult lifetime, I am really proud of my country . . ."
In 2004, when Senator John Kerry of Massachusetts ran against the incumbent President George "Dubya" Bush, his wife, Teresa Kerry became a target. She was attacked relentlessly by the media when she told a disrespectful reporter to "shove it." And when she said that Laura Bush had never held a "real job," the conservative media showed no mercy on her.

Even Fil-Am Republicans called her a "lukarit."

Yeah, the conservative hate-mongers loved to hate Hillary Rodham Clinton. They loved to hate Teresa Heinz Kerry. Will they also love to hate Michelle Obama? They do already. For saying: "For the first time in my adult lifetime, I am really proud of my country," they have already lashed out at her. Cable news shows played her words in an endless loop of outrage.

They have called her "Obama's Bitter Half" and "Mrs. Grievance." Fox News last week called her "Obama's Baby Mama," a slang term for an unwed mother. Recently, there are rumors about the "WHITEY" comments that she has made. Although said to be unsubstantiated, they have appeared on the Web repeatedly and the bloggers and hate-mongers have had a field day bedeviling her.

"There is dirt and lies that are circulated in e-mails, and they pump them out long enough until finally . . . a mainstream reporter, asks me about it," Barack Obama said. "That gives legs to the story. Frankly, my hope is people don't play this game."

Hey, Mr. Obama, welcome to the GAME of politics. As Bill Clinton said, "Politics is contact sports." And, as Ms. Hillary told ya before, "If you can't take the heat, get out of the kitchen."

The game had just begun, Mr. Barack HUSSEIN Obama. The Republican attack machine will soon be all over you and your darling, scowling wife, Michelle. Contrary to what your supporters say, she's no Jackie O. **JJ**

Getting to Know the Real Mrs. Cindy McCain

The political battle line has also been drawn between two ladies. Now that Barack HUSSEIN Obama is the Democrat's presumptive nominee for the race to the White House and John McCain is the GOP's, either Cindy McCain or Michelle Obama would be the next First Lady of America.

Who's your choice?

Michelle is a Princeton grad and a product of Harvard Law School. Pretty impressive, huh? Ivy Leaguer and all. She was a full-time scholar in both schools, paid for by the United States of America. YET in her senior year at Princeton, she wrote a thesis that stated that America is a nation founded on "crime and hatred" and that whites are "ineradicably racist" people.

Talking about being an ingrate.

She also said that there was "no doubt in her mind that as a member of the Black community, I am obligated to this community and will utilize all my present and FUTURE resources to benefit the Black community FIRST and FOREMOST."

The way I understand that is IF she becomes America's First Lady, we, who would be merely on the periphery, would just fight over the crumbs that fell on the wayside underneath the dining table.

That's what we know about Mrs. Michelle Obama. Of course, we also know about the staged "DAP" or the fist bump she and her husband gave each other, when Barack Obama clinched the Democratic nomination a couple of weeks ago.

Now, what do we know about Mrs. Cindy McCain?

The answer to that question was sent to me by Mrs. Becky Belbis of Palos Hills, Chicago. Becky is the bubbly, vivacious, curvaceous wife of my cuz, Manuel. And the reason I said, "curvaceous" is because Becky is a devotee of "Curves." Curves is a gym exclusively for women. My cuz said that ever since Becky started going to that gym. "it's been like embracing a different woman." I knew exactly what my cuz meant when he said that. My wife is also a devotee of Curves and the Air Climber. Me, I am a devotee of the living room couch.

Feminist critics who write her off as a 'stand-by-your-man" shrinking violet are selling her short . . . for Mrs. McCain more than meets the eye.

Enough tsismis . . . Let's go back to Mrs. Cindy McCain. This is what Becky sent me and I quote:

Yes, Mrs. McCain is the perfectly coifed blonde standing dutifully behind Senator McCain during his speeches. And yes, she wears stylish clothing and carries a Pravda purse. And it's true she doesn't say much. But feminist critics who write her off as a 'stand-by-your-man" shrinking violet are selling her short . . . for Mrs. McCain more than meets the eye.

While Obama's wife has been hating America, complaining about the war and undermining our troops serving in Iraq and Afghanistan, McCain's wife has been worrying about her sons who actually are fighting or planning to fight in the war on terror. One, in fact, was until a few months ago deployed in Iraq during some of the worst violence.

You don't hear the McCains talk about it, but their 19-year-old Marine, Jimmy, is preparing for his second tour of duty. Their 21-year-old son, Jack, is poised to graduate from Annapolis and also could join the Marines as a second lieutenant. The couple made the decision not to draw attention to their sons out of respect for other families with sons and daughters in harm's way.

Cindy also says she doesn't want to risk falling apart on the campaign trail talking about Jimmy who was so young when he enlisted she had to sign consent forms for his medical tests before he could report for duty and potentially upsetting parents of soldiers who are serving or have been killed.

The McCains want to make sure their boys get no special treatment. Same goes for their five other children, including a daughter they adopted from Bangladesh. During a visit to Mother Teresa's orphanage there, Cindy noticed a dying baby girl. The orphanage could not provide the medical care needed to save her life. So she brought the child home to America for surgery she desperately needed.

The baby is now their healthy, 16-year-old daughter, Bridget.

Though all seven McCain children, including two whom Senator McCain adopted during his first marriage are supportive of their father, they prefer their privacy to the glare of the campaign trail. Another daughter, Meghan, 23, helps him behind the scenes.

Cindy McCain not only cherishes her children, but also her country, which in an election year filled with America-bashing, is a refreshing novelty. She seethed when she heard Michelle Obama's UNPATRIOTIC remarks that she only recently grew proud of America. "I am very proud of my country," Mrs. McCain asserted.

Mrs. McCain also is a hands-on philanthropist. She sits on the board of "Operation Smile," which arranges for plastic surgeons to fix cleft palates and other birth defects. She also helped organize relief missions to Micronesia. During a scuba-diving vacation to the islands, Mrs. McCain took a friend to a local hospital to have a cut treated. She was shocked, and saddened, by what she saw.

"They opened the door to the OR, where the supplies were, and there were two cats and a whole bunch of rats climbing out of the sterile supplies," she recalled. "They had no X-ray machine, no beds. To me, it was devastating because it was a U.S. Trust Territory."

As soon as she returned home, she arranged for medical equipment and teams of doctors to be sent to treat the island children.

Michelle may contribute to CARE, which fights global poverty and works to empower poor women. Mrs. Cindy McCain sits on its board . . . Unquote.

Cindy McCain is also a former rodeo queen and cheerleader, with a master's degree in special education from the University of Southern California. She's the heiress to a wealthy family in Phoenix, Arizona, to Hensley and Co., one of the largest distributors for the brewing giant, Anheuser-Busch. One of her passions is travelling the globe, doing world-wide charitable work.

Yes, that silent, perfectly-coifed blonde standing behind Senator John McCain during his speeches would make a fine First Lady, don't y'all think? Yes, indeed, absolutely, I think so, too. **JJ**

Senator Obama: "I am now the man . . . this is my moment, my time"

Finally, it's over. At long last, Barack HUSSEIN Obama is now the presumptive Democratic nominee for President, who would be going against Senator John McCain in the November presidential general election. It's a history-making event they said, because Mr. Obama is the first African American to head a major-party ticket and the nominee for President of the United States.

Yikes!

It's been a hard fought nominating battle for both Mr. Obama and Ms. Hillary. Looking back, there are many "could haves" and "should haves" and questions of "why."

For instance: I don't want to sound like a sour grape but Ms. Hillary SHOULD and COULD HAVE won the nomination, if only EACH of the delegate count in Florida and Michigan votes were counted fully as one full count, NOT half a count each!

Editor's Notes: Jesse Jose is a retired US Navy chief journalist and a former deputy sheriff in Florida. He has written for several military and civilian publications, including the "Pacific Star and Stripes", "Navy Times", "All Hands", and other AP/UPI-oriented civilian newspapers all over the country.While in the Navy, he won three Chief of Information (CHINFO) Merit Awards for writing and the Thomas Jefferson Award for a photo feature and investigative reporting. He lives in Seattle, Washington.

Also, WHY were the "uncommitted" delegates in Michigan given as delegate count to Mr. Obama when his name was not even on the ballot?

At first, the Obama camp kept harping that the delegates count in Michigan should NOT be counted because Obama's name was not on the ballot.

But after the committee of dunces of the National Democratic Party decided that the delegates count could be counted, the "uncommitted" votes were given to Obama, plus four more that they took away from Ms. Hillary. When this happened, nobody from the Obama camp or from the boot-licking, lapping, biased media said a word, silently acquiescing to the blatant unfairness of the decision.

And, that, did Hillary in!

So, at a rally last Tuesday night in St. Paul, Minnesota that many people said, "looks more like a revival than a rally," Sen. Obama orated before a chanting, cheering and worshipping audience: "Tonight we mark the end of one historic journey with the beginning of another—a journey that will bring a new and better day to America . . . This is our moment. This is our time. Our time to turn the page on the policies of the past. . . ."

Yikes!

I watched all this unfold on CNN, sitting in my living room next to my wife.

"*Parang si* Martin Luther King *kung magsalita 'to*," I said to her.

"*Ganyan ang style ng mga itim*," she answered. "Orate *ng* orate.

"*Kanino naman kaya kinopya 'yun* speech *na 'yun*?" I asked.

"*Baka kay* Jesse Jose," my wife said. "*O, ilipat mo na sa soap ko, kay Piolo Pascual, yung 'Lobo.' Malapit ng matapos yun.*"

My wife is a registered Democrat, but she said that she's not going to vote for Obama. "I don't trust him," she said. "*Iboboto ko si* McCain. And it's not because Obama is black. But because of his inexperience. He's got nothing to show for. What has he done for this country? What has he accomplished? What is he compared to McCain?"

I think a lot of Americans feel the same as my wife, whether they're Democrats or Republicans . . . and that includes me.

In his speech that evening, Obama had some kind words for Ms. Hillary. "She has made history not just because she's a woman who has done what no woman has done before," he said. "But because she is a leader who inspires millions of Americans with her strength, courage and her commitment to the causes that brought us here to night."

When I heard that, I wanted to laugh, because I don't think Mr. Barack HUSSEIN Obama felt that way. I bet ya, Obama said to himself: "Finally, I slammed this tenacious bitch off my back . . . I am now THE man. I am free at last. At long last, indeed, I am now the man, the first Black Man, who can rule White America. Allah is great! Pastor Wright was right!"

Yikes!

Ya, I am a bigot. But I am no hypocrite though.

"I want the nearly 18-million Americans who voted for me to be respected, to be heard and no longer to be invisible"—Senator Hillary Clinton

It might look finally over, but Mr. Obama still faces a daunting task of uniting the Democrat Party. Ms. Hillary said she'll helped Obama, but she said this: "You know, I understand that a lot of people are asking, 'What does Hillary want? What does she want?'"

She then enumerated a list that included "ending the Iraq War," and "improving the economy" and "providing universal health care to all Americans." Then in pointedly clear words unmistakably directed at

Obama, she added, "I want the nearly 18-million Americans who voted for me to be respected, to be heard and no longer to be invisible."

Mighty words. Is Ms. Hillary asking Obama for half of the spoils? Perhaps, the VEEP position?

DREAM TEAM: While there's a lot of drama, suspense and excitement in electing either the FIRST BLACK or the FIRST FEMALE president, combining both Obama and Hillary into the so-called DREAM TEAM, might be too much of a CHANGE for the electorates of America to handle.

"Besides," wrote Nicholas Von Hoffman in the *Toronto Star*, "would a President Obama really feel comfortable with two power-hungry Clintons pacing the halls of the vice president's mansion? At a bare minimum, he would have to insist that Chelsea Clinton be installed in the White House as his official taster."

Hey, why not install Mr. Obama's favorite 20-year pastor, Reverend Jeremiah Wright, instead? Or perhaps, so as the White House wouldn't look too black in the Obama Administration, Rev. Michael Pfleger? You know, that white pastor, who was a guest at Obama's church recently and mocked Ms. Hillary while the church's all-Black congregation clapped and cheered and jumped like monkeys to edge him on.

Kadiri to death *naman*. That calls for three yikes. Yikes! Yikes! Yikes! **JJ**

Barack Obama:
the Joker, the Flip-flopper and the Liar

Obama, the joker . . . At a rally in Maryland, packed with Obambis, Senator Barack Obama said that Hillary Clinton says he's not tough enough to take on the Republican attack machine.

"I have to explain to people, I am skinny but I am tough," he recited. "Yes, skinny, I am wily. Don't mess with me. Let's bring it on. Who they get? John McCain?"

Then so as to draw attention to Senator McCain's age, Obama added, "Listen, I respect John McCain for his half-century of service to this country. But he is on the wrong side of history now."

As if on cue, clapping, hooting, laughing came thundering from the crowd.

They loved him. They worshipped him. They responded to his jokes outrageously.

They chanted: "Obama! Obama! More jokes! More jokes!" Obama, the joker, indeed.

"Having lashed himself to the ridiculous, unprecedented promise of unconditional presidential negotiations—and then having compounded the problem by elevating it to a principle—Obama keeps trying to explain," *Washington Post* Columnist Charles Krauthammer wrote in his column this week. **Obama, the flip-flopper . . .**

At a July debate 2007 debate . . . Mr. Obama was asked: "Would you be willing to meet separately, without preconditions, during the first year of your administration, in Washington or anywhere else, with the leaders of Iran, North Korea, Syria, Venezuela, Cuba in order to bridge the gap that divides our countries?

Obama answered: "I would. And the reason is this, that the notion that somehow not talking to countries is punishment to them—which has been the guiding diplomatic principle of this administration—is ridiculous."

In a September 2007 press conference . . . Mr. Obama was asked again if he would meet specifically with President Ahmadinejad (pronounced Ah-Mad-In-The-Head).

Mr. Obama said: "Yeah, nothing's changed with respect to my belief that strong countries and strong presidents talk to their enemies and talk to their adversaries. I find many of President Ahmadinejad's statements odious and I've said that repeatedly. And I think that we have to recognize that there are a lot of rogue nations in the world that don't have American interests at heart . . . blah, blah, blah . . ."

In December 2007 . . . Mr. Obama said he was not afraid "of losing a propaganda war" by reaching out to leaders of rogue nations. "Strong countries and strong leaders," he proclaimed, "speak with their adversaries. I always think back to JFK's saying that we should never negotiate out of fear, but we shouldn't fear to negotiate . . . blah, blah, blah . . ."

This month . . . on MSNBC's "Meet The Press," moderated by that boot-licking, Mongoloid-looking host, named Tim Russertt, Mr. Obama said: "I have consistently said that we've got to talk DIRECTLY to Iran, send them a clear message that they have to stop, not only with their potential funding of militias inside of Iraq, but they also have to stop funding Hamas, they have to stop funding Hezbollah, they've got to stand down on their nuclear weapons . . . blah, blah, blah . . ."

This week . . . he took back all his words and said he would NOT necessarily meet with Ahmadinejad. As quoted in a news report by Reuters, these are Mr. Obama's exact words:

"There's NO reason why we would necessarily meet with Ahmadinejad before we know he's actually in power. He's not the most powerful person in Iran . . ."

Say what now, Barack? You pulling our leg, again? Or, you're just full of IT? Or, is that a new dance step that you're dancing now? Dance, Barack, dance!

"Having lashed himself to the ridiculous, unprecedented promise of unconditional presidential negotiations—and then having compounded the problem by elevating it to a principle—Obama keeps trying to explain," *Washington Post* Columnist Charles Krauthammer wrote in his column this week. "On Sunday, he declared in Pendleton., Ore., that by Soviet standards, Iran and others 'don't pose a serous threat to us.' The next day in Billings, Mont., he said: 'I've made it clear for years that the threat from Iran is grave.'" Obama, the flip-flopper, indeed.

In Barako lingo, "metastatic gaffe" is defined as a lie that begets another lie, that begets another, until it becomes a clusterf . . . k of lies, ala-Bush. Obama, the liar, indeed.

Obama, the liar . . .

In his many debates with Ms. Hillary, Obama points to Ms. Hillary as having supported the Iraq war by voting in favor of a resolution to invade Iraq, and he didn't. The impression that one gets is that he has voted against the Iraq resolution.

Never once did he mention that he had not voted against the resolution. How could he? He was NOT even a U.S. Senator when the resolution was passed!

True, he has spoken about it as an Illinois senator in 2002. And, he said in 2003, that he would "unequivocally" oppose the $87-billion war funding being considered at that time. Yet, as soon as he got elected to the U.S. Senate in 2004, he had supported every funding bill for Iraq to the tune of $300-billion.

Also, he has not followed through on his opposition to the war. Until January 2007, when he started campaigning for President, he has not sponsored a single legislation to end the war or to bring the troops home.

In fact, in June 2006, he voted against Senator John Kerry's proposal to remove most troops from IraqU.S. mistakes there." within a year calling it an "arbitrary deadline" that could "compound previous

As Mr. Krauthammer of the *Washington Post* said, his rhetoric has given rise to a "new political phenomenom," called, "the metastatic gaffe: the one that begets another, begets another, begets. . . ."

In Barako lingo, "metastatic gaffe" is defined as a lie that begets another lie, that begets another, until it becomes a clusterf . . . k of lies, ala-Bush. Obama, the liar, indeed. **JJ**

On Hillary Winning Kentucky, Sen. Ted Kennedy and Astrology

Obama's inexperience does more than irritate me, it frightens me. The job of the U.S. President is not an entry-level position . . .—Shannon de Rubens, a Hillary Clinton supporter

So, where are we? Y'all know what happened in Kentucky this week, right? Once again, Ms. Hillary clobbered Mr. Obama. She scored a 35-point win there after trashing Obama by 41-point margin in West Virginia last week.

So okay, Senator Obama won Oregon. One for her and one for him. That split decision left Mr. Obama with 1,949 delegates overall, out of 2,026 he needed to secure the nomination. Ms. Hillary had 1,769.

Three contests remain: on June 1st in Puerto Rico, which has 55 delegates. Then two days later on June 3rd, in Montana, with 16 delegates and in South Dakota, with 15 . . . a total of 86 delegates.

But there ain't no way, Mr. Obama CAN win enough of these delegates to clinch the nomination because of the proportional way which Democrats award delegates.

If they count the delegates in Florida and Michigan, two states that Ms. Hillary clearly won, then she would come out as the winner.

So, where are we? If they count the delegates in Florida and Michigan, two states that Ms. Hillary clearly won, then she would come out as the winner. But will they count the votes from these two states? We'll find out on May 31st.

They should count those votes! They must count those votes! Sure, these two states violated the rules by holding their primaries early . . . but all votes must be counted, no matter what! In a campaign stop in Boca Raton, Florida, Ms. Hillary said:

"Now, I've heard some say that counting Florida and Michigan would be changing the rules. I say that NOT counting Florida and Michigan is changing a central governing rule of this country—that whenever we can understand the clear intent of the voters, their votes should be counted."

I agree. All of America should be heard.

Majority of Americans have voted and the majority voted for Ms. Hillary. Senator Obama merely won the caucuses, which are not the correct representation of the will of the voters. Senator Hillary has won fair and square most of the primaries, all the big states and all the swing states and the battleground states. She has received the most votes. It's simple as that. Also, the superdelegates should listen hard to this:

"The states I've won total 300 electoral votes. If we had the same rules as the Republicans, I would be nominee right now," said Ms. Hillary. "We have different rules, so what we've got to figure out is who can win 270 electoral votes. My opponent has won states totaling 217 electoral votes."

Keep talking, Ms. Hillary. Keep fighting. There are multitudes of us out here, who are behind you. As long as you're in, we gonna be fighting with you. This fight is not over 'til the fat lady sings.

ON SEN. EDWARD KENNEDY: So, it's a cancerous brain tumor that had caused the seizure of Senator Kennedy. See what happens when you endorse Mr. Obama? Just kidding. That's a bad joke.

When I getting my wife and my two boys to the U.S. and the immigration people were "dilly-dallying" on their return, I wrote Senator Kennedy a letter. He responded quickly. He said he'll look into the matter. Sure enough, not long after that, my family was here with me.

I like Ted Kennedy. I like the Kennedys. They have done a lot of good things for this country, this great country that I have adopted and learned to love. I think Ted Kennedy is one of America's most-enduring-and-endearing political figures.

When I was trying to get my wife and my two boys back here to the U.S. and the immigration people were "dilly-dallying" on their return, I wrote Senator Kennedy a letter. He responded quickly. He said he'll look into the matter. Sure enough, not long after that, my family was here with me.

I like his stand on immigration, health care, labor law, Vietnam, Iraq, and campaign finance and ethics laws. I consider him a LION, who roars his liberal views, without fear. I admire Sen. Ted Kennedy. I admire the Kennedy family. And I especially admire President John F. Kennedy and his Camelot-like administration. It was the best of times in America.

Ted Kennedy is the last son from his generation of a famed political family. When his older brother, John F. Kennedy won the presidency in 1960, Ted Kennedy stepped into his Senate seat and has held that seat ever since.

It was said that the Kennedys is a "cursed" family. The eldest son, Joseph, a bomber pilot and the one who was really being "groomed" to become president by the Kennedy patriarch, was killed in World War II airplane crash. Then John was assassinated in Dallas in 1963. Five years later, in 1968, Robert was also assassinated in California while campaigning for President.

Because Sen. Ted Kennedy has somehow touched my life, I fervently hope that the prognosis of "malignant brain tumor" is not as ominous as it sounds. He'll be in my prayers.

All seven seers shared a "sense of foreboding" and agreed that Mr. Obama's "chances of actually taking office is kind of funky."

ASTROLOGY & PREDICTIONS: At the United Astrology Conference this week in Denver, Colorado, attended by hundreds of devotees from 44 countries, its seven top forecasters predicted that Mr. Obama will defeat Sen. John McCain and win the presidential general election.

But all seven also shared a "sense of foreboding" and agreed that Mr. Obama's "chances of actually taking office is kind of funky." And that the stars looked "dicey" in this report.

"There are things that are going to happen in the next couple of months that could turn into something different than we think it is right now," said Shelley Ackerman, a well-known New York City astrologer, who is a frequent guest on TV and radio shows.

Also, they said that "in the year 2009, President Hillary Clinton will change her mind about abortion and become pro life." Not only that. "In the year 2010, after Hillary's election, as prophesied in the Torah, the Bible and the Quran, as well as Nostradamus, World War III will erupt against the Arab Nation."

In their predictions, Hillary's and Obama's names were mentioned as prez. So, who's gonna be IT? I think it's all phooey. What do y'all think? **JJ**

Ha, ha, ha, Hillary Clobbers Obama in West Virginia

He (Obama) has sown doubts about his ability to win white, working-class votes.—David S. Broder, Washington Post

How sweet, how deliciously sweet . . . Those CNN, MSNBC and NBC talk heads and precocious *kuno* print pundits and Democratic Party leaders were ALL wrong about Hillary. They counted her out and they were proved wrong.

Very wrong!

Their constant whining about Hillary needing to get out of the race and allow B. HUSSEIN Obama to move on is not only insulting, to say the least, but also a momentous stupidity.

If Obama were such a strong candidate, he would have ALREADY won the 2,026 delegates he needs to be declared the winner. He would have reached that number ALREADY long before now, especially with the large amount of money he has spent on this campaign.

But he has not. He's still floundering.

On the other hand, burdened by debt and under heavy, relentless pressure to quit, Ms. Hillary YET scored another resounding victory, this time last Tuesday in West Virginia. And surely that cast doubt on whether Mr. Obama—for all his millions of dollars raised, pledged delegates won and winning momentum—is ELECTABLE in the November general election.

"The bottom line is this: The White House is won in the swing states, and I am winning in the swing states," Hillary told a celebrating crowd in West Virginia. "I am more determined than ever to carry on this campaign. . . ."

Go for it, Ms. Hillary.

I am with you all the way, and millions of others out there, too. You're the candidate who speaks to our hearts, our intellect and our souls. To us, you're the leader of leaders and the BETTER candidate than Mr. Obama.

We have seen your dignity, your strength of character, your PRIDE in America and your confidence in us as a people. We have seen your ability to rise above the rhetoric of politics.

Most of all, we have seen your GRIT as a fighter and that brought out the fighter in us, too . . . instilling in us the belief that we can do better, and we will!

Ms. Hillary has won the swing states, the big states and the battleground states, like New York, Pennsylvania, Ohio and California—and of course, Michigan and Florida.

MATHEMATICALLY IMPOSSIBLE: It's been said over and over that mathematically speaking Ms. Hillary has lost and that Mr. Obama is now the Democrat presumptive nominee. As I write this, Mr. Obama has 1,887 delegates to Ms. Hillary's 1,718. To clinch the nomination, 2,026 is needed.

Mr. Obama has also now surpassed Ms. Hillary in the superdelegates count and slowly but surely, more are jumping to Obama's side. The latest superdelegates count is 267 for Obama and 256 for Ms. Hillary. About 253 are still uncommitted.

But beyond that there's another math that we should also look into. Ms. Hillary has won the swing states, the big states and the battleground states, like New York, Pennsylvania, Ohio and California.

According to national polls, IF Ms. Hillary becomes the nominee, this would be the math of the electoral votes in the general election this November: Clinton, 280. McCain, 258. If Mr. Obama becomes the nominee: Obama, 254. Mccain, 273. **Conclusion:** Clinton beats McCain; McCain beats Obama.

Also, the African-Americans who clearly support Senator Obama ONLY makeup 11% of the general election voting population. And, women who make up the majority of Mrs. Clinton supporters are within the 55% of the voting population. And white men who support Mrs. Clinton make up the 45%.

If y'all wanna talk about math . . . that's THE math, the OTHER math, that many have chosen to ignore. In this math, if Mr. Obama goes against Mr. McCain, Obama loses. If Ms. Hillary runs against Mr. McCain, Ms. Hillary wins. That's also the math the superdelegates of the Democrat Party, who will name the nominee, will have to think hard about.

EDWARDS ENDORSES OBAMA: A day after Ms. Hillary routed Mr. Obama in West Virginia, John Edwards, the former North Carolina senator, the man who claims to champion the poor and sports a $400 haircut, endorsed Mr. Obama.

So, one loser endorses another loser. Who cares?

Former Senator Edwards said that Mr. Obama has NOT been around "long enough" to have much of a political track record of credibility.

Or shall I say, one pretty boy endorses another pretty boy. And what does this white pretty boy want from the black pretty boy? The VP slot perhaps? According to news reports, in January, Mr. Edwards said he would not accept a vice-presidential post or a Cabinet position from Mr. Obama. "No, absolutely not," he said. But PRIVATELY, he told friends he would consider the role of VP . . . or perhaps, the position of Attorney General. Hmmm. . . .

When he was still campaigning as a presidential candidate, Mr. Edwards had criticized Senator Obama for "voting ABSENT" 100 times while serving in the Illinois Legislature" and for "taking money from political action committees." He also said that Mr. Obama has NOT been around "long enough" to have much of a political track record of credibility.

But last Wednesday, the two PRETTY BOYS were both lovey-dovey to each other. They hugged and kissed and exchanged kind words to each other. Mr. Edwards said Senator Obama "stands with me" in championing for the poor and in "cutting poverty in half within 10 years. . . ."

Yeah, right. The man who vows to cut poverty in half pays $400 for a haircut. Hmmm. . . . I wonder how much Mr. Obama pays for his? And how much does he give for tips to his lady hairdresser?

Does he call her "sweetie," too?

Hmmm. . . . How sweet *naman*. **JJ**

Hillary Clinton:
"The race to the White House goes on"

"I am staying in this race until there's a nominee. I'm going to work hard as I can to become that nominee.—Ms. Hillary Clinton

Here are other "Quotable Quotes," as heard on the campaign television coverage:

> "***I don't think he's*** (B. HUSSEIN Obama)
>
> ***qualified and when the cream comes to the***
>
> ***surface . . . if he's elected President, I think***
>
> ***he's going to be a disappointment.***"—A North Carolina voter
>
> "***I can't stand him. He's a Muslim. He's***
>
> ***not even pro-American as far I am***
>
> ***concerned.***"—An Indiana voter

First, the good news. A very exciting good news that I wanna share with y'all. It's about my son, Chris. Well, perhaps to others, it won't be that good of a news. To them, I say: Hey, eat your BITTER, sour hearts out! Yes, indeed, I've got something to brag about my son . . . again.

Again? Yes, again.

This time, Chris, a reporter/weekend anchor for CBS 5 (KGWN) in Cheyenne, Wyoming has won first place this year's "BEST ANCHOR" award, given by the Wyoming Association of Broadcasters. Last year, if I may say so, he won two awards: one for "Best News" . . . and the other, for "Best Breaking News." KGWN covers Southeast Wyoming, Northern Colorado and the Nebraska Panhandle.

Editor's Note: To read more on Chris Jose's awards, please go to Jesse's Son Wins Wyoming Broadcasters' Awards

For those doubters, to see is to believe, right? Punch in www.kgwn.tv on your screen, and then click on the slot that reads "meet the team." To see him report, punch some of the videos that he had reported. To see him anchor, punch the videos on late Saturday and Sunday evenings, and Monday mornings. Enjoy his movie star good looks. Like father, like son. But, my wife said: "*Kamukha ko yata 'yan.*" My wife is right. *Buti na lang.*

IT'S ABOUT RACE: Okey *ngarud*, that's enough *yabang*. Let's go back to the race between Ms. Hillary and Mr. Obama. So, Mr. Obama won a resounding victory in North Carolina on Tuesday and ran closely behind Ms. Hillary in Indiana.

And who said this race to the White House is not about RACE? It stinks to high heavens of racial conflict between Black and White.

Just like in South Carolina, Georgia, Alabama, Louisiana and all those southern states heavily populated by Blacks, Mr. Obama's performance in North Carolina was, once again, bolstered by a strong Black vote! He garnered over 90% of those voters in that state, where Blacks accounted for one in three voters.

Ms. Hillary continued to draw her strongest support from Whites, working class whites, that is, and women . . . and old farts, like me. In Indiana, according to The New York Times, about 8 in 10 voters were white and just over 1 in 10 were black. Six in 10 of the whites voted for Mrs. Clinton, while 9 in 10 blacks favored Mr. Obama. And about

I in 10 whites said RACE was a factor in their vote and they voted overwhelmingly for her

As one Obama supporter said: "People, if they have a prejudice—no matter what it is, whether it's religious, racial or whatever—are going to use them to justify NOT voting for him."
Days before the primaries in North Carolina and Indiana, the Obambis voiced concern that Reverend Wright's blasphemous curses and comments on America, would damage Mr. Obama's chances. As one Obama supporter said: "People, if they have a prejudice—no matter what it is, whether it's religious, racial or whatever—are going to use them to justify NOT voting for him."

Tit for tat! Lo and behold! Same thing goes with Senator Hillary!

Right after all the primary votes started coming in North Carolina, the OBAMBIS gleefully announced: "***Dingdong! The witch is dead! The wicked witch is dead! Let's sing a song! The wicked witch is dead!***" And so they did. They gloated and sang their songs with glee.

On CNN, where I watched the election results, all the BLACK news analyst *KUNO*, commentators, contributors all wore a toothy smile. Then, when the Indiana result came in later in the evening, their toothy, happy smile changed into toothy, dumpy snarl.

It's funny, I think, how those so-called mainstream broadcast journalists or whatever you call them, show their bias and blatant dislike for Hillary Clinton. It's laughable how their eyes bugged out and their mouths turned motor-like whenever Senator Obama is put in a bad light. It's so hilarious to watch them get on, how their mouths rat-tat-tat overtime, especially that time when Ms. Hillary won Pennsylvannia. Ron Allen and Jamal something and Brazille whatever her last name was . . . were hot and on the warpath. Now, they jump and whoop with joy.

Senator Obama's 20-year association with Reverend Wright calls into question his MORAL COURAGE and TRUTHFULNESS. At first he refused to denounce him, but when he was pressured, he denounced him and said he was "appalled" by his words.

ON BIGOTRY: Leonard Pitts, Jr., a syndicated columnist of *The Miami Herald*, said in his recent column: "***If you condemn bigotry when it is turned against people like you, but tolerate it when people like you turn it against someone else, you forfeit all claim to the moral high ground. You are a HYPOCRITE acting only from narrow self-interest.***" Mr. Pitts, by the way, is Black.

Call me a bigot. I don't like Mr. Obama.

Because to me, his 20-year association with Reverend Wright calls into question his MORAL COURAGE and TRUTHFULNESS. At first he refused to denounce him, but when he was pressured, he denounced him and said he was "appalled" by his words. We heard different versions as to when he knew him and what he knew about him. It also calls into question Mr. Obama's JUDGMENT in calling Mr. Wright, his pastor, mentor, friend and uncle. This uncle was his "inspiration" for his book, "Audacity of Hope."

To me, Barack HUSSEIN Obama is the creation of Rev. Jeremiah Wright. And I trust neither of them. One is the other. A replica of the other. Mr. Obama once said: "***I can no more disown him (Wright) than I can disown my white grandmother***." But for political reason, he was able to. That's scary. A man like that is untrustworthy.

For America's sake, Ms. Hillary must fight on. She must learn now how to walk on water. And I believe she will. JFK was in the same situation in 1960. He fought on and won. Like him, she will. Yes, she will! **JJ**

Hai Naku, Talo na si Obama

It's a done deal.

Talo na si Barack HUSSEIN Obama.

He can now go back to Kenya.

That above three lines there, by the way, is called Haiku, a Japanese method of writing a poem and telling a complete story. A Haiku to be called a Haiku must have a beginning, a body and an ending, and a moral message. And that one there, I think, has all the characteristics of the ultimate Haiku.

Do you agree? You don't have to.

Do you agree though with Bob Herbert of the *New York Times* when he said this? "For Senator Obama, the re-emergence of Rev. Wright has been devastating. The senator has been trying desperately to bolster his standing with skeptical and even hostile white working-class voters. When the story line of the campaign shifts almost entirely to the race-in-your-face antics of someone like Mr. Wright, Mr. Obama's chances can only suffer.

"Beyond that, the apparent helplessness of the Obama campaign in the face of the Wright onslaught contributes to the growing concern of the candidate as WEAK, as someone who is unwilling or unable to fight aggressively on his own behalf . . ."

Right on. As Ms. Hillary said, "Yo, Barack! If you can't stand the heat, get out of the kitchen!" Or, as Bill, the Big Dog, would say, "Politics is contact sports."

If he can't fight his own WACKO pastor, who seems to be out to destroy his chances to be president of the United States, how can he, B. HUSSEIN Obama, if he becomes president, fight those other WACKOS overseas who are out to destroy America, like Kim Jong, "the Ill" of North Korea and "Ah-mad-in-the-head" of Iran . . . and that awful man, with the awful-looking beard, who wears a rag on his head, named Osama Bin Laden, and whose first name sounds like Barack HUSSEIN Obama's last name.

Obama, Osama . . . Osama, Obama, ain't that almost like, as Erap used to say, "SAME-SAME"? I know I repeat myself, too. But, what da heck, nobody is perfect. I know, too, that Mr. Barack HUSSEIN Obama is NOT a Muslim, but with a middle name, like HUSSEIN, it's kind of hard to believe that he's not. Also, the name, Barack, is a Muslim name, which means, "blessed." And no matter how blessed the man is, I still don't think I would want a man named, Barack HUSSEIN Obama, to be the president of the United States of America.

For one thing . . . America, not God Damn America, but God Bless America, would the laughing stock of the world. The other thing, which is the most important thing, is that Mr. Obama ain't capable to be president. He ain't got the EXPERIENCE, and we're finding out that he's also a WEAK man.

Not only that. After the primaries in Pennsylvania, though very little has changed in the superdelegate count, a number of those delegates have expressed concern over Mr. Obama's INABILITY to do well among blue collar working-class voters, Catholics and women."

Those voters would be the ones who would do the bidding as to who would be the next president. In other words the UNELECTABILITY of Mr. Obama in the general election in November has now been exposed.

Also, the BIG states, the BATTLEGROUND states, like California, Texas, Ohio, Michigan, Florida and New York have been won by Ms Hillary. These states would be calling the shots for Hillary in the general election.

True, Mr. Obama has won more states than Ms. Hillary, but they're only the little, bitty states, like Rhode Island and such. And most of the wins by Obama were the caucuses, which are undemocratic and error-prone in its process, so it's NOT really the true reflection of the voters. For instance here in my state of Washington, 10 per cent ONLY of Washington's registered voters participated in our caucuses. If that's the case, what's the thinking of the silent 90 percent?

My wife and I went to our neighborhood caucus. I wrote about it in one of my past columns, and had described it as a total clusterf-k!

And true, Mr. Obama has won more popular votes than Ms. Hillary and he has garnered more pledged delegates than Ms. Hillary, BUT Ms. Hillary has more SUPERDELEGATES under her belt than Mr. Obama . . . and the rule is: The superdelegates (consisting of 800 or so party officials and elected lawmakers that belong to the party) name the nominee!

If only the mainstream media has been more forthright and more openly honest in coming out right away with Mr. Obama's wacko 20-year PASTOR and MENTOR, godamming America and blaming America for all the woes of the African-Americans, the AIDS and all, and 9/11 as America's "chickens coming home to roost," and America as not the great, noble USA, but the "USKKKA," the voters of America, I am sure, would not have taken a second look at Mr. Obama.

If only America knew Mr. Obama's true relationship with Tony Rezko, that Chicago crook, who helped him his buy his VERY expensive house . . .

If only America knew his close association with Bill Ayers, the founder of the Weather Underground network . . .

If only America knew his wife, Michelle's "SEPARATIONIST" view and intellectually-refined racism that she practiced during her college days at Princeton and advocated in her college thesis . . .

If only America knew and saw the photos of him with his arms crossed while the national anthem is played or the Pledge of Allegiance is recited . . .

If only America knew that he PLAGIARIZES his speeches . . .

If only the media had been more responsible and had exposed Mr. Obama earlier for what he is, he would never have won any states at all! We were deceived! We were had! We were gypped! But no more. He's been exposed.

So, in Japanese Haiku:

It's a done deal.

Talo na si Barack HUSSEIN Obama.

He can now go back to Kenya.

In the Filipino vernacular: Hay naku. **JJ**

Bitter you, Bitter me and the Bitterness of Michelle Obama (Now a Nasty Debate Among FilAms in IL)

So, are you bitter? According to B. HUSSEIN Obama, those people who live in "small towns" and who "cling to guns and religion" are "bitter" people.

(**NEWS FLASH!** The writings of Jesse Jose about Sen. Barack H. Obama have created a tempest among Filipino Americans in Chicagoland. Some of the online-debate participants have e-mailed what one community leader termed as "garbage posting." Some of the postings are reproduced in the "Users' Comments" portion of this article.)

While discussing blue-collar workers at a San Francisco fundraiser, Mr. Obama said: "You go into these small towns in Pennsylvania and . . . the jobs have been gone for 25 by years and nothing's replaced them. And it's not surprising then; they get BITTER, they cling to guns or religion or antipathy to people who aren't like them or anti-immigrant sentiment as a way to explain their frustration."

Hey, Mr. Barack HUSSEIN Obama, sir, with all due respect, I live in a small old town, too, here in Auburn, Washington, and many have also lost their jobs. But I don't see them sulking and moping around . . . looking BITTER.

Nor do I see them bash immigrants around or show antipathy to me, who look different from them. In fact, this town is a welcoming town.

As Ms. Hillary said, you, Mr. B. HUSSEIN Obama don't really get it that we, the people from small towns, "cling to religion" because we "value" our faith. And we "cling to guns" because many of us "enjoy hunting or collecting or sport shooting."
I don't know if my neighbors own guns, but I own two handguns, a revolver and a semi-automatic, and a shotgun, remnants of the "tools of my trade" as a cop, and I go to the shooting range now and then to blast away at targets . . . and I don't think I am BITTER because of that. I shoot, simply, because, I enjoy, shooting at targets.

And, I go to church every Sunday and on days of "obligations" for Catholics. I am a member of Knights of Columbus. I sing with the church's choir during special holidays masses. I am an usher. I am a lector. And I don't think I am BITTER, because of those things that I do for my church and God!

As Ms. Hillary said, you, Mr. B. HUSSEIN Obama don't really get it that we, the people from small towns, "cling to religion" because we "value" our faith. And we "cling to guns" because many of us "enjoy hunting or collecting or sport shooting." And our choice for a President is someone who "stands up" for us and not someone who "looks down" on us.

THE BITTERNESS OF MICHELLE OBAMA: This was sent to me by Tom Bonzon, a reader of my column and a recent cyberspace friend from Virginia, with a note that reads: "She is just as bad as her pastor." That pastor, as y'all know is Rev, Jeremiah Wright. Tom told me that this piece appeared in the Newark, New Jersey community newspaper, "The Star Ledger," written by Kelly Heyboer. It was titled, "Thesis—Michelle Obama aka Michelle LaVaughn Robinson."

"In her senior year at Princeton, Michelle Obama, the wife of Barack Obama stated that America was a nation founded on **'crime and hatred.'** Moreover, she stated that whites were **'ineradicably racist.'** The 1985 thesis, titled, 'Princeton-Educated Blacks and the Black Community' was written under her maiden name, Michelle LaVaughn Robinson.

"Michelle Obama stated in her thesis that to **'Whites at Princeton, it often seems as it, to them, she will always be Black first . . .'** However, it was reported by a fellow Black classmate, 'If those Whites at Princeton really saw Michelle as one who would always be Black first, it seems that she gave them that impression.'

"Most alarming is Michelle Obama's use of the terms 'separationist' and 'integrationist' when describing the views of Black people. Mrs. Obama clearly identifies herself with a 'separationist' view of race. She wrote: **'By actually working with the Black lower class or within their communities as a result of their ideologies, a separationist may better understand the desperation of their situation and feel more hopeless about a resolution as opposed to an integrationist who is ignorant to their plight.'**

"Mrs. Obama writes that the path she chose by attending Princeton would likely lead to her **'further integration and/or assimilation into a white cultural and social structure that will allow only me to remain on the periphery of society; never becoming a full participant.'**

"Michelle Obama clearly has a chip on her shoulder.

"Not only does she see separate black and white societies in America, but she elevates Black over White in her world.

Editor's Note: There is a joke going around in Southern California that OBAMA is the acronym for "Only Black Americans May Apply."

"Here is another passage that is uncomfortable and ominous in meaning: **'There was no doubt in my mind that as a member of the black community, I am obligated to this community and will utilize all my present and FUTURE resources to benefit the Black community *FIRST* and *FOREMOST*.'**

"What is Michelle Obama planning to do with her future resources if she's First Lady that will elevate Black over White in America?

"The following passage appears to be a CALL TO ARMS for affirmative action policies that could be the hallmark of an Obama administration: **'Predominantly white universities like Princeton are socially and academically designed to cater to the needs of the white students comprising the bulk of their enrollments.'**

"The conclusion of her thesis is alarming.

"Michelle Obama's poll of Black alumni concludes that other Black students at Princeton do NOT share her obsession with blackness. But rather than celebrate, she is horrified that Black alumni identify with our common American culture more than they value the color of their skin. She wrote: **'I hoped that these findings would help me conclude that despite the high degree of identification with whites as a result of the educational and occupational path that Black Princeton alumni follow, the alumni would still maintain a certain level of identification with the Black community. However, these findings do not support this possibility.'**

"Is it no wonder that most black alumni ignored her racist questionnaire? Only 89 students responded out of 400 who were asked for input.

"Michelle Obama does not look into a crowd of Obama supporters and see Americans. She sees Black people and White people eternally conflicted with one another. The thesis provides a trove of Mrs. Obama's thoughts and world view seen through a race-based prism.

"This is a very DIVISIVE view for a potential First Lady that would do untold damage to race relations in this country in a Barack Obama administration. Michelle Obama's intellectually-refined racism should give all Americans pause for deep concern. . . ." **JJ**

B. HUSSEIN Obama's List of Lies Goes On and On . . .

A laughter a day keeps the witches away. So, let's laugh first. I read this somewhere, but I can't remember where. It's so hilarious, I think, that I just have to share it with y'all. It's about the characters in that classic book and movie, "The Wizard of Oz" and their parallel resemblances to some of America's political leaders.

Here goes . . .

George W. Bush—the Scarecrow that has no brains.

Dick Cheney—the Tin Man that has no heart.

Ms. Condi Rice—the Dorothy who has no home.

Karl Rove—the Cowardly Lion

Bill Clinton—the Blowback who gets blowed!!!

Har! Har! Har! Okey *ngarud*, enough of that to keep the witches away.

FIFTY LIES AND COUNTING: What follows was sent to me by Jesse Farrales of Chicago, but who's more famously known in Chicagoland as the "Debonair." He said this was posted on www.Politicalforum.com by "Latisha" and all the LIES here have been verified for its truthfulness by a group of his computer-savvy friends.

Also, I've seen some of them printed in mainstream newspapers and used and re-used as background information by many mainstream columnists. I've used some of them myself in my past stories. There are 50 of them. But since my space is limited, I couldn't use them all.

So, here goes. Enjoy. Get mad. Smear feces on my photo. I don't care. What I care is that my readers, and whoever I can reach in America, would know who B. HUSSEIN Obama is.

He said his father was a "***goat herder.***" **A lie**. Obama's father was a privileged, well-educated man, who worked for the Kenyan government.

He said his father was a "***proud freedom fighter.***" **A lie**. His father was part of one of the most corrupt and violent governments Kenya has ever had.

He said his "***grandmother has always been a Christian.***" **A lie**. She does her Salat prayers at 5 a.m., according to her own interviews. Not to mention, Christianity wouldn't allow her to have been one of the 14 wives to one man.

He said his name is "***African Swahili.***" **A lie**. His name is Arabic. Baraka, from which his name, BARACK, was derived from, means "blessed" in that language. The name, HUSSEIN, is also Arabic and so is the name, OBAMA.

He said, "***I never practiced Islam.***" **A lie**. He practiced it daily in his early school years. He was registered as a Muslim and kept that faith for 31 years, until his wife, Michelle, convinced him to convert to Christianity, so he can run for office.

He said, "***I was fluent in Indonesian.***" **A lie**. Not one of his teachers said he could speak the language.

He said in one of his books, "***An Ebony article moved me to run for office.***" **A lie**. Ebony has yet to find the article that he mentioned. It does not, and never did, exist. He said, "***A Life magazine changed my outlook in life.***" Another lie. It does not, and never did, exist.

Editor's Note: Perhaps the tombstone of Mr. Obama's political grave can read: "Here LIES a man who never told a lie . . ."? (With apologies to Poet-pundit Fred Burce Bunao, who penned the original inscription way back in the 1980s.)

He said to vote as "***PRESENT***" in the Illinois legislature is a "common" thing. **A lie.** It was common for him to vote 'PRESENT.' He had under his belt 130 NO VOTES when he served as a state senator in Illinois.

He said, "***I passed 900 bills in the State Senate.***" A lie. He passed 26 bills, most of which, he did not write, but handed to him by a fellow Senator to assist him in his future bid for higher office.

He said he was a "***PROFESSOR***" of Constitutional Law at Harvard. **A lie.** He was a SENIOR LECTURER, on leave.

He said, "***Without me, there would be no Ethics Bill in Congress.***" **A lie.** He did NOT write it, he did NOT introduce it, he did NOT change it . . . nor create any Ethics Bill at all in Congress.

He said, "***I took on The Asbestos Altgeld Gardens Mess.***" **A lie.** He was merely a part of a large group of people who remedied Altgeld Gardens. He wanted to take all the credit to himself that in one of his books, he left out all the other people's names who worked with him.

He said, "***I have always been against Iraq.***" This, I think, is the biggest **lie** of all! He was NOT even in the U.S. Senate as an elected senator when the invasion of Iraq happened. So, how could he claim that he VOTED against the war? When he became a Senator, he voted for every funding bill for Iraq to the tune of $300-billion. Until January 2007, when he ran for President, he has NOT sponsored a single resolution or legislation to end the war or to bring the troops home. And, he seems to be stepping back now from his proposed withdrawal date of U.S. troops from Iraq.

He said, "***I have always supported Universal Health Care.***" **A lie**. His plan will leave us all, the taxpayers, to pay for the 15,000,000 who do not have to buy it.

He said, "***I am as patriotic as anyone.***" **A lie**. He won't wear a flag pin on the lapel of his jacket and place his hand over his heart while America's national anthem is played.

The list goes on . . . and on.

He also said that he did "***run ads in Florida.***" That's **a lie**. He allowed national ads to run 8 to 12 times a day for two weeks. He also said, "***I won Michigan.***" He did not. He said, "***I won Nevada.***" He did not.

He said, "***I want all votes to count. I want America to decide.***" **A lie.** He prefers caucuses that limit the vote, confuse the voters, force a public vote, and only operate during small windows of time.

Yeah, the list of Mr. Obama's lies goes on . . . and on.

Does Hillary lie, too? Of course. She had regaled audiences with tales of a dangerous landing under sniper fire in Tuzla, Bosnia 12 years ago and then running for cover. None of this happened. When CBS provided the tape, she confessed that she "misspoke." But her list of lies does NOT go on and on, UNLIKE that of B. HUSSEIN Obama's list that goes on . . . and on. **JJ**

Feedbacks and Comments on My Stories on B. HUSSEIN Obama

Let's take a quick break *muna* from B. HUSSEIN Osama, oops sorry, I mean, Senator Obama. I cannot seem to remember how to spell correctly Barack Hussein's last name. Osama's and Obama's names sound and look so much alike. And, as y'all know Osama is America's public enemy number one, and Obama is America's frontrunner in the Democratic Party's presidential nomination. And as Erap would say, "*SAME-SAME.*"

Can you imagine a name like Barack HUSSEIN Osama, I mean, Obama, as the President of the United States of America? Saddam HUSSEIN would be rolling over in his grave with laughter and Osama Bin Laden would be giggling his butt off in his cave.

Really, I don't think America would allow that. Would ya? So okay, as I said, let's take a break muna from this guy.

Now and then, we, *KUNO* writers, get awesome and fabulous comments for our writings. And when that happens, all the pain and all the agonies of writing and the time spent on it become all worth it. This particular comment came from a Chicagoan, named Don Azarias. He wrote:

"Hi Jesse,

"Your most recent Cup 'O Kapeng Barako column is a gem. I think it is one of the best writings that you have penned since I started reading your column. You spoke the truth and nothing but the truth.

And, let's face, the truth hurts . . . especially when it comes face to face with people like Senator Barack Obama, Tony Rezko and Reverend Jeremiah Wright who try to be what they are not.

"What you wrote was so brilliant, so elegant and unassailable.

"Keep it up!

"(Signed) ***Don Azarias"***

Not all readers of my column agree with me. In fact, many hate me, curse and despise me. One lunatic even mailed a disfigured, feces-smeared of my photo and a typed hate letter along with it in unprintable language.

When I got this letter I was so *kilig to the bones* that the first thing I did was to share it with my *Bestpren*, Yoly T. of Chicago and said: **"Check this out!"**

Yoly answered: ***"Don is like that. He'll tell you what he honestly thinks—suwerte mo at bilib siya sa 'yo."***

I asked: "***Ikaw, hindi ka ba bilib sa akin***?"

Yoly answered: "***Bestpren, need you ask? Hindi ba obvious? Of course naman . . . bilib na bilib***!!!"

I answered: "***Ako rin. Bilib na bilib sa 'yo.***"

This next comment came from Singapore, from a lady there named, Dr. Carmelita C. Ballesteros, a teaching fellow at the National Institute of Education, Nanyang Technological University. She wrote:

"Dear Ka Jesse,

"I was so intrigued by the news item re Rev. Jeremiah Wright's venomous sermon and Obama's so-called eloquent defense that I took precious time out from my hectic teaching schedule to watch on YouTube both speech events.

"I agree with you, Ka Jesse. Rev. Wright sounded like a WACKO. And Obama didn't impress me at all. Modesty side, I can deliver a far more passionate speech than Obama. Ha, ha, ha! I was an orator, declaimer, and debater from high school till college. I can also write original speeches. There was nothing uplifting nor inspiring in Obama's delivery or content. Certainly doesn't come anywhere near Dr. King's "I have a Dream" speech.

"Ka Jesse, please continue with your de-construction of Obama. It isn't about an oratorical contest, is it? If it were, I'm sure Denzel Washington can do a better job.

"Cheers,

"(Signed) ***Carmel****"*

Now this one came from Allan Albert of California. He's also columnist. He wrote: "*Makes you wonder if he just* ***"vehemently condemned" the statements of Reverend Jeremiah Wright, for, you know, political showmanship.***" And this, from a guy who signed himself, "Ikocen": "***Great piece. Too bad the USA press will not publish this honest assessment of one political hack.***"

A reader said: "(It is) one of the best writings that you have penned since I started reading your column. You spoke the truth and nothing but the truth . . . the truth hurts . . . especially when it comes face to face with people like Senator Barack Obama, Tony Rezko and Rev. Jeremiah Wright.

Of course not all readers of my column agree with me. In fact, many hate me, curse me and despise me. One lunatic even took the time to send through the mail a disfigured, feces-smeared of my photo and a typed hate letter along with it in unprintable language. Though he tried to sound like an American, I knew right away he was a Filipino in the way he constructed his letter. *Carabao English kasi, eh*. And, like all COWARDS, he didn't sign his name!

Here's another letter, disagreeing with me, quoted en toto: It's a decent, intelligent letter, I think, compared to some of the crackpot letters I've gotten in the past:

"Did you actually watch the whole video? The "chickens coming home to roost" comment was not by Wright, but his quoting the US ambassador. If you are going to put so much emphasis on it, you better get your facts straight before you start mouthing off. Look it up, watch the video.

"I find it SPOOKY that people use his middle name like you do . . . it's a name given to him at birth. So . . . that makes him a terrorist?

"Or, if he were a Muslim, then he would be a terrorist?! Muslim = terrorist to you?

"The complete ignorance of posts (columns) like these, scare me a lot more than one politician. They show a mass of people who can be led like sheep into a raging frenzy of hate and bigotry, while turning a blind eye to any FACTS that may be shown to them.

"To me, that's scary. That's back to the Middle Ages."

This guy signed himself off, "joesassmonkey@gmail.com." Hey, Joe (whatever your name is), thanks for your comment. Good luck to your boy, B. HUSSEIN Osama, oops, I mean, Obama. Bet ya, he's gonna lose. **JJ**

A Judas, an Indian Chief and Senator Obama's Speech on Race

The KNIVES are out. The first one to strike was "the Hispanic." That's right . . . the governor of New Mexico, Bill Richardson. Describing to the press the tense conversation he had with Ms. Hillary that he would endorse Barack HUSSEIN Obama, Governor Richardson said, "Let me tell you: We've had better conversations."

I wonder what Senator Hillary told him. She probably gave him the "ice." Mouthfuls of it. Hey, they don't call Ms. Hillary Rodham Clinton, a "chilly bitch" for nothing.

But Governor, sir, with all due respect, what do you expect? You're a lousy SOB and big-time backstabber. You were a close ally, a special trusted friend and a bosom buddy of both Bill and Hillary. And not too long, you and Bill even had a six pack and watched the Super Bowl together and y'all probably talked about NOT only of football scores but also your scores with floozies together.

And, you gave your word that you'll be supporting Ms. Hillary all the way. And if you remember, sir, when Bill Clinton then was the President of the U.S. of A and you were just an unknown Mexican American, he took a liking on you and elevated you to the national stage and named you his energy secretary . . . then ambassador to the United Nations. Then when you wanted to be a governor of your state of New Mexico, they helped you realize that dream.

The Mexican Americans, I know, they know how to return favors. But you are an ingrate, sir, and a poor role model to all Mexican Americans, and for that matter, to all Americans, hyphenated or not.

After all the good things that the Clintons did for you, you sucked up to B. HUSSEIN Obama and said of him: "There's something special about this guy. I've been trying to figure it out, but it's very good."

I dunno about that. I don't see anything "special" about B. HUSSEIN Obama. But whatever, I am sure, Mr. Obama had already figured you out that if you can backstab the Clintons, who gave you so much, you can just as easily backstab him. You're the living picture of Judas Iscariot . . . sir.

AN INDIAN CHIEF AND HIS BRAVE: Let me pass on this little story to y'all. I think it answers the BLACK ANGER that Mr. Obama talked about in his speech on race and on his pastor's venomous remarks.

INDIAN BRAVE: "Chief, I heard your wife ran away, your son died and your house burned down."

INDIAN CHIEF: "There are two wolves within me, fighting for control of my heart and soul. One says that I must fight and rage against the injustice of life. The other says I must forgive and move on."

BRAVE: "Which wolf will win?"

CHIEF: "The one I feed."

So, which wolf within him this pastor feeds? And what's the remedy for this BLACK ANGER? Reparations? Affirmative Action? Apologies on a national level? Free college-level education in Ivy-League Schools? Minority-owned contracts? Welfare, Medicare, SSI and other special privileges?

What is the remedy for that ANGER?

How about free drugs and Cadillacs?

Reverend Wright, I think, should take a lesson from that Indian Chief. Mr. Obama can use that lesson, too. Instead of justifying his pastor's venom, he should have advised the Black Man of America to learn how "to wrest control of his heart and soul, forgive and move on" . . . and rage no more

OBAMA'S SPEECH ON REV. WRIGHT'S VENOM: I suppose y'all heard Senator Obama's speech defending the hateful, inflammatory sermons of his pastor. Many said, it was "awesome" and a "once in a lifetime" speech . . . and "John F. Kennedy-like."

Oh, please. Gimme a break. B. HUSSEIN Obama ain't no John F. Kennedy. I must say though that it was a beautiful speech. He surely knows how to deliver a speech. But it hardly makes up for having spent 20 years as a member of a church that's anti-American and blatantly racist . . . and for regarding his WACKO preacher the most reverential figure in his life.

In that speech, Mr. Obama publicly acknowledged for the FIRST TIME that he had heard those inflammatory remarks from Wright while he was in church. Previously, he said, he had NOT heard. Then, he was confronted with evidences, he took his words back and said, "Oh yeah, I heard."

The LYING has begun.

How many more lies will we hear from this man who aspires to be the President of the United States of America? How many more "awesome" speeches will he deliver to deceive America? And how many more times will he get caught in his lies? Is he a George W. Bush in the making?

Who is this man who we all know as Barack HUSSEIN Obama? Is he the silver-tongued orator who speaks so convincingly of unity and hope and understanding between the races?

Or, is he the one who gives generously to Jeremiah Wright's church and sat in the pews of that church for 20 years, listening to his pastor's message of RACIAL HATE and anti-American views?

In describing Senator Obama's speech, Charles Krauthammer, a *Washington Post* columnist, said: "It's the Jesse Jackson politics of racial grievance, expressed in Ivy League diction and Harvard Law nuance. That's why the speech made so many liberals commentators swoon: It bathed them in racial guilt, while flattering their intellectual pretensions. An unbeatable combination. . . ."

In ghetto lingo: Right on, baby! 'Bama's B.S. ain't gonna wash. **JJ**

NOT God Bless America!
No, no, no, G . . . D America!

I will stand with the Muslims should the political winds shift in an ugly direction.

In Barack Hussein Obama's book, "Dreams Of My Father"

It's a BONEHEADED kind of thing and childish, too, but I keep hearing in my mind's ear that old Filipino ditty that goes, ***"Beee, buti nga! Beee, buti nga! Buti nga! Buti nga! Buti nga!"***

And that's probably because, bone by bone, Barack HUSSEIN Obama's skeletons are coming out now from his closet . . . and spooking America.

First, there's this guy, named Tony Rezko, a Chicago crook, a slum lord, a big-time contributor and a close associate, who helped purchase a very expensive home for him.

Then came the "endorsement" of Louis Farrakhan of his presidential bid. As y'all know, Mr. Farrakhan is the honcho of the Black militant group, Nation of Islam.

Mr. Obama said his message of HOPE is to unify the country across racial and party lines. We have been duped!

Then this NAFTA thing, where he declared that whatever he said about it in his speeches and debates against Ms. Hillary were just for "political" showmanship, nothing else. Can you imagine that?

Then out came the "mother" of all spooks: Rev. Jeremiah Wright, Mr. Obama's pastor for 20 years at the Trinity United Church of Christ on Chicago's South side, who HATEFULLY proclaimed in one of his sermons:

"The government gives them the drugs, builds bigger prisons, passes a three-strike law and then wants us to sing 'God Bless America.' No, no, no, not God Bless America, God damn America, that's in the Bible for killing innocent people . . . God damn America for treating our citizens as less than human. God damn America . . ."

As we all know, what this loony said about America are NOT in the Bible. He must have smoked some kind of a weed that Senator Barack used to smoke . . . when this pastor spat those words. I didn't make that up, you know, about the drug part.

Senator Obama used to snort crack and coke and smoked them weeds. He, the great B.O. himself, said it in one of his books . . . Hey, I used to smoke them weeds, too. So I can't really condemn him for that. But like Bill, I didn't INHALE. Honest. But let's not talk now about my honesty. Let's talk about Senator Barack's spooks.

So, when this "mother" of all spooks showed its ugly, scary face to America, Mr. Obama immediately called Wright's statements "completely unacceptable and inexcusable" and didn't reflect the kinds of sermons he had heard from this preacher and that such statements been the "repeated tenor of the church . . . I wouldn't feel comfortable there."

Yeah, right. Mr. Obama had repeatedly and religiously attended the services of that church for 20 years. He had said and written that Reverend Wright had been his "mentor" and "spiritual adviser." This pastor had officiated at his wedding with Michelle and had baptized their two daughters. Come on now, no one would remain a loyal, faithful, tithing member of a church where its teachings offend you.

And, according to *The New York Times* Columnist William Kristol, Rona Kessler, a journalist who has written about Mr. Wright's ministry, claims that Mr. Obama was in fact in the pews at Trinity when Reverend Wright blamed the arrogance of the 'United States of White America' for much of the world's suffering, especially the oppression of Blacks.

Also, Mr. Obama must have heard this on the Sunday after 9/11, when Reverend Wright spewed this venom: "We bombed Hiroshima, we bombed Nagasaki, and we nuked far more than the thousands in New York and the Pentagon, and we never batted an eye. We have supported state terrorism against the Palestinians and black South Africans, and now we are indignant because the stuff we have done overseas is now brought right back to our front yards. America's chickens are coming home to roost . . ."

Obama said he "vehemently condemned" those statements. "They in no way reflect my attitudes and directly contradict my profound love for this country," he said.

Okey *ngarud*, but Mr.Obama has stated publicly that the Reverend Jeremiah Wright was the "inspiration of his book, "Audacity of Hope." He even called him his "uncle" in that book.

"I found a solace in nursing a pervasive sense of grievance and animosity against my mother's race . . . that hate hadn't gone way," Obama wrote, blaming "white people—some cruel, some ignorant, sometimes a single face, sometimes just faceless image of a system claiming power over our lives. . . ."

In his book, "Dreams of my Father," Mr. Obama wrote: "I'd never emulate white men and brown men whose fates didn't speak to my own. It was into my father's image, the Black Man, son of Africa, that I'd packed all the attributes I sought in myself, the attributes of Martin Luther King and Malcom X, Dubois and Mandela."

"I was trying to raise myself as a Black Man in America," he added, "and beyond the given of my appearance, no one around me seemed to know exactly what that meant . . ."

I don't EXACTLY know what that meant either. Why raise yourself ONLY as a Black Man in America? Why this pervasive sense of grievance and animosity and HATE up to now? Why emulate only the attributes of great Black Men? And, why speak only for Black-Americans? Why not for all Americans? Mr. Obama said his message of HOPE is to unify the country across racial and party lines. We have been duped!

And, if Barack Obama was inspired in anyway by a BIGOT named Jeremiah Wright, ask yourself: How good is this JUDGMENT, which he brags, that he has.

Is it a childish, boneheaded judgment? Or, is it a version of the Filipino ditty, "*Buti nga*?" **JJ**

"Pundit-in-chief" daw si Barack Hussein Obama

Let me tell y'all first right quick that it wasn't me who coined that word: "Pundit-in-Chief." I am not that bright to be able to invent such a word. It was Mr. Bush, our current commander in chief, who coined that word. And because of Mr. Barack HUSSEIN Obama's soaring and inspiring and PLAGIARIZED speeches, that fool a lot of people, I agree with Mr. Bush. I don't usually agree with Mr. Bush, but this time, I do.

Mr. Bush can be so very witty at times. Just like that time when he ordered our troops to find Mr. Saddam HUSSEIN. He said then of HUSSEIN: "He can run, but he can't hide." That was very witty and creative, I think.

Now Mr. Bush tells us that Mr. Barack HUSSEIN Obama is a "pundit-in-chief." That's also very witty and very creative, I think. As witty and creative in coining Karl Rove's nickname, "Turd Bloosom."

HILLARY CLOBBERS BARACK: That was the banner headline that screamed in every newspaper all over the country Wednesday. A friend, a colleague, and I'm sure, one of my fans, too, send me an email late Tuesday night right after the results of the primaries in Ohio, Texas, Vermont and Rode Island came out . . . and she gushed: "Hooray! I knew she will win in Ohio and Texas and in Rhode Island, too."

So I emailed her back and said: "Hey, long time, no hear. It's hooray, indeed! We're going on, we're going strong and we're going all the way . . . back to the White House. Hillary to the Oval Office. And Bill to the Oral Office. Let the good times roll once more. Hooray!"

I know. I am such a nasty, dirty old man.

Seriously now, after 12 straight losses, Ms. Hillary's victories sent a message to the Obama juggernaut that clearly says: "Hey, Barack, my boy, not so fast! I could still beat you and I will."

And, she will. Her victories in Ohio and Texas, according to her advisers, were enough to keep her in the race at least through Pennsylvania's April 22 primary even IF Obama has more delegates.

And the results Tuesday, says The New York Times "bring doubts and questions about Obama's electability in key swing states like Ohio that Democrats are eager to carry in the November general election."

Not only that.

Hillary has also won the powerhouse Democratic states of California, New Jersey and New York, but also major and key battleground states like, Arizona, Nevada, New Hampshire and New Mexico . . . and this could persuade the superdelegates—the party's hundreds of leaders who have a vote on the nomination—to stop abandoning her for Obama.

In other words, Hillary is now the "hope" candidate. And this battle between her and Obama could go all the way to the day of the national convention in Denver, Colorado in August. Hillary said she'll soldier on to that day. "I am a doer, I am fighter, I am a champion," she proclaimed. Indeed she is. She's been a politician who has been a known quantity for 16 years now. She's been attacked from all sides, and she has always managed to prevail and win against all odds.

Each time her detractors think she's down, like after Iowa, for instance, or South Carolina, or the February primaries, Hillary has found ways to come back up. She's like that mythical phoenix that keeps rising from the ashes of her defeats.

I truly think that only a fighter, a strong leader and a smart tough-minded woman, like Hillary, can get this country out of the filthy mess created by the Bush/Cheney/Rove administration. Eloquent, inspiring, empty, and COPIED speeches of Obama will only lead to failure and despair. Barack ain't got what it takes.

To me, he's just a mirage created by a fawning media and by MSNBC talk heads, especially that one with a Mongoloid-looking fat face, named Tim Russert.

IGNORANT REMARKS: Have y'all heard what Mr. Obama said on CNN? I kid you not. Not on the Filipino CNN (Coconut News Ngayon) either, but on the mainstream CNN, Larry King Live talk show. Obama was talking about the Army. He said: "You know, I've heard from an Army captain who was a head of a rifle platoon—supposed to have 39 men in a rifle platoon. Ended up being sent to Afghanistan with 24 because 15 of those soldiers had been sent to Iraq . . .

"As a consequence, they didn't have enough ammunition, they didn't have enough Humvees. They were actually capturing Taliban weapons, because it was easier to get Taliban weapons than it would to get properly equipped by our current commander in chief. . . ."

These are stupid, ignorant remarks. Ask any soldier, any lowly grunt and he'll tell ya in between a cuss word or two that Barack Obama knows NOT what he talks about.

First of all, captains don't lead platoons. Lieutenants lead platoons. Captains lead companies, consisting of three or four platoons. Secondly, platoons are not divided and sent to different war theaters. They have trained together, so usually, they go to war together. Thirdly, it's dangerous and a big no-no to be using captured enemy weapons. The strange popping sound of the enemy weapons being fired is a magnet for "friendly" artillery fire from afar.

Lastly, our troops are well equipped. They may not have the armored Humvees and bullet proof vests, but compared to other soldiers, they are the best-equipped soldiers in the whole world. Also, ammos are plentiful . . . always. Believe me, I know. I was a soldier, a lowly grunt, once, in a long ago war.

And who was this Army captain that Mr. Obama had talked with, anyway? Captain Kangaroo? Yes, indeed, Mr. Bush is right to call Mr. Obama, "PUNDIT-IN-CHIEF." For his empty words soar, like a balloon, full of helium, spiraling toward the sky. **JJ**

Obama Wins the Nomination, McCain Becomes the President!

Lifting whole passages from some else's speeches is NOT change you can believe in. It's change you can Xerox. . . .—Sen. Hillary Clinton

In a college campus somewhere, two friends, a black dude and a white dude were shooting the breeze and having fun jiving with each other. After a while, the white dude said, "Gotta take off, dude. I'm gonna be late for class." "What?" said the black dude. "Since when has that ever mattered to you?"

"I know," the white dude answered. "I'm putting my slack cred at risk. But this class is actually inspiring!"

"What is it?" asked the black dude.

"English 129," said the white dude. "'The Poetry of Barack Obama.'"

"What?" said the black dude. "That's the hottest course on campus. How did you get in?"

"On HOPE, I guess," the white dude said.

"That WORKS?" said the black dude. . . .

Y'all got it? Get the drift? Yes, I plagiarized it from the political cartoon, "Doonesbury," by Garry Trudeau. Hey, if Barack Obama can blatantly plagiarize his soaring, inspiring speeches that the OBAMBIS can swoon on, I, too, can plagiarize my Kapeng Barako column that y'all can moon on.

OBAMA, THE ORATOR. SO WAS HITLER: Whether you believe in his politics or not, everyone, almost everyone, agrees that Sen. Barack Obama is the best orator among the current crop of presidential candidates.

As Jack Shafer, the editor of the online magazine, Slate, wrote: "Barack Obama bringeth rapture to his audience. They swoon and wooble, regardless of race, gender, or political affiliation, although few understand EXACTLY why he has this effect on them."

Such is the power of Mr. Obama. Such also was the power of Adolph Hitler. During those times when Hitler mesmerized the Aryan Nation, he also "bringeth rapture to the Germans" . . . and "they swoon and wooble" . . . "not knowing EXACTLY why he had this effect on them."

On a couple of occasions, I took the time to listen closely to Barrack Obama. He got me mesmerized. He's truly a talented orator. But then, after I've listened to him, I asked myself: Now, what did he say? Can he really accomplish that? Can he really do all that?

True, he told me what I wanted to hear, but I didn't hear him tell me HOW he's going to do it. There were no SPECIFICS. True, his words were poetry and he speaks in rhythm and perfect cadences, but he ain't got no beef. He ain't got no specifics in his promises. His speeches ring hollow. As Sen. John McCain aptly said: "Empty, eloquent rhetoric."

Ms. Hillary Clinton may not have poetry in her speeches, but she offers us down to earth solutions to America's problems, and I'd rather believe in that than those dream-like words that Mr. Obama utters.

A PHOTO IS WORTH THAN A THOUSAND WORDS: So, did y'all see that photo of Barack HUSSEIN Obama in that Taliban garb? It was so funny, I think. But, of course, all the OBAMBIS went ballistics over it. They shrilled that it was "fear-mongering."

What's so fearful about that? There's nothing to fear but fear itself. (I copied that sentence, too, by the way. Call me a wannabe Barack). Really, I do think that garb suits Barack to a tee: the turban and the wrap around skirt and all.

It wasn't fearful. It was funny.

But guess what? Barack looks like he's been wearing the garb all his life. Do y'all think he could be a "closeted" Taliban? You know, like those "closeted" gay hypocrite lawmakers, like Foley and Cunningham and all.

Just asking.

Because, you'll never know. With a middle name, like HUSSEIN . . . you'll never know. Ask Mr. Bush. He knows. He used to have a STRANGE fixation on a man named, Saddam HUSSEIN. But, you know, there' also something STRANGE about Barack.

When a presidential candidate refuses to place his hand over his heart when the national anthem is sung and reasons that "47,000 fans at NFL games do not place their hands over their hearts . . ." That to me, is STRANGE.

When a presidential candidate refuses to wear the pin of the United States flag on the lapel of his jacket and says, "that's not patriotic . . ." That to me, is STRANGE.

When a presidential candidate's wife says, "For the first time in my life, I am finally proud to be an American . . ." That to me, is STRANGE.

When a presidential candidate plagiarizes his speeches and says, "Hey, that's no big deal. . . ." That to me, is STRANGE.

When a presidential candidate presents himself as squeaky clean, yet have a close association with a man, named REZKO . . . that to me, is STRANGE.

Let Barack Obama get the Democratic presidential nomination and we'll have John McCain as America's next president. And that to me, won't be STRANGE at all. **JJ**

Barack Obama . . . a Plagiarist?

In her own words, Hillary Rodham Clinton said: ***"Americans have a choice to make in this election. It's about picking a President who relies not just on words, but on work, hard work, to get America back to work, to get America working again for all the people. While words matter greatly, the best words in the world aren't enough, unless you match them with action."***

Barack Hussein Obama responded: ***"Don't tell me words don't matter. 'I have a dream'—just words? 'We hold these truths to be self-evident, that all men are created equal'—just words? 'We have nothing to fear but fear itself'—just words? Just speeches?"***

Beautiful, gorgeous words, aren't they? No wonder those adoring, mindless throng of OBAMBIS were applauding, jumping and gyrating in ecstasy when Mr. Obama boomed those words.

But those soaring, high-faluting, gorgeous-sounding words were not his. They were PLAGIARIZED. Yes, copied, word for word. Yes, they were echoes from a speech delivered by Gov. Deval Patrick of Massachusetts during his own political campaign in 2006 in response to a criticism by a political rival who said that Patrick merely offered lofty rhetoric over specifics.

Gov. Patrick boomed also then: ***"We hold these truths to be self-evident, that all men are created equal'—just words? Just words? 'We have nothing to fear but fear itself'—just words? 'Ask not what your country can do for you, ask what you can do for your country.' Just words? 'I have a dream'—just words?"***

Not only that.

In November of 2007, in South Carolina, Mr. Obama said in one of his soaring and inspiring speeches: ***"I am not asking you to take a chance on me. I'm also asking you to take a chance on your aspirations . . ."***

In June of 2006, in Massachusetts, Gov. Patrick said in one of his speeches: ***"I am not asking anybody to take a chance on me. I'm asking you to take a chance on your aspirations."***

There's more. The mantra: ***"Yes, we can!"*** that Mr. Obama and his supporters chant over and over again in their rallies was also the rallying cry and mantra of Ceasar Chavez and all those Mexican farmers that he led fighting for fair wages and humane living conditions.

Hey, I plagiarize, too. I copy other people thoughts and words, but NOT word for word, or thought by thought. I process their words and thoughts first, scramble them and meld them with mine. All writers and talk heads and pundits all do that. Anybody who says they don't . . . are liars! Also, I am not a big time politician, like Barack, who aspire to hold the most coveted job in the word: the presidency of the United States of America. I am just a small time pundit. Therefore, only, a small time thief, of words.

MS. CONDI RICE AS OBAMA'S VP: There have been talks and speculations by CNN pundits on the Larry King show that Ms. Condi Rice is being considered as Obama's VP. Also, on PBS, on the "Charlie Rose" talk show . . . a guest on the show, a renowned southern black preacher, whose name I didn't get, had said that Ms. Rice would be the "right choice" and that he would be "very delighted to see that happened."

CHARLES BARKLEY FOR SECDEF: On the Filipino CNN (Coconut News Ngayon), there are also talks and speculations by Filipino pundits that Charles Barkley, you know, that former NBA star player and now a motor mouth NBA games commentator should be appointed as Secretary of Defense. Because, they said, when he used to play for the Phoenix Suns, "he played good defense" and was an "awesome power forward man." He was also an awesome barroom brawler.

For that matter, my wife said that Mr. Obama should ask Mr. Michael "His Airness" Jordan to be his ambassador at large to the Middle East. So that instead of sending soldiers to fight and kill Muslims, Barack Obama y HUSSEIN can just send America's NBA players to challenge the Muslims to a basketball game.

Hey, what about Al Sharpton and Jesse Jackson? I wonder what's gonna be their role in Obama's cabinet?

A FRAY BETWEEN TWO WIVES: The presidential nominees for the two major parties have not been named yet, but ALREADY the fight is on between Sen. John McCain's wife, Cindy and Sen. Barack Obama's spouse, Michelle.

It began when Mrs. Michelle Obama made a remark Monday in Milwaukee. She said, ***"For the first time in my adult lifetime, I am really proud of my country. And not just because Barack has done well, but because I think people are hungry for change."***

To which Mrs. Cindy McCain said to a crowd at a rally, alluding to Michelle's remark: ***"I am proud of my country. I don't know about you—if you heard those words earlier—I'm VERY proud of my country . . ."***

When asked about the matter, Sen. John McCain said: ***"I don't think, we have any comment on that, do we? Do you have any comment?"***

With all due respect, Senator, I do. I am a Democrat. But if Sen. Obama wins the Democratic nomination, I'll vote for you. I want somebody tested and ready and experienced to be the President of this country that I love. If I can't have my candidate, Hillary . . . then you're the next best thing. And I think a lot of Americans feel the same way that I do. ***JJ***

Democrat Caucus: A Farce and a Joke

Caucuses are jokes. Democrat caucuses, that is. Last Saturday, when our State of Washington had its Democrat caucuses, my wife and I eagerly went, raring to participate and make our views known. In my Lakeland Hills neighborhood, a suburb south of Seattle, we held our caucus in the small basketball gym of Lakeland Hills Elementary. Many came. So the gym just about overflowed with people. But what really surprised me was the sea of Black faces in that small, packed gym.

I asked my wife, "Where did they all come from? Where are our neighbors?

This is supposed to be an all-white neighborhood." Where they all came from, I don't have any idea.

I would see a Black face in our neighborhood now and then, but usually I don't. There's a Black family that lives several houses up the street from us, but that's it. I don't see them at our neighborhood Starbucks where I usually hang out. I don't see them at our neighborhood shopping plaza. I don't see them at our neighborhood restaurants and fast food stores.

So it was kind of a shock to me to see them all of a sudden, gathered all together in one place in this neighborhood.

"*Siguro* (maybe)," I told my wife, "*mga HAKOT.*"

Editor's Notes: Hakot is a Filipino term for "to bring." Ergo, "hakot delegates" are those brought or bused-in supporters of a particular candidate and who are usually paid and pampered and fed by the campaign organization.

Our neighborhood caucus was a joke, anyway. We got in. Nobody asked who we were. We didn't have to show any ID's. We were given forms to fill out: names, addresses, phone numbers, and our signatures.

Now, check this out: On the form, there was a portion there where it asked if you're gay, lesbian, bisexual or transgender. I kid you not!

I tell ya, the Democrat Party here in Washington is a nosy political party.

Why do they want to know who you're sleeping with? Surely, that's a joke.

Then, on the last slot of the form, we wrote down the name of our preferred candidate.

A Black lady next to me, filling out her form, wrote down FIVE names, then signed five different signatures after those names . . . and on the slot for preferred candidate, wrote down, five times: BARACK OBAMA.

Surely, that's a joke.

When I saw this, I was tempted to get another form, write down also five fictitious names and addresses and phone numbers, signed five different signatures and write down in the slot of preferred candidate, five times: HILLARY CLINTON. You know, as a joke, too.

Well, if that lady could do it, I could do it, too, right? But I couldn't be bothered.

I was getting hot in that enclosed gym. We were getting packed like sardines as more people came. The place was getting noisy and SMELLLY, like a fish market.

It was impossible to carry on a conversation with anybody. So, I grabbed my wife and left.

The following day, I heard on the news that a lot of people said: "The caucus system sucks." "It's horrible." "It's confusing." "It disenfranchises people." "It's undemocratic." "It's pointless." "It turns a lot of people off to politics. . . ."

To me, it was simply STUPID! A farce! And, a joke!

True, as reported by the media there was a "record turnout" and "lines around the block," BUT only an estimated 10 percent of registered voters took part.

If that's the case, who then is the TRUE preferred candidate of the 90 percent of Washington voters? Is that also the case, nation-wide?

OBAMA SWOOPS THE POTOMAC: So, like a red tide swooping down on the yellow peril (that's how it looks like on the map of CNN political pundits), Mr. Barack Obama rolled on to victory Tuesday and captured the Potomac states: Virginia, Maryland and Washington, D.C., adding to eight states his win over Ms. Hillary since Saturday.

And that gave Mr. Obama a lead over Ms. Hillary in pledged delegates, which at last count is over a hundred now as I write this.

According to *Associated Press*, the score is: Clinton, 978; Obama, 1,112. The magic number is: 2,025. Whoever will get that number of pledged delegates would be the nominee.

Let's don't forget, too, the 796 "unpledged" superdelegates—party leaders and elected officials who have an automatic seat at the national convention in Denver—and who could have the last say as to who would be the nominee. Right now, there are 81 superdelegates who have committed their votes for Mr. Obama.

For Ms. Hillary, 109 superdelegates have promised her their support. But we're not in Denver yet. We'll cross the bridge when we get there.

HILLARY'S UNDAUNTED HURRAH: Right now, Hillary is losing. And she might lose again next week in the primaries in Wisconsin and Hawaii, where Obama grew up.

But Hillary remains undaunted. She vowed to take delegate-rich Texas and Ohio, Rhode Island and Vermont on March 4 when those states hold their primaries, as well as Pennsylvania on its April primary.

She said in El Paso: "We're going to sweep across Texas in the next three weeks bringing our message about what we need in America, the kind of President we need on Day One to be commander in chief and turn the economy around . . . I'm tested. I'm ready. Let's make it happen."

That's my girl. She's unbowed. She's got substance. She has withstood attacks from all sides and survived them all. She's got experience. She's got knowledge. She's got intelligence. She's got sensitivity. She'll beat Barack Obama. Then, she'll beat John McCain, the GOP's presumptive nominee. She'll be America's next President. She'll make it happen. **JJ**

Ms. Hillary Rodham Clinton, America's President-in-Waiting

"It did take a Clinton to clean up after the first Bush and I think it might take another one to clean up after the second Bush . . ."—Sen. Hillary Clinton

How true! How true! No doubt about it: Ms. Hillary will be the President who would clean up the mess that Mr. Bush, the Second, would leave behind: a budget deficit, a huge debt, a bankrupt economy, a looming recession, two ongoing wars, an America divided . . . and hated overseas.

Talagang nagkalat ng lagim, ika nga.

No wonder Americans crave for change! And we have a very likeable candidate in the person of Barack Obama, who offers this CHANGE for America. "A change," his supporters chant, "we can believe in."

Really? Can he really? True, he's likeable. I like him, too.

There's a lot to like about Mr. Obama. Handsome, intelligent, Harvard grad, "exotic" upbringing, good dancer with a good rhythm, fabulous speaker, I mean, he's a PRINCE . . .

Seven years ago, America "elected" a very likeable presidential candidate, too, in the person of George W. Bush. Yes, just like Mr. Obama, he was also handsome and wholesome, and a Harvard grad . . . Yes, just like Mr. Obama, he was also a PRINCE. And very likeable. But he turned out to be a frog, who likes to holds hands with Arab princes and say to

America's enemies, "bring it on" and to us, Americans, "we'll stay on course."

And look what happened to America! Yes, let there be CHANGE! But let's listen carefully and read up on issues that truly matters. Let's don't get BLINDED by poetic rhethorics and promises that cannot be delivered.

The New York Times said, "Mrs. Clinton is more qualified right now, to be President . . ." As written in an editorial in *The New York Times* a week ago, "the sense of possibility, of a generationl shift, rouses Mr. Obama's audiences and not just through rhetorical flourishes. He shows voters that he understands how much they hunger for a break with the Bush years, for leadership and vision and true bipartisanship . . ."

But we need more SPECIFICS to go with his amorphous promise of a new governing majority, a clearer sense of how he would govern. . . ."

True and I say again, Mr. Obama does not tell us HOW.

OBAMA/CHIQUITO: Obama reminds me of our own Chiquito, y'all remember him? You know, that Filipino comedian turned wannabe small—time politician in the 70's, who said when asked by a reporter: "Mr. Chiquito, *ano po ba ang plataporma ninyo*?" To which Chiquito answered: "*Ah, hindi ko sasabihin 'yan, baka kopyahin ng mga kalaban ko*." I can't remember now what he was running for, but on the premise that he's not going to reveal specifics of his policies, Chiquito won that election.

But that was Chiquito in the Philippines, and ONLY IN THE PHILIPPINES, y'all know what I mean? Mr. Obama is running for President of the United States of America, and as leader of the world. "The *potential upside of a great Obama presidency is ENTICING," added* The New York Times, "but the country faces huge problems, and will no doubt be facing more that we can't foresee.

The next president needs to start immediately on challenges that will require CONCRETE solutions, resolve, and the ability to make government work. Mrs. Clinton is more qualified right now, to be President. . . ."

I totally agree. "Hearing her talk about the presidency, her policies and her answers to America's big problems," the editorial continued, "we are hugely impressed by the depth of her knowledge, by the force of her intellect and the breadth of, yes, her experience." Right on. *Si Barack ay bubut pa. Magpahinog muna siya.*

A TOUGH FROM CHICAGO: "I try to explain to people, I may be skinny but I am tough," said Barack HUSSEIN Obama to a crowd in Connecticut, with the Kennedys looking on. "I am from Chicago." Really? Then how come he got his butt kicked in California, the biggest prize of the "Super Tuesday"?

And in Massachusetts, the land of the Kennedys, where he got a lot of Camelot-like help. Yeah, they even got Oprah, again, putting on for a show for him, with pals Caroline Kennedy, and Maria Shriver Kennedy, and Patrick and Ted, and Michelle Obama. Even actor Robert DeNiro and singer Stevie Wonder came to join in the gathering . . . and they all pranced on the makeshift stage, putting on a great show for the gawking *masa* and their votes.

Oprah said, "People think I endorsed Obama because he's black. Well, it hurts me that people think that. I endorsed Obama because he's brilliant."

Oprah, my dear girl, whose leg are you pulling?

People ain't that dumb. Of course, you endorsed Obama because he's black. And there are many who have more intelligence than you and Obama put together. Really, I think, it's bad enough that a talk show host is endorsing a politician. Isn't that a breach of conduct?

The same thing goes with Toni Morrison, that beloved black author of the black experience, who years ago dubbed Bill Clinton as America's "first black President."

But now says that's no longer true. So, what's the truth? Mr. Obama maybe poetry, black and beautiful, whereas, Ms. Hillary Clinton is harsh sounding, but she's prose in action and more prepared for the Herculean task of figuring out exactly HOW and WHAT must be done to set things right again in this country. Her abiding, powerful intellect and her EXPERIENCE tell us she's capable of doing that.

She's America's President-in-waiting and commander-in-chief. **JJ**

Speeches, Hugs and a Snub

Jesse Jackson won South Carolina twice, in '84 and '88. And he ran a good campaign. And Senator Obama's run a good campaign here. He's run a good campaign everywhere.—William Jefferson Clinton

Bill Clinton's comment above alludes only to one thing: Jackson and Obama are both BLACK wannabe Presidents of America.

Good grief! Imagine having for President of the United States a Black man, who's not really Black, whose name is Barack HUSSEIN Osama, I mean, Obama. It's now or never, don't y'all think?

Indeed, these are interesting times in American politics. It's drama galore. *Patalbugan at pataasan ng ihi.* So the media, the pundits and talk heads are all going bananas telling the world about it

This past Monday, three things unfolded before our eyes and spilled into our living rooms.

SPEECH & HUGS: First there were the speech and the hugs and the Camelot-like *daw* endorsement that Sen. Edward Kennedy gave Senator Obama. Here's the scenario and the dialogue:

At a rally at American University in Washington, D.C., Senator Kennedy says of Senator Obama: "He will be a President who refuses to be trapped in the patterns of the past. He is a leader who sees the world clearly without being cynical. He is the fighter who cares passionately about the causes he believes in without demonizing those who hold a different view . . ."

Senator Kennedy pauses in his speech here and gives Mr. Obama a hug.

Then Kennedy continues, and in an obvious reference to Bill Clinton's statement that Mr. Obama's anti-war stance was just a "fairy tale," says: "From the beginning, he opposed the war in Iraq. And let no one deny that truth. With Barack Obama we will close the book on the old politics of race against race, gender against gender, ethnic group against ethnic group . . . and straight against gay." Then, he stops again his speech and gives Senator Obama another hug.

"With Barack Obama," he continues, "there is another new national leader who has given America a different kind of campaign, blah, blah, blah, yakity yak. . . ." Sen. Kennedy stops again and gives Senator Obama another hug.

Y'all get what I am driving at? On *yata itong dalawang ito. Panay ang yakapan, eh.*

The day before, Caroline Kennedy, the daughter of President John F. Kennedy, had also endorsed Sen. Obama. She said, "I have never had a President who inspired me the way people tell me that my father inspired them. But for the first time I believe I have found the man who could be that President—not just for me, but for a new generations of Americans."

That's a profound statement. I like Caroline. And I liked her father, John F. Kennedy. And I also liked her uncle, Robert F. Kennedy. And her other uncle they call, Ted. But I have to disagree with her and her Uncle Ted on this one. Even if Mr. Obama could be elected as America's President, I doubt if he could INSPIRE Americans like her father did.

And that's because Barack Hussein Obama is NO Jack F. Kennedy!!! Perhaps Barack was able to inspire Ted and Caroline and many others. But he was not able to inspire all of the Kennedys and millions of others, who are non-Kennedys. Get my drift?

Kathleen Kennedy Townsend, the eldest daughter of the late Robert F. Kennedy said that she, her brother Robert, Jr., and sister Kerry were endorsing Hillary Clinton because "she shares so many of the concerns of my father." So there.

True, Mr. Obama has got the gift of the slurpy, syrupy, silvery tongue. He's an inspirational speaker and a great orator and such. Hitler was also a great orator and such. He was able to move the Aryan nation to join his Nazi Party. Many Germans also believe that Hitler could bring CHANGE. . . . Okay, y'all don't go ballistics on me now. I am not insinuating anything. I am just stating a fact. But if you wanna think otherwise, go ahead, be my guest, it's a free country. A great country, may I add.

OBAMA'S SNUB OF HILLARY: It was moments before Mr. Bush was going to deliver his seventh and last State of the Union Address in that great hall of Congress where America's powers-that-be deliver their speeches . . .

And only hours after Sen. Barack Obama received those passionate and repeated embraces from Sen. Ted Kennedy when that much talked-about SNUB occurred.

Barack and his newly-found Uncle Ted were standing together. Hillary walked into the great hall. Heads turned. "She was impossible to miss in the sea of dark suits and Supreme Court dark robes," said Maureen Dowd in her New York Times column. "Like Scarlett O'Hara after a public humiliation, Hillary showed up at the gathering wearing a defiant shade of red."

As Ms. Hillary reached out to shake Sen. Kennedy's hand, Mr. Obama turned way to talk KUNO to another legislator instead of joining Uncle Teddy in shaking hands with Hillary. Those who saw that intentional snub cringed in embarrassment for Hillary.

The following day, Obama said he was "surprised" to hear news reports of this SNUB. "I was turning away because Claire (that's Sen. Claire McCaskill) asked me a question as Senator Kennedy was reaching forward," Obama explained. "Senator Clinton and I have had very cordial relations off the floor and on the floor. . . . I think there is just a lot more tea-leaf reading going on here than I think people are suggesting."

Ha! Tea-leaf reading, indeed. As we all know, that was a fib. They hate each other's guts. As Ms. Dowd said, "Their relations have been frosty and fraught ever since the young Chicago prince challenged Queen Hillary's royal proclamation that it was her turn to rule." That SNUB was clearly a snub.

That SNUB clearly alludes only to one thing: Barack is merely a BOY in the world of adult politics . . . and politeness. In the Filipino vernacular: *Marami pang kakainin bigas si Barack*. **JJ**

Is Sen. Barack Obama an "Oreo" or a "Brother"?

You know, Senator Obama, it is very difficult having a straight-up debate with you, because you never take responsibility for any vote, and that has been a pattern . . .—Sen. Hillary Clinton

So, for the GOPs this past Saturday, Sen. John McCain, the ex-POW and war hero of the Vietnam "quagmire" won the South Carolina primary, defeating Mike Huckabee, the ex-Baptist minister and Mitt Romney, the ex-Mormon pastor.

This coming Saturday would be for the Democrats and this is going to be a battle royale between Obambi and Billary.

Pundits and talk heads have said that this state would be won by Mr. Barack HUSSIEN Osama . . . sorry, I mean, Mr. HUSSIEN Obama, y Barack. And the reason Mr. Barack will win is because all the black voters of the Democrat Party will come out and vote for their man, named HUSSIEN.

And they said this presidential election is not about RACE?

As Bill Clinton would say: "Gimme a break. That's the biggest fairy tale I've ever heard."

As Bob Herbert, of The New York Times wrote this week in his column: "On Saturday, in a cold, steady rain, voters turned out for the Republican primary. NEARLY ALL OF THEM—close to 100 percent—were white. At a dinner party here Saturday night, I was reminded ruefully by one of the guests: 'It used to be the Democratic Party that was the white man's party in South Carolina. Now it's the GOP. The black people vote next Saturday.'"

And, en masse, may I add.

And they said this presidential election is not about RACE?

As Bill Clinton would say: "Gimme a break. That's the biggest fairy tale I've ever heard."

Of course, it's about race!

Even though Mr. Obama is not completely black—he's half and half, half white, half black—he's nonetheless considered as black. YET, he ain't running in this presidential race on the platform of his being black. Hey, y'all follow me here? I ain't done explaining yet . . .

And because he's considered as black, even though his skin coloring is white, the blacks STILL consider him as a "brother." And in being that, all the black people of America, majority of them, that is, will surely vote for Mr. Obama, because he's black.

That's also why black celebrities are backing him up and endorsing his candidacy. There's Oprah and Denzel and Spike . . . and all the black TV and print pundits and talk heads. I mean, they're all solidly behind their "Brother" Barack. I would, too, if I was black.

Yeah, man, Barack's presidential race is about race.

BIGOTRY IN SOUTH CAROLINA: Do y'all know that the ruling white people of South Carolina still fly their confederate flag down there? That's right! Right there on the grounds of their state capitol in Columbia.

To Black Americans, this flag is a symbol of racism and of the difficult, abhorrent days of slavery. But to whites, it's a symbol of Southern pride and tradition, and of General Lee and of their "genteel" way of life . . . and of that famous blood-curdling rebel yell: heeehaawww!

To me, there should only be one flag that should fly in America: the Star and Stripes. That's it! (We shouldn't even fly the Philippine flag, except inside the Philippine Embassy. To do otherwise would be a display of the well-known Filipino carabao mentality).

Now check this out: Right next to this confederate FLAG that flies in Columbia, S.C., is the statue of Gov. Benjamin Tillman.

Mr. Bob Herbert said, "They still honor Benjamin Tillman down there, which is very much like honoring a malignant tumor. A statue of Tillman, who was known as 'Pitchfork Ben,' is on prominent display outside the statehouse."

Mr. Tillman who served as South Carolina governor and U.S. senator in the early part of the 1920s publicly defended the lynching of blacks. Several thousands of young black men were lynched all over America. The last one was in the early 1960s.

Speaking before the U.S. Senate, Governor Tillman declared: "We of the South have never recognized the right of the Negro to govern white men, and we never will. We have never believed him to be the equal of the white man, and we will not submit to his gratifying lust on our wives and daughters without lynching him."

As Ms. Hillary said, Senator Obama "never took any responsibility for any vote."

"OREO" OR "BROTHER": So, as I was saying, this presidential race of Mr. Obama is about his RACE. But he said he's not running on that issue. That's not my platform, he said. My platform is about CHANGE, he said. About changing the status quo. About changing the mentality of this country. About changing America for the better.

That's fine. Go on then. I am with that.

But does Mr. Obama got what it takes? Or, is he just all talk? All poetry, no prose. From what I understand, when he was a state senator of Illinois, he didn't do anything. He didn't vote on anything. What he was famously known for was in representing Chicago "slum landlords." Then, when he became a U.S. senator, he didn't do anything either. He was physically present during sessions, but he didn't take on issues.

As Ms. Hillary said, he "*never took any responsibility for any vote.*" And, he **FLIP-FLOPED** on his stand on the Iraq War.

If Mr. Obama is truly for CHANGE, I wanna see him change first that blatant bigotry that's on display right in the heart of South Carolina! I wanna see him take down that flag that symbolizes the oppression of his race! I wanna see him demolish that statue of that horrible man who defended the LYNCHING of black men!

If Senator Obama is really a true "brother" and not an "Oreo," I wanna see him take on a responsibility for a CHANGE . . . and tear those symbols down! Then, perhaps, I'll believe in his mantra of "change." **JJ**

Hillary's Cry . . . and Obama's Fairy Tales

Many people have said that the reason Ms. Hillary won the Democratic primary in New Hampshire was because she cried. And that the women all felt sorry for her that they all came out and voted for her and in doing that their "sisterhood votes" overwhelmed the "Obama phenomenon."

What da heck? If that's what it takes to win, hey, why not? This is a country run by "we-men" of all kinds, anyway.

But let's get the story straight though about Hillary's cry: Nope! She didn't cry, she didn't shed any tears, she didn't sob her heart out or went into a crying jag . . .

She "teared up," and got misty.

There is a difference there. Great difference.

Here's how it happened. Hillary had been invited by a friend to join other undecided female voters in a little New Hampshire café. There a woman asked Hillary: "As a woman, I know it's hard to get out of the house and get ready. My question is very personal: How do you do it?"

Hillary struggled for words. Seeing this, the woman rescued her as a friend might and asked: "Who does your hair?"

"Luckily, on special days I do have help," Hillary gamely answered. "If you see me every day, and if you look on some of the Web sites and listen to some of the commentators, they always find me on the day I didn't have help."

Warming up, Hillary then went on to say: "It's not easy, it's not easy. And I couldn't do it if I just didn't passionately believe it was the right thing to do . . ." Then pausing as if to collect her thoughts, Hillary softly said, "You know, I have so many opportunities from this country, and I just don't want to see us fall backwards. . . ."

"Some people think elections are a game, they think it's like 'who's up' or 'who's down'" she continued, her eyes glistening, her voice breaking. "It's about our country, it's about our kids' futures, it's really about all of us, together."

Her eyes glistened. Her voice broke. But she didn't cry. And I really think what she said there in that little cafe in New Hampshire came from her heart. During that moment in time, frozen for eternity, she showed her humanity . . . and her love for this country.

And to those who say that it's a weakness to be emotional about one's country, they are wrong! On the contrary, I think, it's strength. And America saw a glimpse of that strength in Hillary.

She's no "chilly bitch," that's for sure. Nor a witch. She's a highly intelligent, incredibly strong woman and I am sure she'd be the next President of this great country. I believe in her. I believe she can render the CHANGE that we all have been clamoring for.

OBAMA'S FAIRY TALE: When Mr. Bush announced the SURGE of troops last year in Iraq, Sen. Barrack Obama said that he didn't believe that the 30, 000 additional troops would "make a significant dent in the sectarian violence that's taking place there."

But it did make a significant dent. Attacks on our troops have slackened. Iraqi civilian deaths are down. And last month's overall number of deaths, which includes Iraqi security forces, Iraqi civilians as well as our troops, has been the lowest since the war began.

In a recent Democratic debate, Mr. Obama was asked: "Would you have seen this kind of greater security in Iraq if we had followed your recommendation to pull the troops out last year?"

Mr. Obama did not give a direct answer . . . and said that "much of that violence has been reduced because there was an agreement with tribes in Anbar Province, Sunni tribes, who started to see, after the Democrats were elected in 2006, you know what?—the Americans may be leaving soon. And we are going to be left vulnerable to the Shias. We should start negotiating now."

Say what? I think that's a song-and-dance answer. Or, as Bill Clinton said, "the biggest FAIRY TALE I've ever seen."

Or, as William Kristol, a syndicated columnist of *The New York Times*, said, "Last year's success, in Anbar and elsewhere, was made possible by confidence among Iraqis that U.S. troops would stay and protect them, that the U.S. would NOT abandon them to their enemies."

In other words, because the United States sent more troops instead of withdrawing, we are seeing some kind of success in Iraq. In other words, the surge worked! In other words, Sen. Barack Obama was wrong about Iraq.

In other words, as in that song that Frank Sinatra used to croon to us: "Fairy tales can come true, it can happen to you, if you're young at heart . . . tedum, tedum. . . ."

But I think the BIGGEST fairy tales of all time were the reasons Mr. Bush told America why Iraq was invaded: First, it was the WMD. Then, it was democracy. Then, terrorism.

Others said it was the Bush's family honor. Some said it was Islam. Many said, it was the oil. Fairy tales, they were . . . like this story:

A college teacher reminds her class of tomorrow's final exam. "Now class," she said, "I won't tolerate any excuses for you not being here tomorrow. I might consider a nuclear attack or a serious personal injury, illness or death in your immediate family, but that's it. No other excuses whatsoever!"

A smart-ass student in the back of the room raised his hand and asked, "What would you say if tomorrow I said I was suffering from complete and utter sexual exhaustion?"

The entire class is reduced to laughter and snickering. When silence is restored, the teacher smiles knowingly at the student, shakes her head and sweetly say, "Well, I guess you'd have to write the exam with your other hand."

Fairy tales, indeed, like Bush's fairy tales, like . . . Obama's. As Erap used to say: SAME-SAME. In other words, Obama is a Bush in the making. **JJ**

Change? What Kind of Change? Loose Change? Or, Sex Change? (Obama Is the "Oreo Candidate")

I live in an upper middle-class neighborhood in the suburbs of Seattle, in a little quiet town called, Auburn. Majority of the people who live here are whites. It's a welcoming and friendly neighborhood, but also reserved. Most families are also church goers.

I like this neighborhood a lot. I've made a couple of good friends in this neighborhood. It's a typical, small town neighborhood all over America. It's the face of America, I think. I am at home here.

When Barack Hussien Obama won the Iowa caucuses, one of my next door neighbors exclaimed, in horror: "No! No! No! No! No! Absolutely not!"

Another said, in disgust: "Ain't no way a Black Man is gonna rule this country." And, another said angrily: "Nope! We are not going to allow it."

My friend and walking partner, Jerry, said, "I don't think so. I don't think that will happen in America. Not yet, anyhow. Not in our lifetime . . ."

"But Obama is not completely Black," I said. "He's half and half. And, he's no oreo, you know what I mean?

Jerry asked: "What's an oreo?"

"Black on the outside, white on the inside,' I answered.

My wife votes Democrat but she will not vote for Mr. Obama if he becomes the nominee.

In my own household, my wife, who votes Democrat, said: "If Obama becomes the nominee, I'll go over to the other side and vote Republican. That is, if McCain becomes the Republican nominee. If not, I'll just NOT vote at all."

Me? Just like my wife, I'll jump the fence, too, to the other side and go for Huckabee, the preacher. He said that when he becomes America's President, he'll ELIMINATE the IRS, do away with income taxes . . . and taxes on our savings and dividends. The only taxes he'll require are sales taxes.

Eliminate the IRS and income taxes! Woohooo! I like that! Don't you? It's an idiotic idea though. America thrives on taxes. We are able to feed the hungry, the poor and the many "palamunins" of this country from our income taxes.

John McCain, the war hero and American patriot.

I do like McCain. He's a war hero and a true American patriot. I like most of his ideas, except on the war in Iraq. On that issue, he's a CLONE of Mr. Bush.

So really, I dunno . . . about jumping over to the side of the GOOFS, I mean, GOPS.

My two boys, Jon and Chris, are both for Obama. Because of Obama's mantra for CHANGE . . . and of his idealism: an idealism that young Americans can relate to. The idealism of the youth, the inexperienced, the rookie . . . the untested, the "OBAMBIS."

Barack Hussein Obama said, "We are one nation. We are one people. And our time for CHANGE has come."

Right on, my man! Beautiful rhetorics. Obama has a very likeable persona. Eight years ago, we elected a President on likeability, and we got one who misguided America into war and debt!

So, what kind of change is Obama advocating? Loose change? (That's to borrow Bobby Reyes' words, a California pundit and editor of this online magazine.) Or, is it sex change? Or, keep the change?

Mr. Obama, I think, is full of B.S.! He's great orator. No doubt about that. He reminds me of Dr. Martin Luther King. But I need to know exactly how he intends to effect this change. This CHANGE must be more than a political mantra.

In magical words, he said that we need to change the health-care system of America. I agree with that. It's true. It needs to be changed. But HOW? Mr. Obama doesn't tell us. He doesn't tell where he would get the money. He has no plan. He merely offers words, beautiful words that blindside the American OBAMBIS, like my two boys.

Is Senator Obama more arrogant than President Bush?

In awe-inspiring words, Mr. Obama said that when he becomes President and Mr. Osama and his Al Qaedas have been "pinpointed" in Pakistan or anywhere else in this world, he would go in "immediately," bomb the place to smithereens and send in the troops . . . the United Nations, be damned! Really, I thought Mr. Bush was an arrogant man . . .

In poetic words, Mr. Obama said that when he becomes President, on day #1 of his presidency, he's would pull out all the troops from Iraq. Hey, that's fine. Let's get the hell out of Iraq. But Mr. Obama doesn't tell us HOW he's going to pull out the troops from Iraq. You just can't pull out troops from a war zone, with out any specific plans. Or, without caring what would happen in that part of the world when our troops have left. That's irresponsible . . .

I think the CHANGE that Mr. Obama so beautifully talks about is the way he CHANGES HIS MIND on issues.

As Ms. Hillary said: "If you gave a speech, and a very good speech, against the war in Iraq in 2002, and then by 2004, you're saying you're not sure how you would have voted, and then by 2005, 2006 and 2007 you vote for $300 billion for the war you said you were against, that's NOT change . . ."

True, that's not CHANGE! Loose change, maybe. Keep the change, perhaps. I'd rather believe in someone who's READY FOR CHANGE than someone who merely chants poetic, meaningless CHANGE and offers false hopes that lure the young and the naïve. **JJ**

The Iowa Caucuses . . . and Sen. Joe Biden's One-Liners

Today is the much-awaited Iowa caucuses. By the time you've read this, it'd be Friday. The caucuses would be all over. We would all know who the winner is . . . and America's attention would already be in New Hampshire for its primaries. But right now, according to polls, for the Democrats, Senators Hillary Rodham Clinton of New York and Barack Hussien Obama of Illinois are neck-and-neck in the race. Whereas John Edwards, a former senator of North Carolina, is right in there, close at the heels of Clinton and Obama.

The others are just "saling pusa" na lang.

For the Republicans, it's a toss-up between two former governors: Mitt Romney of Massachusetts and Mike Huckabee of Arkansas. As y'all know, Romney is a former Mormon pastor; Huckabee is a former southern Baptist minister.

These two are squaring it off toe to toe. Both claim to be more Christian than the other; closer to Jesus than the other. Their followers chant: "Our Jesus is BETTER than your Jesus." I suppose the group with the better Jesus will win this race.

Who's gonna be their party's nominee, I dunno for sure. It's been said over and over again though by pundits and talk heads that whoever would win in the Iowa caucuses would be THE party's presidential nominee. These caucuses, they say, will sway the whole country and point out who's gonna be the choice of the party.

That's a bunch of B.S., I think.

In Iowa, ONLY 6% of its population go to caucuses. And Iowa has a population of about 2.9 million people and majority are farmers. These bunch of farmers are telling America who's gonna be the nominees of the two major parties . . . and one of them the next leader of the most powerful nation in the world?

Rubbish!

As one political analyst said: "Just as nonrepresentative as Iowa is of the country, Iowa caucusgoers are nonrepresentative of Iowa as a whole."

Also, check this out: I really don't think Senator Barack Hussien Obama will win in Iowa. Most of the people are Christian Conservatives there . . . and RURAL Whites. I really don't think, these people would want a BLACK MAN, with a Muslim name, to be America's president, do you?

Nor, would they want a MORMON, would they?

I believe it's gonna be Hillary Rodham Clinton for the Democrats, because of her entrenched and powerful political machinery. And, Mike Huckabee for the Republicans, because of his kinship with Christian Conservatives.

Now, if I turned out to be wrong . . . well, hey, nobody is right all the time. I am a pundit. Rightly or wrongly, I merely opine.

So, anyway, what are caucuses?

"Caucuses are QUIRKY electoral creations that depart from the usual civics-class ideas about fair elections. They are run not by the government, but rather by the state Republican and Democratic Parties," said The New York Times.

They are "small community meetings in which citizens gather not only to choose candidates but also to conduct local party businesses. And rather than secret ballots, there are public exchanges of opinions."

Like a meeting de abante, in other words.

To Iowans, the 1,781 caucuses in their state are a civic treasure, passed down from one farmer generation to another. The practice was introduced two centuries ago. Caucuses do not conform to one-person, one-vote rule. Ties can be settled by COIN TOSS or picking names out of a hat.

A quirky form of election all right. Well, what do y'all expect from farmers?

COOL QUIPS FROM SEN. BIDEN: You know, I like Senator Joe Biden of Delaware a lot. I think he's a cool guy. In December 1972, one month after his election to the Senate, a car accident killed his first wife and a baby daughter and injured his two young sons. He began a daily commute, from his home in Delaware to work in Washington, D.C. and back—80 minutes each way—so he could tuck his children in at night and be there when they woke up.

That, to me, is THE coolest.

A known jester, he said of Obama, "I mean . . . you got the first mainstream African-American who is articulate and bright and clean and nice-looking guy, I mean, that's a storybook, man . . ."

He also said, "I got tested for AIDS. I know Barack got tested for AIDS. It's an important thing . . . it's not unmanly to wear a condom . . ."

Rev. Al Sharpton answered: "I am also clean. I take showers everyday . . . and I also use condoms."

Sen. Biden once told an Indian man on his campaign trail this: "In Delaware you cannot go to a 7-Eleven or a Dunkin' Donuts unless you have a slight Indian accent . . . I'm not joking."

Commenting on GOP candidate, Rudy Giuliani, the former New York City mayor, "There are only three things he says in a sentence: a noun, a verb and 9/11."

Senator Biden, sir, with all due respect, your jokes are much better than those late-TV jokes of David Letterman and Jay Leno. For your jokes, you get my vote, sir, that is, if you're still around and running after the Iowa caucuses.

Otherwise, it's "BILLARY" for me. Hey, it's two for one. **JJ**

It Was, Indeed—the Year of the Pig

This year is just about done. A few more days it would be over. It was the year of the pig. True to its name, it was a piggish year. A wacky year. A weird year. A scandalous year.

Let's review it.

THE MAN WITH THE WIDE STANCE: "I am not gay," so said Senator Larry Craig after he was arrested in a men's room at the Minneapolis airport in an undercover sex sting. According to the arrest report prepared by the undercover officer, who arrested him, "Craig stated . . . he has a WIDE STANCE when going to the bathroom and that his foot may have touched mine."

Senator Craig also "tapped his foot" against the officer's foot and "waved his hand underneath the partition" of the stalls. The Idaho GOP pleaded guilty to disorderly conduct. At first he intended to quit. Now, he says he'll finish his term.

MADAME'S FAVORITE: Senator David Vitter, another goofy GOP was discovered to have the distinction of being the biggest name and "the number one client" on a Washington, D.C. escort service phone list. Yeah, just like those PACKAGE DEAL escort services that are provided to Japanese tourists in the Philippines.

We heard that Vitter has also the distinction of being "the biggest tipper" for those services rendered to him. Yeah, just like those Japs. This goofy GOP from Louisiana said "God and his wife have already forgiven him," so he's also staying on as a GOOF, I mean, GOP senator.

"SCOOTER" LIBBY: VP Dick Cheney' former chief of staff was convicted for LYING in court in a CIA leak case. He was sentenced to 30 months in prison, but Mr. Bush commuted the sentence, calling it "EXCESSIVE" punishment. Water boarding, yeah, that's excessive.

NEGLECT OF VETERANS: Staff Sergeant John Shannon, a wounded Iraq war veteran testified early in the year about "patient neglect and shoddy conditions" at Walter Reed Hospital, the supposedly premier hospital of the U.S. Army. This scandal cost the hospital commander, an Army general and the Army Secretary their jobs.

It was also a wake-up call to all the civilian administrators of VA hospitals all over the country to get off their butts and pay attention more to vets . . . instead of those "pretty little nurses" in VA hospitals. That's right, shape up or ship out, misters. Do your job. America is number one because of us, vets.

A NASA LOVE TRIANGLE: Navy Commander Lisa Novak's NASA career went tumbling down when she was arrested in Orlando, Florida. Cops say she drove 1,000 miles non-stop from Houston to Orlando to "kidnap and kill" a rival for the love of a fellow astronaut.

So she won't have to go on a BRB during that long drive, she wore a diaper. . . . Crazy love, I tell ya.

A RAPE THAT WASN'T: The rape case against a handful of Duke University Lacrosse players blew up in the face of Prosecutor Mike Nifong. He went from prosecutor to prosecuted when it was found out that he withheld evidences that could disprove the guilt of the accused youngsters. He also said that the DNA that was found at the scene of the imagined "gang rape" was irrelevant to the case.

He was DISBARRED, resigned as Durham County District Attorney and served a day in jail for contempt of court. Last we heard, he now works as a burger flipper at McDonald's.

DON IMUS: His remarks about the players of the Rutgers University women's basketball team got him fired and off the air by CBS. He repeatedly apologized. He practically begged to be forgiven, but "no way," said the Reverend Al Sharpton, "you burn, baby, burn."

But Imus didn't get burn. He returned to the air waves a few months later with ABC radio. His show is now again heard all over the country and he's getting paid mucho millions for it. Reverend Sharpton and company must have burned when they heard this. Burn, baby, burn.

FALLEN STARS: NFL player Michael Vick's bright career as a quarterback was "mauled by pit bulls," when he pleaded guilty to charges of promoting dog fighting on his property. The Falcons suspended him and he was sentenced to 23 months in prison. What a waste! A rare talent gone to the dawgs, so to speak.

Another bright star who fell from grace due to steroid use was three-time Olympic gold medalist Marion Jones. She tearfully admitted that she used steroids . . . after saying repeatedly that she never used those enhancement drugs. Jones pleaded guilty to felony charges, gave up the medals she won at the 2000 Olympic Games . . . and retired from her sport.

She was so beautiful to watch. I cheered for her during the GAMES. I cried with her when she admitted her deception.

GOD AND POLITICS: According Syndicated Columnist Andy Borowitz, Mike Huckabee, a former Arkansas governor and GOP president wannabe, has already picked his VP: Jesus Christ. In every debate that he was in, he never failed to mention Christ's name. The Rev. Pat Robertson, a supporter of Rudy Giuliani, said he was "blindsided" by that news. "I talked to Jesus the other night," said Rev. Robertson, "but he didn't mention anything about it to me."

ET TU, BHUTTO?: Like a "buto," I think Ms. Benazir Bhutto of Pakistan had no brains. There were many assassination attempts and death threats on her before she was shot to death the other day. Why she didn't take the precautions to protect herself from those dangers is to me a sign of utmost stupidity.

Perhaps, she wanted to be killed. Perhaps, she wanted to be martyred. She was the face of America in a country where Americans are not well-liked. She was a symbol of American neo-imperialism in a country teeming with Al Qaedas and Talibans. She was a TARGET, begging to be assassinated. She got her wish. She's now a martyr. . . .

Yeah, this year is just about done. A few more days it'd be over. It was, indeed, the year of the PIG. A scandalous year. A weird year. A wacky year.

Yo, Happy New Year, y'all!!! **JJ**

My Giddy Christmas Thoughts this Christmas

> To suggest celebrating Christmas and having decorations offends Muslims is absurd. Why should Christmas not be celebrated openly and wholeheartedly in our country when a vast majority of our people are Christians?"
> Shayk Ibrahim Mogra, a Muslim leader

I love Christmas, don't you?

The cheer, the décor, the songs, the nip in the air, the shopping for gifts, the Christmas cards that we receive wishing us, "Merry Christmas," the Christmas Tree. And all those twinkling, colored lights that we put up in front of our houses to light up the way for Mary, who is heavy with the Child, along with Joseph . . . as they seek a place to stay for the night.

And, of course, the colorful stories that are told such as this one that I am going to tell ya in a minute. It's not about Christmas, but hey, it's a true story that you can tell, and re-retell to friends at Christmas parties. This was written by a young boy and it won a national prize in FIRST-PERSON ESSAY WRITING many Christmases ago.

It's short and to the point. Read on. And smile there, Sour Face, at Pasko na.

"I took my dad to the mall the other day to buy some new shoes. We decided to grab a bite at the food court. I noticed that he was watching a teenager sitting next to him. The teenager had spiked hair in all different colors: green, red, orange, blue.

"My dad kept staring at him. The teenager would look and find him staring every time.

"When the teenager had enough, he sarcastically asked, 'What's the matter, old man? Never done anything wild in your life?'"

Knowing my Dad, I quickly swallowed my food so that I would not choke on his response. And in that unique classic style that my Dad has, he told the teenager, without even batting an eye:

"'Got drunk once and had sex with a peacock. And I was wondering if you were my son!'"

SEX WITH THOUSANDS OF WOMEN: Wilt Chamberlain . . . you know, that great basketball player in the olden days, once boasted that he had made love to about three-thousand women. Julio Iglesias, that Spanish singer who sung that song, "To All The Girls I've loved Before," which is now a classic, once said, that he had made love to about 6,000 women.

> Editor's Note: Please read a proposal in the User Comments to Jesse Jose about turning Filipino husbands into versions of Wilt and Julio . . .

Now, check this out: Actor Jack Nicholson claimed that he had made love to 900,000 women! Gawd, Jack . . . when did you ever had time to pee?

VIAGRA FOR VOTES: Have y'all heard that in Thailand, candidates there for political office are using Viagra, instead of cash, to buy votes. Yeah, that's a fact. I heard it on the Filipino CNN (Coconut News Ngayon). I wonder what they use now in the Philippines to buy votes.

By the way . . . I heard there's something much more potent than Viagra that was discovered in the Philippines. It's called AMPALUNGAY. It's ampalaya and malungay mix together and the KATAS from these two vegetables when consumed, mas grabe daw ang resulta kaysa sa Viagra. This was concocted by LASTIKMAN. Hmmmm. I must go to the Philippines soon and check out this Philippine-made katas.

THE GALAXY OF VENUS/CHICAGO: Meanwhile, American scientists are learning about Venus, "where it can be 457 degrees Celsius in the summer, with winds up to 225 miles per hour." And in the winter, it's like living in a freeze box or in an igloo. In other words, basically like Chicago, without the Sears Tower.

BUMPER STICKERS: I have a new car bumper sticker on my Toyota truck. I've placed it just below my "SUPPORT OUR TROOPS" sticker, next to the U.S. FLAG sticker . . . and it reads, "BUCK FUSH." Those three stickers make three statements that I truly believe in.

A VOTE FOR HILLARY: Y'all remember Gennifer Flowers? Yeah, that floozy, who in 1992 said she had "a long, adulterous affair with Bill Clinton." She said that she may vote for Hillary. "I can't help but want to support my own gender," she said. She also purred that Senator Joe Biden, a wannabe President of the United States of America, "is a very sexy man." Perhaps, Ms. Flowers would also like to have "a long, adulterous affair" with Senator Biden?

OBAMA'S DRUG USE: Christmas season is not only the season for giving, it's also the season for apologizing. Senator Hillary Rodham Clinton, America's president-in-waiting, apologized personally to Senator Barack Hussien Obama for a top adviser's public remark on Mr. Obama's youthful DRUG USE.

The adviser, William Shaheen was quoted by *The Washington Post* to have said that the goofy GOPS "would probably go after Mr. Obama for having used cocaine and marijuana." Shaheen went on to suggest that the GOOPS, I mean, the GOPS would probably question, too, whether Mr. Obama "shared drugs with others or was a dealer."

I think the question that should be asked, is: DID HE INHALE?

Y'all forgive me for being giddy with this column. It's the Christmas season, *kasi. Okey ngarud, Maligayang Pasko sa inyong lahat. At yung mga galit sa akin: PEACE na.* **JJ**

On Oprah, CIA Tapes and Romney's Mormonism

So, Oprah is supporting Senator Barack HUSSIEN Obama in his run for the White House. Y'all forgive me please for being such an ignoramus, but who the heck is Oprah? {glossarbot=disable}
Kapangalan ng tsimay namin noon araw 'to, eh. Oprah rin ang pangalan. At maitim din. . . .

Really, I don't think that Oprah has the stature or the pull or the weight to catapult Mr. Osama, I mean, Mr. Obama to become the President of the United States of America. I don't think she's capable of doing that. Sure, thousands of people came to see her in Iowa, in New Hampshire and in South Carolina. Sure, people came to show their support for Mr. HUSSIEN, I mean, for Mr. Barack HUSSIEN Osama, I mean, Obama. But I think they came more, for the spectacle of it all, y'all know what I mean?

DESTROYED EVIDENCES OF TORTURE: So, the CIA destroyed videotapes of torture techniques of two senior al-Qaeda detainees, AFTER telling a federal judge that no such tapes existed. The CIA said they destroyed the tapes "to protect the identity" of the CIA torturers that were on the tapes.

When queried by reporters about the matter, Ms. Dana Perino, Mr. Bush's mouthpiece, said the President had "no knowledge" of CIA torture tapes of terrorist suspects. Of course, Mr. Bush has "no knowledge" of it. He has "no knowledge" of much of anything at all!!!

ON MITT ROMNEY: As y'all know he's a Mormon. And a lot of people consider the Mormon religion as a "cult." When asked during an interview about the teachings of Joseph Smith, the founder of Mormonism, Romney said church officials should answer those questions. "You know, they're probably the right folks to give you the answers to questions related to a bunch of Mormon teachings," he said. "What I can tell you is that the values of my faith are founded on Judeo-Christian principles."

HUMANS CAN BECOME GOD: If Mormonism was founded on Christian principles, why then the practice of polygamy for a long, long time in the church's history? And why then the barring of Blacks from full rights of membership in the church until 1978?

Joseph Smith founded the Mormon religion in the 19th century as a "restoration" of what he considered to be "a true Christian church." Mormons do not believe in the concept of the unified TRINITY. They believe that God has a physical body and that human beings can eventually become God. And that people can be baptized after they have died. And that the Garden of Eden was in Missouri.

Perhaps, to others, it's a mystifying religion. But to me, it's scary. Especially that part where it says that "humans can eventually become God."

By the way, do y'all know that Mr. Romney was an erstwhile pastor of his church? In the Catholic religion that's equivalent to a Bishop. And, if he becomes President, he said, he will continue to believe "in my Mormon faith" and will endeavor to live by it. To me, that's truly scary.

THE SPEECH: In his SPEECH last week, Mr. Romney said: "What do I believe about Jesus Christ? I believe Jesus Christ is the son of God and the savior of mankind."

He also said that "religious tolerance would be a shallow principle indeed if it were reserved only for faiths with which we agree." And then he added this caveat: "My church's beliefs about Christ may not all be the same as those other faiths." Those are brilliant and eloquent words. But are they true? Or are they merely political words? Words that deceive, in other words.

He also said that "polygamy is not a part" of his faith. Yet his grandparents practiced polygamy . . . and he vowed that he will always abide by the "faith of my fathers."

So, where's this guy coming from? He also asserted that "freedom requires religion and religion requires freedom." I don't think so! Religion has been the enemy of freedom! Think Taliban! Think Spanish Inquisition! Think Philippines when it was ruled by the Spanish friars for so long!
People have likened the SPEECH of Mr. Romney to that of President Kennedy in 1960 about his Catholicism. There is NO COMPARISON at all. Romney said that religion has a place in the public domain and that the Constitution rested on a "foundation of faith."
He said, "In recent years, the notion of the separation of the church and state has been taken by some well beyond its original meaning. They seek to remove from the public domain any acknowledgement of God. Religion is seen as merely a PRIVATE AFFAIR with no place in public life. It is as if they are intent on establishing a new religion in America—the religion of secularism. They are wrong!"

John F. Kennedy emphasized the separation of church and state and called religion a "private affair."

President Kennedy said, "I believe in an America where the separation of the church and state is ABSOLUTE—where no Catholic prelate would tell the President (should he be a Catholic) how to act and no Protestant minister would tell his parishioners for whom to vote . . . where no man is denied public office merely because his religion differs from the President who might appoint him or the people who might elect him . . .
"I believe in a President whose views on religion are his own PRIVATE AFFAIR, neither imposed upon him by the nation or imposed by the nation upon him as a condition to holding that office."

Right on!

Mr. Romney is the one who's wrong. His Mormonism ain't for me and he ain't no John F. Kennedy. I believe in the separation of church and state. That to me, is America. **JJ**

Religion in Politics: is it Right or Wrong?

RELIGION is at its best when it is furthest from political power. The power to send armies to war, to rule every aspect of our lives, to tell us what to wear, what to think, what to read—when religion gets hold of that, WATCH OUT! Because trouble will ensue. . . .

So says Philip Pullman, who wrote "*His Dark Measures,*" a trio of fantasy novels that has sold over 15 million copies since the first volume, "*The Golden Compass,*" was published in 1955. It has been turned into a radio drama, a hit stage play in London and now a movie, starring Nicole Kidman and David Craig. It soon hopes to take the place of J.K. Rowlings' Harry Potter books and movies.

So . . . if what he said is true about religion, no wonder we got into trouble in Iraq. Before invading Iraq, Mr. Bush said he had talked with God about it and heard His voice.

Mr. Bush heard God's voice? Or, did he hear voices?

There's a difference there. My wife, who is a psycho-therapist, told me that when a person HEARS VOICES, watch out! That person is "delusional," and trouble, for sure, will ensue.

IRAQI DEATHS: According to IRAQIBODYCOUNT.ORG, since the 2003 invasion, the documented deaths of INNOCENT Iraqi civilians have now reached the count of 88,812.

If that is true, then we have committed GENOCIDE!!!

A QUESTION AND ANSWER: In a recent White House press conference, veteran journalist and syndicated columnist Helen Thomas asked Dana Perino, the mouthpiece of Mr. Bush, this question: "Do we kill innocent Iraqi civilians?"

Dana Perino answered: "Helen, I find it really unfortunate that you use your front row position bestowed upon you by your colleagues to make such statements . . . It is an honor and a privilege to be in the briefing room, and to suggest that we, at the United States, are killing innocent people is absurd and very offensive."

What a STUPID arrogant woman! Hey, Ms. Perino, truth hurts and can be offensive, but it's NEVER absurd. Also, have you heard this off-the-cuff remark by Mr. Bush in 2005 when asked how many Iraqi civilians have been killed by our troops?. He said, "So far, we'd killed 30,000 . . . more or less."
It's almost 2008, how many now have we killed?

BECAUSE OF RELIGION, A BOY DIES: Yeah, it's true. Here in Seattle, a 14-year-old boy died after refusing blood transfusions in his fight against leukemia. The boy objected to receiving blood because it ran counter to his beliefs as a Jehovah's Witness. A Superior Court Judge affirmed the boy's right to refuse the treatments because he said the eight-grader was MATURE ENOUGH to make the decision.

That's kind of weird, I think. At 14, you're not mature enough to buy cigarettes and liquor, and you're not mature enough to vote . . . or even mature enough to have sex, but you're mature to make that decision to die because of your religion? That's one of the weirdest things I've heard. But Seattle, just like Chicago and California and Florida, has a lot of weirdoes of all kinds.

FOR DEMOCRACY'S SAKE: So as to preserve democracy in Pakistan, President Pervez Musharraf stepped down from his post as Pakistan's military commander-in-chief. The following day, he was sworn in as a civilian president.

So as to also preserve democracy here in America, shouldn't Mr. Bush step down, too, as commander-in-chief?

THE SURGE, A SUCCESS: So the so-called SURGE of U.S. troops in Iraq is working. Violence is down. Casualties are down. ONLY 36 of our troops were killed there last month. Piece of cake. Thirty six? That ain't nothing. It's not our children that are getting killed over there. It's other people's children. It's other people's husbands and wives. It's other children's dads and moms. So, why should we care, right?

But as Americans, we, at least, need to ask ourselves the questions Mr. Bush refuses to answer: Is America signing on to keep the peace in Iraq indefinitely? If so, how many American and Iraqi deaths a month would be an acceptable price? IF NOT, what's the plan for getting out? And do we keep on spending $10 billion a month to maintain this "peace"?

A SHINING MOMENT FOR SENATOR JOHN MCCAIN: Last week in my column, I wrote about the CNN/YouTube debate of the goofy GOPs.

But I forgot to mention that Mr. McCain said a couple of things that I truly liked. His stance on TORTURING terrorist suspects is commendable: "DON'T! We are better than those people. . . ."

I also like his stance on immigration. After mentioning the failed effort of the Senate to pass a bill, portions of which included the temporary guest program and the pathway to citizenship for illegal immigrants already living here in America, Senator McCain said . . . so very eloquently, I think:

"What we've learned is that the American people want the borders enforced. We must secure the borders first. But then . . . we need to sit down as Americans and recognize these are God's children as well, and they need some protections under the law and they need some of our love and compassion. . . ."

That little speech was interrupted with a standing ovation. God was mentioned and Christian conservatives loved that little speech.

And, so did I. I am no goofy GOP or a Christian Conservative though. I am a Democrat, but I keep my mind open to Republican ideals.

So, is RELIGION at its best when furthest from politics? Or, is RELIGION a part of American politics and of our daily lives? Is Philip Pullman wrong? What do y'all think? **JJ**

On Treason, Obama, IQ and Acrobatic Sex

"Little minds are interested in the extraordinary; great minds in the commonplace."—Elbert Hubbard

I don't know how y'all feel about it, but I think it's treason.

Yes, TREASON!

Scott McClellan, Mr. Bush's former White House mouthpiece, has released excerpts from his book, titled, "What Happened," with startling information implicating Mr. Bush, VP Dick Cheney and Karl Rove in the OUTING of CIA agent, Valerie Plame . . . and LIES that they said to justify attacking Iraq, a country that posed no threat whatsoever to our nation's security.

If we are to flourish as a democratic country with all the checks and balances, these people who have trashed our Constitution, given away lives of so many of our soldiers, killed thousands of innocent Iraqi citizens and drained our treasures almost to the point of bankruptcy MUST be held accountable. They must be indicted and tried in court . . . IMPEACHED and sent to prison.

Nobody should be exempt or above the law.

(Editor's Note: Please see related article, a satire
Top Ten Reasons Why Senator Obama Is a Foreign-Relations Expert)

ON OBAMA'S FOREIGN POLICY EXPERIENCE: Speaking in IOWA last week, Senator Barack HUSSIEN Obama boasted that his "exotic upbringing, his Kenya family and his years of growing up in different countries has given him the opportunity to see the world with more understanding," and helped form his "judgment" in resisting the war in Iraq.

""I spent four years living overseas when I was a child living in Southeast Asia," he said. "If you don't understand these cultures then it's very hard for you to make GOOD FOREIGN POLICY DECISIONS. Foreign policy is all about judgment."

BUT Senator Hillary Clinton didn't buy that. Knowing that Obama's foreign policy experience is as thin as his physique, she pounced on him and told a crowd in Iowa: "With all due respect, I don't think LIVING IN A FOREIGN COUNTRY between the ages of 6 and 10 is foreign-policy experience."

Right on! I don't care what y'all call Ms. Hillary: "Witch," "Bitch," "Chilly Hilly," "Her Royal Thighness," or whatever. One thing for sure, she's no dingbat. She's got wit. She's quick on her feet. And, she's got . . . grande cojones, figuratively speaking, of course. Mucho bigger than Obama's. Or even that of Giuliani's, the GOP frontrunner for the presidential nomination.

Ms. Hillary is gonna beat them both! One at a time. First Obama, then Giuliani. Bet me and I bet ya, you gonna lose.

If this country is stupid enough to elect another Republican President, then this country deserves anything it gets.

"With all due respect, I don't think living in a foreign country between the ages of 6 and 10 is foreign-policy experience"—Mrs. Clinton

According to a national survey, African-American voters favor Hillary Clinton more than Barack Obama. The New York senator was viewed favorably by 83 percent, compared to Obama's 70 percent. One of the reasons for Clinton's lead in this poll was the economic success African-Americans experienced during her husband's time in the White House.

The other reason is obvious, but it's too POLITICALLY INCORRECT to say. But, if I must say it: Yes, the other reason is because he's BLACK and his middle name is HUSSEIN. And I don't think America is ready for an African-American President, whose middle is HUSSEIN.

ON HILLARY'S VP: Did y'all hear? Bill Clinton, always out front, already is saying that Hillary's running mate should be Kucinich. Elizabeth Kucinich, that is. Okay, it's a bad joke. Sorry.

A PARDON FOR A TURKEY: So, we learned that Mr. Bush, again, this year, pardoned a turkey Thanksgiving Day. When he was governor of Texas, he never pardoned nor delayed an execution of a death row inmate in any given day.

IQ'S OF RACES: The science of modern genetic had found evidences that the races are not, strictly speaking, the same. Repeated testing conducted on different continents show racial variations in IQ. Whites have an average IQ of about 100, while Africans and African-Americans average from 70 to 85 . . . and, Asians, from 106 to 113.

Critics content that IQ testing is based on WHITE, EUROPEAN SOCIAL NORMS. If that's the case, why then do Asians do best of all? Another question, if y'all don't mind: Are Filipinos Asians or Hispanics? In our history books, we've claimed that we are of the Malay race. What da hell is the Malay race? It rhymes with palay. And palay connotes the *magsasaka* and his carabao. . . .

ACROBATIC SEX: According to a news alert from China, doctors there are warning their countrymen NOT to try to imitate the acrobatic sex scenes in Ang Lee's movie, "Lust, Caution," lest they suffer "unnecessary physical harm." The movie is about a love affair during World War II and it's very popular in China. Moviegoers have flooded the theaters to watch the uncensored version.

A hospital official said, "Most of the sexual maneuvers are in abnormal body positions. Only women and men that have gymnastics or yoga experience are able to perform them."

I've always wanted to be a movie star. If only Ang Lee had given me the opportunity to a screen test, with all my yoga skills and experience, I could have starred in that Chinese movie. No such luck yet. But I am not giving up hope. Until that day when I hit the big screen, I'll just keep on practicing my yoga . . . behind close doors.

By the way, did y'all watch on CNN the You Tube Debate of the goofy GOPS that was held in St. Petersburg, Florida Wednesday night? Aside from Ron Paul, all of them were CLONES of Mr. Bush, mouthing off what he has been saying and will be saying till the end of his term: WE'LL STAYON COURSE!!!

And I repeat: If this country is STUPID enough to elect another Republican President, then this country deserves anything it gets!—**JJ**

Sumbich . . . How Do We Beat the Bitch?

So, call me a jester. I have another joke. Told to me by a friend. A special friend. He's also my next door neighbor. Well, not exactly next door. Almost. He lives just around the corner from my house, about five houses down the street.

Like me, he's also retired. He's a retired truck driver. He used to drive, cross country, those long, huge 18-wheelers. He's 70 years old.

He's also my walking partner. His name is Jerry Lytle. He's got a little friendly, affectionate dachshund, named Molly. And a genteel, lady-like wife, named Marilyn. And a son, named Bruce, who is a freelance photographer for National Geographic.

From Monday to Friday, rain or shine, at exactly 3:30 p.m., Jerry is at my door, ringing my doorbell, and knocking on my door. He would knock and knock . . . until I would open the door to tell him, "I'd be right out."

He's like a clock, always on time, on the dot, at 3:30 pm, not a second less, not a second more.

And we would walk around the neighborhood, on sidewalks, on walking trails, up and down hills, on running tracks, round and round, in our two neighborhood parks.

We would walk for miles. Three miles, five miles, seven miles sometimes, when the sun is gloriously out and we are both feeling good. One solid hour we would walk. Hard walk. Power walk. Jerry is in real good shape. In a much better shape than I am.

And while we walk, we would talk. We would talk and talk about everything under the sun. Politics, current events, family values, race, sex, books, the war in Iraq, our aging bodies, anything that comes to mind, anything that we fancy, in any descriptive words, in any words that we feel like using . . . no holds barred. We freely use the F words and the N words and all the forbidden and politically incorrect words in this world.

And yes, we would gossip, too, about our neighbors. And, we would tell jokes to each other. Dirty jokes, good jokes, racial jokes, awful jokes, corny jokes . . . anything goes. And we would talk loud, too, because both of us are hard of hearing. And we would laugh outrageously at our jokes . . . cackle and burp, hoot and fart.

I thoroughly enjoy our walks and our talks and our jokes. He told me this joke the other day, titled SUMBICH:

"A filthy rich South Florida man decided that he wanted to throw a party and invited all his buddies and neighbors. He also invited Leroy, the only redneck, in the neighborhood.

"He held the party around the pool in the backyard of his mansion. Leroy was having a good time drinking, dancing, eating shrimp, oysters and barbecue and flirting with all the women. At the height of the party, the host said, 'I have a ten-foot, man-eating gator in my pool and I'll give a million dollars to anyone who has the nerve to jump in.'

"The words were barely out of his mouth when there was a loud splash and everyone turned around and saw Leroy in the pool! Leroy was fighting the gator and kicking its butt!

"Leroy was jabbing the gator in the eyes with his thumbs, throwing punches, head butts and choke holds, biting the gator on the tail and flipping the gator through the air.

"The water was churning and splashing everywhere. Both Leroy and the gator were screaming and raising hell.

"Finally Leroy strangled the gator and let it float to the top like a dime store goldfish. Leroy then climbed out of the pool. Everybody was just staring at him in disbelief.

"Then the host said, 'Well, Leroy, I reckon I owe you a million dollars.'

"'No, that's okay, I don't want it,' said Leroy.

"The rich man said, 'Man, I have to give you something. You won the bet. How about half a million bucks then?'

"'No, thanks. I don't want it,' answered Leroy.

"The host said, 'I insist on giving you something. That was amazing. How about a new Porsche and a Rolex and some stock options?'

"Again. Leroy said no.

"Confused, the rich man asked, 'Well, Leroy, then what do you want?'

"Leroy said, 'I want the name of the SUMBICH who pushed me into the pool.'"

Heeehawww!!!

BTW, y'all heard about this? It's true. I am not making this up. About a week ago, a woman bluntly asked president wannabe, Sen. John McCain, at a GOP rally in South Carolina:

"So, how do we beat the bitch?"

McCain chuckled and said, "Excellent question."

Though later on, McCain said he respects Hillary Clinton, aka "the Bitch," I think, just like that woman who asked the question, Senator McCain revealed his own true feelings about Ms. Hillary with that immediate chuckling response.

And I bet ya, Senator McCain—and all the goofy GOPs—also have the same unspoken, unrevealed question on their minds: "Sumbich . . . how do we beat the bitch?"

Hey, y'all know what I mean? I am a jester, you see. **JJ**

A Turkey Story for Thanksgiving Day

Gobble-gobble . . . Is this the way a turkey sounds? Or does it cluck like the way a chicken clucks . . . like kuk-kuruk-kuku. Or is that a Filipino yodel?

I don't really know.

A long, long time ago, when I visited the world-famous San Diego Zoo in California, I've seen turkeys in their man-made natural habitat, but I didn't hear any of them do the cluck-clucks nor the kuk-kuruk-kukos.

What I've seen was that the male turkeys preen a lot and show off their brilliant feathers to the all drab-looking females scattered around . . . and they mount the females from behind, like a rooster would.

So I assumed that turkeys must be of the fowl species. But the male human species sometimes do mount from behind, too. So, I don't really know.

What I do know is that male turkeys are promiscuous.

Because I observed that right after mounting a female, the male turkey nonchalantly walks away. And minutes later, it's preening again in front of another female . . . yes, for another mounting.

And I learned that day that the main preoccupation of male turkeys was to preen and show off and mount all the females in town . . . and I envied them. Because that's the kind of life I'd like to have in my second life on earth.

But, of course, like everything else in life, there are hazards of being a turkey.

Before I forget, here's my joke for the week . . .

And this is the merry joke I'll tell to my friends. It's about what Little Johnny saw . . . no, not at the zoo, but in the woods . . .

One day, Little Johnny saw his daddy's car pass by the school playground and go into the woods. Curious, he followed the car and saw Daddy and Aunt Jane in a passionate embrace. Little Johnny found this so exciting that he could not contain himself as he ran home and started to tell his mother:

"Mommy, I was at the playground and I saw Daddy's car go into the woods with Aunt Jane. I went back to look and he was giving Aunt Jane a big kiss, then he helped her take off her shirt. Then Aunt Jane helped Daddy take his pants off, then Aunt Jane . . .

At this point, Mommy cut him off and said, "Johnny, this is such an interesting story, suppose you save the rest of it for our Thanksgiving dinner. I want to see the look on Daddy's face when you tell it tonight." (***The story's conclusion is at the end of this column . . .)***

Come Thanksgiving Day, you can end featherless and roasted golden brown on a platter, laid on one of America's dinner tables, prayed over, and then consumed by the whole family that came together for the sole purpose of gobbling you up.

Come to think of it, I wonder why the Indians of ancient America chose the promiscuous turkey to give to the Puritans to feast on in their first celebration of Thanksgiving Day.

Could it be that the American Indians, who showed the ignorant Puritans how to farm corn and how to cook and eat turkey, were really making fun of them, perhaps saying among themselves: "Let's give these Puritans the promiscuous turkey to eat, so they'll loosen up a little? Then we'll show them how to smoke the hallucinogenic PEACE PIPE . . . and then later, show them, too, how we, Indians, do Thanksgiving parties."

It must have been quite a party that first Thanksgiving Day. There must have been a lot of whooping and jumping around the campfire and going in pairs behind bushes. And it must have been a happy co-existence between the Puritans and the Indians after that.

The relationship soured after more Puritans came and the land grabbing begun. The more land the Puritans grabbed, the more land they want.

Then came Manifest Destiny (the slaughtering of the American Indians), and their forced relocations to reservations, and as y'all know, this is one of the ignoble chapters of American history.

Come to think of it, too, why do we, Fil-Ams, celebrate Thanksgiving Day? It's not even in our culture. We are not even descendants of the Puritans or of the Indians. What we ought to be celebrating should be called, Arrival Day. You know, the day we arrived here in America.

That's the EVENT that we should be thankful for. Like the Puritans, America for us, was the Promised Land.

And I consider myself blessed that I am here. And that my family is here. And that through hard work and perseverance, my wife and I pursued and captured the promise of this land, that we call the American Dream.

And I am thankful that my children grew up here and are now part of mainstream America, thinking like one, walking the walk and talking the talk of the natives.

Yes, I am thankful, I am blessed, and because of that, I celebrate NOT the Puritans' Thanksgiving Day, but my Arrival Day.

And when friends come to my dinner table this year to partake on the devouring of my oven-roasted PROMISCUOUS turkey, we'll drink red wine. And y'all know how it is in celebrating important days of our lives: We toast each other, we drink up and the more you drink, the more you get merry. And the more you get merry, the TALKS and the DYOKS get merrier.

And here's the concluding episode of Little Johnny's story . . .

At the Thanksgiving dinner table, Mommy asked Little Johnny to tell his story: "I was at the playground and I saw Daddy's car go into the woods with Aunt Jane. I went back to look and he was giving Aunt Jane a big kiss, then he helped her take off her shirt. Then Aunt Jane helped Daddy take his pants off . . .

"Then Aunt Jane and Daddy started doing the same thing that Mommy and Uncle Bill used to do when Daddy was away in the Army . . ."

Gobble-gobble. Happy Thanksgiving, y'all!!! JJ

Whatever Happened to the FilVets' Bill? And a Tale of Two Presidents: Ahmadinejad and Bush

I've got a couple of questions first: Whatever happened to the FilVets issue? There used to be cacophonies of voices and noises and fanfare about it. Now, nothing . . . not a sound is heard, not a word. Not even a lost voice in the wilderness.

Did it die a NATURAL DEATH in Congress? All those people who were gung-ho about it are now all tameme. Did they all die a NATURAL DEATH, too, from high blood pressure? Or, did they all perish from stab wounds? You know, from stabbing each other on the back.

And, what happened to that clown, what's his face name? Yeah, Filner. That guy na mahilig manguto ng mga Pinoy. Mga biglang nagsipaglahong lahat. Parang ningas kugon, ika nga. Oh, well, as I've said, it ain't gonna pass.

Here is an Update: Both Senator Akaka and Congressman Filner have, through their respective assistants given me the latest update on the FilVets' Equity Bill (EB). According to Sharon Schultze the office of Congressman Filner is feverishly working to schedule a vote on the EB this month (November). I asked Sharon if it's at all possible to have it scheduled before November 11 to give our celebration of Veterans Day more significance. She said they will try but cannot give me a definite promise. She said, however, that oncethe EB is scheduled, it is assured of passage. The same assurance came from Senator Akaka's office. We are all hoping this happens before November 11 so let's keep on praying that the Lord may will it as we have prayed. Sharon promised to keep me posted and I shall inform you and the team accordingly. By Col. Romy Monteyro (Ret.)

MAHMOUD AHMADINEJAD (pronounced AH-MAD-IN-THE-HEAD), the president of Iran, has gained international attention because of his defiance to America and contempt for Mr. Bush, and for his outrageous statements about the holocaust and the Jewish people.

But make no mistake. This little punk is only all bark and bluster. According to Intelligence Reports, "he does not control Iran's nuclear program, its military or its foreign policy." The bite and the power belong to its supreme leader, Ayatollah Ali Khamenei, and the 12-member Guardian Council of religious leaders, who can VETO any bill Iran's parliament passes.

Yeah, that's right, almost like the Bush government. Congress passes a bill, approved by the people, and Mr. Bush vetoes it. You know, just like the way he vetoed SCHIP, the health insurance for America's poor children. And, just like the way he vetoed the wishes of the American people to bring the troops home from Iraq.

Sometimes I wonder who's the real AH-MAD-IN-THE-HEAD. Perhaps, we have two AH-MAD-IN-THE-HEADS in this world.

Now . . . will anyone be amazed if George W. Bush orders a preemptive attack on Iran before the presidential election, using that vote to justify aggression in defense of America and to swing the election to the goofy GOPS? What do y'all think?

BTW, I overheard this snatches of conversation at my favorite Starbucks hang-out:

First Voice: "Ironic, isn't? Bush promised to restore DIGNITY to the Oval Office after Bill Clinton . . ."

Second Voice: "That's right . . . instead he became our first TORTURE president, trashing our standing around the world . . ."

Third Voice: ". . . And now it may be a Clinton who cleans up his mess!"

First Voice, Second Voice and Third Voice in UNISON: Ha! Ha! Ha!

ANOTHER BUSH LAP DOG RESIGNS: Karen Hughes, one of the last members of Mr. Bush's Texas inner sanctum, who was given the job of "reversing America's plummeting image abroad," announced that she'll resign. The job that was created for her: Director of the State Department Public Policy Programs. The budget allotted to her: $900 million a year.

But, public polls show that the "image of the United States declined SUBSTANTIALLY in the Muslim world . . . and elsewhere overseas . . . during Mr. Bush's presidency." And the numbers have not improved during Hughes two-year stint. In some cases, it had gotten worse. Political media experts contend that Hughes was "too focused on defending Bush's foreign policy and not on selling U.S. values and culture."

A lap dog is a lap dog is a lap dog. GOOD RIDDANCE to this Texas lap dawg. That was a waste of taxpayers' money. Yours . . . and mine. They could have given that money to the FILVETS instead.

PANTIES FOR PEACE: I kid you not. This "Panties For Peace" is a campaign on behalf of democracy in Myanmar (formerly known as Burma), and it's growing in momentum world-wide. By mailing packets of women' underwear to Myanmar embassies around the world, activists hope to defeat the ruling junta by exploiting its superstitious beliefs that contact with ladies personal garments will sap a man's strength.

Ha! Can you imagine that? Junta yata ng mga bakla 'yun. Hey, do you know what will sap my strength? Not ladies panties, that's for sure. Do you wanna know? Do I have to spell it out? It also begins with the letter, "P."

BILLIONS OF DOLLARS MORE: Do y'all know that Mr. Bush asked Congress to appropriate $196 billion in emergency funding for the wars in Iraq and Afghanistan? That's $46 billion more than the $150 billion that he requested earlier this year. The additional money would cover

Bush's TROOP SURGE . . . and upgraded armor-plated vehicles built to withstand roadside bombs.

Close to 4000 of our troops have now died in Iraq, majority from roadside bombs. Hundreds of thousands of our troops have been maimed for life, majority from roadside bombs . . . FINALLY the Decider had said our troops there need armor-plated vehicles to protect them from roadside bombs.

Ah-mad-in-the-head, indeed! **JJ**

Ya, God Bless America!

A Mexican, a Filipino, and a redneck girl are in the same bar.

When the Mexican finishes his beer, he throws his glass into the air, pulls out his pistol, and shoots the glass to pieces. Then he says, "In Mexico our glasses are so cheap, we don't need to drink with the same one twice."

The Filipino, who claims to be always "angat sa mundo," and who can never be outdone in anything, downs his beer, throws his glass into the air, pulls out two pistols and shoots the glass to pieces. Then he says, "In the Philippines, we have so much glasses made of crystals that we don't need to drink with the same one twice either."

The redneck girl, cool as a cucumber, picks up her beer, throws her glass into the air, whips out her sawed-off shotgun and shoots the Mexican and the Filipino. Ka-boom! Ka-boom! Then . . . catching her glass, setting it on the bar, and calling for a refill, she says, "In America, we have so many illegal Mexicans and Filipinos that we don't have to drink with the same ones twice!"

Ya, God Bless America!

TALKING ABOUT SHOTGUNS: VP Dick Cheney became fodder for late—TV comedians last year when he accidentally shot his companion during a hunting trip in Texas. Mr. Cheney thought his companion, Attorney Harry Whittington, was a "quail about to take off into the air." So Mr. Cheney aimed quickly and shot the quail. Bull's eye! The quail, I mean, Atty. Whittington was hospitalized for six months for treatment of wounds in his torso, neck and face.

This past Monday, Mr. Cheney picked up his shotgun again for an outing in New York's Hudson Rive Valley . . . and he had asked former New York City mayor and president wannabe Rudy Giuliani to be his hunting companion. Mr. Giuliani was reported to have said. "No way, Hosay. I am no quail. Maybe Dick should ask Al Sharpton instead." Ya, God Bless America.

I COULD CARE LESS WHAT Y'ALL SAY ABOUT MR. GIULIANI. I like him. True, he' a "flawed man." He admits that. Who isn't? He's no jerk though. Not like you know who . . . you know, that "bring it on" guy. In a recent speech, Mr. Giuliani invoked, as he often does, Ronald Reagan's admonition that "my 80 percent friend is not my 20 percent enemy." "My belief in God and reliance on his guidance is at the core of who I am, I can assure you of that," Giuliani said. "But isn't it better for me to tell you what I believe rather than change my positions to fit the prevailing wind?" I believe when Mr. Giuliani said that, he was referring to his rival to the Republican presidential nomination, Mitt Romney. You know, that Mormon guy, who keeps flip-flopping depending on the prevailing wind. Giuliani has called for a constitutional amendment declaring MARRIAGE TO BE BETWEEN A MAN AND A WOMAN and decried the "holocaust of liberalized abortion." He said, "We do not have the right to move the standards of God to meet cultural norms. We need to move the cultural norms to meet God's standards." Ya, God Bless America!

THE HOLISTIC APPROACH: When a dentist here in Seattle was accused of fondling the breasts of 27 female patients, he told the judge that he was "merely manipulating the women's pectoral muscles to relieve jaw pain caused by temporo-mandibular joint disorder." Say what? Hey, before we go any further, can we check this guy's diplomas? You know, just to make sure they aren't, like, from some dental schools in the Philippines." Ya, God Bless America!

DON IMUS IS BACK: Y'all remember him, right? Yeah, that same Don Imus, who was fired six months ago by CBS Radio for referring to black female basketball players of Rutgers University as "nappy-headed ho's." Well, he was hired by New York City's WABC radio. The station will pay him $5-million a year, and plans to syndicate and broadcast his show across the country. Ya, God Bless America!

CALIFORNIA BURNING: Te-dum, tedum . . . I've seen fire and I've seen rain, tedum, tedum . . . I've seen rain that I thought would never end . . . tedum, tedum . . .

No, I am not singing. I am comparing. The fires last week that raged in Southern California presented parallels to Hurrican KATRINA that hit the Gulf Coast two years ago.

Here we have two natural disasters, two regions, two cities . . . and TWO STADIUMS where evacuees took shelter: The Qualcomm Stadium in San Diego and the Superdome in New Orleans.

At the Superdome, there was chaos, filth and overcrowding. There were no beds and blankets. Bathrooms were not working. Supplies were scarce. People have to scrounge for food and water. There were rapes, lootings and killings. FEMA had their thumbs up their asses.

At Qualcomm, it was orderly. There were plenty of beds and blankets and piles of donated clothing. There was FOOD GALORE and plenty of water. So many people gave generously that some of the offers of gifts were turned away. San Diego's mayor said there were almost as many volunteers as evacuees in the stadium. There were counselors that the evacuees could speak with. Even massages were offered.

Thanks for the volunteers . . . because FEMA, again, had their thumbs up their asses, even FAKING news briefings and conferences . . .

Ya, God Bless America! **JJ**

Feedbacks and Comments on My "Kissing Cousins" Column

Writing is agonizing. For writers, wannabe writers and even kuno writers (that's me), there's nothing more thrilling and satisfying than receiving feedbacks and comments on stories that we write.

We crave for those comments. We long for those feedbacks. We want to know if we're being read. We want to hear from readers. Because you see, we are a bunch of INSECURE egomaniacs.

Seriously now, I did receive several comments for my story last week, "Dining in Carmel . . . ites." If you missed that, hey, shame on you!

The first to comment was my favorite cuz, Manny Belbis of Chicago. He's not only my favorite cuz, but also my number one fan of my Kapeng Barako column in the Windy City. He wrote this en toto. I didn't change, delete nor add any words.

"Hey, pare ko! This is beautiful. I think I am reading your spiritual side, my cuz. Haysoooos, with character, with tenderness, with sensitivity, with passion for life, with bountiful love for people. . . ." (Signed) ManWell.

His wife, Becky, wrote, too:

"Dear Jesse . . . Read your story and enjoyed it. It was very detailed and interesting. Readers like these kind of stories because it is very TOUCHING, SENSITIVE and HONEST. I am sure people will find it very interesting because it is very rare that people get to be invited inside a monastery, but much more getting invited to dinner. We felt much honored to be included in Sister Grace Marie's dinner invitation. Thanks a million.

"Sister Grace Marie emailed me and I had responded and thanked her for such an opportunity to witness her vows. We will never forget that momentous day. Praise the Lord! Looking forward in three years time to attend the FINAL VOWS.

"Also, thank you so much for your hospitality. You and Maribel were just awesome hosts. The 'care basket' was great. What a great idea! Ayos na ayos. Wala kaming masabi. At a scale of 1 to 10, that weekend with you guys was a 20!!! Again, thank you very much. We are lucky to have COUSINS like you and Maribel. Love." (Signed) Manny and Becky.

Then came these letters from the NAVARROS of Vancouver, Canada. Tessie wrote first:

"Maraming salamat sa masarap na lunch at saka sa sobrang tamis ng mga Asian pears. At siyempre sa sobrang pag asikaso ninyo sa amin. Pasensya na at naubos ang mga bunga.

"Natutuwa ako at nagkita-kita tayong muli. Sabi ko kay Rey ay dapat talaga na pupunta kami, kasi para na itong reunion mg mga magpinsan. Kaya Friday ay tumawag siya sa office nila na di siya papasok ng Linggo. Masaya tayong lahat at iyon ang mahalaga. Nagkaroon ng bonding ang magpipinsn kahit sandaling oras lang.

"Nabasa ko ang MAGANDANG column mo at buong buo ang kwento doon. Sayang di kami kasama sa "DINING IN CARME . . . ites."

"Again, thank you very much. Ingat kayo lagi. With you in prayers." (Signed) Tess.

Then Lolet:

"I enjoyed reading your write-up of the event last Sunday. The prayer of Ate Gace is VERY TOUCHING. I love it. Thank you for sharing this with us." (Signed) Rosalie Fedalizo, DataWave Services, Canada, Inc.

Cristy, for Cristina, but who we fondly call, "Matutina" or "Miss Universe" wrote this:

"Hello there, Mr. Jesse . . . Hope everything's well with you and Ate Belle. Yes! Yes! Yes! I read it! Ang galing galing . . . inggit naman ako. Mukhang ang sarap ng handa ni Sister Grace. And the song, 'AVE MARIA' of Mr. Manuel . . . saying hindi namin narinig. Sana pala nagparinig siya ng isang sample while we were there at your house.

"But anyway, siguradong nagustuhan ng mga ka sisteran doon sa Carmelite monastery yung kanta niya.

"That was a VERY NICE ONE, Mr. Jesse. Take care and stay well. Regards to Ate Belle." (Signed) Tina.

Sister Grace Marie wrote, too:

"Dear Jesse . . . Thank you very much for sharing your story. You have written BEATIFULLY of your wonderful experience. Last Sunday's event was truly a great blessing from the Lord to all of us. He blesses us so, not because we deserve it, but because He is all Good and all Love. Let us give thanks and praise to Him in all that we do. . . . All the sisters enjoyed your story and said that you're a very good writer." (Signed) Grace.

So, those were the comments and feedbacks of my KISSING COUSINS on my story last week. But, I think, the crowning comments came from my two publishers: Yoly T. of Chicago and Bobby Reyes of California.

When I told Yoly T. in an email about all the feedbacks, she said:

"Hi Bestpren . . . I am glad that everybody liked your story. You're an awesome storyteller is all I can say. . . . Sige, gotta cook breakfast for me and my Bartolytes." (Signed) Yoly.

And, this from Bobby Reyes, excerpts of which read:

"Hi, Ka Jesse. . . . Congratulations for this fine article that you penned. I like in particular your excellent use of metaphors such as describing the Asian pear trees "pregnant with fruits." But, I bet that the solemn occasion to a perfect family reunion could have been better if the hosts served Kapeng Barako, right?" (Signed) Bobby Reyes.

For a KUNO (sic) writers like me, nothing could be better than feedbacks and comments, such as these. For the agony of writing becomes ecstasy. **JJ**

A Blessed Day, A Special Day:
"Dining in Carmel . . . ites"

"This is like dining in heaven," I told those smiling nuns.

But I am going ahead of my story. So, let me begin from the beginning.

This past Sunday was another special day for my sister in law, Sister Grace Marie. She took her first vow as a "bride of Jesus." You see, she's a nun in the Carmelite monastery in Shoreline, a quiet little town just outside of Seattle.

Two years ago, she had her "Clothing Day": A day when she was clothed in the habit of a Carmelite sister and assumed the name, Sister Grace Marie.

There are two vows a Carmelite nun has to take. This past Sunday was the taking of her first vow. Three years from now, she would again take another vow, which would be her final vow to becoming a nun. And that's called, the "SOLEMN VOW."

So, I suppose, she's halfway there.

There was a special early morning mass and we were ALL there to witness and hear her declare her vow and share in her HEAVENLY joy: my wife, Maribel, Sister Grace Marie's only sister; my son, Jonathan; and all their cousins from Vancouver, Canada. There was Cristy, ebullient as ever. There was Rey and his wife, Tessie and their 16-year-old son, Rico. There was Lolet and husband, Caloy and their 10-year-old son, Chad.

My cuz, Manuel, and his wife, Becky, flew in from Chicago to be with us, too. That day became a family get together day and a RARE, happy occasion. For all of them are KISSING COUSINS. So you can just imagine all the kissing that happened that day.

To me, a kiss is NOT just a kiss. A kiss, if not Judas-like, can melt away hurts and TAMPUHANS, especially among kissing cousins.

St. Joseph's Carmelite Monastery Chapel, a quaint-looking chapel, located on the grounds of the reclusive-looking monastery, where Sister Grace Marie took her vow, was packed to a full house. The angels must have heralded the occasion, because aside from us, many faithful parishioners also came to partake in the joy of Sister Grace Marie.

Father Robert Egan, celebrated the mass and officiated Sister Grace Marie's vow-taking. Midway in the mass, I was CHOSEN to lead the PRAYER INTENTIONS. We prayed to the Lord for "our family and for all families in the world." We prayed that the Lord "help us mend all the BROKEN RELATIONSHIPS in our lives and make us merciful and forgiving."

We prayed for Pope Benedict XVI. We prayed for the bishops and pastors of the Church. We prayed for our nation and our nation's leaders.

Most especially, we prayed for all the Carmelite sisters of that community. And with all my heart and with all the ELOQUENCE I can muster, I uttered into the microphone: "Dear God, we ask you to bless them for all the sacrifices and prayers they offer for all the peoples and for peace in our world. Let us pray to the Lord!"

Loud and clear, I heard all the sisters, sitting in a secluded section of the church, unseen by the parishioners, say: "Lord hear our prayer!" Their voices rose above that of the congregation that gathered that day.

It was a beautiful gathering, I think. It was solemn, joyful, blessed . . . and mysterious. I felt "cleansed" when I exited that little quaint chapel.

A reception followed, hosted by Sister Grace Marie. There was a long line of people wanting to see her, hug her and tell her, "congratulations."

So, there were more HUGGING and KISSING. And there was coffee and sweets . . . and suman. I grabbed a couple of suman and a cup of coffee and circulated among the people. Many told me I did a good job reading the prayer intentions. "Ah," I said, "that's because an angel came, took my hand and helped me lead our prayers."

Lunchtime came. We invited our Canadian cousins to lunch. We went to a Mongolian Grill place and occupied the longest table there. Food abound. Laughter abound. Earthy jokes abound. My cuz, Manuel and earthy, ebullient Cristy traded jokes. And we, the spectators, roared with laughter, egging them on.

Then . . . Maribel said, "Tayo muna sa bahay, magkape." So, we trekked to my house. I proudly showed them my lush backyard full of fall flowers. There's an Asian pear tree, pregnant with ripened fruits. I plucked one of the fruits to give to my cuz. He took a bite. The juice ran down his chin. All of a sudden, there was a commotion of picking all the ripened fruits. My Asian Pear tree was stripped. . . .

After the coffee and more laughter, they all went home with bags full of Asian pears. A flurry of more kissing and hugging came on as they said their long goodbyes at the door . . . then again, on the driveway of my house.

My cuz and his wife, Becky, and Maribel, Jonathan and I were especially invited to dinner inside the monastery. So we headed back there. At the hallway, we were greeted by NINE smiling nuns: Sister Sean, the prioress of the monastery, Sister Michael Marie, Sister Emmanuel, Sister Agatha, Sister Teresa Benedicta, Sister Susan Elizabeth and Sister Miriam.

Their beatific smiles were contagious.

The airy dining area overlooks a well-tended garden. There were huge, colorful flowers that grazed the window that were "plucked from the garden," said Sister Grace Marie. On the walls, pictures of saints and unknown-to-me long-ago nuns to watch over the diners. There were three round tables. We sat in the biggest round table there, which was gaily-decorated with flowers. On my plate sat a colorful paper napkin, arranged like a big bouquet of flowers.

Sitting with us were: Father Egan, the celebrant of the morning mass; Father James Reichmann, who, like Father Egan, is also a Jesuit priest and a lecturer of theology and philosophy at Seattle University, Sister Sean, Sister Susan, Sister Grace Marie, Nancy, the church's choir soloist and her husband, Al Rustad . . . and my cuz, Manuel and wife, Becky. The two other tables were occupied by the rest of the nuns and a couple of benefactors.

The menu: Seafood salad, sweet potato casserole, stuffed baked zucchini, pineapple upside down, homemade ice cream, fruit salad, See's chocolates and fresh fruits platter.

A feast, an eye-popping feast, indeed! Led by Sister Susan, we prayed over the feast . . . then, salivating, I dove into the feast.

At my first bite of the casserole, I tasted something exquisitely delicious. "Heavenly," I muttered. There were bottles of merlot and shirraz from Chile and Australia that we could help ourselves with.

That I did, generously. Heavens! It was potent!

And the more I took a sip of the shirraz, the more the food tasted heavenly. I consumed three full glasses of that potent heavenly wine. I heard easy, flowing conversation all around. But my focus was on the food. I was pigging on the feast, GLUTTING AND SINNING in front of the nuns and priests.

Then, Sister Grace Marie made an announcement that Manuel was going to provide a little entertainment: he's going to sing. I clapped noisily and added: "My cuz used to be the understudy of Luciano Pavarotti."

My cuz gamely got up and belted the song, "Ave Maria." While my cuz sang, I looked around. I saw different reactions. Some were amazed. Some were amused. Some were mesmerized. Some had their eyes closed as if in prayer. I was slurping the nuns' homemade ice cream.

I felt good. I was having fun. I felt like I was in heaven, partaking in a feast at Jesus' table.

When I finally gulped down two cups of strong coffee, I said aloud to no one in particular: "I think I am going to write something about this. In fact, I already have the title for my story: 'Dining in heaven.'"

"May I make a suggestion?" Father Reichmann replied. "How about, 'Dining in Carmel . . . ites'?"

"Yes, why not?" I said to him. Thus, the title of this story.

Then . . . Sister Sean announced that we were all going upstairs to say the night prayer. We all sat in a small, darkened room, holding lighted candles. We stood up. We bowed. We sat again. We prayed. We recited psalms. We sang the hymn, "Shepherd me, O God." I sang with gusto. I felt happy, singing and praying to Jesus with all these beautiful people.

Then . . . Sister Grace Marie prayed this:

"Almighty father, thank you for this glorious day of my simple profession. Thank you for calling me to be a BRIDE OF YOUR SON. I am most unworthy. Because You love me and have mercy on me, I am what I am today.

"Oh, Holy Spirit, please grant me the grace to remain faithful to you and to love Him as I ought. Thank you for all the people in my life, my sisters in Carmel, my family, relatives and friends. Bless each one of them. It is through them that You love me.

"Oh, Holy Spirit, please grant me the grace to love them as I ought. All Glory to the Father, and to the Son and to the Holy Spirit. Amen. Good night, my dear Jesus. Good night, my dear Mother."

And, good night to y'all, too, dear readers. It was a blessed day, a special day. Thank you for reading my story. **JJ**

Hysterical hysterics of Desperate Housewives

The hysteria has now died down. But at its peak, it was hysterical. Over and over, we heard words like:

"It's a SLUR!"

"It's RACIST!"

"It's an INSULT to the Filipino people!"

"It's a denigration of the educational system in the Philippines! It's a putdown for Fil-Am doctors schooled in the Philippines!"

The call to arms was: SUGUD, MGA KAPATID!!! And like our Katipuneros before us, with our TABAKS, sugud we did.

Greedy Fil-Am lawyers screamed: "Let's sue! Let's sue! Let's get some PERA out of this!"

Y'all know what I am talking about, right? Yeah, that Sunday soap opera on ABC, popularly known as, "Desperate Housewives." America's favorite soap. And my wife's, too. From what I heard, America's first lady, Mrs. Laura Bush, never fails to also watch it.

For those of you who might have missed it, in a segment that was aired two Sundays ago, Susan, played by Teri Hatcher goes in for a medical checkup and is shocked to learn when the gynecologist who examined her told her that she may be "going through a menopause."

The dialogue went like this:

Doctor: "Listen, Susan, I know for a lot of women the word 'menopause' has negative connotations. You hear 'aging,' 'brittle bones,' 'loss of sexual desire.'"

Susan: "Ok, before we go any further, can I check these diplomas? Just to make sure they aren't, like, from some medical school in the Philippines."

Bingo!

Like thunder and avalanche combined, ABC was inundated with wrathful calls, emails and letters from Fil-Ams and Filipinos . . . and some TNTs.

"A statement that devalues Filipinos in healthcare is extremely unfounded, considering the overwhelming presence of Filipinos and Fil-Ams in the medical field," they cried.

True. I agree. But . . . here's my take:

"Mga kabayan, welcome to America! Where opinions are as diverse as its people. Where opinions are jokes, and jokes are opinions and can be said FREELY, without fear. Love it or leave it!

"It was a joke, plain and simple. It wasn't a slur. It was an opinion, in the form of a joke. It was a joke, period . . . perhaps, kind of stupid, like many other stupid jokes we've heard before. Mas grabe pa nga yung mga dyoks tungkol kay Bush. Masyadong naman tayong balat sibuyas. Get over it.

"Count your blessings for being in America. As the song says, "Enjoy na lang kayo and have a good time."

Or as a certain Art Tolentino said in an online debate of this issue: ". . . Their right to say is protected under the First Amendment. Making fun of another country's education system is NOT racist or discriminatory as defined by Civil Rights Act Title VII. This is NOT slander because the defense for slander is the truth. The (script) writer can claim he is referring to something he read somewhere about Philippine diploma mills. You (Fil-Am doctors) cannot prove damages to your career because you guys are some of the best and highest-paid doctors in America."

Right on.

Mr. Tolentino added that if a "Fil-Am doctor somewhere can prove he got fired from his job or his patients left him because of the 'Desperate Housewives' remark, then he can sue and the jury may award him some monetary restitution. I doubt it. Lighten up. Give it a rest."

I agree.

And, as **Colonel, Frank Quesada**, Ret., a columnist in another Fil-Am publication in California, said: ". . . the issues served as a focal-and-uniting exercise in not letting the culprits get away with it.

"I believe our kababayans have made their point. A public apology sufficed. . . . To belabor the subject, is like beating a dead horse. Grandstanding it in court, in my opinion, becomes superfluous. I don't see any money in it."

Right on, Colonel. Cheers.

And to ABC: Love those lovely "DESPERATE HOUSEWIVES," especially THAT flighty, silly Susan. It would be her to ask and say: "OK, before we go any further, can I check these diplomas? Just to make sure they aren't, like, from some medical school in the Philippines."

Tee-hee. It's a silly joke from that silly Susan, that's all. **JJ**

Odds and ends . . . and Alzheimer's

The world is like a mirror: frown at it and it frowns at you. Smile and it smiles, too.—Herbert Samuels

So, Newt Gingrich, another disgraced GOP Speaker of the House during the time of Pres. Bill Clinton, finally said he's not running for president. He predicted that a Democrat will win the White House in 2008.

Hey Newt, that's a given! And it's gonna be that woman that y'all have been demonizing. Yeah, Hillary Rodham Clinton.

That's right, sir, THAT woman whose husband, Bill, you and Tom Delay, the Bible thumper and Senator Larry Craig, the foot thumper, tried so hard to also demonize as a big time womanizer, crook and even a murderer.

Now check this out: Do y'all know that men's restroom stall in the Minneapolis airport where Sen. Craig was arrested for his "wide stance" is now a TOURIST SPOT?

I tell ya, America teems with hypocrites . . . and sickos.

So . . . from what I've been hearing there are now SIX branches of the U.S. military that are now fighting in Iraq: the Marines, the Army, the Navy, the Air Force, the Coast Guard . . .

And BLACKWATER, that mean, lean KILLING machine of Iraqi civilians.

So, the warmongers, I mean, the war supporters of the Iraq War have boasted that the SURGE is working because the month of September has the lowest levels of American casualties since July of last year. Only 66 U.S. soldiers have died.

Piece of cake, right? ONLY 66! That ain't nothing. Also, the month of September brought ONLY 400 attacks on civilians and Iraqi and coalition forces. That's right, ONLY a couple of hundreds car bombings, ONLY a hundred killings and murders, and ONLY a handful of beheadings . . . hey, that ain't nothing! Piece of cake, huh?

So, White House spokesman Tony Snow quit his job over his low salary daw. And so did Michael Jackson at the Homeland Security. Both earn $168,000 a year. It doesn't look really good when two employees of the Bush Administration can't make ends meet on a salary that's four or five times higher to that of an average American household.

Hey, have a heart, would ya, and cut those poor guys and their families some slack?

BTW, according to the Washington Post, George W. Bush once asked: "IS OUR CHILDREN LEARNING?"

Now he has an answer. "CHILDRENS DO LEARN," he said.

I kid you not. The setting was an education event at the Waldorf-Astoria Hotel in New York where Mr. Bush was taking credit for advances students have made in the National Assessment of Education Progress.

Bush was proudly citing the federal government report that showed improvements in math and reading among grade schoolers. Mr. Bush said: "Report shows CHILDRENS do learn when standards are high and results are measured."

Really, I thought Erap's kanto boy English was atrocious. Pero mas grabe itong si Bush. Daig pa si Erap, eh.

Recently, I was diagnosed with AAADD. That's Age Activated Attention Deficit Disorder. This is how it develops:

I decide to water my garden. As I turn on the hose in the driveway, I look over my car and decide my car needs washing. As I start toward the garage, I notice that there is mail on the porch table that I brought up from the mailbox earlier.

I decide to go through the mail before I wash the car. I lay my car keys on the table, put the junk mail in the garbage can and notice that the can is full. So I decide to put the bills back on the table and take out the garbage first.

But then I think, since I am going to be near the mailbox when I take out the garbage, I may as well pay the bill first. I get my checkbook, and see that there is only one leaf left. My extra cheques are in my desk in the study, so I go upstairs to my desk where I find a Cup o' Kapeng Barako that I had been drinking.

I see that my coffee is cold, so I decide to go downstairs in the kitchen to put my coffee in the microwave to warm it up. Then I head downstairs trying to remember what I was going to do.

Get the pattern? If this isn't you yet, your day is coming! Growing older is mandatory. Growing up is optional. But laughing at yourself is THERAPEUTIC . . . so, I laugh at myself a lot.

A study of elderly people suggests that those who see themselves as self-disciplined and organized achievers have the lowest risk for developing Alzheimer's than people who are less conscientious. And that social connections and stimulating activities, like doing crossword puzzles are preventive measures for this disease.

But according to researchers, for prevention, nothing beats reading and writing a column, like mine . . . So, right on, I write on. And YOU must read on.

Oh sh—! I just remembered. I left the water running in the driveway! Gonna go. Bye. **JJ**

A Kinship with Blacks; a Cheer for Hillary & Sally

The other day when I went to my favorite neighborhood Starbucks to get my daily jolt of caffeine and to read my favorite newspaper, **The New York Times**, the girl barista who I suppose only wanted to be friendly, asked me, "What's your nationality?"

I've been asked this question before. Several times, in fact. So I now have a response that I have fine tuned to a tee.

First, I gave the girl my best smile, and then I said, "Ah, my dear, actually, I am half-white and half-black. From the waist up, I am white and from the waist down, I am black . . . and I got rhythm."

Then after a short dramatic pause, I said, "And in Chinese, my name is Hung Lo."

Whether that poor girl was amused, shocked, or scandalized, I couldn't tell, but she gave me a look that says: "You dirty old man!" Yes, I know, I am such a bastard. I shouldn't be scandalizing Starbucks' baristas. So I promised myself that next time I am in there, I'll behave.

But really, I do feel a KINSHIP with blacks. When I was in the Navy as a steward, I've worked with them and lived with them in the same berthing compartments aboard ships. They called me, "homey" or "homeboy" and sometimes, "cuz" or "bro."

(Editor's Note: Here are some of the reasons why probably our columnist, Jesse Jose, feels so much kinship with Black Americans. QUOTE. The Filipinos treasure the exploits of the more-than 6,000

Buffalo soldiers that America sent during the Filipino-American War from 1899 to 1901. At least 20 of the Buffalo soldiers defected to the Filipino Army and they died fighting for Philippine freedom and democracy. When peace was declared on July 4, 1902, by then President Teddy Roosevelt, more-than 1,200 of the Black-American soldiers stayed behind and married Filipino brides. UNQUOTE. To view the entire article, please click on this link http://www.mabuhayradio.com/content/view/351/51/.)

I had a lot of fun being with them. We laughed a lot. We told outrageous stories and jokes to each other and laughed outrageously.

And we laughed at those dorky white officers we served on ships' wardrooms. To their faces, we addressed the white officers as "sirs" or "misters." Behind their backs, we called them "dorkies" and "honkies."

That was in the 60's. From that experience, I've developed a feeling of KINSHIP with blacks and that good feeling of kinship has remained inside of me.

So, I take it personal when I heard about this "whites only" shady tree at a high school in Jena, Louisiana, where black students could not go and hang out. When one black student had the temerity to go under this tree, the white kids hung nooses from this tree. In return, six black students beat up a white student for it and got into real trouble and will do time in prison . . . while those white students who hung the nooses skated. The charge against those black kids: ATTEMPTED MURDER. The injury sustained by the white kid: A black eye and a minor concussion.

Attempted murder for giving somebody a black eye? Indeed, I take that personal. Because that's lopsided Dixie justice. Y'all know what I mean?

And, I take it personal when in Tulsa, Texas, 38 blacks were convicted of drug dealing on a sole, personal, and perjured testimony of a white cop known for describing black people as "niggers."

And, I take it personal when in Paris, Texas, a black girl shoved a teacher's aide and was given seven years prison time by a judge who had earlier given probation to a white arsonist.

And, I take it personal when white people say that "blacks and other 'coloreds' are of a savage, yet simultaneously childlike, lower order and that if anyone sought to mix blacks and whites, whites must resist by any means possible."

And, I take it personal when people say that "inequalities because of skin color is now an ABSURDITY that we have left in the 50's" . . . because that's not true! Because those things that I mentioned above happened only most recently. Not way back in the 50's. But now. Year 2007.

A cheer for Hillary and Sally

This week, Ms. Hillary Clinton, the Democratic presidential front-runner and United States president in waiting unveiled her proposed health-care plan, calling for mandatory universal coverage for 47 million uninsured Americans.

Under this proposal, Americans with employer-provided health insurance would be allowed to keep it, while the UNINSURED would be required to purchase public or private coverage that would be subsidized by the federal government at the cost of $110 billion. The gist of her plan is to require everyone to enroll, and setting it up so that the insured would never lose AFFORDABLE coverage, even if unemployed.

"Part of our health-care system is best in the world, and we should built on it," Clinton said. "Part of the system is broken, and we should fix it."

How true! If it ain't broke, don't fix it. But it's broke. So, right on, Ms. Hillary, you go, girl, come 2009, fix it, please.

Did y'all see on TV the Emmy last week? Did y'all hear what Sally Field said? While accepting lead actress award for her TV role as a mother of a soldier in Afghanistan, Ms. Field tried to make a statement about women and war. But as y'all know, the only thing viewers heard was: "Let's face it. If mothers ruled the world, there would be no god. . . ."

Fox, which aired the show, took the cameras off her and CENSORED the rest of her sentence, which ended, ". . . damn wars in the first place!"

Yeah, Miss Sally, you go, girl! Pox on Fox! And, on Bill O'Reilly, too. **JJ**

Is General David Petraeus Mr. Bush's "water boy"?

Are we going to continue to invest American blood and treasure at the rate we're doing now—***Sen. Chuck Hagel (R-Neb)***

True, with all those colorful medals, he looks awesome and handsome in his Army uniform.

True, with all those glittering stars on his shoulders, he looks splendid. And when he walks, he swaggers.

And true, he holds a doctorate from Princeton. And a Princeton grad is looked upon, as a prince.

He was likened to "David." The princely, biblical David.

At his Senate confirmation hearing in January, he was described as "the quintessential military professional, a credible, independent voice," who WOULD STAND ABOVE the political fray between the Democrats and the Republicans.

But when he came back last week to Capitol Hill to report on the war, his image changed.

The ***quintessential general*** . . .

The ***military professional . . .***

The ***credible, independent voice who would stand above political frays and in-fightings . . .***

The ***David . . .***

The ***princely, biblical David . . .***

Turned out to be Mr. Bush's ***WATER BOY.***

For he exactly **ECHOED, MOUTHED, REPEATED** what Mr. Bush has been blabbering all along: "***STAY ON COURSE!!! We'll fight them there, so we won't have to fight them here.***" That same, old, STUPID strategy that's slaughtering many of America's brave, splendid, young men . . . and draining America's treasure ($10 billion a month).

In January, Mr. Bush ordered 30,000 more U.S. troops to Baghdad for six months to tamp down the sectarian killings there so that the Al-Maliki government would have the chance to create a stable government. And, he minted Gen. David Petraeus as overall commander of the war.

Last week, Petraeus came back with his report and asked Congress to give that strategy MORE TIME to work. He said the added 30,000 troops can be rolled back by mid-July 2008 . . . 18 months AFTER Bush ordered the SURGE. That would leave 130,000 U.S. troops in Iraq more than five years after the invasion.

Petraeus said that the U.S. forces could ALL go home as soon as they could hand over the responsibility to Iraqis ***"as the situation and Iraqi capabilities permit."***

Sen. Lisa Murkowski (R-Alaska) said: "That sounds identical to what President Bush has been saying all along, that U.S. forces will drawdown as the Iraqis are able to stand up."

Sen. Hillary Clinton (D-N.Y.) said Bush ordered Petraeus to "***implement a failed policy,***" adding that "***civilian deaths and car bombings in Iraq have risen***" and that "***U.S. casualties have been greater in 2007 than in 2006***" and "***meanwhile Osama Bin Laden, the mastermind of the 9/11 attacks remains at large and his terrorist network is gaining strength in Pakistan.***"

"The reports that you provide to us really require the willing suspension of disbelief," Clinton added.

Sen. John Warner (R-VA), asked Petraeus if his recommendations would make America "safer."

Gen. Petraeus at first evaded the question by saying: "***Sir, I believe that this is indeed the best course of action to achieve our objectives.***"

Warner asked the question again. Petraeus answered, "***Sir, I don't know actually.***"

For his testimony before Congress, war critics have dubbed Gen. Petraeus "his generation's Gen. William Westmoreland," the overall commander of the Vietnam quagmire. He has been called "General Betray Us." He has been accused of "cooking the books for the White House," just like the way Gen. Westmoreland cooked the books for the Nixon's White House.

Others, like Tom Engelhardt, an online columnist and a fellow at the Nation Institute, called Petraeus "the Paris Hilton of generals" and a "vain media darling with almost no credibility."

Jon Stewart, host of Comedy Central's "The Daily Show," said Petraeaus testimony means that "***the president's been right the whole time.***"

In other words, General Petraeus merely echoed, mouthed and repeated what Mr. Bush has been saying all along: STAY ON COURSE!!!

In other words, General David Petraeus is Mr. Bush's water boy.

Time magazine columnist Joe Klein eloquently wrote this week in his column: ". . . ***George W. Bush's credibility on Iraq is non-existent. And so he has placed David Petraeus, an excellent soldier, in a position way above his pay grade. He has made Petraeus not just the arbiter of Iraq strategy but also, by default, the man who sets U.S. policy for the entire so-called war on terrorism. . . .***"

Yeah, exactly, a water boy! A highly-decorated, excellent water boy! **JJ**

Did the Wrong Eagle Land in Iraq?

The **Koran** says: "For the wrath of the Eagle cleansed the lands of Allah, and there was peace . . ." But did it refer to the American Eagle? We will discuss the matter of the Eagle at the end of this column.

In the meantime, I heard this on **CNN** (*Coconut News Ngayon*). Yes, the other CNN, as coined by my fellow journalist, Romy Marquez, of San Diego, California.

TV Reporter: "So, Senator, what have you done for IMMIGRATION?"

Senator: "We have voted to have Alberto Gonzalez deported."

Hey, you can't call yourself progressive-minded if you ain't got no sense of humor and you don't know how to laugh and your face has a scowl and a permanent sour look. Y'all get my drift?

Okey ngarud, now check this out: One early evening inside a typical American family home. Dinner's just over and the family gathers around a photo album, looking at the photos, remembering what they did this past summer on their vacation trip. The dad said, "*. . . And here we are during our delay at the Chicago airport and there's us delayed in Denver." And the mom said, "And here's us during our Newark delay. . . .*"

We're still at the airport.

While going through an airport during one of his many trips, President Bush encountered a man with long hair, wearing a white robe, and sandals. He was holding a staff.

Mr. Bush went up to the man and said, "Aren't you Moses?"

The man never answered, but just kept staring straight ahead. Again, Mr. Bush, in a loud voice said, "Moses!"

The man just kept staring ahead, never answering the President.

President Bush pulled a Secret Service Agent aside. He pointed to the robed man and asked the Agent, "Doesn't that man look like Moses to you?"

Again, the President yelled, "Moses!" And again, the man stared ahead and did not answer.

The Secret Service Agent went up to the man in the white robe and whispered, "You look just like Moses? Are you Moses?"

The man leaned over and whispered back, "Yes, I am Moses. However, the last time I talked to a BUSH I spent 40 years wandering in the desert, and ended up leading my people to the only spot in the entire Middle East where there is no oil."

Heee-hawww!

We're still at the airport . . . at the Minneapolis airport, that is. It's 12:45 past midnight, do you know where your children are, I mean, which toilet stalls your senators are in?

A foot tapping: Tap, tap, tap. One, two, three. The tapping foot touches another foot in the next stall. Now we see a hand reaching underneath the divider . . . waving.

And that hand was the hand of Senator Larry Craig, a conservative Republican from Idaho, who was arrested in June for propositioning an undercover cop in Minneapolis International Airport. According to police reports, Craig tapped his foot against the foot of the man in the next stall and ran his hand beneath the divider. These signals are used by men seeking SEX in public restrooms.

The man in the adjacent stall that Craig waved to was an undercover cop.

Of course, Craig denied that he was gay and that his foot accidentally touched the officer's because he has "a wide stance."

Really?

That wide?

Oh my.

These goofy GOPS, I tell ya.

Craig is the latest GOP senator that had been exposed with ethical and moral problems. Senator Ted Stevens of Alaska is now being investigated for his "relationship" with a contractor and Senator David Vitter of Louisiana had been linked to a prostitution ring as a "regular" customer.

So, Mr. Bush's hand-picked commander in Iraq, General David Petraeus, had said this week before Congress that the U.S. military objectives "are in large measures being met" and that Bagdad is now a lot "safer" and that "sectarian killings have declined."

BUT in a poll of Iraqis conducted by ABC News, the BBC and the Japanese network, NHK, 70 per cent of Iraqis said security in their areas and in the whole country as a whole have worsened.

And that about 65 percent said the "U.S. invasion was wrong" and that the "coalition forces should leave now." And that attacks on U.S. forces is "acceptable." Yeah, but never mind what the Iraqis think and say to us.

We'll stay on course . . . and kill more of them.

The following verse is from the Koran (9:11): "For it is written that a son of Arabia would awaken a fearsome Eagle. The wrath of the Eagle would be felt throughout the lands of Allah and lo, while some of the people trembled in despair still more rejoiced, for the wrath of the Eagle cleansed the lands of Allah, and there was peace."

Wrong! It was no Eagle; it was an Ass! And there was a quagmire!

BTW, did y'all note the Koran's verse number? **JJ**

A Conversation with Lourdes Ceballos About the FilVets

Y'all can call me a pariah. I don't give a damn. A couple of weeks ago, I had this online conversation with Lourdes Ceballos about the Filipino veterans (FilVets). Lourdes is the veep of the NPC/PhilUSA of Chicago, a group of press people kuno in the Midwest. She's a fine lady.

She and I had this exchange of e-mails, which I quote en toto. "Well, Jesse . . . Now that you mention the 'FILVETS' Equity and the reference you had months ago previously written about its monetary aspect and 'Kung-Fu fighting each other,' among the NPCers, I like to remind you that from the first e-mail you sent about your view on the veterans' funding, I responded to you that there is another Bill which does not make the Filipino vets concerned only with money. The other Bill is just as vital (as) and less contentious than the demand for dollars of the Equity Bill.

"This is the Filipino Veterans Family Reunification Bill which seeks to bring over soon the immediate family members already petitioned legally by our Fil-Am vets. It provides family values, security and yet requires not a single cent of outlay from the US Congress. This Bill has never been the target of Kung-Fu fighting anywhere, by 'Holy Cows,' 'Buffoons,' 'Crusaders,' in the NPC-PhilUSA, not even in the USA Congress.

"This is why I understand and sympathize with your view that the FilVets plight should not be perceived only as equity-for-$$$ Kung-Fu battle, but as a Holy Crusade for morals or money. (Signed) Lourdes."

My response: "Hello Lourdes . . . Well said. How are you? Been so long, huh? You guys miss me? I don't miss any of you. There was so much buffoonery going on within the 'Society of Buffoons' that I just had to make my exit then. Just like what Romy Marquez had done most recently. It's him that the BUFFOONS were after this time.

"Have you read that play, 'The Crucible,' written by Arthur Miller? What the BUFFOONS of the NPC-PhilUSA have done mirror the essence of that play.

"As to that FilVets Family Reunification Bill . . . that bill, my dear, has been shot down. That's already KAPUT in Congress. I don't understand why the families of the FilVets deserve that kind of special treatment anyway. Why couldn't they get in line just like everybody else?

"I had to get in line when I got my family over here . . . and I am a VET, too. A war vet in the U.S. military at that, with 20 years of active service!

"The next bill that's going to be shot down is the FilVets Equity Bill. And I really do think it should be shot down!

"I don't think the FilVets deserve that PENSION that the Holy Crusaders of this bill have been asking for so long. Because . . . yung mga Kano nga na lumaban din sa guerra are not getting this pension that you guys have been harping about. Yung mga Pinoy vets pa kaya?

"The Holy Crusaders of this bill are out of their minds if they think this bill would get passed in Congress. To get a pension from the U.S. Military, the service member must serve at least 20 years of active duty. The FilVets have only served the duration of WW II, and that's only four years

"Anyway, why are we so fixated on this issue? Wala na ba tayong ibang issue kung hindi 'to? Representative FILNER, et al, and the rest of his cohorts . . . 'yan mga 'yan, nang-uuto lang ng mga Pinoy.

"Our own Fil-Am community leaders fighting KUNO for this cause are the present-day Dons Quixote. And they're all beginning to look like clowns and buffoons, too, Kung-Fu fighting each other . . . stepping on each as they clamber up the ladder for recognition. Parang mga alimango't alimasag in a bucket, pulling each other down. You know what I mean?

"These FilVets are not really KAWAWA, as we claim them to be. They get Medicare/Medicaid, VA care, Social Security benefits, SSI, food stamps, welfare money, free apartment housings . . . the whole smear, the whole care package. They get more benefits than I do. Perhaps, even more than many U.S. Vets I've seen panhandling on street corners. Ngayon gusto pa ng pension. Susmaryusep!!! (Signed) Jesse.

I didn't get any response from Lourdes. Y'all can call me a pariah for my opinions. I don't really give a damn. **JJ**

Confession of a Crazy Columnist

People tell me I am crazy.

I have a confession to make: I am crazy. I think I can see lots of heads nodding out there. Yeah, well, nobody is perfect. Each one of us has a flaw or two. I have many, and my biggest flaw is that . . . I am crazy.

Read on and I'll tell you why.

A couple of weeks ago, a dear reader from Kansas, **Tom Martires**, wrote: "I like the way you write and I like your sense of humor. You're funny . . . and very articulate. I like to write, too, but I am not as articulate as you. What school did you graduate from?"

Hmm, I thought . . . a fan.

So, I wrote back: "I attended the University of Santo Tomas and San Sebastian College, in Manila, UConn, Connecticut College, Syracuse University, Palm Beach College and many others, but I've always considered UST as my alma mater. I have a doctorate and an HONORIS CAUSA in the Kuma Sutra."

Tom replied: "You're well schooled. What is the Kuma Sutra? Also, may I ask, what's your hobby?"

"The Kuma Sutra is a form of a Hindu philosophy. It's a very physical philosophy actually," I answered. "But it's also spiritual, emotional and mental. You have to be totally focused when applying this philosophy in real life . . . because it takes the whole self to practice the techniques and its various sets of principles. You practice this philosophy only with someone you're physically and emotionally in tuned with. Your partner does not have to be knowledgeable with the techniques."

"The techniques can be easily taught," I said. "It's an exhausting philosophy to apply, but very satisfying and fulfilling. When you do it well, you and your partner can both attain Nirvana. Nirvana, in layman's term, is the joy and the bliss of a heavenly, mutual climax.

"The Kuma Sutra is also my hobby," I went on. "I used to be a macho dancer, but I've retired from that."

Tom replied: "You're crazy . . ." See, I told ya, I am crazy.

Now, this one came from a U.S. Border Inspector, named Yoshi. My wife and I often go to Vancouver, Canada, to visit her relatives there and participate in orgies of eating, talking and gossiping. It's only a three-hour drive from Seattle to Vancouver, and the ride is pretty and scenic all year round. So, on a whim, we often go. I always enjoy the ride and the orgies. It's crossing the border that sours the joyride and the orgies. The Border Guards ask too many questions.

Questions like: Where are you from? Where do you live? What's your citizenship? Why are you here? What's your occupation? What's the purpose of your visit? How long are you going to stay? Did you buy anything? What do you have in the trunk of your car? What are you bringing into the country? Etc, etc.

STUPID, irritating, Gestapo-like questions.

And I have to answer all their questions respectfully. Because those goofy-looking Border Inspectors on the American side work for a goof, named Michael Cherrygoff (sorry, I can't spell his last name). But y'all know who I am talking bout . . . you know, that Homeland Security honcho, who looks like a clone of CNN TV pundit, Larry king.

On the Canadian side of the border, the Guards there work for a cretin, I think. And whoever you work for is who you are . . . and vice versa.

The Border Guards, for some reason, always suspect me as a terrorist. It's probably because of my Erap-like mustache (Erap was my hero in my kanto-boy days) and from the way I look at them as they grill me with their IDIOTIC questions: I always look at them . . . cross-eyed.

So, they always pick on me. A couple of weeks ago, on the way back to the American side of the border, I decided, for a change, to pick on one of them. As we approached the guard shack, I noticed that the inspector looked Japanese. So, I asked him: "Are you Japanese?"

"No," he curtly and officiously said, "American!"

In pidgin English and pointing at myself, I said, "Me, too, American." Then I gave him the thumbs up sign and said, "Amerika-nese numbah one!"

He looked pissed. He barked an order, "Let me see your passport and open the trunk of your car." I showed him my U.S. passport and flicked the trunk open. He closely scrutinized my passport, held it against the light and flipped through the stamped pages of my travels to various countries in Europe and Asia. Then, he went to inspect the trunk.

"There are dead body parts in there," I said.

"What!" he said, looking at me, his slant eyes widening in disbelief. I looked back at him, with my own semi-slant eyes . . . and I crossed 'em for effect.

That perturbed him even more.

For a second or two, he touched his automatic pistol in his holster, like he was gonna draw. For a second or two, I touched mine, too, a magnum .357, like Clint Eastwood's, which was stashed under my seat. And I thought that day was gonna be a Clint Eastwood "make my day, punk" kind of day for me.

For eternity-like seconds, my mind entered another time, the Japanese Occupation in the Philippines, and in my mind's eye, I saw a Jap in an

Imperial Army uniform, whose face was my parents' oppressors and I blew him away with three wire cutters, his dead body parts plastering the walls of his sentry shack.

It was surreal . . .

Until that Jap, wearing a U.S. Border Inspector uniform, spoke up again and said, "What did you say was in your trunk?"

"Dead body parts," I said. "They're in the big silver pot." I couldn't see what he was doing from where I was sitting, but he must have lifted the lid off the pot of our PABAON, because the garlicky smell wafted into the air.

"Those are dead body parts?" he asked.

"Yes," I said. "Dead body parts of a pig, and the concoction is called, ADOBONG BABOY . . ."

"DOROBO?" he asked.

"No," I said, resorting, again, to pidgin English. "You, Dorobo! That, Adobo. Me, adobo eater, yummy, yummy, like sushi . . ."

At the mention of the word, sushi, Yoshi's slant eyes, slanted to slits. I stared back at him, crossed my eyeballs, uncrossed 'em and crossed 'em again. Then I wiggled my ears, one at a time.

Then I farted, LOUD. That did it. He said: "You're crazy . . ."

The crossing barrier to America flew up. I stepped on the gas and roared away, roaring with laughter. As I savored my mirth, Maribel said: "You're crazy . . ."

See, even my wife tells me I am crazy. **JJ**

On Australian law and the Filipino flag

Mag-dyok muna tayo.

So finally we've found out that last year Mr. Bush was successfully treated for Lyme disease. But according to Seattle Times columnist Ron Judd, "the president was said to be mystified, as he's more of a lemon guy."

Tee-hee!

Okay . . . now that Karl Rove, "the Brains of Mr. Bush," had also called it quits, I wonder what we'll find out about him. What lies and what crimes, unknown yet?

And, how will the "puppet" survive now without the "master puppeteer"? The dismal failure of the Bush Administration, is Bush's, but Rove mapped out the road that brought him and this nation to this decline. Instead of "Brains," I think the name, "Turd Bloosom," befits him more.

Buh-bye, Karl Rove. On your way out of the White House, don't let the screen door hit you where the dog should have bit you.

Umm, honest, I didn't say that "buh-bye and dog" part. Washington Post columnist Eugene Robinson has that for his lead in his column this week. And I thought it was a beautiful lead. Simple, truthful and straight to the point.

Okey ngarud, I wanna be serious now. This piece was sent to me more than a few times by different people. The last one who sent it was my dear cuz, Manny Belbis of Chicago, who asked me: "Any comment on this Australian law? Do you agree?"

Here's the piece:

A day after a group of mainstream Muslim leaders pledged loyalty to Australia and her Queen at a special meeting with Prime Minister John Howard, he and his misters made it clear that extremists would face a crackdown.

Treasurer Peter Costello, seen as heir apparent to Howard, hinted that some radical clerics could be asked to leave the country if they did not accept that Australia was a secular state, and its laws were made by Parliament.

"If those are not your values, if you want a country which has Sharia law or a theocratic state, then Australia is not for you," he said.

In a separate nationally-televised speech, Prime Minister Howard said: "IMMIGRANTS, NOT AUSTRALIANS, must adapt. Take it or leave it. I am tired of this nation worrying about whether we are offending some individuals or their culture . . .

"I am not against immigration, nor do I hold a grudge against anyone who is seeking a better life by coming to Australia. However, there are a few things that those who have recently came to our country, and apparently some born here, need to understand. This idea of Australia being a multi-cultural community has served only to dilute our sovereignty and our national dignity. And as Australians, we have our own culture, our own society, our own language and our own lifestyle.

"This culture has been developed over two centuries of struggles, trials and victories by millions of men and women who have sought freedom.

"We speak mainly English, not Spanish, Lebanese, Arabic, Japanese, Rusian, or any other language. THEREFORE, if you wish to become part of our society . . . LEARN THE LANGUAGE!

"Most Australians believe in God. This is not some Christian, right wing, political push, but a fact, because Christian men and women, on Christian principles, founded this nation, and this is clearly documented. It is certainly appropriate to display it on the walls of our schools. If God offends you, then I suggest you consider another part of the world as your new home, because God is part of our culture.

"We will accept your beliefs, and will not question why. All we ask is that we accept ours, and live in harmony and peaceful enjoyment with us. . . . We are happy with our culture and have no desire to change, and we really don't care how you did things where you came from. By all means, keep your culture, but do not force it on others.

"This OUR COUNTRY, OUR LAND, and OUR LIFESTYLE, and we will allow you every opportunity to enjoy all this. But once you are done complaining, whining, and griping about OUR FLAG, OUR PLEDGE, OUR CHRISTIAN BELIEFS, or OUR WAY OF LIFE, I highly encourage you take advantage of one great Australian freedom, THE RIGHT TO LEAVE."

I told my cuz that "I totally, completely, and absolutely agree with this Australian law . . .

"And, therefore, the practice of raising the Philippine flag on the streets of Chicago or on any street in America, to celebrate Philippine Independence Day and show KUNO our loyalty and patriotism to the country that we already left behind for good . . . is to me, a STUPID practice. And that practice should be banned. There should only be one flag in America that should be raised, and that's the Star and Stripes."

My cuz fired back: "I don't agree with that. The flag is only a symbol of the country where we came from. We Filipinos accept and adhere to the laws of this land. We do not reject the customs and tradition of this country. We pledge allegiance to its flag, we pay our taxes, we assimilate with mainstream America, we embrace its three forms (branches) of government, we do not preach its destruction. Pare ko, we love our adopted country, but we must not also forget where we came from." (Signed) Manuel.

I replied: "Pare ko . . . Well said. But how come we are the only ethnic people who are doing this practice in America? To me, that shows that we have NOT fully integrated yet into mainstream America. Mga taga-barrio pa rin tayo. I don't see the Japanese, the Chinese, the Koreans or the Italians or the Jews raised their flags here in America to commemorate their country's Independence Day . . .

"I really think that in this country, there should only be ONE FLAG, ONE LANGUAGE, ONE PLEDGE OF ALLEGIANCE . . . just like in Australia. That's my stand! America is our country now. She takes good care of us. So let's give her our complete and absolute loyalty.

"The Philippines? Yes, of course, let's remember her with fondness. But we must now cut the restraints of her umbilical cord, so we can leave the barrio behind." JJ

Laughing at the Ugly Face of Racism

A pious man explained to his followers: "It is evil to take lives and noble to save them. Each day I pledge to save a hundred lives. I drop my net in the lake and scoop out a hundred fishes. I place the fishes on the bank, where they flop and twirl. 'Don't be scared,' I tell those fishes. 'I am saving you from drowning.'"

That came from Amy Tan's last book, "Saving Fish from Drowning," before Alzheimer's struck her down.

It reminded me of Pandak and the Filipino people. The pious leader is Pandak and the fishes are the Filipino people. It could be Bush and the Iraqi people, too. But that's not my story today.

It's about RACISM: America's dark and dirty little secret. Though it's no longer blatant as it used to be, it IS alive and well.

This was written not too long ago by one of my favorite columnists, Leonard Pitts, Jr., a Pulitzer Prize winner and a syndicated columnist of The Miami Herald: "My youngest son was arrested last year," he began.

"Police came to my house looking for an armed robbery suspect, 5-feet-eight-inches with long hair. They took my son, 6-foot-3 with short braids.

"They made my daughter, 14, fresh from the shower and dressed for bed, lie face down in wet grass and handcuffed her. They took my grandson,

8, from the bed where he slept and made him sit on the sidewalk beside her.

"My son, should it need saying, hadn't done a damn thing. In fact, I was talking to him long distance—I was in New Orleans—at the time of the alleged crime. Still, he spent almost two weeks in jail. The prosecutor asked for a high bail, citing the danger my son supposedly posed.

"A few weeks later, the prosecutor declined to press charges . . . There was no robbery, he said. The alleged victim had picked a fight with the perpetrator, lost, and concocted a tale. A surveillance video backed him up. The jury returned an acquittal in a matter of hours.

"But the damage was done. The police took a picture of my son the night he was arrested. He is on his knees, hands cuffed behind him, eyes fathomless and dead. I cannot see that picture without feeling a part of me die. So I took personally what William Bennett said . . ."

"For those who might have missed it," Pitts added, "former Education Secretary and self-appointed arbiter of all things moral, said on his radio program that if you wanted to reduce crime, 'you could . . . ABORT every black baby in this country and your crime rate would go down. That would be an impossible, ridiculous and morally reprehensible thing to do, but your crime rate would go down.'"

That's BLATANT, RAW RACISM!It reminded me, too, what former First Lady Barbara Bush, the MOTHER of George W. Bush, said about the mostly Black New Orleans evacuees of Hurricane Katrina who were temporarily living in the Houston Astrodome in Texas.

I mentioned this before in a previous story, but I think it bears repeating. She said: "What I am hearing, which is sort of scary, is they all want to stay in Texas. Everyone is so overwhelmed by the hospitality. And so many people in the arena here, you know, were UNDERPRIVILEGED ANYWAY, so this is working very well for them."

That's also BLATANT, RAW RACISM!

And so is the word, "MACACA." Macaca is a French word for monkey. Former Republican Senator George Allen used that word to describe a man of Indian descent while campaigning last year for his senatorial seat. As y'all know, Allen lost his seat to now-Senator James Webb.

People who are racists, such as William Bennett and Barbara Bush and George Allen and many others . . . may not realize what they are doing. They have learned to accept negative qualities that are found within a race and ignore anything to the contrary. They have formed a personal conviction that prejudging is the right and acceptable way to think.

Racists are tragic, abhorrent people. But what's more tragic and abhorrent is they tend to pass on their way of thinking to their children.

And just like Mr. Pitts and his children, my children and I have also experienced racism in this country. It would be too long to enumerate all of them on this page, so I can only tell you the best. Yes, THE best . . . because I laughed at its ugly face. It happened two summers ago.

I was in my front yard, wearing scruffy cut-offs, an old sleeveless shirt and a sweat-stained buri hat, tending to my flowering plants and mowing the lawn and such, when I heard a car pulled over the curb in front of my house.

A man's voice called out: "Hey, Chico! Chico!"

I turned toward the voice, stopped what I was doing and ambled over. The car was a shiny, brand new Lexus and there inside was a white family of four: the man who called out and his gorgeous-looking wife and two young children in the back.

I took off my buri hat, stood humbly before them and said, "Si, senor?"

"You speak English?" the man asked.

"Beri leetle only, senor," I said, indicating with my thumb and forefinger how little was "leetle" and it was very little.

Then he asked, "How much do you charge for mowing lawns?"

I took a long look at the man's good-looking wife and winked at her . . . then I looked at the man straight in his eyes and said in a perfect American accent that I could muster:

"I don't charge cash, pal . . . only in kind. Whenever and wherever I mow lawns for anybody, I get to sleep with the lady of the house." The lady of the house sitting in the car giggled. She seemed to like the idea. I smiled at her. Then I laughed in the man's face . . . at that ugly face of racism!

Racism roared away.

I ambled back to my flowers to have a deep sniff of their earthly scent. **JJ**

Sen. Hillary Clinton: A President-in-Waiting

Did y'all watch the Democratic presidential candidates "YouTube" DEBATE Monday night on CNN? Those questions aired and fielded to the candidates were tough and direct, unusual and emotional . . . thanks to a new format that put the questioning in the hands of the voters themselves who sent in home videos through the Internet, instead of the usual questions asked by polished news anchormen, the debate was down to earth.

First, a dyok.

A Barako dyok, that is.

This was sent to me by my cuz, Manuel, who is a fellow Barako. If you don't fall in this category, please mosey on to the next page, because I don't think you'd have the depth or the intelligence to understand and appreciate this dyok.

We've heard about people having guts or balls. But do you really know the difference between them? In an effort to keep you informed, the definition for each is listed below.

Guts—is arriving home late after a night out with the guys, being met by your wife at the door, with a broom in her hand, and having the guts to ask her: "Are you still cleaning, or are you flying somewhere?"

Balls—is coming home late after a night out with the guys, smelling of perfume and beer, with lipstick on your collar and slapping your wife on the butt and having the balls to say, "You're next!"

Medically speaking, there's no difference in the outcome, since both ultimately result in death. (Smile, Sour Face).

Okey ngarud . . . enough of that.

Questions that are on everybody's mind on race, same-sex marriage, Darfur and the Iraq war were asked.

Some questions put the candidates on the spot in a personal way . . . questions like, Is Sen. Barack Obama truly black? Or . . . is Sen. Hillary Clinton feminine enough by American standards or so feminine that those Arab leaders could never take her seriously?

Mr. Obama said he "never has to explain how black he is when trying to catch a cab." I think that was a good answer and it drew hoots, whistles and applause.

But Ms. Hillary drew the strongest applause for her reply to the question about whether she would "be taken seriously" as a female President in Arab and Muslim countries where people there view women as "second-class citizens."

She said she has met with kings, prime ministers and sheiks and "I believe there isn't much doubt in anyone's mind that I can be taken seriously."

After noting that many major nations have female leaders, like Germany and Chile, she said, "I have noticed that their compatriots on the world stage have taken them seriously. I think it would be quite appropriate for a woman President to deal with the Arab and Muslim countries on behalf of the United States of America."

Amen to that. I liked that answer.

Speaking of the GENOCIDE in Darfur and on the plight of the children there, I also liked what Sen. Joseph Biden, Jr. of Delaware, said: "Those kids will be ALL dead by the time diplomacy is over."

The most revealing moments, I think, for the candidates was when they were asked if they would work in the White House as President for a MINIMM WAGE of $5.85 an hour rather than President's annual salary of $400,000.

Former Sen. John Edwards said, "Yes." Senator Hillary answered, 'Sure."

Sen. Chris Dodd said he would NOT, because he has "two young daughters to send to school." Senator Obama said, "Yes." And added that "we can afford to work for the minimum wage because most folks on this stage have a lot of money." Then addressing Senator Dodd, he said, "You're doing all right, Chris. You don't have Mitt Romney money. . . ." Senator Biden joined the fray and said: "I don't have Barack Obama money either."

The last question came from a lesbian couple, who asked if the candidates would "allow us to be married," followed by a minister's question who asked former Senator Edwards to explain his opposition to gay marriage.

Rep. Dennis Kucinich said he "supports gay marriage. Senator Dodd and Governor Richardson said they're for "civil unions, with full marriage rights."

But former Senator Edwards said he felt an "enormous personal conflict over gay marriage." And that it would be "wrong" to use his own faith to justify the issue and "impose" his own religious belief on other people." Sounds like an old John Kerry line to me.

On the Iraq war: I liked all their answers and their stand on it: Let's bring the troops home!!! But it was Representative Kucinich's rhetoric that reverberated clearly and drew the longest and loudest applause when he castigated his fellow candidates and said that the Democrats have FAILED America when they joined the Republicans in funding the war.

The best rhetoric though came from the quietest one on the stage and the least well-known, former Sen. Mike Gravel, when he said this, or something to this effect: **"There's nothing more worst than soldiers dying in vain in Iraq, but MORE soldiers dying in vain there. . . ."**

But I think it was Ms. Hillary who stood out among the eight candidates. I really think she will WIN the nomination. She put on a sterling performance. She's knowledgeable. Her words were superb and sincere. Her quick wit and intelligence surfaced to the core. She presented her arguments well. She was eloquent.

Obambi, I mean, Senator Obama next to her, looked naïve and inexperienced. The others, Edwards, Biden, et al, looked like her entourage.

Yes, even with that coral-colored jacket she had on, Ms. Hillary already looked . . . **PRESIDENTIAL!**

Undoubtedly, assuredly, she's America's President-in-waiting, for January of 2009. And that's no dyok. **JJ**

Men Gossip More Often Than Women?

It must be true. I read it in a tabloid that men, macho men, big hairy men and hunky, muscled men, or even those little men amongst us, GOSSIP MORE than women.

He, he, he. I think that's funeeee. But it's true. That's what it says in this tabloid I've just read.

We, men, may call it "locker-room banter, or "networking," or maybe, "keeping in touch." But in form and substance, it's called, simply and truly, GOSSIP! And, men do it everyday. Hey, I do it. Well, not everyday. Maybe, every other day. PLEASE don't tell me that YOU don't do it or had never done it. Because . . . you're lying, bro.

This juicy tale are findings of the Social Issues Research Centre (SIRC), a non-profit think thank based in England. It defines GOSSIP as "chatty talk among friends," and the "process of informally communicating value-laden information about members of a social setting."

Further quoting this tabloid, the Center's other findings are:

. Men are likely to gossip with work colleagues, love partners and female friends.

. Men gossip about work, politics or other highbrow topics less than 5-percent of the time, unless (check this out) women are present! Then the proportion of male conversation increases to impress the women.

. Men spend much more time than women talking about themselves . . . and that gossip is the mutterings of the powerless.

Even the Academia and Wannabe Journalists

And now hear this, teachers! Ken Stewart, a former professor and now a family-and-marriage therapist in Minnesota, said the worst gossip mills is ACADEMIA, "with a lot of smart people with a lot of time on their hands who are not as powerful as they'd like to be."

For example, when someone else gets the promotion to full professor, sharing dirt on him or her isn't kind, but it sure is comforting. (Like those kinds of gossips, I suppose, among Fil-Am journalists, or for that matter, even among wannabe journalists).

This study also found that "while women are more likely to talk bout RELATIONSHIPS, when it comes to nasty, vicious, backstabbing information about other people, men do that JUST AS MUCH as women."

But according to this study, there's a bright side to gossip, too. Men are not really that CYNICAL at all. Most are genuinely interested in other people.

"Gossip," said Stewart," is a way of creating a network of information, a way of saying, 'I heard about something that made me curious.' In that sense, it's a good thing. It knits together community."

So, with that in mind, let me share this interesting GOSSIP from "Uncle Ben" Giovanelli of Chicago. Last week I emailed him and said that I mentioned him in my column and that I incorporated a couple of his DYOKS he sent me.

He wrote back: "Thanks Bro . . . I hope they have a sense of humor. Oh well, it was a good change of pace for Fil-Ams. We live with enough pressure and confusion in our lives, we all need to take a break from our EGOS. We all take ourselves much too serious.

"Hey, by the way, have you taken in Michael Moore's new film, "Sicko"? It's about how the medical and drug companies are running the USA . . . and how some members of Congress are filling their pockets by special interest groups to evade any chance of change.

"I, along with the entire audience went from a HIGH, of a standing ovation to a LOW, of some outright crying and some sniffles. The movie has balls as does the producer. I say, good job, Michael Moore!

"I also picked up a conversation between Wolf Blitzer of CNN on the 'net, about how that Indian Doctor, Sanji Gupta tried to discredit Moore's assertions in his movie. It was quite a heated debate. Check it out. Oh, well, enough for now. Keep the faith, Bro. Over and out." (Signed) Uncle Ben.

Good gossip, **Uncle Ben**. Clean as a whistle . . . got anything "UNCLEAN"? Just kidding.

Romy Marquez's Breaking News

This is another good gossip. Last week, my prolific and highly-esteemed colleague, Romy Marquez cc'd me a copy of his latest story before it saw print, **"BREAKING NEWS: Filner Exposes Scams in FilVets' Ranks**," with a note that reads:

"Good morning to all . . . It seems scammers are all over the place that even Congressman Filner complains about them. Here's the latest development in our community. Thanks and best regards." (Signed) Romy Marquez.

After reading Romy's story, I wrote him: "Pare . . . Thanks for the heads up. Good story. This is the way I see it: the FIGHT now seemed to be for self-serving recognition . . . of who should be the SUPREMO of this fight for Filvets Equity, with Representative Filner acting as JUDGE and JURY. You know, just like the fight between Aguinaldo and Bonifacio. They fought for the same cause, YET they were insanely jealous of each other.

"Pare, para sa akin . . . this FilVets issue has too many cooks who are cooking the broth. Kaya and labas diyan: GELE-GELE."

Romy responded: "Well, they can fight for whatever. But the outstanding issue remains the scam being perpetrated on the hapless veterans. Pare, mahirap na ang mga ito, ginagatasan pa!"

If these emailed exchanges are dubbed as gossips, then gossip is a good thing. If it's a way of creating a network of information, or a way of knitting together our community, or a way of keeping in touch, then I am all for it.

Let's gossip on!

Hey, got one to share? Psssst, I got one. **JJ**

Are Democrats Faggots? Ask Ann Coulter.

I think I am having an attack of the so-called writers' block. I don't know how to begin this story.

RANDOM THOUGHTS keep coming into my head. I couldn't focus on one thought, snare that thought and develop it into a story. My mind keeps jumping from one thought to another.

Perhaps, if we DYOK first, it might help me get out of this rut and jumpstart my old lethargic mind. These were sent to me by "Uncle Ben" Giovanelli of Chicago. The first one gave me a chuckle; the second one, a hyena's howl.

Here's the first: "At a cocktail party, one woman said to another, 'Aren't you wearing you wedding ring on the wrong finger?' Answered the other, 'Yes, I am. I married the wrong man.'"

Here's the second: "A lady inserted an ad in the classifieds: **HUSBAND WANTED**. The next day, she received a hundred letters. They all said the same thing: 'You can have mine.'"

Ain't that a riot? Hey, Uncle Ben, thanks for the laughter. We, Fil-Ams, need to laugh more at corny dyoks. We are too serious and too grumpy and too sour. I, too, have a dyok. It's true and written in haiku:

"Bush lied. People died.

"Memories faded. Scooter skated."

Lest we forget, the number of deaths of our troops, as I write this, is now: 3, 602 . . . and counting! The wounded: over 27,000 . . . and counting! And half of these wounded can never function as normal human beings again! On the part of the Iraqis: hundreds of thousands of dead and wounded . . . and counting!

A RANDOM THOUGHT: As to Scooter, y'all know him, right? I. Lewis "Scooter" Libby, was a White House aide and was VP Dick Cheney's chief of staff. Mr. Bush, the Decider, intervened to keep Scooter out of prison by commuting the former aide's 30-month prison term. Scooter was convicted of LYING to federal prosecutors about his role in a White House leak of a covert CIA agent's identity. I suppose, LIARS and THIEVES, and birds of the same feather, flock together . . .

ANOTHER RANDOM THOUGHT: Do y'all know that according to a study conducted by three University of Indiana scholars, Fox News pundit Bill O'Reilley's daily commentaries contain an average of 8.88 instances of name-calling per minute, or one INSULT every 6.8 seconds . . . and that his favorite defense from insults hurl back at him at him is: "So's your mother!" Reilly, you motherf . . . !!!

Hey, what about that ultra-conservative WACKO pundit named, Ann Coulter? She shrilled that former North Carolina senator and president wannabe John Edwards and all Democrats are "FAGGOTS" and snickered that Hillary Clinton has "chubby little legs."

Coulter, as described by syndicated columnist Maureen Downey, is a "cheap character assassin in black sheath and heels . . . a Paris Hilton of the right, admired as much for her blonde good looks and her short skirts as her unapologetic viciousness against Democrats."

In other words, she's vile and she's got bile.

But I did look closely at Hillary's legs. It's true, she's got "chubby little legs." And Sen. Edwards do look like a pretty little "faggot" with that coif.

ANOTHER RANDOM THOUGHT: When it comes to the war in Iraq, said David Broder, of the Washington Post, there's a "major disconnect between public opinion and Washington reality."

Every poll now indicates that MOST Americans think Iraq is not worth the loss of American lives. Yet despite of Mr. Bush's veto of a military-spending bill that included timetables for troop withdrawals, Democrats ain't doing nothing.

May I ask: Is the will of the people being THWARTED? You bet it is!

But Broder said, "In a word, yes—but not indefinitely. The beauty of our constitutional system is that while the President runs the military, the people pick the President. And history shows that wars do end when the American people say they must."

So if the war in Iraq doesn't wind down with Bush still in the White House, "rest assured," Broder added, "the endgame is almost certain to happen in 2008, when we elect a new commander in chief."

So, as we wait for 2008, we'll count the dead and the wounded and watch helplessly as the spiraling violence, carnage and mayhem unfold before our eyes and spill into our living room.

I think that's sick. I think our Democratic leaders are all paranoid of being seen as doves and the "cut-and-run" type. I really think they all have been NEUTERED, and that Ann Coulter maybe right when she said that: "DEMOCRATS ARE FAGGOTS!!!"

PS: Hey, I think my writers' block is gone. **JJ**

On Fairy Tales and Filipino Fairy Godmothers

It's the Fourth of July as I write this. Are y'all enjoying those different display of fireworks? Hmmmm. I thought my own fireworks were bad, but they're nothing compared to the fireworks other people are generating somewhere else. Y'all know what I mean?

It's soooooo petty and soooooo potty.

It's so funeeeeeee . . .

And, it's so sad!

It's the picture perfect FAIRY TALES that we should NOT tell our children at all. We should all be ashamed.

Talking about fairy tales, I recently received this email from Bobby Reyes, the editor/publisher of the on-line magazine: www.Mabuhayradio.com.

"Dear Ka Jesse: Did you know that the NaFFAA national chairperson, Alma Q. Kern, lives in Seattle? One of her best supporters, Anita Sese, lives also in Seattle.

"Perhaps you may want to interview both ladies for your next column or a special issue of it. Ms. Kern has refused to talk to me even online and can you please ask her why? Ms. Anita is known online as the "Fairy Godmother." Perhaps she is the godmother also of Perry Diaz, whom your best friend, Joseph Lariosa, called the "PerryTale writer." Mr. Diaz' column is called PerryScope. I will forward to you Ms. Anita's emailed comments about the NaFFAA scandals. If you want to interview Perry Diaz, his email address is perrydiaz@aol.com.

"Mabuhay and good luck with the interviews. (Signed) Bobby M. Reyes."

I answered: "Hello Bobby . . . Let me formulate some interview questions for these three people that you mentioned. I'll probably ask them their opinions on the series of exposes that you've written on the "NaFFAA crooks." I'll ask them, too, what they think of you and also ask Ms. Kern why she doesn't want to talk to you. I'll tell 'em that their answers won't be CENSORED and that this interview would really the best opportunity to voice their sides . . . on whatever.

"I'll ask Perry Diaz why he's called a "PerryTale writer" by Joseph Lariosa. I'll also ask Ms. Sese why she's widely known online as the "Fairy Godmother."

"I hope they respond. It'd be fun reading for sure. Okay ngarud, Bobby, take care. (Signed) Ka Jesse.

I wrote Perry Diaz first. "**Hey Scoop,**" I said. (I call Perry, 'Scoop,' because of his column, PerryScope and in the way he "outscoops" us, Fil-Am journalists, in getting the news).

"How are you, my friend? What's you comment on the attached emails between Bobby Reyes and me? Have you read his latest exposes on "NaFFAA crooks" and his story, "How some NaFFAA NEOs hijacked the NAFVE" on his online magazine?

"Hey, I want to incorporate your comments in my next Kapeng Barako column, together with the comments of Ms. Kern and Ms. Sese. That is, if these two ladies are game. You game, buddy? Fair and square 'to. Let's keep it clean a little. It's for publication, you know. Take care and talk to you later. (Signed) Jesse."

Here's Perry Diaz' response, en toto.

"Hi Jesse . . . Glad to hear from you, my friend. You've weathered the storm that came your way. My hats are off to you. As a journalist you're free to express your opinion unless it violates the rights of others, which you didn't.

"Now, there are journalists in our midst who should be called "calumnist" instead of "columnists." I call them "medialante" for using the media to malign other people. But when a journalist criticizes the work of a fellow journalist, that's the lowest a journalist could go. First, I believe that a journalist should respect the opinions of other journalists, whether he or she agrees or not. Have you heard of a physician criticizing another physician, or a lawyer another lawyer? That is "professionalism" and journalists should act professionally as well.

"I never heard or read Joseph Lariosa criticize my work. Perhaps I missed his postings. However, after Bobby said that Joseph called my column 'Perry Tale,' I emailed Joseph to confirm what Bobby said, but he never responded. However, if Joseph really said that, all I can say is that he is entitled to his own opinion, which by the way, is only a minority of one. The 3,600+ subscribers of my eNews bulletin, 'BALITA-USA' love my articles. The comments I receive from them spoke highly of my work. Today, I have some of the most prominent journalists/writers in the Philippines contributing to BALITA-USA.

"Bobby titled his story, 'How some NaFFAA NEOs hijacked the NAFVE?' In his article, he especially attacked Jon Melegrito and myself. First of all, how can we hijack NAFVE when NAFVE was our creation? Jon, myself and about 50 others, including representatives of the Philippine-based WWII veterans created it in December 2006 at a summit at the Philippine Embassy in Washington, DC.

"And let me tell you a SCOOP (you can publish this if you want). When Bobby Reyes posted his suggestion that a summit be held in Los Angeles (his turf, kuno), I contacted Doy Heredia and someone at the Philippine Embassy that we should PRE-EMPT Bobby by calling for a summit at the Philippine Embassy in Washington, D.C. Within two days, the summit was announced (sponsored by Ambassador Gaa and NaFFAA). Bobby was invited, but he refused to attend (maybe he cannot go through the security check points at the airports for lack of ID). I know that Bobby will hate me more for this. But what the heck? He is at war with us, right? All the best. (Signed) Perry."

I also wrote Ms. Kern and Ms. Sese to seek their comments. I haven't gotten any response from Ms. Kern yet. Maybe, NEVER at all. Ms. Sese DELETED my email. Oh, well, can't win them all. You win some, you lose some. You slay some dragons. Some dragons slay you, like in draconian FAIRY TALES that our children shouldn't ever be told. **JJ**

Chicago's Fil-Am Press Club Threatens Legal Action Against This Web Site

Editor's Note: The National Press Club of the Philippines affiliate in Chicago recently censured and wanted to sanction columnist Jesse Jose. Mr. Jose, however, resigned from the press club before any sanction could be meted out. The following e-mail was sent by a certain Esperanza Talavera Sanchez to the Illinois-based Filipino-American press club in defense of Mr. Jose. More commentaries at the end of this article, as this web site has reprinted the "dialogue" among the parties involved in the controversy. The issue now is whether a press club has the right to censure and/or sanction a member for views expressed in a column that some club officers find racially or morally offensive?)

Hereunder, Dear Readers, is the threat from an officer of the Philippine National Press Club of Chicago to call for an immediate legal action against the editor of this online publication. And the editor's reply follows.

In a message dated 6/11/2007 4:44:05 PM Pacific Daylight Time, Tingjoven writes:

Bobby,

The NPC list serve is a private, NOT A PUBLIC list serve. You have no right to publish the private conversations of a private entity (where you do not belong) without the entity's permission.

YOU HAVE VIOLATED OUR RIGHTS!

TO ALL NPC MEMBERS OF THE EXECUTIVE BOARD:

This calls for an immediate legal action.

Thank you.

Ting Joven
Treasurer
NPC USA

Dear Ting:

I welcome any legal action that you and/or the NPC Executive Board may wish to pursue at the soonest possible time.

If you do not know history, any press club belongs to the so-called Fourth Estate, which is unofficially the fourth branch of government in a democratic country. The Fourth Estate has, therefore, public-benefit functions, duties and responsibilities. Because you are a public-benefit entity, any member of the public may demand transparency from your press club and all media organizations. And when you started sending by e-mail the various messages about the Jesse Jose brouhaha, your dialogue became public domain. Ngarud?

Bringing me to court will make my day.

Mabuhay,
Bobby M. Reyes
Editor
www.mabuhayradio.com

The columnist, Jesse Jose, is phenomenal and irreverent. His viewpoint stings but with merit. He is one columnist who never runs out of readers.

You became indignant for his differing views on the FilVets and other ethnic minorities. You were of one mind that he committed a grave offense and sanctioned him. You were relentless in your efforts in assailing his character.

It was such a comedy and a tragedy. You all met and had an inquiry. Was Mr. Jose present during the inquiry? Was an invitation extended to him to be physically present or be available by phone during the time of the inquiry? Then his rights have been gravely violated if the responses were no to those questions.

It was also a comedy and a farce. You sanctioned Mr. Jose who was no longer a member of your group during the so-called inquiry. It is so sad that you would not stop hounding him. When is the end to this harassment?

I am a taxpayer. I do hope that Mr. Jerry Clarito, a duly-elected official, did not use government time in sanctioning and assailing Mr. Jose. I do hope too, that the named elected official has other programs to pursue for his constituents other than the FilVets issue.

The war in Iraq rages. A thousand soldiers have died and will continue to die *(Editor's Note: Actually more than 1,500 American soldiers have died as of today, June 10, 2007).* Families will continue to mourn. Funds are running out for this war and in aiding the families of the fallen soldiers. What a shame to seek on-going monetary funding for the FilVets while the soldiers in Iraq don't even have armored body vests and vehicles for their protection!

There are so many pressing issues in the community that awaits leadership. You have wasted too much time and efforts rebuking a person who has different outlook and viewpoints from you.

Thank you,

Esperanza Talavera Sanchez **JJ**

Three-thousand, Four-hundred Ninety-four . . . and Counting!

First, I must say this: I agree with my MegaScene colleague, Ting Joven of Chicago, with what she said in her column last week that if you're being talked about, you're "an important person."

And I must be a VERY important person.

Because I am the "talk of the town" in Chicago right now. Yeah, I am the buzz of the town and I am not even from that talkative, gossipy town. From what I understand, the TALK has been going on for so long. I must really be THAT important.

The officers and members of Chicago's NPC-PhilUSA, a group of press and "de-pressed" people that I used to belong to, are all wagging their tongues about me.

Believe me, when press and de-pressed people wag their tongues, the whole town is all ears and follow suit to wag their own tongues. So there's a lot of wagging going on. But I LOVE BEING WAGGED ABOUT!!!

What do they talk about? Heck, I dunno. Probably everything about me, including the size and length of my . . . shoes. And whether I have two lefts or two rights. And why do they talk about me? Heck, I dunno that either . . . I'll take that back. That's a lie. I DO know. But I won't tell you that now, because it'd be another story, a MIDGET story. And as Bruce Lee said in one of his classic movies: "I am not gonna bother myself with midgets."

Okay, enough already of this mundane talk.

Let's move on and talk about what we really NEED to talk about: IRAQ!!! Yes, Iraq and the escalating violence there . . . and the escalating deaths of our troops in that God-forsaken land. Yes, this war is getting bloodier! Car bombings are more frequent than ever. The IED's are getting deadlier. And the Iraqi insurgents are getting better, smarter and meaner in slaughtering our troops.

Yes—as I write this—it's now THREE-THOUSAND AND FOUR-HUNDRED NINETY-FOUR . . . and COUNTING!!!

The month of May was the deadliest month for U.S. troops in two and a half years. One-hundred twenty seven young, brave Americans were killed over there. This month, on its first three days alone, 16 soldiers have already been killed! But we ain't seen nothing yet.

Mr. Bush said America should brace itself for more casualties this summer. This summer, to say it bluntly, many more of our troops will die. Many more Iraqis—men, women and children—will die, too.

There will be many more car bombings to kill Iraqis. There will many more IED's exploding to kill and maim our soldiers. There will many more bound and tortured and hog-tied dead bodies of Iraqis that will be found in the alleys and side streets of Baghdad. There will be many more kidnappings, murders, carnage and mayhem.

There will be more bombs from U.S. warplanes that will fall in Iraqi cities and towns and kill Iraqi mothers and their babies. Do y'all know that the bombings of Iraq had not stopped? There were more bombs dropped this year than last year. That's a fact.

My God, what have we done to this country? What have we done to these people? They didn't hurt us. There are "terrorists" there now, because WE ARE THERE! We are OCCUPIERS of that country . . . hated and loathed.

Sad. Truly sad. Maddening. Frightening. I am running out of words on how to describe this war. The word, "STUPID," I think, is the perfect word to describe it. Because, it's so pointless! I cannot see any justification for it.

Let's move on . . .

Now that British Prime Minister Tony Blair has announced his departure this June from Downing Street, we're getting the TRUTH about his feelings toward the Iraq war and the "DYSFUNCTIONAL" Bush Administration. The London newspaper, "The Guardian" reported that Blair AGONIZED over the war, and asked his political secretary: "Do you think we will ever be free of this?"

It's clearly known now that Blair was so "frustrated" with Donald Rumsfeld's tactical mistakes in conducting the war. The Guardian quoted a Downing Street insider, who said that "Tony was literally tearing his hair out . . . he could see what needed to be done, but he did not have the levers."

Bloody hell, Sir Blair! What part of "pooh-del" didn't you understand?

Moving on . . .

As y'all know, Mr. Bush is in "Old Europe" now mending fences with allies there. Better late than never. There's plenty of work to be done to repair the damage inflicted on America's moral leadership by the debacle in Iraq and by the sordid images of . . . "Abu Ghraib." Y'all remember those OBSCENE photos, right?

Mr. Bush, from what I understand, is also having a lover's spat with his other pal there, Russian President Vladimir Putin. They're squabbling about the placement of U.S. MISSILES . . . something like that. Both are talking tough to each other.

Not to worry. These two are PALS. They already have made plans to meet in Maine sometime in July. According to my own pal, Seattle Times columnist Ron Judd, the "two world leaders plan fireside chats to shoot the breeze on their favorite subjects: fishing, clearing brush . . . and SUBVERTING their nation's Constitution."

On a final note . . . So, "Scooter" Lewis Libby, VP Dick Cheney's former chief of staff is going to prison for 30 months . . . for LYING and obstruction of justice. Y'all know the story, right?

"Truth matters," said Special Prosecutor Patrick Fitzgerald, who doggedly prosecuted this case. Libby was one of the prime movers to the planning and execution of the Iraq war that has cost America dearly in BLOOD and treasures.

Not counting the rivers of BLOOD that the Iraqi people have shed, its THREE-THOUSAND FOUR-HUNDRED NINETY-FOUR killed U.S. troops for us. And, COUNTING! **JJ**

To Be a Journalist . . . Is to Be a Swordsman

With wit and irreverence, Frank McCourt, the Pulitzer Prize winning author of "Angela's Ashes" and "'Tis," wrote in his third memoir, "Teacher Man":

"'Yo, teacher man . . .' Joey again.

"'Joey, I told you my name is Mr. McCourt, Mr. McCourt, Mr. McCourt.'

"'Yeah, yeah. So, mister, did you go out with girls in Ireland?'

"'No, dammit. Sheep. We went out with sheep. What do you think we went out with?'

"The class explodes. They laugh, clutch their chests, pretend to fall out of their desks. This teacher. Crazy, man. Talks funny. Goes out with sheep. Lock your sheep. . . ."

I am no teacher man. Nor do I do sheep. Haven't even tried it. But that passage from McCourt's book brought to mind the three people who taught me what I know about journalism.

When I was a military journalist, writing and sending stories to AP-UPI and other mainstream newspapers around the country and still VERY wet behind the ears, three seasoned journalists took the time to mentor me.

The first was Bruce Dart, who eventually became a Washington Post political writer in the 70's and 80's.

The second was Alex Hailey, who eventually wrote the book, "Roots."

And the third was Gagne (I can't remember his first name now). He was my editor in the 70's when I worked as photo-journalist for the Seventh Fleet Public Affairs Office. My buddies and I secretly called him, "the Frenchman" because of his French name. He was brutal. He had a way of reducing 10 sentences in drafts of my stories . . . into one sentence. His favorite expression was: "Re-do this story." He eventually became a city desk editor in one of the metro dailies in Pennsylvania.

And though I met them in different times and in different "foxholes" of my military journalism life, they basically said the same thing. "Jesse," they said, "Journalism is not like writing a college composition for your English teachers. In journalism, you write for news readers. Keep your sentences short. Keep your paragraphs short. Five sentences at the most. Use simple words. Be precise and concise and brief.

"Talk to your readers. Tell them the news, but don't over-tell them. Don't insult your readers' intelligence by over explaining. Get in and get out of your paragraphs. Tell them the five W's of the news—who, what, when, where and why. Keep moving, doling out your info one at a time.

"Don't try to impress your readers with big, long words. Use short words instead.

"And, don't lecture. Don't make that mistake. Readers resent being lectured at. You're a news writer, a journalist, NOT a lecturer. And avoid clichés. Invent your own.

"And remember this: the most important punctuation in journalism is the PERIOD. Verbiage is garbage.

"If you're going to make a cut at somebody, don't hesitate, don't dilly-dally, do it with force, do it without fear and do it with finesse. Don't make a mess. Do it clean. One cut, two cuts, that's it, then flick the blood off from your sword and sheath your sword.

"A true journalist is a master swordsman. He's a true warrior. He's FEARLESS. Now, go out there, killer, and score some kills."

As a young pup then, I listened in awe to the words of these writing gods. I took their advice to heart. I became a true swordsman. I scored numerous kills. They were NOT journalistic kills though. I was a knucklehead. They were kills, nevertheless, in the form of "birds, chicks and broads."

They told me, too, to read, read and read. "Read books. Read novels. Read the classics," they said. "Read magazines and all kinds of newspapers . . . and if, one day, you might want to become a columnist, read newspaper columnists. And study how they write."

That I truly took to heart. I closely read the late Doroy Valencia, the late Jack Anderson and the late Mike Royko. I studied their style and the way they construct their sentences and paragraphs. And I noticed that what they have in common were their simple, short sentences and their simple, short paragraphs.

Now my favorite columnists are Maureen Dowd and Bob Herbert of The New York Times, Howard Pitts, Jr. of The Miami Herald, and Molly Ivins of the Dallas Star. (Ms. Ivins passed away not too long ago.) All four are Pulitzer Prize winners and all write active, simple, short sentences.

I also took a liking to reading Hemmingway, John Steinbeck and Isabel Allende and Philip Caputo. I read all of their books. For thrillers, I read Ken Follett, Nelson DeMille, John Grisham a little bit of Tom Clancy. What these authors have in common are their short, simple, straightforward sentences.

For fun, I read bestsellers. Mitch Albom's books are the bests of the best. I tried the old classics, but they tremendously bore me. Maybe, I am not there yet. Maybe, I haven't reached that plateau yet. Maybe, I am still a knucklehead. I've a penchant for the old Pilipino classic, "Tiktik." I remember them as exciting extracurricular readings while I was a student at Araullo High in Manila and as a journalism student at the University of Santo Tomas.

But yo! readers, I don't mean to impress you with tall tales of my life. I am just passing on to young pups lessons that I've learned when I was still wet behind the ears as a journalist, listening in awe to my three writing gods, Bruce, Alex and Gagne, "the Frenchman."

And that to be a journalist is to be a swordsman, but not in the way I became, whose journalistic kills were merely birds, chicks and broads, and therefore, NOT really a writing god, but merely an irreverent wannabe. **JJ**

Yo, America! Where's Your Outrage?

Mag-dyok muna tayo.

This is for my fellow senior citizens. My wife sent it to me with a note that says: "Sweetheart, please tell me this won't happen to us."

Here it is. Enjoy.

"A little old lady was running up and down in a nursing home. As she walked, she would flip up the hem of her nightgown and say, 'Supersex.' She walked to an elderly man in a wheelchair. Flipping her gown, she said, 'Supersex!' "He sat silently for a moment or two and finally answered, 'I'll take the soup.'"

Now, I'd like to share with you a couple of feedbacks from my story last week, "Farewell, Falwell . . ."

The first one read: "WOW is all I can say, Mr. Jesse. You seem to be the Filipino version of Jesse James, shooting all the bullets in your six-shooter at the Conservative Christians. But it is your right to write as you damn please . . . according to the First Amendment.

"More power to you, JJ, although some of your friends (our mutual pals?) in Chicago refuse to read your column. . . ."

Well, it's to their loss if they don't read my column. Some of my PALS in Chicago are TOXIC creatures, anyway. With toxic creatures, you stay away from them . . . as far away as you can. Their REFUSAL to read my column brought to mind "THE THREE MONKEYS," where one has its hands covering its eyes, the second has its hands covering both ears, and the third has its hands covering its mouth.

They don't wanna see, they don't wanna hear, and they don't wanna talk, except to each other. Among monkeys, the practice is: monkey see, monkey do, monkey talk. Read between the lines. I have no further comment.

The second feedback read: "Hold on, Jesse. People, including columnists, are not supposed to speak ill of the dead. You lambasted the Rev. Falwell, who cannot defend himself because he is six-feet under the ground. . . ."

Yes, I suppose I shouldn't be doing that. But as a journalist, it's my duty to tell the evil deeds of this man. The truth of the matter, so to speak.

Former Philippine President Ferdinand Marcos, who died a long time ago, is still spoken ill of as a "debased ruthless dictator," who "raped and looted" the Philippines for 20 years. He's still a cursed man. And the ills that beset the Motherland are still being blamed on him. Poor Apo.

The same thing goes with Idi Amin, who was once Uganda's president. People still denounce his madness and cruelty. And so with Hitler and Stalin and Pol Pot and the rest of those EVIL people that came into this earth.

These people are now long dead, yet we still speak ill of them. Their evil words and deeds are still topics in books and movies. Their stories are told over and over again, for in the telling and re-telling, we hope to become more aware and watchful of wannabe despots and Rasputin's. . . .

So much for the past. Let's go to the present.

So, despite the fact that majority of Americans want a pull-out timetable for the Iraq war, the Democrat-controlled Congress didn't get a war-spending bill with a withdrawal deadline past Mr. Bush. That's sad. I wouldn't call it a compromise, because it isn't! I wouldn't even call it a promise to continue the debate, because it isn't! I would call it what it is:

an OUTRIGHT FAILURE! Didn't we, the people, speak as one? Didn't we say: "Let's bring the troops home!" Didn't we say that this war is a STUPID war?

Didn't we say our troops there are dying needlessly? It's now over 3,466 . . . and counting! This past Memorial weekend as we celebrated an extra day-off from work, TEN American soldiers were killed. Then SEVEN more on Tuesday, and FOUR more this Wednesday, making the month of May the DEADLIEST month for U.S. troops in two and a half years. Didn't we say that this STUPID war has been draining America's treasures? It's now $300 BILLION . . . and counting! And that's not to mention that contentious war-spending bill of $120 BILLION, approved by Congress and signed off by Mr. Bush.

Didn't we say that this war was a war of choice by Mr. Bush? That the reason for it was based on his OUTRIGHT lies. Didn't we say we are sick and tired of this war? And that we wanted to end this war NOW? Aren't we a government OF, BY and FOR the people? Why is it then that our common will AS the people was thwarted?

Last week those Democrats in Congress who rode into power on a pledge to stop funding the NEEDLESS and STUPID war in Iraq voted overwhelmingly to continue funding it. Liars! They all lie! Politicians of the Right, Left and Center are all the same! *Mga nang-uuto lang, ika nga.*

Yo, America! Where's your outrage? **JJ**

Farewell, Falwell . . . Paul and Alberto, too

I've been looking at the race for the Republican presidential nomination, and I've come to a disturbing conclusion: Maybe we've all been too hard on President Bush.

No, I haven't lost my mind.

Bush has degraded our government and undermined the rule of law; he has led us into strategic disaster and moral squalor. But the leading contenders for the Republican nomination have given us little reason to believe they would behave differently. Why should they?

The principles Bush has betrayed are principles today's GOP, dominated by movement conservatives, no longer honors. In fact, rank-and-file Republicans continue to approve strongly of Bush's policies—and the more UN-AMERICAN the policy, the more they support it . . .

Oh, my goodness!

Of course, I didn't say that. Paul Krugman, a syndicated columnist of The New York Times said that in his recent column. I couldn't have written something so blunt, so true and yet as profound as something like that. I wish I could have. I've thought about it. But I was not able to verbalize it.

BTW . . . have you heard that Democrats and a sizable number of GOPs in Congress and in the U.S. Senate are calling for a NO-CONFIDENCE VOTE on Attorney General Alberto Gonzalez, saying he has become "too weakened" to run the Justice Department? Not only because of those politically-motivated firings of those eight federal prosecutors. But also because when he was still the White House legal counsel of Mr. Bush, Gonzales was found out to have visited the sickbed of then-Attorney General John Ashcroft in 2004 to pressure Ashcroft to APPROVE THE LEGALITY of Bush's eavesdropping program, which Ashcroft refused to do. To eavesdrop on Americans, in America, without warrant, is against the law. When Mr. Bush appointed Gonzalez as America's top law enforcement officer, thousands and thousands of Americans were wiretapped without warrants. My goodness!

BTW . . . have you also heard that Mr. Bush is expected to quickly nominate a replacement for DISGRACED and now FIRED World Bank GIRL-CRAZY president Paul Wolfowitz, the former "architect" of the Iraq War and former assistant to the former Secretary of Defense, Donald Rumsfeld, who was also FIRED?

According to the Beltway Boys of Fox News that as soon as Mr. Bush hears from his talent scouts, there would be a nomination . . . and guess where those talent scouts have looked? From the International Arabian Horse Association, where the famously DISGRAFUL "Brownie" of FEMA was recruited . . . and then FIRED for doing "a heckuva of a job" during Hurricane Katrina.

My goodness!

Now, check this out. I've been hearing a lot of goofy GOPs and talk heads on Fox News falling all over themselves, saying what a great and religious man of God Televangelist Jerry Falwell was. As y'all know he passed away last week. I'll never wish death on anybody. That's only for MANGKUKULAMS. But I don't mourn his death. I think he was an evil man. During the 60's civil rights movement, he called the CIVIL-RIGHTS movement the CIVIL-WRONG movement. And that Dr. Martin Luther King, Jr. was "not a sincere" man of God. He preached that God meant for "Negroes to serve Whites." He embraced the APARTHEID regime of South Africa, under President P.W. Botha and denounced Bishop Desmond Tutu as a "phony."

During an evangelical conference in 1999, Mr. Falwell said that the "anti-Christ' was a "male Jew alive in the world today." He also said that

"Tinky-Winky" of the children's TV show, "Teletubbies" was a "gay role model." And, he had denounced, loud and clear, Prophet Muhammad as a "terrorist." And that "AIDS is the wrath of God upon homosexuals." He told Christians that it was their "duty" to jump into the political fray. And they did, with millions of them registering and voting for the first time in 1980 . . . that helped put President Ronald Reagan into the White House.

After the 9/11 terrorist attacks, Mr. Falwell said, "I really believe that the PAGANS, and the ABORTIONISTS and the FEMINISTS and the GAYS and the LESBIANS and the ACLU . . . all of them who tried secularize America, I point the finger in their faces and say, 'You helped this happen.'"

My goodness!

As syndicated columnist Leonard Pitts Jr., said: "This Christianity's moral purview was reduced to two issues: abortion and homosexuality. It had nothing to say about feeding the hungry, housing the homeless, helping the helpless." "Worse, it was mean, smug and self-satisfied," Pitts added. "The language of faith, forgiveness and forbearance became the language of demonization, marginalization and objectification." Indeed, he was a demon on this earth. He preached hate.

So, farewell, Mr. Falwell. Good riddance. You, too, Mr. Wolfowitz . . . and soon you, Senor Gonzales. **JJ**

Jesse's Son Wins Wyoming Broadcasters' Awards

(Editor's Notes: We decided to change the article's title, as indeed the achievements in broadcasting of our columnist's son deserve to be the focus and not just his birthday. We congratulate the Jose Family for Chris' success in American broadcasting. Yes, Jesse, Chris is your son, in whom you are well pleased—to use a Biblical phrase.)

I have some good news. It's about my son, Chris, a broadcast journalist for CBS News Channel 5 in Cheyenne, Wyoming.

Good news to good friends and supportive relatives, that is. But NOT too good, I am sure, to sour grapes, would-be friends and green-eyed kin.

My wife got hold of the news first. From work, she called me and said, "*Yung anak mo, katatawag lang, nanalo na naman ng dalawang* award."

"Which one?" I asked, pride and excitement rising in me.

"The Wyoming Broadcasters Association Awards. One for "Best News Story" and the other for "Best Newsbreaking Story," said my wife.

"*Ang galing naman*," I said. "He just started working there . . ."

"I know. *Kasi mana sa akin*," my wife said. It's true, I thought.

"*At saka, kamukha pa ng mama niya. O, di ba*?" my wife added. *Buti na lang*, I also thought. For true indeed, my wife is a looker. Sexy pa.

So, upon hearing the news from our son, my wife told the whole world about it . . . and within seconds, thanks to modern technology, the whole world knew about it, too.

She heralded the news this way:

"Hi . . .

"I would just like to share our joy. Chris was awarded two prizes by the Wyoming Broadcasters Association. He won the 'Best News Story,' and the 'Best Newsbreaking Story.' We are so proud of this boy."

And I, on my part, heralded the news this way: I forwarded what my wife wrote and then wrote in this brief note.

"Hello Everybody . . .

"Just some good news to share with. Take care y'all . . ."

From Wyoming, to Washington, to Chicago, to Canada, to Florida, to New York and California . . . all the way to the Philippines, the news traveled and crisscrossed. Twice. Perhaps, even thrice, because I am sure, my wife's sister and Chris's aunt, Sister Grace Marie of the Carmelite Monastery in Seattle, heralded the news, too. Yes, perhaps, even all the way to Rome . . . and to all the angels in heaven, who watch over my son.

My brother, Soc, an assistant movie producer, screenwriter and director in the Philippines, wrote back:

"Dear Kuya . . .

"Your pride is contagious! It spilled over here. Congrats, Chris! Soc."

Many wrote back to us. Maribel's friends, my friends, kin and clans and relatives, sharing in our joy. My Bestpren, Yoly, said something about DNA's. One said something about "the PROOF is in the pudding." Another said something about "FRUITS not falling too far from the tree."

Whatever . . .

Here's the proof and the DNA . . . and the fruit. Punch on your computer screen: www.kgwn.tv. Then click on the left hand side that says "Meet the Team," and you'll see the photos of the CBS 5 Wyoming team. Click on my son's photo . . . and therein you'll read this:

"Chris joined the CBS News Channel 5 team in August of 2006. Since his arrival, Chris has covered stories ranging from breaking news to politics. Chris was first on the scene when a natural pipeline explosion scorched more than 800 acres in southwest Cheyenne. Chris EXCLUSIVELY covered the heated 2006 US House race when Republican Barbara Cubin narrowly beat Democrat Gary Trauner.

"He also investigated and uncovered the most dangerous neighborhoods in Cheyenne.

"Chris was born and raised in South Florida, but most recently lived in Seattle, Washington. He attended the Edward R. Murrow School of Communication (Washington State University) and graduated with a degree in Broadcast News and a minor in Sport Management in June 2006. During his time in college, Chris was honored six times by the Murrow School with his highest honor being the EXECUTIVE AWARD for his work at the campus television network, Cable 8 Productions.

"Chris started his television news career as an intern at KIRO (CBS) in Seattle and also worked for Sports Radio 950. He also had the honor to represent SONY during the 2006 National Association of Broadcasters Convention in Las Vegas, Nevada.

"Chris first got the journalism bug at 10 years old from his father, a photojournalist in the Navy. . . . Chris is an active member of the Asian American Journalists Association."

If y'all want to see him in action, click on the videos. He reports from the field, Monday to Wednesday. He anchors on Saturdays and Sundays. He's off on Thursdays and Fridays.

Hey, what can I say? There's the proof, the DNA . . . and the fruit. Eat it, but don't choke on it, please.

Wednesday this week, May 16, was my son's 23rd birthday. I call him, "Bam." Bam for "BAMBINO," because when he was still a baby, his Lola Meny thought she looked like the revered Bambino. I shortened it to Bam, and began to pronounce it as "bomb" when he turned 15 and became a high school basketball star player and a "bombshell" to giggly girls and love-struck women.

His mom calls him, "Babe." Bam or Babe, it all means the same, because it all boils down to: "Love ya, Bam . . . or Love ya, Babe."

Happy Birthday, Bam!!! Love ya. This is my gift to ya. Take care.

And this, dear readers, is my good news to all of ya: my Bam, my son. **JJ**

On Barack Hussein Obama

Is that who-you-ma-call, Barack HUSSEIN Obama?

You know, that good senator from Illinois.

He wants to be the next President of the United States of America? *Susmaryusep! Sa pangalan na lang, talo na 'to, eh.*

True, he was a Harvard-trained lawyer and a Harvard law professor. And that he was a prominent civil-rights lawyer and activist. And a very active legislator in the State of Illinois and a highly visible senator in the US Senate.

True, he gleams on national television and he's a darling of the press, and wherever he went, people flock to see him and listen to him speak. He's got the stature of a rock star, and he's a great orator, eloquent and charismatic.

True, he's handsome, intelligent and he says the right kind of things . . . things that the American people love to hear.

Me, included.

When questioned about his THIN FEDERAL RESUME as a public servant, he said: "I think the one thing the American people require of their president is good judgment. In most of our lives, we hope that more experience gives better judgment—but not always. Dick Cheney and Donald Rumsfeld had an awful lot of experience, but displayed poor judgment in this Iraq war . . . so part of the measure I have to take is, do I feel I have the judgment to take the toughest job on Earth."

Sharp, beautiful, gorgeous words.

These, too, are ENDEARING words: "The true desire of all mankind," Obama said, "is not only to live free lives but lives marked by dignity and opportunity, by security and simple justice."

I also like his stance on the Iraq War: "Let's get the troops out! No 'ifs' or 'buts.' Let the Iraqis solve their own problems. The SURGE of U.S. troops there is an escalation of the war that will surely result in more deaths, more violence and more hate for America. The solution to the quagmire in Iraq should be a political solution, NOT a military solution. Bring Iran and Syria and the whole region to the TALKING table and let's all formulate a solution."

I like that kind of solution to problems: Let's talk. Let me hear you. And hear me out, too. Let's work it out. Let's compromise.

Let's change our vocabulary and talk about America seeking JUSTICE, which is a fundamental Muslim concept, rather than DEMOCRACY, which is interpreted as a code word for America's support for dictatorial governments that run RIGGED ELECTIONS.

Yes, let's talk. Guns and bombs are the tongues of goons and morons.

Let's use words. Soothing words. Humble words. NOT stupid and arrogant words, like: "Bring it on!"

But may I ask, can Barack bring America together? And will America bring on Barack? Or to put it bluntly: Is America ready for an African-American to become its President?

I doubt it! Not yet . . . or, maybe, even, NEVER!

Let's face it. Let's get real. This is the United States of America, where WHITE MEN rule. Will they really relinquish that power to rule?

This is a nation YET where XENOPHOBIA is the common mental disorder of many!

As Leonard Pitts Jr., a Pulitzer Prize winner columnist recently wrote: "Barack Obama is a black man with a Muslim name who would be seeking the presidency in a historically RACIST nation currently at war against Muslim extremists."

Amen to that.

"One wonders if there is enough handsomeness, intelligence and charisma in the world to overcome all that," Pitts added.

Nope.

It ain't the time yet for a man named, Barack HUSSEIN Obama, to become President of the United States of America.

And for that matter, not even for that man named, John McCain, who I think will win the Republican nomination, who then will go against Hillary, who, I am sure, will win the Democratic nomination. Senator McCain is Mr. Bush's clone. A loser, for sure.

Even Rudy Guliani, the former mayor of the city of New York and the leading GOP contender in recent polls will surely lose, too. Because though NOT exactly a Bush's CLONE, he's a Bush's LAPDOG.

Clones and lapdogs . . . are same-same.

So, it's gonna be Hillary Rodhan Clinton, aka "Billary." Hey, two for one! Two bright minds of the land, tilling together. She said, "I am in. And I am in to win." She will.

"I was born into a middle-class family in the middle of the country in the middle of the last century," she cooed recently in her flat Midwestern twang to several hundreds of people—mostly mothers and their daughters—in IOWA . . . and they loved her.

In every American's home, it's always been the woman who rules. We men, just pretend. If Nancy Pelosi now has the gavel to put ORDER in the once unruly HOUSE full of naughty boys, Hillary will soon hold the HELM to steer America back to Bill's economic boom years and happy, peaceful times, without wars.

Osama, I mean, Obama, Barack HUSSEIN Obama, that is, has got a long, long wait yet. **JJ**

Is Jesse Jose "A Little Brown American?"

For my views, many people hate me. I've been called "OJ," as in Obnoxious Jesse . . . and a Filipino daw, with a "crab mentality" and who, instead of shooting at the enemy, I turn my rifle around and shoot at fellow Filipinos.

I've been called a "narrow-minded bigot."

I've been called a "foul-mouthed S.O.B."

I've been called a "little brown American."

A few had even threatened me with physical harm. Some want to "sanction" me and ban me from writing and muzzle me from expressing my views.

I am too "dangerous" *daw*. Someone, a friend, who used to be a friend, that is, but who became a foe because of my views, even wished me "grave illness" and "death." Kind of scary. And kind of sad.

But, I think, it's more of a SCREAM, like a YIKES scream. Y'all know what I mean? Yes, funneeeee and soooooo deliciously laughable.

The most laughable and the most STUPID comment, I think, was when I was called "a little brown American." Of course, I am an American . . . and proud of it. And, of course, I am brown. Tan, golden, and brown . . . and proud of it. I am not LITTLE though, like many "little Filipinos."

I am tall, dark and handsome, like the way Poldo Salcedo used to look. And, with my bigote and perfumed hair pomade, you could also say I am an Erap look-alike in his heydays as an actor. Eat your hearts out, heh, heh, heh. I am kind of old now, and I keep my stash of Viagra near my bed. But you know what they say about men getting on with age, they truly know how to get it on. OLDER, BOLDER, SEXIER, they say. I kid you not. And surely, quality is better than quantity.

Yes, make no mistake. I am not what-you-ma-call a "little brown American." I am an American, period. You and I are now in America. This is NOW our country. Let's think like an American. And let's talk like an American. And let's walk like an American. And show our complete and total LOYALTY to America . . . like a good American.

I am not saying that we should forget our ethnicity and do away with our cultural heritage. Let's keep it in our hearts and practice it. But let's don't be too CONSUMED with our Filipino-ness. I think that is wrong! Let's be an American first, and second only as a Filipino.

Let's stop saying: "I am a Filipino." Because, really, who cares if you say that in America?

Let's stop singing that stupid song: "*Ang Pilipino angat sa mundo.*" Because it projects to the world our sense of inferiority complex and our inadequacy. Let's prove first that the Filipino is *angat sa mundo*, then let's sing it!

Let's toil for this country as an American. This country that takes good care of us. In this country, our accomplishment as a person should be what we should sing about.

And, as that great American, John F. Kennedy, once said: "Ask not what your country can do for you, ask what you can do for your country."

To me, that means, let's don't be a BURDEN of this country. Let's don't take advantage of the WELFARE system of this generous country.

If you are one of them who do, shame on you! Get a job, pal! And get a life! I didn't mean to give lecture here. Got carried away a little with that "little brown American" bit. I am getting off my soap box now. But remember, I am not LITTLE. Brown, yes. American, yes. And Filipino, yes, but "beri leetel" only . . . you dig?

In other words, my heart and soul is Filipino, I cannot change that. Nor do I want to change it. But my mind is American and my loyalty is to America.

As to those other descriptions, *kulams* and curses that were heaped on me, hey, what can I say? This is America. The land of the free. Your land and my land. The land of free speech. The land of many Americans, black, white, yellow, giants and midgets, as well as those . . ." little-minded brown Americans" within its midst.

Yes, I am hated for my views, but now and then, a comment from readers would come my way and warm my heart. This one came from someone in California, named Allan. I am not making this up.

I'll quote him en toto:

"Hi Jesse,

"Love your post. Light, funny, yet deeply profound. It's almost poetic . . . Keep up the good work."

Signed) Allan.

For my views, some people love me, too. **JJ**

John Edwards' Haircut Boggles Jesse Jose's Mind

It boggles the mind! It boggles the mind!

May I ask: Where do you get your haircut?

I am a cheapo, so I get mine from Great Clips. A haircut there costs $15. But as a senior citizen, Tina, my Vietnamese barber, charges me only $12. With coupons, $9. But she does such a good job trimming my hair and telling funny stories about Vietnam in her lilting, accented sing-song voice that I usually give her $15. And that to me is splurging on a trim.

So when I heard that former South Carolina senator and president wannabe John Edwards pays $400 for his trims, I felt violated, I felt like that there was something not right with that, I felt inadequate.

I even felt hate for this man. No, not hate, probably envy . . . no, not envy. I just couldn't pinpoint it. There's something, something that's very wrong and very disturbing to me. Four-hundred bucks for a haircut?

It boggles the mind.

"*The common man, not to put too fine a point on it, doesn't pay $400 for a trim,*" said Leonard Pitts, a syndicated Miami Herald columnist.

I think Pitts pinpointed my mixed-up emotions on the matter.

"*Granted, John Edwards is a wealthy man,*" Pitts said, "*and he can pay whatever he wants for a trim. But those of us in the cheap seats are likewise entitled to think his pricey coif sends a message jarringly at odds with the populists theme of Edwards' campaign.*

"After all, this is the guy who likes to style himself the SON OF A MILLWORKER, standing up for the common man. . . ."

Yes, I think that's it. The man is a FAKE! This son of a mill worker is no common man. He's a fancy man. A pretty, pansy, fake. Fakes, people and things, no matter how pretty, should be done away with.

I am now taking a hard look at the African grandson of a goat shepherd: Barack Obama. He seems more in the know how to get it on with the common man. He's got the moves. And he's got game. I like his beliefs. It's more aligned with the hopes and beliefs of the common man. Also, I like goats and I have a kinship with goat shepherds. My grandfather on my father's side was a goat shepherd.

I remember those days of old when I would occasionally visit him in Piddig, Ilocos Norte, he would butcher one of his goats and make PINAPAIT that was so heavenly to the taste that up to now I still consider this Ilocano dish as something like food for the gods.

Moving on . . . and this is something for the gods, too: Recently dug-up World War II-era documents show that after its surrender, Japan also set up "COMFORT WOMEN" brothels for American soldiers. The brothels, similar to the ones used by Japanese soldiers, also coerced women into prostitution, with "tacit approval" from the U.S. occupation officials.

The documents show the brothels were rushed into operations as U.S. forces poured into Japan in 1945. The rationale was "to create a breakwater to protect regular women and girls." In other words, to contain the U. S. occupation forces from committing widespread rapes and sexual assaults on Japanese women, they opened up brothels to provide cheap sex for them. "The COMFORT WOMEN," the report read "had some resistance to selling themselves to men who just yesterday were the enemy, and because of differences in language and race, there was a great deal of apprehensions at first . . . But they were paid highly, and they gradually came to accept their work peacefully."

Indeed, those generous American soldiers with their dollars, American cigarettes and nylon stockings to give, any girl in war-torn countries would have bedded with any of them.

But a year later, Gen. Douglas MacArthur shut all the brothels down, reasoning that the practice is NOT only "embarrassing" for the folks back in America, but also "IMMORAL for the troops."

Ha! It boggles the mind, the immorality of it all, and the pomposity and hypocrisy of this otherwise great World War II warrior.

MacArthur, during this time, conducted his tryst with his own private COMFORT WOMAN that he kept at the posh Manila Hotel . . . a widely-known whispered "secret" in Manila circles.

Moving on again . . . and time is really a-moving on. Today, May 1st, as I write this, marks the fourth anniversary when Mr. Bush declared that "major combat operations" in Iraq had ended.

Well, it ain't over yet, that's for sure.

The violence, the killings, the chaos, and the deaths of our soldiers continue to escalate.

Last month, at least 104 more of our troops have perished in this war, making April, according to news reports, "the deadliest month so far this year and the sixth deadliest of the war." Three-hundred and forty-eight (soldiers) have already been killed this year.

Compared to last year and the year before, the deaths of our troops have TRIPLED. This increase in deaths is the result of a STUPID PLAN by top military brasses in Iraq when they began moving troops from huge fortified bases outside of Baghdad to small, vulnerable outposts in the city.

This plan daw was to secure the city of Bagdad. It boggles the mind, this plan. In all, 3,351 of our troops, and counting, have now been killed in Iraq.

Enough! The war is LOST, for God's sake! We are just sending those soldiers to the slaughterhouse! We, the American people, have spoken! Let's bring the troops home!

Last week, Congress had passed a $124-billion spending bill that would force U.S. troops to begin withdrawing from Iraq by October 1st, with a goal of a complete pullout six months later. Mr. Bush said he's going to VETO it. True to his word for a change, Mr. Bush vetoed it today! Nancy Pelosi's Democrats do not have the two thirds majority to override this veto.

So, the war stays on course! How many more of our young, brave soldiers are going to die in this STUPID war? How many more bucket of tears are going to be shed by their loved ones? Is it all worth it?

It boggles the mind! It boggles the mind! **JJ**

A Crazy Carnage at Virginia Tech

Crazy, I tell ya.

Last week, when Seung-hui Cho, an Asian-American immigrant of Korean descent and a creative writing senior student at Virginia Tech, committed the deadliest shooting rampage in a school campus in US modern history, TV pundits, news commentators, print and broadcast, shrilled: What was the motive? What was the motive? What was the motive?

For heaven's sake, there was no motive!

The guy was sick. He was mentally ill. He was hearing voices, telling him to kill, kill, kill! He was insane. He was a monster, from-Jekyll-to-Hyde monster, who had to kill simply because he had to.

Cho killed 32 people, and himself. According to news reports, Cho first shot and killed two fellow students in his school dorm, then headed across the school's sprawling campus to kill 30 more students and teachers in a building where classes were being held. But there was a TWO-HOUR INTERVAL between the two shootings.

During this lag, Cho went back to his room, took a video of himself, brandishing his guns and spitting his mad epithets at the world. Then he packaged the whole thing, went to a post office and sent the package to NBC News in New York. Crazy . . .

Meanwhile, the police who were investigating the first shooting were running around like chickens with their heads cut off and their thumbs up their butts . . . FAILED to give the alarm that the killer was still on the loose! FAILED to secure the campus! And consequently FAILED to protect those students and teachers from Cho's killing spree.

Talking about police stupidity, that's the height of it. When Cho began his second rampage, students were walking about on the campus and many classes were in session. Cho simply entered one of the buildings and walked in one classroom and shot the teacher and students and walked out.

Then he walked in another classroom and shot the teacher and students and walked out. Then, again, he walked in another classroom and shot the teacher and students and walked out. And, AGAIN, in another classroom, he shot and killed more. Then, he shot himself.

Where were those fat cops? (I saw pictures of some of those cops on TV and in the papers carrying the dead bodies off after the carnage and the majority were FAT! And, I mean, really, FAT-FAT!) Can't really blame those cops for their INABILITY, can ya? Now, don't y'all get me wrong again? I am not prejudiced against fat people. Only against FAT and STUPID COPS. Because, let me put it this way, can they really protect me? Or you? And our families?

Anyway, back to Cho. As I said, the guy was crazy. But before he went completely bonkers, there were signs. Many signs.

A year ago, two female students called Virginia Tech police and complained that they were being "hounded" and "stalked" by Cho, with repeated phone calls, IMs, and notes. They did not know Cho and did not want to know him. He had no friends. He was a loner.

In class, some of his female classmates also complained that Cho were taking pictures of their legs with his cell phone from under his desk. The teacher of his writing class told university administrators about his weird demeanor in class and his DISTURBING, violent and profanity-filled writings. "Duh," they said.

One of Cho's roommates had, at one time, called police to say that Cho "seemed suicidal." "I don't think at the time you could have said he's definitely going to shoot someone. But we had talked about he was likely to do that if there was someone that was going to do it," said the roommate.

Officers went to speak with Cho. He was referred to a local health center, and then by order of a Virginia judge, sent to a psychiatric care hospital. The judge's order read that Cho was "mentally ill and in need of hospitalization, and presents an IMMINENT DANGER to himself or others . . . so SERIOUSLY MENTALLY ILL as to be substantially unable to care for self, and is INCAPABLE of volunteering or unwilling to volunteer for treatment."

The CRAZY thing about this judge order was an asterisk that also read: "The alternatives to involuntary hospitalization and treatment were investigated and were deemed suitable. I have found that there is LESS RESTRICTIVE alternative to involuntary hospitalization and treatment in this case . . . and I, therefore, direct that the person named receive an OUTPATIENT TREATMENT."

In other words, Cho's case "fell through to the crack." After a couple of days, he was released from psychiatric care. After being adjudicated as DANGEROUS and mentally ill, he was set free. Crazy . . .

Then, he bought those guns and ammos, and the rest is now America's nightmarish history. The gun shop owner where he bought the weapons from said there ain't nothing on Cho that could prevent him from buying guns. Any kind of guns, for that matter. Yeah, even assault guns. On guns, the NRA rules this country.

Crazy, I tell ya. But who? Cho . . . or us? **JJ**

U.S. Vets Come First, Before the FilVets

Cups runneth over, cliches runneth over, but anger boils over.

My anger seethed and boiled over when I read a press release by the National Alliance for Filipino Veterans Equity (NAFVE) in the NPC-Phil USA list serve. It was titled "61-year long wait for Filipino veterans may be over with Congressional majority support for Filipino veterans equity."

In parts, it read: "The House of Representatives Veterans Affairs Committee Chair Bob Filner and Chair of the Congressional Asian Pacific American Caucus Mike Honda (D-CA) announced the unprecedented progress that has been made by the Filipino Veterans Equity Act (HR 760) in a national teleconference . . . In the call, they reaffirmed their commitment to funding the bill and praised the Filipino-Americans' leadership on this bill since its introduction . . ."

That's fine.

The teleconference was co-hosted by Rep. Mike Honda and NAFVE, a national coalition of organizations working for full equity for Filipino World War II veterans . . .

That's fine, too, and more power to NAFVE.

It continued: "Rep. Honda commended the veterans for their service to the United States and issued a clear call for passage of the bill . . ."

Then Honda said daw, "A promise made should be a promise kept, especially when it comes to veterans. If we are to be a legislative body dedicated to ideals of justice and dignity, then it is IMPERATIVE we honor the promise made to Filipino veterans, and restore their benefits . . . we have prioritized the plight of the Filipino WWII veterans as a top legislative goal."

That's when I hit the roof, seethed and boiled over.

The press release was forwarded by my friend and NPC-Phil USA colleague, Jerry Clarito, so I addressed my anger to him, with copies to all members of the list serve and many others.

I told Jerry: "It was an ignorant and hypocritical statement by Representative Honda. If it is imperative that the United States honor the promise made to the FILVETS, then it is also IMPERATIVE that the United States take care of it own veterans. But it has not."

Has he heard of Walter Reed?

If the legislative body of the United States is truly dedicated to its ideals of justice and dignity, then the promise they told us, U.S. military retirees and our families, of free medical benefits for the rest of our lives, should also be kept. But it did not.

Right after I sent that brief e-mail, volleys of e-mails fired back at me. The first came from Jerry; the other was from Lourdes Ceballos. The other e-mails came later, condemning me for my views.

What follows is my reply to Jerry and Lourdes:

"Lourdes and Jerry, I am not a member of that list serve that you mentioned, the Military Retirees Grass Roots Group, whose members according to you complain DAILY of the broken promises made to them by the US government, Congress, the White House . . . I have never heard of that group. But as a U.S. military retiree myself, I join them in deploring the broken promises made to us, veterans.

"The U.S. government did promise free lifetime medical benefits for us and for our families, if we serve for 20 years. Many of us served because of that promise. But that promise was not kept.

"They also promised us that if we get injured and disabled while on active duty, and the disability is service-related, we would get free lifetime medical care . . . and a pension. True, that was kept. But the pension was within poverty level and the medical treatment in military and VA hospitals had been shoddy.

"The expose on Walter Reed, the U.S. Army's premier hospital, by the Washington Post, on how our INJURED and disabled and brain-damaged soldiers were mistreated, was a blessing to many fellow veterans.

"It brought to light the SHODDY, and sometimes non-existent follow-up care, that those war-injured veterans of the Iraq and Afghanistan wars received. Pardon my French, but those war-injured veterans were treated like sh—t!

Hopefully, this will have a whirlpool effect and they would look into the disgraceful treatment given to veterans in other military and VA hospitals all over the country.

That was the reason why I said Representatives Filner and Honda and all those other morons fighting KUNO for the FilVets are all a bunch of hypocrites because their attention are focused only in helping out the FilVets. I think these two clowns are merely out there to get Fil-Am votes.

Nang-uuto lang, ika nga.

The attention and the cry for help should not only be for the FilVets. That is wrong! It should be for ALL veterans, who fought for America!

Charity begins at home! America is our home now! Before helping out the FilVets, we should help out the US Vets first!

To me, the FilVets issue is moot. Through the years, it had been rejected over and over . . . YET we keep on begging, like those beggars ng mga makukulit in front of Quiapo Church and other churches all over the Philippines. I am sorry to say, but we, Fil-Ams, have become mendicants, too, because of the FilVets issue.

I do not want any part of that!

My primary concern lies with my fellow U.S. vets. My sympathy is with them. My loyalty lies with America first. To me, the problems that exist with the care of wounded U.S. vets should be the utmost concern. Because that is the real INJUSTICE!

Perhaps, the FilVets Equity issue is also an injustice. Is it really? Or, are we only after the money? Whatever . . . The cry for help by U.S. vets must come first before those of the FilVets. **JJ**

In the NEVERLAND of Free Speech

So, what in God's name is a "nappy-headed hos"? First time I've heard it.

It's a racial slur, some people said.

Really?

Puh-lease. What does it mean? How did it become a slur? In what lingo?

According to news accounts, Don Imus, a syndicated national radio talk host of WFAN-AM in New York City, owned by CBS, uttered those words to describe members of the mostly-black Rutgers University women's basketball team, the day after the team played but lost the NCAA women's basketball championship game against Tennessee.

Imus' show is broadcast to millions of people on more than 70 stations and on MSNBC and CBS television networks.

Imus was talking about the game on his show with producer Bernard McGuirk, and it went like this:

"That's some rough girls from Rutgers," Imus said. "Man, they got tattoos. . . ."

"Some hardcore hos," said McGuirk.

"That's some nappy-headed hos there, I am going to tell you that," Imus then intoned.

Now, maybe I am naïve, but why are those words that were exchanged between Imus and McGuirk offensive and interpreted as racial slurs?

The Rev. Al Sharpton, a Black civil-rights activist and a radio pundit himself, said they were. "Somewhere we must draw the line in what is tolerable in mainstream media," he said. "We cannot keep going through offending us and then apologizing and then acting like it never happened . . . we've got to stop this."

Stop what? Free speech?

The Rev. Jesse Jackson, another Black civil-rights activist and leader of the RainbowPUSH Coalition, said, "If he has to use that platform to insult and degrade then we have the moral obligation to picket NBC and to protest."

Protest what? Free speech?

"If he can violate us in that platform in the name of free speech," Jackson added, "we'll be picketing NBC in the name of free speech."

Long live free speech then. In America, free speech in any form can never be curtailed. So I say, march on, Reverend.

Meanwhile, in IRAQ, a "democracy" on the march, according to Mr. Bush, there are some free-and-fiery speeches going on, too.

This one came from an enigmatic Iraqi leader, who has emerged from the chaos of the war there: Muqtada al-Sadr. He's a Muslim cleric and commands an enormous following among Iraq's majority Shiites and has close allies in the Shiite-dominated American PUPPET government of Prime Minister Nouri al-Maliki.

He said: "You, the Iraqi Army and police forces, don't walk alongside the OCCUPIERS, because they are your archenemy. God has ordered you to be patient in front of your enemy, and unify your efforts against them—NOT against the sons of Iraq. You have to protect and build Iraq."

If I may practice, too, my right to FREE SPEECH, I'd like to say: Hey, I like this guy. He's got chutzpah. Yeah, but that doesn't mean I sympathize with the enemies of my adopted country. Nor am I an unpatriotic sonamagun. I love America. I've laid my life for America as one of its warriors, and I'll do it again and again to defend this nation's way of life and all its freedoms, especially its most cherished freedom . . . to FREE SPEECH.

Last week, when CNN's Wolf Blitzer asked Senator and president wannabe John McCain about the nightmarish situation in Iraq, McCain said: "You know, that's where you ought to catch up on things, Wolf. General Petraeus goes out there almost everyday in an unarmed Humvee."

McCain added that Americans can now walk safely in "many parts" of Baghdad.

Blitzer then asked CNN's Baghdad correspondent, Michael Ware, a hook-nosed, beleaguered, but tough-looking journalist, the same question.

"To suggest that there's any neighborhood in this city where an American can walk freely is beyond ludicrous,' said Ware. "I don't know what part of NEVERLAND Senator McCain is talking about . . ."

In the NEVERLAND of free speech, probably.

McCain also boasted that when he recently visited Baghdad with other GOP politicians, they drove from the airport to a central Baghdad marketplace, mingled with shoppers and haggled over the price of rugs, without any incident . . . or getting blown up by suicide bombers.

But what Mr. McCain didn't tell us was that while there in that marketplace, they all wore heavy body armor and heavily-armed American soldiers in their armored Humvees encircled the marketplace.

Also, American snipers nearby closely watched the crowd from concealed, strategic places. And U.S. helicopters hovered above.

And, how long did they stay in that marketplace? Exactly ONE HOUR, if y'all care to know. Yes, exactly one hour, no more, no less . . . In the NEVERLAND of free speech.

That day, four American soldiers on their EXTENDED tour of combat duty were killed in Baghdad. Another four, the following day. Over the weekend, ten: Bringing to 3,280 and COUNTING the number of our soldiers who have died there . . . In that NEVERLAND of free speech.

And if y'all wish to also call me a "nappy-head hos," fine with me. This is America, the NEVERLAND of free speech. **JJ**

London's Olympic Games: My Take

I watch the London Olympics, do you?

It's thrilling to watch the world's Olympians in action. It's awesome to watch them performing in their peaks. It's touching to see the winners' bright, happy smiles when receiving their medals . . . and heartbreaking to see the open tears, flowing on the faces of the losers.

I've also watched the opening ceremony, did you?

It was *daw* a "hilariously quirky Olympic opening ceremony, a wild jumble of the celebratory and the fanciful; the conventional and the eccentric and the frankly off-the-wall. . . ."

That's true. It was a dizzying spectacle. There was even James Bond himself escorting the Queen in a helicopter ride into the arena, then jumping out in a colorful parachute, from that helicopter when his mission was accomplished. There was Paul McCartney, singing "Hey Jude" and leading the world's Olympians and spectators in singing that classic song of the Beatles. And altogether, they swayed as one with the swaying tune of the song.

Yes indeed, there was unity . . . peace and brotherhood that day.

And Britain presented itself to the world as something it has often struggled to express: "a nation," it was said, "secure in its post-empire identity."

Whatever that means, I dunno.

And, if, as New York Times columnist, David Brooks, puts it in his column, the Opening Ceremony "mimics peace," but the games that follow, "mimic warfare." That's true. Through fierce competition, the games separate the elite from the mediocre. It's war. It's country against another country. And in war, heroes are born. In war, the goal is to defeat the enemy. There are 204 countries involved in this war. And about 11,000 combatants.

In war, as in the Olympics, the goal is not to win friendship, but to "demolish the enemy." And, to win!

And, to get that GOLD! Not the silver. Not the bronze. The Gold! In a competition, there's only one winner. The silver and bronze medallists are both losers. Their medals are only *pangpalubag-loob* for their ferocious, but lost fight, against the true winner, the gold medallist. The Gold medallist reigns supreme.

NINE GOLD MEDALS FOR CHINA: As I write this, three Asian countries are among in the top of the list who have who have won medals. Gold medals, that is. China has gotten the most, with nine. South Korea, two. And Japan, one.

What have the athletes of the Motherland won so far? I haven't even heard any mention of any of them, competing in any games . . . and I think that's pathetic. *Kulelat na naman ba tayo?* I thought the Filipinos are *"angat sa mundo"?* That's what we keep on saying and singing and screaming to the world.

It would have been a good time—the perfect time—to show the world that the Filipino is "angat sa mundo."

Oh, well, how deep is the (Philippine) well? So shallow *naman. Mas malalim pa ang baha. . . .*

OPENING CEREMONY: In the opening ceremony, I waited patiently for the Philippine contingent to appear. I wanted to see the Motherland's athletes, how they look and how they would prance and dance, and proudly wave the *bandila.* When the narrator of the ceremony started naming and presenting the countries that begin with the letter "P," I stood up and walked close to the TV screen, to see our own *kababayan* athletes better and to yell a cheer for them.

Finally they came on. Now, you see 'em, now you don't. For three seconds flat, a couple of athletes representing the Motherland were seen on camera. I saw the flag being waved weakly by a *kababayan,* wearing a poorly-designed *BarongTagalog,* with a *salakot* on his/her head.

At nakasimangot pa.

I couldn't even tell if the flag bearer was a he or a she. When I googled it, I found out the bearer's name was Hidilyn Diaz, a she. And a 21-year-old weightlifter *daw.* She should've waved that flag strongly, proudly and happily. But she did not. There were eleven Philippine athletes *daw,* but these eleven were not captured by the camera that I saw on TV.

Yes, now you see 'em, now you don't. That's how the Opening Ceremony presented the Philippine contingent. How disappointing. The narrator of the ceremony mentioned the name of Pakyaw though. But what's Pakyaw name got to do with the Olympics? He was not even a competitor.

BARONG AND SALAKOT: Also, why the *Barong* and the *Salakot?* The *Barong* is a formal wear, worn usually in important social or official functions. And the S*alakot* is worn while tilling the land in the rice fields, under the hot, blazing sun. To me, that's an odd combination of clothings to wear in presenting the Philippines. I am at a lost as to the symbolism of this oddly-paired attire to present to a world-wide audience.

Bonga ka, 'Day, they were not.

It was a drab attire, I think, and as I said, poorly-designed, compared to the attires that the other group of Olympians of other countries, had worn. They all looked resplendent, their attires, I heard, designed either by Armani or by Ralph Lauren . . . and check this out: Made in China, too!

Whereas, the Pinoys' attire, looked pathetic, made *daw* in the Philippines! That's what I saw. I didn't make that up. I am not "Mitt, the Twit." (Y'all know why Mitt Romney was called a "twit" by the Brits, when he was in London, right?)

Oh well, how deep is the tweeting well? Tweet it *ngarud,* Dear Readers. That's all. **JJ**

EPILOGUE

Dear Readers, let me offer this story as the epilogue of this book. It's about my dear friend, Ray Burdeos. Ray was the person who pushed me to put together this book.

This story is also an intimate conversation between two long-lost friends and a quick over-the-shoulder glance of the past.

A Stroll Down Memory Lane with Ray L. Burdeos, a Book Author, and a Friend from Another Lifetime

Ray Burdeos is a friend, a long-lost friend from another lifetime. He's also an author. He writes books. About Filipinos who have served in the U.S. Navy and U.S. Coast Guard. His latest book, **"Pinoy Stewards in the U.S. Service: Seizing Marginal Opportunity"** is his fourth and latest book.

I met him in the early 70's in New London/Groton Submarine Base in Connecticut while I was stationed down there as a Navy submariner. I've just changed my rate then from a First Class Navy Steward to First Class Journalist, and had become the editor of the base newspaper, called the "Dolphin."

Ray wasn't a Navy submariner. He was a "Coastie." A Hospital Corpsman, stationed then at the U.S. Coast Guard Academy, working as a Clinical Laboratory Technician. The Submarine Base and the Coast Guard Academy are separated by the Thames River, the river where the old diesel boats and fast attack submarines that were homeported there, traversed out to sea.

Those years were young years for both of us.

I met Ray when a bunch of us Fil-Ams in that town who were in the Navy and Coast got together and formed the very first Filipino-American association there. We were a merry group, plenty of parties and picnics and all . . . and gossips and intrigues, too, of course. Friendships flourished. There were many happy, memorable times.

Then, I got transferred out overseas, to the Navy Base in Subic Bay, Philippines, working as photo-journalist for the Seventh Fleet Public Affairs Office. From that part of the world, we would send out our stories and photos to military publications and hometown newspapers, and the Associated Press (AP) and United Press International (UPI) would sometimes pick up our stories for national publications. I was at the height of my career as Navy journalist during those years. I garnered awards.

I had no idea what happened to Ray. I supposed he also thrived in his Coast Guard career and went up the ranks.

Memories are long, so to speak, for decades later, someone from that past emailed and told me that Ray had written a book, titled **"The Steward and the Captain's Daughter."** I got hold of the book . . . and Ray's email address. I told him I enjoyed reading his book. It's about his love affair with the daughter of the captain of one his ships he was on. We exchanged emails. He encouraged me to write my own book, too. He said I've got the "tools" to write my own book, having been trained as a journalist in the Navy.

I said, I'll try . . . And I did try. But completing the book never got to fruition.

Ray and I moved on again with our own lives. Another decade passed. Then I heard from Ray again. He said he had written his fourth book. We began emailing each other, once more.

He wrote:

Jesse . . . I have been trying to contact you last year, but I didn't get any response from you. I wrote my fourth book about Filipinos in the U.S. Navy and Coast Guard who did well starting as stewards and later were able to change their rates. You are one of them that I was interested to write about. The title: ***Pinoy Stewards in the U.S. Sea Services: Seizing marginal Opportunity.*** *Look it up in the Internet www.amazon.com or www.bn.com. That's Barnes and Noble.com.*

How's you book coming? (Signed) Ray.

I answered:

Hello Ray . . . It's good to hear from you. I didn't get that email of yours from last year.

Your fourth book now? Congratulations! I don't remember at this moment the title of your first book that I've read. I know I still have it somewhere in one of my littered bookcases. I thoroughly enjoyed reading that book. It was a love affair with your captain's daughter, wasn't it? That book reminded me of one of my many love affairs while I was in the Navy. But I was never successful in seducing a ship captain's daughter, just like you did. You are, indeed, a fine seducer of women.

You're also a fine writer.

I started writing my own book after you've told me that I should write one, too. I got to Chapter 7 . . . and then my computer crashed, and everything I've written so painstakingly got all deleted. And I couldn't retrieve any of it. It was an autobiographical novel of my life in the Navy. It began when I received that calling card to report for testing in Sangley Point, Cavite. I have reached that part where I found myself working in the officers' wardroom aboard my first ship, the WW II aircraft carrier, USS Intrepid, CVS 11.

When all that writings got deleted, I focused more on writing my weekly column, "A Cup O' Kapeng Barako" and on personality profiles for the Philippine Time/MegaScene, a Chicago-based hard copy magazine. But I had a falling out with the publishers. Now I write primarily for an on-line publication, www.mabuhayradio.com and kept the name of my column. Several Fil-Am publications reprint my column.

My bluntness in telling-it-like-it is had garnered a lot of enemies for me that I've earned the name "OJ," as in Obnoxious Jesse. Believe it or not, I even get cursed out, I mean, really literally cursed with obscene words and names.

But I just laughed at them. I loved it, for that means, I am being read. Cursed out and hated, but read nevertheless. I suppose many of my readers love to hate me.

What I have in mind now for a book is perhaps a collection of the best and my most hated writings. I need a publisher who would do this for me. What do you think? Any suggestions?

I would like to read your latest book, and all those books you've written. Can you please send them? And please tell me how much it will cost, and I'll send a check to you. Okay Ray, take care now and talk to you soon. (Signed) Jesse.

Ray's response:

Jesse . . . Hey, that's a terrific idea, "the best and my most hated writings" into a book. That title alone will grab someone's attention. I am looking forward to see that in print.

About publishing your book, go to the Internet and just type AUTHORHOUSE. COM and it shows everything about publishing a book. That's the one I used. In the application for publishing, there's a question about who suggested to you to use their services. Just mentioned my name . . . They'll give me 100 dollars for recommending you.

Publish that book now!

About my books, the only one I have is the latest one. I'll send you one . . . a gift. I got two reviews on that. One is by Amazon.com and the other by Allen Gaborro, A Fil-Am writer, based in San Francisco, California. In that book, I wrote something about you . . . It's on page 67. The only complaint I have about this book, is the "typos." The printer did a poor job on this one. (Signed) Ray.

I answered:

Hello Ray . . . I got your book. I've began reading it. I read that portion about me. Sayang, we were not able to get together. Anyway, thank you for mentioning me and for your kind words.

Right after I retired from the Navy in January 1981, I went back "home" to the Philippines to use my GI Bill . . . and while attending a summer

Literature class at my old alma mater, the University of Santo Tomas in Manila, I met a woman there, named Maribel, the teacher of that Lit class. It was love at first sight, if there's such a thing. Perhaps, it was lust at first sight. Whatever. I was mesmerized by her beauty and vivacious personality. I fell head over heels in love, and in lust. . . .

Meeting her and falling in love with her erased the memories of my past loves with other women. It was a whirlwind courtship and romance. Two months later, we were married.

A year later, we had a son and named him Jonathan. The following year, she gave birth to another son and named him Christopher. I consider my wife and my two sons as precious gifts from God, in my new life.

We settled in Baguio City, where I became the editor of the Camp John Hay Newsletter. When they closed down all the U.S. military bases in the Philippines, I came back to the U.S., went to Florida, where I became a Martin County deputy sheriff. And with my wife and two boys, we settled in a little, quiet town, called Palm City.

When I retired from the Sheriff's Office, we all came up here to the Northwest and settled in Auburn, Washington, a quiet suburbs of the city of Seattle. To keep myself busy and out of trouble, I began writing again. Thus, "A Cup O' Kapeng Barako was born. I enjoy writing. It has become a pleasurable hobby for me.

I am talking too much about myself, ha?

I'll always remember you in your dress blue US Coast Guard uniform. You were in your uniform that day when we began forming that first Filipino American Association in the New London/Groton/Norwich area. You looked so reserved, a perfect gentleman in uniform.

In your latest book, in that portion where you told your own story and unexpectedly met your ship's "Captain" once again, who became then the "Admiral" of the Eight Coast Guard District Command, you should've asked him about his daughter. But I understand your "fear" for not asking about her. But you know, I'll always wonder what happened to her. Her name was Kim Bullard, right? That part of your life story was very "touching" to me. I think I also know the reason why you didn't become a warrant officer. Perhaps, that Admiral hindered you.

Well, Ray, thanks for sending and autographing your book for me. It was interesting and compelling reading. It'll be one among my collections of precious books.

I want to shout this out, loud and clear: Yes, despite all the prejudice and the discrimination that we, Filipinos, in the U.S. Navy and Coast Guard went through during those times, there were many of us who were able to overcome those hardships and became successful in our chosen fields of our military careers! We showed the Navy and Coast Guard establishments that we, Filipinos, were indeed, intelligent high achievers!

Take care now, my friend. (Signed) Jesse

POST RETIREMENT & A REVIEW OF RAY'S LATEST BOOK: Upon retiring from the U.S. Coast Guard as a Chief Hospital Corpsman, Ray attended the University of Texas in Galveston and earned a Bachelor of Science Degree in Health Care Administration. He eventually became the manager of the Department of Defense Outpatient Clinic at St. Mary's Hospital in Galveston. And like me, he's now fully retired.

In a review by one of the writers of Amazon.Com of Ray's latest book, it reads:

"This book shares personal and compelling stories of a unique group of Americans and I was surprised to find myself wrapped up in one story long after my expected bedtime! As I read, I felt like I was getting to know the Chavez family; maybe it was the letters from Zack's children or perhaps the story of trying to marry as bi-racial couple, I am not sure. But I am sure that this glimpse into the lives of men who left their homes seeking opportunities was compelling.

"The writing is not stellar (there were even typos), but it felt more real that way. I recommend this book. . . ."

I, too, recommend this book. To me, there's only one word to describe Ray's latest book: TOUCHING! Touching because, in a way, it's my story, too. Touching because Ray considers me as a friend. The autograph on his book, that he gave me, reads, *"To Jesse . . . A good friend back in the seventies at Groton Submarine Base. (Signed) Ray L. Burdeos."*

Touching, because, it's a stroll down memory lane. **JJ**

Edwards Brothers Malloy
Thorofare, NJ USA
April 2, 2013